D

Nikolai's Fortune

NIKOLAI'S FORTUNE

Solveig Torvik

A McLellan Book

UNIVERSITY OF WASHINGTON PRESS

Seattle and London

Nikolai's Fortune is published with the assistance of a grant from the McLellan
Endowed Series Fund, established through the generosity of Martha McCleary McLellan
and Mary McLellan Williams.

Additional support was provided by the University of Washington
Department of Scandinavian Studies Publication Fund.

University of Washington Press
P.O. Box 50096, Seattle, WA 98145
www.washington.edu/uwpress

Library of Congress Cataloging-in-Publication Data

Torvik, Solveig.
Nikolai's fortune / Solveig Torvik.
p. cm.—(New Directions in Scandinavian Studies)
ISBN 0-295-98563-1 (acid-free paper)
1. Norway—History—German occupation, 1940–1945—Fiction.
2. Norway—Emigration and immigration—Fiction.   3. World War, 1939–
1945—Norway—Fiction.   4. Mothers and daughters—Fiction.
5. Norwegian Americans—Fiction.   6. Women immigrants—Fiction.
7. Finland—Fiction.   8. Oregon—Fiction.   9. Idaho—Fiction.   I. Title.
PS3620.069N55   2006   2005016962

For
Brita Kaisa Kurola
1880–1966

in loving memory

CONTENTS

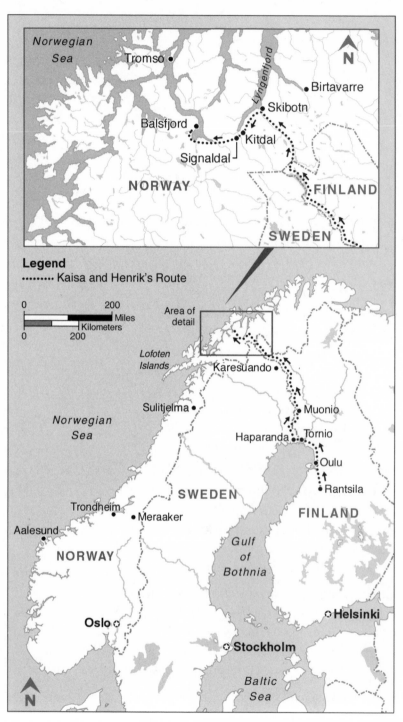

Map by James McFarlane

PROLOGUE

The Nazis invaded Norway on my first birthday.

On April 9, 1940, their warships slipped slyly into Oslofjord under cover of darkness, and at first blush of northern light, their warplanes roared over Oslo's rooftops. They came, so they said, to save us from the British. Dumbfounded Norwegians could only gape in innocent wonder as wave after wave of steel-helmeted Germans goose-stepped smartly onto Norwegian soil, the chilling strike of their jackboots ricocheting on cobblestone streets.

"April ninth" became symbolic shorthand for bitter national tragedy. And as a young child, I secretly worried that my mother nurtured dark suspicions that this day of Nordic infamy was somehow of my doing. And for all I know, perhaps she did. Who can say? Always assiduous in assigning blame, she was an unfathomable, ungovernable force of nature, fierce and willful, a whirling dervish of conflicting emotion and raw energy. Her tiny physical presence swelled to dominate any room she was in, leaving no space for moderating influences—even those of her own indomitable mother, my beloved grandmother, Kaisa.

My mother Berit was guided by the dictates of superstition; my father Edvard leaned to logic. He was a dapper, dark-haired charmer—when he chose to be. His was a classically droll Norwegian sense of humor, shackled to a temper as ungovernable as my mother's mercurial moods. He drank infrequently but not well.

My father was a mischievous, irrepressible storyteller, and as a child I could not get enough of his tales of being chased by rats through the streets of Leningrad or seeing a sailor's hand bitten off by piranhas in the Amazon. He was a machinist in the Norwegian merchant marine and had the misfortune of being aboard a ship in home port on the day of the invasion. The Nazis confiscated the Norwegian fleet and its crew. When my father occasionally came home for visits during his years of indentured servitude to the Führer, we two would sit companionably together on the green daybed in the cramped living room of our tiny sod-roofed cottage overlooking the fjord, I shy and adoring of this dashing stranger who held me spellbound with improbable tales.

My favorite story—and one that elicited dark scowls of disapproval from my mother—was how during the invasion he had braved Luftwaffe fire to fetch me home from the Oslo hospital where the stork had dropped me. But why I had been left to languish in the hospital for months after the initial delivery, like an unclaimed package sent to the wrong house, was never addressed in his fanciful account of my induction into the family. And neither of my parents would explain to my satisfaction how it came to be that I was born in Oslo when my parents' home had always been a long way up the coast in Aalesund. Uneasy, I filed away these questions as children do when stumped by inexplicable riddles. They were prickly burrs embedded in our tightly woven familial tapestry.

Ours was a family bound by an unacknowledged credo: if a thing remains unspoken, it does not exist; if pain is given no voice, it lacks power to harm.

But I didn't know any of that then.

What I did know of our family history was what I saw in our photo album, which I pored over whenever I was confined indoors. Here was Father with his crewmates on the deck of an ice-encrusted ship in Greenland, and here were the sweet-eyed seals they hunted, awaiting their doom on the ice floes. Here were Mother and Father on their wedding day, he smirking tipsily, she with lips pursed disapprovingly—a look with which I already was all too well acquainted. Here was Mother as a fashionably turned out young woman assuming stilted, theatrical poses for the camera, and here was Father, debonair in his homburg and three-piece suit by the canals of Venice.

Mother usually enjoyed explaining the stories behind these photographs, but she always turned aside my questions about one of them—a small formal portrait of my grandmother Kaisa with the four eldest of her eight children. Grandmother, who in other photos is a ramrod-straight, handsome, self-possessed woman exuding strength and dignity, here sits almost unrecognizable with unhappy children at her side. She's stony faced, defeated, her eyes haunted. Mother, at eight the oldest child, has a shockingly truculent, angry expression, her eyes puffy, the corners of her mouth turned down. Uncle Karl, the oldest boy, looks sullen, hollow-eyed and withdrawn, nothing like the kindly, good-natured man I would one day come to know. All of them look hungry and ill used.

I was curious about two other photos Mother seemed reluctant to discuss. In one, she's standing in a grassy field on her grandparents' farm in a narrow valley called Kitdal in North Norway. She's dressed in what we then called Lapp clothes, holding a reindeer by the harness, smiling broadly. With her dark brown hair and eyes, flat cheekbones and pointed nose flaring wide at the bottom, she looked exactly like the Lapp lady cradling a baby on a postcard in our album. Grandmother had sent this postcard to Mother while on a visit to Kitdal. The first time I saw it, I thought the lady was Mother. When I said so, she laughed strangely, not exactly offended and not exactly pleased. Lapps, or Sami as we now know to call them, were not, I would come to learn, considered civilized, respectable people like ourselves. But Mother apparently liked this picture of herself in Sami clothes; she had it enlarged so it filled the whole page of the album. All she would say about it was "I was born on that farm."

Another portrait piqued my curiosity, mostly because Mother was so evasive about the exotic-looking woman smiling coquettishly into the lens. This was her cousin Inga. There was also a small snapshot of the two of them together on a fine summer's day in North Norway before I was born. They're standing in fancy dresses in the middle of a dirt road, a sharp mountain peak looming above them. I would come to treasure that image.

My curiosity about family photos was not limited to those in our album. Overseeing all our gatherings in Grandmother's cozy living room was the portrait of a dark-haired, fine-featured, serious-looking man with a mustache who stared watchfully down at us from the wall. This was Grandmother's father, Nikolai.

"He went to America and got rich," Mother told me, both pride and derision in her voice. When I asked why he went to America without Grandmother, she warned me not to be so nosy. But he hung there on the wall, a potent, puzzling presence, and I persisted in my questions. One day Mother finally relented, stiff with exasperation.

"Grandmother's mother—her name was Marie—and Nikolai were never married," she managed to say. "Your grandmother was born in Finland." Being a Finn was shameful, I knew, though it wasn't clear why. Grandmother herself never mentioned Finland or her father.

"Nikolai wanted to marry Marie, but his family wouldn't let him," Mother went on. "They were rich landowners and she was just a poor servant girl on their farm. They fell in love and Nikolai was desperate to marry her. But his father refused. His family had a wife picked out for him, someone of his own station, and they wouldn't hear of it. They kicked Marie off the farm when they found out she was going to have a baby." Her eyes flashed furiously at this injustice.

"Nikolai was so angry and upset that he went to a place in America called Astoria, where he got rich." Pride crept back into her voice. "He had a store and a big farm there." She paused dramatically.

"Many years later, Nikolai came back to Finland to see Marie. He told her he wanted to give her money because she was so terribly poor. And he told her he wanted Grandmother to inherit everything he had because he and his wife had no children." She paused to savor this moral triumph.

"But Marie threw him out of the house," she concluded proudly, her voice ringing with righteous satisfaction.

I savored this story and turned it over and over again in my imagination, quietly studying the face of the man on the wall. What was he like, then, this Nikolai? How could he have gone to America and left Grandmother behind?

As it happened, we were about to do the same. As long as I could remember, Mother had a cherished mantra: "When the war's over, we're going to America." She had joined the Mormon church and longed to settle in Zion. And there she meant to find and restore to my grandmother her rightful inheritance from Nikolai's long-lost fortune. She assured Grandmother of this whenever the unhappy subject of our departure came up, but Grandmother only shook her head in despair.

The prospect of leaving Grandmother filled me with acute dread. She was the loving, steady center of our existence. She trudged in worn, quiet dignity between her apartment and the fish cannery, where she stood stirring boiling vats of sauce, preparing fishcakes, or wielding a fillet knife on the day's catch. When we grandchildren came round to the cannery door begging for treats, she sneaked warm, butter-browned fishcakes to us before shooing us away, an indulgent smile tugging at her mouth.

Her humble kitchen was only big enough for a small painted table, cupboard, counter, cold-water sink, stove, and three wooden chairs. But in that small room overlooking Borgundfjord we lived much of our lives. It was the spiritual locus of our family, the place I would hold fast in homesick memory from far across the sea. When I first returned to Norway after an absence of fifteen years, I was astonished at what a tiny, stark room that kitchen really was. It had been so warm and safe when the world outside was filled with evil and danger.

In January of 1949 my mother, father, and I joined yet another great wave of immigrants fleeing Europe for the fabled dream of America, leaving my heartbroken grandmother and our grieving relatives, dressed in their funeral best, waving forlornly on the dock in Aalesund. We set our feet in the footprints of those who had gone before, sailing over an unruly Atlantic and then tracing by Greyhound bus the pioneer path across a vast, snowbound continent to our new home in Idaho.

Obsessed with finding Nikolai's fortune for Grandmother, Mother pressed me into service as soon as I could write in English. We sent countless letters to Oregon as well as to Canada, where we knew he had disembarked, asking for proof of his life and death. Slowly the empty replies came back. Nothing. No trace of his life, no evidence of his death.

"Don't they keep records of people in this country?" Mother fumed. "I know he died a rich man. He must have left a lot of money behind. It can't just have evaporated into thin air."

But Nikolai and his fortune had done just that. He had vanished.

Forty years after my first attempt to find Nikolai, I determined to try again. By then both Mother and Grandmother were dead and Nikolai had been lost to our family for more than a century. As a journalist, I was confident that I now had the skills I had lacked in childhood to solve the mystery of Nikolai's life.

I wanted to put his story to rest not only because I was still intrigued to know what had happened to the man who had so captured my imagination as a child, but for my mother. Even though she was dead and I myself had no interest in Nikolai's fortune, I felt I owed it to her to complete the quest that had been so central to her life.

So I set out to recapture a story all but lost to memory, yet one traceable in the archives of the astonishingly detailed factual records of clerics and census takers. I began in the small village of Rantsila, Finland, where Grandmother was born. The first of her family to return there, I was warmly welcomed by her distant kin, who showed me where she and her mother Marie had lived their lives.

As I uncovered the real story of Grandmother and Marie's life in Rantsila, I found myself sitting as an honored guest one Sunday morning in the same imposing church where Marie more than a century before had been forced to face the congregation in order to be publicly denounced for the sin of bearing Grandmother out of wedlock.

The parish pastor, who had shown me the records of what had been done to Marie, informed the small group of worshippers that I had come to Rantsila to learn about my great-grandmother's life. And, he said, my quest had inspired the topic of his sermon that day: the forgiveness of sin. It was unclear to me, however, whether the sin most properly proposed for forgiveness was Marie's or that of the church for its inhumane treatment of her.

I set out from Rantsila one hundred and one years to the day after Marie sent her twelve-year-old daughter Kaisa on a nearly five hundred-mile winter journey on foot over the mountains of Lapland to her new home in the arctic landscapes of North Norway. I followed my grandmother Kaisa's route in pursuit of the story of her life.

This time, I found Nikolai—and uncovered his life's real circumstances.

What I could never have imagined is that this quest also would uncover my own long-hidden ethnic identity.

Ours was a family of secrets, beset by cruel cycles of separation. These secrets, and the shame that roiled silently in their wake, reached across three countries and an ocean to hold four generations in thrall.

My quest for Nikolai was driven in part by my desire to understand the events that had helped to shape my incomprehensible mother. But, above all, I wished to honor my grandmother by recording her life and capturing her place—one all too common for women of her time and station in Scandinavia—during a compelling, little-known moment in history.

The major events in *Nikolai's Fortune* actually happened, and, with minor exceptions, the characters and their fates are real. While Books I and II are crafted as historical fiction based on fact, Book III segues into memoir in order to bring full closure to this book of multigenerational consequences.

Three women tell their stories of broken bonds between mothers and daughters. *Nikolai's Fortune* begins with Marie's story as my grandmother might have told it—if only I had bothered to ask.

MAJOR CHARACTERS

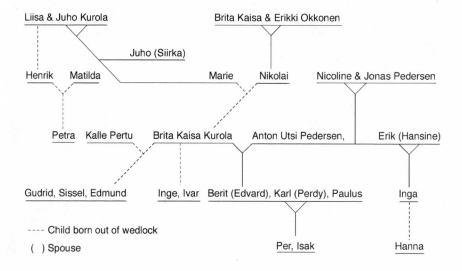

Liisa & Juho Kurola

Brita Kaisa & Erikki Okkonen

Juho (Siirka)

Henrik   Matilda

Marie   Nikolai

Nicoline & Jonas Pedersen

Petra   Kalle Pertu   Brita Kaisa Kurola   Anton Utsi Pedersen,   Erik (Hansine)

Gudrid, Sissel, Edmund   Inge, Ivar   Berit (Edvard), Karl (Perdy), Paulus   Inga

---- Child born out of wedlock

( ) Spouse

Per, Isak   Hanna

Starting in the early 1800s in Finland, these members of five
generations appear in *Nikolai's Fortune*.
Drawing by James McFarlane

BOOK I

THE ROAD OF THE FOUR WINDS

Kaisa

They've erected statues to us now, both my mother and me.

Hers graces an old hayfield in a small Finnish village on the flat, pitiless plain that was Ostrobothnia's buttery. Shaped in stone, a young woman stands prettily poised over her butter churn. "Dairy-maid" they call her—now.

Mine overlooks the inner harbor of a sea-stained fishing town in Norway. Bent over a barrel, head bound in a scarf, an old woman salts down the day's catch. But no blood oozes from those bare, bronzed hands; no wet winds pierce that sagging spine. "Herring Wife" they call me. I too have been called much worse. Much, much worse.

But that, of course, was long before lives such as ours became works of art.

ONE
MEETING NIKOLAI

The bare birches guarding the lonesome road to Rantsila were rigid with ice that dusky November afternoon and when the biting wind rustled their branches, they chimed sweetly in the stillness.

But Nikolai didn't care about cold or chimes: he was eighteen.

My mother Marie, twenty-six and mother of a two-year-old daughter named Sofie, first caught sight of him that fateful day in 1874 through the frosty windowpane of his parents' cottage. She happened to glance up momentarily from the table where she was kneading bread dough in a large wooden trough and saw a tall young man with a woven birch knapsack slung over his shoulder striding up the snowy lane as if he owned the place.

Though I was not even a twinkle in either of their eyes, I can imagine their meeting in exquisite detail, from the smell of the bread to the crunch of Nikolai's footsteps on the frozen ground. Imagining this scene, I feel almost as if I am there witnessing mutely the events that led to my birth. But back then she was not my mother; she was Marie, a vibrant young woman about to fall deeply in love with a dark-haired, handsome dreamer.

"Who's that?" Marie asked, startled by the unfamiliar figure marching purposefully into the farmyard. Squinting, Brita Kaisa peered out the tiny window, wiping her hands on her apron. A radiant smile washed over her face.

"Great heavens, it's Nikolai!" She rushed to the door and threw it open, her arms flung wide in welcome.

"Nikolai! Nikolai! Is it really you, son? You've grown so tall! And look at you. You're nearly frozen!" she admonished as she released him from her embrace.

He smiled as he stepped into the room and slipped off his knapsack.

When he removed his wool cap, a heavy shock of dark hair fell over his forehead. The fit of his threadbare but well-kept clothes suggested just the touch of a dandy.

"Oh, I'm so glad to see you," Brita Kaisa laughed, brushing away a tear. "Are the others all right? Has anything happened?"

"They're all well," he assured her.

A year earlier Brita Kaisa and her husband Erikki and their twin teenage sons and only daughter Grete had moved to Rantsila from nearby Tyrnava. For the sake of her family's welfare, Grete had agreed to marry a man sixteen years her senior, and, in fair exchange, her father Erikki was allowed to rent a cottage and farm a small plot of his new son-in-law's land on favorable terms. The couple's oldest son Matti and his wife had stayed behind in Tyrnava, as had Nikolai.

With Grete often unavailable, Nikolai's arthritic mother had sought permission from Marie's employer for the young dairymaid to help with a late, last round of fall baking. Marie was fond of her neighbor Brita Kaisa, and not just because she was one of the few villagers who still treated her decently. Brita Kaisa reminded Marie of her own mother, who had died for want of the round, flat rye loaves with holes in the middle that they were about to bake and string on poles to hang under the cottage's low ceiling. No birch bark was added to this dough. This year the harvest had not failed them.

"Just wait until your father sees you!" Brita Kaisa exclaimed heartily, as if to assure Nikolai of his welcome. "He and the twins are working in the woods."

"That's why I came," Nikolai said ruefully. "There must be some work for me here. There's nothing in Tyrnava. Anyway, it was time for me to leave, Mother."

"Oh," Brita Kasia sputtered when Nikolai's questioning gaze fell on the petite, comely woman wrestling with the dough. "This is Marie Kurola. She's been such a help to me since Grete got married." As Brita Kaisa beamed at her, Marie tucked a strand of black hair under her scarf, wiped her hands on her white apron and smiled tentatively.

Nikolai acknowledged Marie silently, nodding in her direction. He scrutinized her with dark, intense eyes, glanced down at Sofie, who clung timidly to her mother's skirts, and then for the briefest moment stared quizzically into Marie's face. She felt the familiar burn of shame creep up her throat and into her cheeks. She dropped her eyes and turned back to her bread dough.

But Marie couldn't help stealing another look at Nikolai as he settled himself by the fire with a bowl of warm porridge. Firelight danced in his hair and eyes, washing across a finely shaped nose and high, well-formed cheekbones. He was a handsome young man, Marie thought, older than his years perhaps. Something about him was different, that much she sensed. There was some restlessness in him, something unsettled. Something unsettling.

He may have felt her eyes on him. He looked up from his porridge and held her gaze. Then he suddenly smiled at her with warm, sparkling eyes. Cheeks flushing again, Marie bent over her dough, unaccountably shaken. As soon as she could, she made her escape back to the nearby farm where she lived and worked as a dairymaid.

Marie didn't see Nikolai again for weeks and was glad of it. She had every reason to be wary of male attentions. She didn't want to think about what she had seen in his eyes. As time passed, she persuaded herself that she had imagined or misunderstood it. But just in case she hadn't, Marie avoided visiting Brita Kaisa, who soon sent word complaining of her prolonged absence. It was Christmas morning before Marie saw Nikolai again.

Christmas was the highlight of our year in those days because it meant two blessed days of rest. The plank floors of our cottages had been scrubbed with sand and water, and on Christmas Eve, straw was brought inside to cover them as a reminder of the Christ Child's birth. In good years, food in such abundance as we never saw the rest of the year made its way to the table: breads, porridge, potatoes, ham, rice pudding—all washed down with sweet rye beer and coffee brewed from roasted rye kernels.

Parishioners were summoned to Christmas service long before dawn. The church bell in the tall belfry adjacent to the magnificent wooden church in Rantsila chimed at six a.m. for a service lasting a good three hours. Since fines could be levied against those absent from church on high holy days, the farms emptied of all but those who were ill or left behind to mind them. The richest landlords and their most lowly "*renki*"— male hired hands—and "*pika*"—servant women such as my mother— squeezed into horse-drawn sleds to dash through icy darkness down snowy lanes with only stars, and sometimes the moon, to light the way. Straw was strewn on the floors of the unheated church, which seated upwards of eight hundred souls and at Christmas was stuffed with sleepy worshippers stiffly adorned in their best attire. Lest any of us nod off during the interminable devotions, a stern functionary roamed the aisles armed with a long pole to sharply rap anyone who dared succumb to slumber.

The last place Marie wanted to be was in this church, but she had no say in the matter. Holding Sofie close, she found an inconspicuous seat in a back corner and, with eyes hard and angry, grimly studied the ornately carved pulpit with its parade of saints, steeling herself against the searing memory it provoked. When she noticed Nikolai trailing down the aisle behind his parents and the twins, she looked away, but not before Nikolai shot a quick, slight smile in her direction. He whispered something to Brita Kaisa, who turned to greet her with a broad smile. Marie smiled back, suddenly ashamed of neglecting a good friend. The whole thing was ridiculous; she would have to make amends. She had few enough friends in this world. She could ill afford to lose one as sweet as Brita Kaisa.

While the pastor belabored the occasion, Marie struggled to keep her eyes from settling on the back of Nikolai's head. Once, about halfway through the pastor's droning sermon, Nikolai turned to smile mischievously at her. She smiled back, then bit her lip in instant regret.

"Are you mad? What can you be thinking?" she silently reproached herself. She knew then that she must put an end to this foolishness for good and all. So, when at last the pastor had exhausted himself and the relieved worshippers rose to flee, Marie determinedly threaded her way through the crowd toward Brita Kaisa.

"I've missed you, Marie," Brita Kaisa chided good-naturedly when Marie grasped her hand in greeting.

"Oh, I've wanted to visit you but it's been hard to get away. There's been so much work, and Sofie has been sickly," Marie answered, shading the truth. She turned to Nikolai, who had hung back beside his mother while the others moved outside. "Have you found work then, Nikolai?" she asked evenly.

He nodded. "I'm over at the Mattilas', helping with the wood." He looked directly at her, but she found nothing alarming in his face. Surely she had misjudged him.

"Will you be able to stay on there in the spring?" She was determined that her voice sound natural.

His brow furrowed. "I don't know if they'll need me." If he remembered anything about what she thought had passed unspoken between them at that first meeting, he gave no sign. Good, then; that was it. She had imagined it.

"I'll come as soon as I can," Marie promised Brita Kaisa as they made their way out to the churchyard. A light snow was falling, softening the gravestones in the adjoining cemetery. Nikolai paused on the church steps to admire the carved wooden statue of the church's famous Poor Man, his huge arms held out in solicitation of alms for the needy. A large iron lock was affixed to his massive, hollow chest. Unlocking it to retrieve the alms was a solemn event overseen by a handful of the congregation's most trustworthy members. The offerings were used to support destitute old people who lived in the village poorhouse, which sat in a sloping field not far from the church.

"I've heard talk of him," Nikolai said, nodding at the statue and casually dropping a coin into the wide slit in the Poor Man's chest. He cleared his throat self-consciously. "We'd all be grateful for a coin if we came to suffer such a fate, God forbid," he added.

Marie nodded wordlessly. Nikolai seemed a proper, God-fearing sort; he went up a bit in her estimation. She herself had no coin to offer, but that didn't stop her from feeling guilty to be standing there empty-handed. The habit of feeding the Poor Man was well ingrained among the residents of Rantsila, who were perhaps a bit over-proud of the fame he brought their village.

It had not been so long ago that the church annually auctioned off destitute, homeless villagers to the lowest bidder. The farmer who accepted the least pay from the church for this transaction got another pair of hands to help with the unceasing labors of Finnish husbandry. And the destitute got a roof over their heads and food in their bellies— a not altogether heartless arrangement, as I have come to appreciate.

Despite my mother's vow to put her interaction with Nikolai on an even keel, several weeks passed before she dared visit Brita Kaisa again. Thoroughly embarrassed by her neglect and ashamed of an unbidden, overheated fantasy, she went with Sofie and found Brita Kaisa home alone, standing over the table rolling newly-washed laundry with one of the round wooden presses that served as an iron in those days.

"Has Nikolai got work?" Marie asked casually after they had gossiped by the hearth for awhile.

"He's still at the Mattilas' place. He's very restless, though. It's not what he'd hoped for."

"Umm," Marie nodded.

"I don't know what's to become of him really," Brita Kaisa fretted. "He's not like the other boys. Much more dissatisfied with everything. He's always been that way. He reads too much. But then he always did better in school than the others. The pastor said he was so clever that he should consider the church for his vocation. But Nikolai wants something more from life, though I must say he's taken the church more seriously to heart than his brothers and sister ever did."

"Oh, he'll settle down soon enough, I expect."

"You think so?" Brita Kaisa sighed. "I hope you're right. But he's completely unrealistic. He's desperate to have a farm of his own. Can you imagine? Where would he get such a thing even if he had the money, I ask you? There's no land left in Finland, not for the likes of us, anyway. Nikolai has such grand dreams, such impossible ambitions. I'm afraid he's going to be hurt by them. And his father is exasperated with him." She clucked her tongue, worry wrinkling her brow.

"He sounds like my half-brother, Henrik," Marie said soothingly. "No one could do anything with him, either. My father got upset every time Henrik came home."

"Isn't Henrik still in Ruija?" Brita Kaisa asked, using the Finnish name we used for North Norway.

"Oh, yes. He'll never come back to Finland. Except on his rounds, of course. You should hear him carry on about it! There's nothing so grand as his beloved Ruija," Marie chuckled.

"I hope Nikolai never gets ideas into his head about traipsing off to Ruija," Brita Kaisa frowned. "But he's always full of new dreams. I don't know where he gets them."

Dogs barking in the yard abruptly broke off their conversation. Brita Kaisa quickly stepped to the cupboard to fetch wooden bowls for the porridge that bubbled in a large pot over the fire, and moments later Erikki, Nikolai, and the twins came through the door. Deep in conversation, they barely acknowledged the women. As they seated themselves at the table to be served, Erikki and Nikolai resumed what apparently had been an unhappy exchange.

"I'll just have to go to work in the city for real wages, Father," Nikolai said earnestly. "There's no help for it. I hear there are jobs in the mills and on the docks in Oulu and Kemi . . ."

"Oulu and Kemi! How can you talk of living in places like that?" Erikki snorted. "Why can't you be satisfied staying here and making the best of it like the rest of us?" he demanded crossly.

Nikolai slumped over his bowl, frustration tightening his face. "You know why, Father. We've been over this so many times. How else can I earn money for land of my own?"

"Why does it have to be your own? Why can't you be thankful to have a roof over your head and bread on the table like the rest of us? What does it matter if it's another man's land so long as it feeds you?"

"I can't say why! It just does!" Nikolai snapped. He pushed his bowl away and jumped from the table, cheeks flaming. He stomped out the door, slamming it behind him.

The awkward silence in the cottage ended when Sofie began to whimper. Marie seized the moment to say a hasty goodbye and stepped quickly out into the snowy farmyard. She saw Nikolai leaning back against the barn, his arms tightly crossed over his chest. There was no ignoring him; she had to walk right past him. She fought the urge to say something comforting and lost.

"My father and my half-brother Henrik used to have this same argument," she told him quietly, pausing a short distance away.

"Oh? And how did that end?"

"Henrik went to Ruija to make his fortune."

"And did he?"

Marie smiled. "Not quite yet. He comes home nearly every year, though, to tell us it's within his grasp. But I don't think he really wants to settle down. He's a peddler and enjoys the wanderer's life."

"A peddler?"

"He walks great distances—from here to the northernmost tip of Norway, selling and trading things he makes. He's full of stories." She smiled again, warmed at the thought of Henrik's cheery disposition.

"I'd like to meet him sometime," Nikolai said, unfolding his arms and stuffing his hands into his pockets. "Do you think I could?"

Marie paused uncertainly, fearful she'd gone further than intended.

"Well, he hasn't been home in awhile, but he'll probably come this year . . ."

"Will you send word when he comes ?" he persisted. "I'd really like to hear about Ruija."

"Well . . . of course, Nikolai."

She was as good as her word. When Henrik arrived at his family's farm early that spring, Marie stopped by to tell Brita Kaisa that Nikolai could accompany her home if he wished. "But warn him that it's a long walk," she cautioned.

"It's a longer walk to Ruija," Brita Kaisa snorted. "I don't know what's to become of that boy, Marie. His father won't thank you for this, but I thank you for your patience with him anyway. I hope he soon comes to his senses."

"Oh, it's no trouble," Marie managed to say. "Henrik will like him."

Nikolai was waiting for her under a tall birch by the side of the road, whittling on a stick in the gentle morning light. He had turned nineteen; a mustache framed his upper lip.

"I hope you don't mind if I come with you," he said by way of greeting when Marie and Sofie stopped shyly before him. There was a disarming hint of uncertainty in his voice.

"Please yourself, Nikolai. But it's a very long way."

"I don't mind, Marie. I like your company." He smiled warmly at her, and her chest tightened.

She set a wicked pace that forced Sofie to trot along beside her as fast as her little legs could run. Not until she began to whimper did Marie slow down, and then a laughing Nikolai scooped up the child and set her across his shoulders. They marched along like that, following the lazy curves of the Siikajoki River as it wound among lush farm fields in the morning stillness—Sofie with her arms wrapped tightly around Nikolai, Marie striding purposefully at his side, nearly mute. Nikolai prattled easily with Sofie, who chattered happily, thrilled with the attention. He tried without much success to engage Marie in small talk.

"What do you think, Marie?" he finally demanded when they had tramped along for the better part of an hour. "Everyone else thinks I'm a fool for wanting my own land, but I can't see a future here without it.

I'm afraid that if I stay here without land to call my own, I'll die as poor as the day I was born."

"I don't know, Nikolai. But I do know you have to follow your heart or you'll never be happy."

He gave her an odd look, as if something was on the tip of his tongue. But neither spoke again until they reached the turnoff, a narrow wagon rut that twisted away from the river and up a gentle rise in the landscape toward the farm. Here the cultivated farmland gave way to thin forest. Still they kept going, deeper into the trees, up and down rocky little hills that led into wet marshlands where they had to pick their way along a footpath of logs strung between soggy islets of tufted grass.

"I had no idea it was this far out," Nikolai muttered when they stopped to rest on the crest of a small rise. Before them lay a rolling expanse of rocks and scrubby trees and the cold, still waters of a lake. "There's nothing out here but marsh and rocks. And water."

"This was all the land that was left when my father wanted a piece of land to call his own. You can see for yourself what kind of soil this is," she said as Nikolai climbed a small boulder for a better look.

"And even then, poor as it is, he couldn't really call it his own," he retorted grimly.

"My brother Juho has to wear marsh shoes to harvest his pitiful hay crop," Marie continued, alluding to the flat, wooden ski-like contraptions worn by Finland's bog farmers in those days. "No matter how many dikes he builds, he can't get the water out of here. It seeps over everything. Even his sorry excuse of a horse wears marsh shoes so she won't sink into the muck."

"This is what I mean, Marie," Nikolai said, jumping down from the boulder to stand beside her. His voice was filled with urgency. "This is exactly the reason I have to go somewhere else if I'm ever to have a decent life. Don't you understand? There's nothing left here. The land's all used up."

She understood all too well.

My grandparents, Liisa Hukkanen and Juho Heikisson Kurola, were as poor as the rest of the luckless Finnish cotters whose fortunes were tied to those of the wealthy farmers upon whose lands their rented cottages stood. My grandmother moved to Rantsila from the nearby village of Pulkkila in 1838, when she was twenty. Shortly after, she gave birth to my half-uncle Henrik.

I have every reason to appreciate what my grandmother must have faced when she left home to give birth to an illegitimate son.

My grandfather had tried to make a living in the seaport of Oulu, the largest town in our district, but he moved back home to Rantsila in 1845. A year later, he married my grandmother, then six months pregnant with his child, and took Henrik in as his own. Their first two babies died in infancy. So Henrik, my mother Marie and her younger brother Juho—named after his father—were Liisa and Juho's only surviving children.

My grandfather was just as determined as Nikolai to have his own plot of land to farm. But Ostrobothnia was crowded even in his day and productive land jealously hoarded. Fifteen years into his marriage, my grandfather succeeded in persuading a wealthy landowner to let him try his hand at clearing trees and draining marshland out on the isolated shores of Lake Mankila. Pelts saved from years of hunting were traded for an abandoned grain drying shed; this ramshackle hut became the family home. Meager savings, hoarded for nearly twenty years, provided a down payment on a worn-out horse. On this unpromising foundation my grandfather's dream of simple survival was built.

Finland in those days was held in the twin thrall of famine and the unpredictable yoke of the Russian czar. But we landless peasants were triply cursed: we also were dependent on the whims of the landed gentry for our very existence. Among our kind, want of daily human necessities had long since crushed hope of better lives, even among the most dull-witted of optimists. Yet the lot of the farmers who owned the fields and forests in which we toiled in endless servitude only got better as ours grew worse.

Despite the hard times, the church insisted on our education, such as it was: four years of schooling starting at age ten. We were expected to learn to read and write, master our sums, and, most importantly, memorize the blessed catechism. The parish pastor regularly visited each farm to ascertain whether the inhabitants could recite it. Public disgrace was the dread weapon he used to enforce church strictures. It wasn't uncommon in those days to find a grown man who had failed to recite correctly sitting under the dining table with an empty bowl on his head, put there by the pastor for punishment.

My mother Marie had an aptitude for schooling that she did not pass on to me. Nothing but the best marks were set down beside her name in the thick, leather-bound volumes in which the most intimate details of our miserable lives were duly recorded by church clerics. When my turn came in the classroom, a succession of cow pie marks were dropped across the page beside my name, a demeaning symbol used to signify the worst that could be said of a student. For me, school was a preview of hell on earth. My classmates never ceased tormenting me and I could never concentrate on the lessons.

My half-uncle Henrik, energetic, footloose and curious about the world, had drifted away in search of a more rewarding life by the time I was born. "Who is satisfied with little remains poor," was his favorite proverb, so he pushed ever farther north in hope of leaving poverty behind. First he labored on the docks at Kemi. Then he moved on to the colorful, ancient settlement of Tornio, where the Tornio River rushes down from the mountains to empty into the northernmost tip of the Gulf of Bothnia. There he lay on his stomach on a sailing sled on the frozen gulf, shooting seals for their fur. But the irresistible lure of the Arctic pulled him farther north, up the Tornio River valley into the wild, barren steppes of Lapland.

Season after season, meanwhile, my mother exhausted her youth in fields and barns and kitchens, scrubbing, cooking, weaving, knitting. She milked cows, churned butter, shoveled manure. In summer, she raked the hay and piled it into those neat, cylindrical stacks that only Finns seem able to master—there was none of this careless throwing of hay willy-nilly across wires strung between poles in the sloppy manner these self-satisfied Norwegians are so proud of, I can tell you that. No, the hayfields of Finland were works of art: row upon precise row of nicely rounded humps of sweet hay dotting deep green fields flat as a lefse. Small wooden sheds for storing the dried hay stood evenly spaced in every field. And interspersed amongst these sheds were large wooden windmills for grinding the grain crops. The whole effect was to give the countryside a settled, friendly look, one quite different from the stony landscapes of Norway.

Or so I remember it.

I can still see my mother in those hayfields, scarf tightly wrapped around her dark hair, rake flying, the breeze billowing her long, full skirts. I remember her at the river's edge among the wooden tubs, fiercely beating laundry with a wooden paddle. And I can see her strong hands working flax under an August sun after the dainty blue flowers had withered on their stems. The flax stalks were put into soaking tubs and hung in the sauna to dry. On cozy winter evenings, after the stalks had been squeezed on a wooden press, Mother sat at the loom on the women's side of the cottage—men kept to their side and women to theirs—and wove the flaxen strands into cloth. But most of all I remember her standing over the wooden butter churn, both calloused hands firmly grasping the paddle, pumping smoothly up and down, up and down, hour after hour, sweating as she fought the heavy milk into rich butter. Even at this backbreaking task, my mother stood erect, defiantly proud.

She always treated me tenderly. I can't remember her ever speaking a cross word to me, and she always found time to pull me close at the end of the weary day. Perhaps it was because she understood from the outset what she would have to do.

TWO

MARIE'S PAST

Mother had not always been a *pika* churning butter in another woman's kitchen. In 1866, when Marie was eighteen, long before she met the man who would be my father, a grim life took a wrenching turn for the worse. Late, killing frost ruined much of the harvest. In those days, Finns lived from harvest to harvest; there was little to tide them over through an unproductive season. Less food found its way to the family table with each passing day. Mother told me that my grandmother Liisa grew thin and weak but refused her rightful share of the scant portions.

"You must eat," Grandmother would say, pushing a bowl of thin gruel toward her husband and children. "You must keep your strength for the fields," she insisted. "How else are we to live?"

"But there's nothing in the fields to harvest!" Grandfather would protest helplessly.

Starvation stalked the village. The poorest succumbed to sickness and the weakest died in alarming numbers. The church bell tolled frequent funeral salutes—three chimes for a woman or child, five chimes for every man. The bodies piled up faster than they could be buried. The constant ringing of church bells only intensified the fears of those left alive to hear it.

Marie learned to improvise in the kitchen as the other women did: she mixed soft, pulpy birch bark with a precious handful of flour or dried peas, if any could be found. If not, she made do with moss.

"Birch bread," Marie smiled grimly when, full of shame, she set this infamous dish before her father and brother. For six hundred years famine-ridden Finns had dined on birch bark to survive when times demanded. The men chewed it stonily, without comment, humiliation burning in their eyes. My grandmother wouldn't touch it. She lay in a narrow cot by the fire, face turned to the wall. Her family could only watch as she sank deeper into herself, refusing to be roused, feverish eyes bulging from hollow sockets. My mother meanwhile plodded from barn to kitchen and back, nursing her mother, attending by rote to the family's daily needs, dogged in the face of crushing adversity.

On a bitterly frosty November afternoon in 1866, my grandmother died in the family cottage of malnutrition and old age. She was forty-eight. The ground was frozen, so her body was stuffed into a sack and lowered into a large open pit in the churchyard. There the bodies lay piled upon one another awaiting burial at spring thaw.

The shock of the family's loss was cushioned by their exhaustion. Unable to mourn properly, they fell into a cheerless routine, driven through the winter by one goal: procuring the next meal. When word of his mother's death eventually caught up with Henrik, he came home in time to help with an alarmingly late spring planting. While they tensely awaited the healing heat of summer, he found work on a charitable works project, paid for by one of the rich men in the village, building a road to an outlying hamlet. Each worker carried a bag into which at the end of the day was dumped his wages: one cup of flour. It kept them alive.

But summer never came. The ice never completely melted from the lake, and the marshy humps of soil held frost nearly all summer. Full-blown famine spread across the land. Often feverish, sapped of strength, Marie struggled weakly through her chores, hoping for the day when a successful crop would be harvested, praying she would live to see it.

Meanwhile Henrik and his half-brother Juho stumbled over one another, often at swords' points. Finally, Uncle Juho snapped. It happened in the fall, when it had become clear to my mother that their rations would not see them through the winter no matter how much birch bark she used. Only a few rye loaves still hung under the ceiling, and just a handful of dried peas and a few moldy potatoes remained in the cellar near the sauna.

"We'll have to kill the cow," Grandfather told them, anguish playing across his beaten face. His hair had turned snow white and his shoulders were perpetually slumped. "There's no help for it."

"But if we eat the cow, we'll have no milk! And then what shall we do come spring?" Juho exclaimed in alarm.

"Better once too much than always too little," his father answered bitterly, quoting the old proverb. "God in his own good time will have to provide for us, but it seems we have to get ourselves through this winter."

Juho grimaced angrily. "We'd have enough if there weren't an extra mouth to feed in the house," he spat out.

"Juho! We'll not have such talk in this house! The poorest stranger is welcome to share our last morsel and the warmth of our hearth. You know that. Surely you don't begrudge your brother what you'd willingly offer a stranger?"

"Brother, indeed! He comes here only in times of trouble, when he can't feed himself by wandering footloose and carefree across the countryside. Then he expects us to provide for him. But what about those of us who stay home and take responsibility?" He glared defiantly at Henrik, who sat quietly by the fire, his head bowed.

"That's enough, Juho!"

"No, it's all right," Henrik said, rising. "He's right. I shouldn't have stayed so long. Next time I come home, I'll make sure it's not in time of trouble."

The next morning Marie bade Henrik a sorrowful farewell. He had treated her with solicitous kindness ever since she was a tiny child. "Where will you go this time?" she asked forlornly as he threw his worn birch knapsack across his back and pulled on thick woolen mittens.

"Back north, of course. It's the only place a man's got a chance."

"I wish you could stay. It's so good to have you here, Henrik."

He opened the door and spat into the piercing wind that whipped at the snow piled against the cottage wall. It was freezing; the river that he used as a road would be ready. He smiled affectionately at her as he pulled his battered hat over his ears.

"I only came back to look after you, Marie," he answered gruffly. "I wanted to be sure you're all right. You've grown into a fine woman. Any day now you'll have a man of your own to look after you."

"Try to send word to us so we know where you are and that you're well. And come back soon."

"I'll be back. Don't worry so. Things will get better." They hugged awkwardly and then he was gone, head held high, whistling his way out of the farmyard.

But things did not get better. The roads became ever more crowded with ragtag beggars in search of food and work, an army of the dispossessed cut loose from ancestral villages and familial ties. Many followed Henrik's route up the Tornio Valley to the heights of Lapland and down to the fish-rich fjords of Ruija. Those with land to plant stayed behind, sowing scarce seeds with hearts aching in their throats, reaping meager harvests while the bile of despair gnawed in their bellies.

Then one chilly June day in 1871, Marie's father dropped stone dead in the barn. Overnight Uncle Juho, now twenty-one, became the man of the house. It didn't improve his temperament.

"What's to become of us now, I ask you?" he complained to Marie shortly after their father had been laid to rest. The tiny cottage, which somehow had accommodated them all so cozily, suddenly had grown awkwardly crowded with just the two of them.

"Well, you'll be marrying Siirka soon," Marie replied with false cheer. Juho and the warmhearted Siirka, as sweet as he was sour, had recently become betrothed.

He scowled. "You should be marrying soon yourself. Who are you waiting for, anyway? A czar's son?"

Marie flushed. It was a familiar, sore subject. Though she was tiny, backbreaking work had made my mother strong and self-confident—and probably a little cheeky. She always held herself erect and brooked no nonsense from anyone, especially the young village louts, as she liked to call them. Perpetually weary, she hoarded for herself what little unburdened time she had and gave a frosty welcome to unsubtle suitors who from time to time found a thin pretext for dropping by the cottage. As a result, she was considered pretty enough but altogether too haughty and dour.

Meanwhile the clergy, alarmed by the growing number of young men who, inspired by hard times, spent drunken evenings carousing and playing cards, imposed a curfew on the village. Any man caught out after ten P.M. was issued a fine; if he were a *renki*, his master was required to pay it. And since a tax had been levied on dancing establishments in an effort to discourage them, courting was fraught with new perils.

For her part, Marie was glad for the church's interference; she hated being pestered.

"Seriously, Marie, there's already talk that you hold yourself too good for any of the local lads. I think your time to marry has come; we must pray it hasn't gone as well. It won't do to put on such airs. They just despise you for it."

"Why are you carrying on so?" Marie snapped. "I'll not get in your way, and I'll thank you to stay out of mine. Can't we just mourn Father in peace?"

"Well," Juho growled, "I will be wanting to marry soon, as you say. And Siirka will want to be mistress of her own kitchen."

His words fell on her like leaden weights. So, just like that, the day she long had so dreaded had finally arrived. She searched Juho's face for a sign, hoping she had misunderstood. He wouldn't look at her. Neither spoke for a long time.

"What do you want me to do?" she finally asked quietly. "What can I do? I can't produce a husband from thin air, especially not in times such as these. And I won't marry just anyone to get a roof over my head. I won't!" She glared defiantly at him.

"Then you should find a permanent post. We can make some inquiries. The Widow Kangas always needs help . . ."

"The Widow Kangas? Are you mad? There's a good reason she always needs help!"

"Talk to her," he urged, ignoring her protests. "It's one of the finest farms in the village, after all, and there's no want of food at that table, famine or no famine. And you'd have some *markkaa* at the end of the year to show for your trouble, which is more than you'll ever have staying here." He smiled weakly, trying to make light of it. "And who knows? The widow's sons will be needing wives themselves soon, I should think."

"They won't be picking them from the likes of us, as you very well know!" she snapped. She glared at him, fighting hot tears of helplessness. Poor as it was, the ramshackle cottage had been a refuge from such people as the Kangases and their demands. However humble, here, at least, she was mistress of her own kitchen. She worried the situation over in her mind for several sleepless nights. But it was true: she had postponed the inevitable as long as she could. She didn't want to end up the old maid sister-in-law, the daughter destined to remain a spinster because she couldn't entice a husband to provide her with her own kitchen. Finland was full of such women; they were the butt of endless jokes and objects of scorn and pity. She had seen the misery such unhappy, spiteful women caused in cramped households all over the village, and she had no intention of becoming one herself. If she were to keep her self-respect, she would have to clear out and leave the cottage to Juho and his wife. She had the right to stay as long as she wished, of course; that much protection the law did afford her.

The law also obliged her family to provide for her, so it wasn't as though she was in danger of becoming an object of charity, she assured herself. But she was too proud to stay where she wasn't wanted.

The Widow Kangas's farm was nicely situated on a little rise overlooking well-tilled, well-drained fields. The house, barn, and outbuildings sat in a square facing inward to the central farmyard; only the sauna stood, as was customary, a way off from the other buildings to protect them in case it caught fire.

The Widow, a spectacularly wrinkled presence, made it her business to oversee the servants as well as her two shiftless sons, neither of whom she trusted to take charge of the farm. She hectored them, one and all, servants and sons, from daybreak until long past dark. As a consequence, her servants came and went with great regularity. In those days, servants signed on for a year's work each November; they were not paid until the year was out and the harvest safely put away for winter. Most stayed put year after year if they found conditions tolerable. They were to be grateful for a place to sleep by the kitchen fire and barely enough food to keep hunger at bay. But as soon as the Widow's servants had their annual wages in hand, most of them fled.

As she had feared, Marie was hired on the spot. She'd hardly settled into her new surroundings when she became aware that the sneering dullard Paavo, the Widow's youngest son, was eyeing her unpleasantly at every opportunity. A cold chill went through her the first time she noticed him in the doorway of the barn, leering at her through his blond forelocks. She pulled industriously on the cow's teats, squirting warm, foaming milk into the bucket. She hoped he'd lose interest when he saw she paid him no mind.

Just then one of the renkis stopped to say something to Paavo, and they both laughed. "Fine teats on that one, wouldn't you say?" Paavo smirked.

She set her jaw and moved on to the next animal, but he persisted. "Are you too good to answer when your employer speaks to you?"

"No," she mumbled, heart racing.

He came closer. "I've heard you set a fine price on yourself," he continued threateningly. "You're a servant here. You'll do as you're told." He gave her a hard look, then turned on his heel and strutted off.

He had frightened her, but there was nothing she could do about it. Who could she tell? And who would care? Certainly not the Widow. And Juho? He'd think she was trying to find an excuse to come home. She could only hope for the best. She was heartened, as time went on, that Paavo didn't confront her again, though he often turned up unexpectedly to stare insolently at her as she went about her chores.

One uncommonly hot summer day Marie was sent alone into the field farthest from the house to finish raking up a last bit of hay. She was lost in thought, raking methodically, apprehensively weighing the merits of her circumstances. "Juho's right about one thing, at least," she told herself. "I shan't be starving when the bad times come again, anyway."

Heat steamed up from the moist, sweet grass and sweat soaked her dress. She took off her scarf and wiped her face with it, then decided to cool down for a few moments in the shade of the nearest hay shed. These well-designed sheds had two opening doorways on opposite walls so the hay wagon could be pulled in from the front, unloaded, and then driven straight out the back. Marie sank down against the wall near the front doorway and gratefully closed her eyes. She had rested there only a moment when he grabbed her shoulders from behind.

She shrieked, but Paavo clamped a hand over her mouth and dragged her roughly into the shed. He pushed her into the moldy, prickly remnants of last year's hay and threw his legs across her body, pinning her under him.

"Don't fight me, slut. Who do you think you are? You think you're too good for me, is that it?" he hissed. "Scream and they'll find us, and you'll be the worse for it." While he ripped at her clothes and his own, she twisted frantically under his weight. She wriggled both arms free and raised them to his head, wrapped her fingers around his ears and ripped sharply downward. Yowling, he reared back and punched her with a fully knotted fist across the mouth. Her head snapped sideways, and a moment later, she felt him pierce her. A scream of agony and fury rose in her throat but he muffled it with his hand.

"Paavo! Where are you?"

There was no mistaking that voice. It was the Widow, very near.

He cursed and groaned, pumping his hips in great frenzy.

"Paavo! I need you, you lazy cur!" She was upon them, so close Marie could hear her footsteps crunching the stubble. "Paavo! Where are you?"

At the moment he exploded inside her, Paavo's hand fell from Marie's mouth. She sucked air and screamed.

"Paavo!" his mother roared from the doorway.

Wide-eyed, he leaped backwards to his feet, panting rapidly and pulling on his trousers.

"You worthless pig!" his mother shouted "You're just like your father!" She seized the rake and whacked him across the shoulders. He fled out the back doorway.

Marie lay in the rotting hay, sobbing convulsively. The Widow stood over her, still clutching the rake, her face knotted in a fearsome scowl.

"And you! I'll have no more whoring out of you!" She spat in disgust, ignoring Marie's swelling face. Long, sob-wracked moments passed before Marie sat up to glare bitterly at the Widow.

"He attacked me! He *attacked* me! I didn't do anything wrong!"

The Widow frowned. "You're a good worker, I'll say that much." She paused, then added decisively: "Paavo won't bother you again. I'll see to that."

Marie pulled herself to her feet, chest heaving, and leaned unsteadily against the wall. "He won't, that's true enough. I'll strangle him with my bare hands while he's asleep in his bed if that's what it takes." She didn't recognize her own voice.

The Widow's eyebrows flew up, but Marie didn't care; she shook with rage. Waves of nausea washed over her and tears coursed down her cheeks. All she wanted was to escape from this place. But where could she possibly go? And how could she tell Juho?

She didn't tell him until she had to, just before Christmas, when it had become inescapably apparent that she was carrying a child.

"How could you let this happen!" Juho shouted when she came home to stand, humiliated, in the doorway of the family cottage to beg for shelter. "You disgrace our parents! You disgrace me!" Furious, he turned his back to her while Siirka hovered nervously in the shadows

"Juho, it wasn't my fault! He forced me! I fought him but there was nothing I could do! Nothing!" Her voice shook with anger, hurt and desperation.

He wheeled to face her accusingly. "Then why didn't you tell me when it happened? I could have done something . . ."

"What? Just what exactly would you have done, Juho? Demand that he make me an honest woman? I'd die first! Besides, when I told the Widow, she refused to believe it was his child—even though she saw with her own eyes what happened. She called me a whore and threw me out. 'You're just looking for a respectable father for your spawn,' is how she put it."

Juho sighed deeply and patted her awkwardly. "All right, Marie. I believe you. Shush, now. Shush." Sobbing, she collapsed into Siirka's arms.

My sister Sofie was born on my grandfather's farm May 6, 1872, in the sauna, as was the custom. For the next forty days, my mother was permitted no contact with anyone. She was not allowed to eat with others or to touch them. In the eyes of the church she, like all women who gave birth, whether married or unmarried, was considered unclean and thus to be shunned by chaste, God-fearing souls.

But, weakened as she was by a difficult childbirth, it was not until Sunday, July 21, that my mother faced her crowning humiliation.

It was a lovely day. Celebratory sunlight streamed in through the high, arched windows of the church as if to mock the moment. My mother sat stiffly in a chair placed on a low platform facing the parishioners who had assembled to do their duty. The pastor towered above her on his pulpit. Today my mother was to be held up to public scorn as an example of the basest of sinners. Face aflame, she sat as still as the carved saints adorning the massive pulpit while the pastor's accusations roared in her ears. Fighting nausea, she gripped the seat of the chair tightly with both hands, steadying herself under a thundering torrent of recriminations.

There had been growing numbers of such scenes in the church in Rantsila in recent times. With each newly-fallen woman, the pastor—a thin, pale man whose eyes were devoid of the barest flicker of compassion— grew more frenetic in his exhortations.

"Man is an imperfect creature, by his very nature too easily tempted to sin," he warned. "But woman, she is ordained to be the guardian of his virtue. Should she fail in that sacred duty, as did this poor sinner, we shall all be lost!" He paused for effect. "But there is hope, even for such sinners as this." This was the moment they were waiting for. On cue, Marie stood to face the worshippers. She swallowed and wet her lips; her throat was so tight she was sure no sound could escape it.

"I confess the sin of having a child out of wedlock," she said tonelessly. Her voice was barely audible in the deep silence, but a sigh of satisfaction rose from the packed pews. When the ordeal was over, the subdued congregation filed out. But Marie remained standing until the pastor approached her.

"Come back tomorrow to receive absolution," he told her curtly. She knew what that required: a candle in one hand, money in the other. Uncertainly, she searched the back pews for Henrik, who emerged from the shadows, glowering, and took her arm. His eyes were narrow glints of fury.

"I'm sorry, Marie. I never thought I'd see a day such as this," he muttered through clenched teeth as he led her outside.

"I'm sorry for the shame that has fallen on our family, Henrik. But it wasn't my fault. Why can't anyone understand that?" She was determined not to cry. Or vomit.

"I know, Marie." He guided her past the prying stares of the last handful of gloating worshippers who were waiting for a closer look at a certified sinner. The men leered at her knowingly; the eyes of the hard-faced women shot her through with venomous daggers. One of the women spat in front of her as she passed.

"Slut!" hissed another.

She and Henrik kept walking, heads high, to where Juho's horse and decrepit wagon were waiting, but Marie's knees were wobbling. Now that it was over, she was afraid she would faint. It was some time after they were safely seated in the wagon before she could speak. When she did, her voice trembled.

"I know that Juho, in his heart of hearts, still thinks it was my fault, that I could have done something to stop it. He says he believes me, but . . ."

"Never mind him, Marie. He's a fool. Always has been."

"I'm so glad you're here, Henrik. I couldn't have gotten through this without you. Can't you stay this time?"

"I'm through with this place for good," he answered angrily. "As soon as the rivers freeze up, I'll go back north."

Marie fought back the tears. Her reputation was ruined. With her good name destroyed, any hope of attaining what precious little she otherwise could have expected from life was gone. And none of it was her fault. Whenever she thought of the injustice of it all, a blind fury seized her and her whole body shook.

What was to become of her?

"They'll be needing help over at the Suorsas'," Juho announced one evening just after the New Year. "And they're willing to take a servant with a child."

Marie had sensed this was coming. They had been closed inside the tiny cottage with one another for months and the evenings were long. Marie tried to keep herself and the baby out of the way and allow Siirka to reign in the kitchen, but the inevitable tensions were wearing on them all.

"What choice do you have?" Juho demanded irritably. "They know your work well enough. No one's ever said a word against you on that score. Besides, they can't be too particular."

"Neither can I," Marie acknowledged bitterly.

Elsa Suorsa was a Swedish skinflint who had never been heard to utter a good word about any Finn. She had a haughty seventeen-year-old daughter named Anna and a morose, henpecked husband named Viho, who kept out of their way the best he could. The Suorsas were notorious for their un-Christian frugality, and their servants were poorly fed.

"You must know I tolerate no improprieties," Elsa warned meaningfully when Marie, her stomach a tangle of tense knots, presented herself at the farmhouse door to petition for work. That day my mother became one of two hired hands attached to the Suorsas' farmhouse. While not so fine as that of the Widow Kangas, the Suorsa farm had a thin forest of pine and fir and undulating fields draining toward the river. The farmhouse was unpainted, but its windows were trimmed in white, as were all the better houses in the village.

Marie's primary responsibilities were the cows, the milk and the butter. But in truth, she spent her days in an unending cycle of chores in the barn, kitchen and fields. There were chickens and pigs to feed; sheep to be sheared to make woolen dresses, coats and blankets; rye to be harvested, then cured in drying sheds, threshed into flour in wooden windmills and baked into loaves. The work never stopped, each task to its season, day in, day out, year upon exhausting year.

Marie's only respite was when she was dispatched to assist Brita Kaisa, and that was only because Brita Kaisa, a skilled knitter, paid Elsa Suorsa in knitted socks in exchange for Marie's services. But Marie would gladly have helped Brita Kaisa for free had it been up to her.

At first, Marie hung Sofie in a large basket from a peg in the Suorsas' kitchen ceiling while she worked. Later, she plunked the toddler down through a round hole in a wide plank attached to four wooden legs. With Sofie safely trapped in this clever enclosure, Marie sprang from chore to chore. She and her child slept between coarse blankets on the lower bunk of a cot near the kitchen hearth. Since she was the only female servant, she and the baby had the bed to themselves. The manservant, forty-seven-year-old Johan Frantsila, slept above them, huddled next to the chimney.

"Times surely can't be so bad that it's come to our having to hire strumpets," had been Johan's greeting when Marie arrived for her first day of work. "And with a babe in arms to boot." He spat disdainfully and strode off, leaving Marie standing wordless, flushed with shame.

Johan Frantsila was just another victim of his country's hard times, but he took it with singular bad grace and rancor. He had developed a private theory to explain why he and his Finnish countrymen were suffering so: it was the fault of the Swedes.

It was not enough that they had come, centuries since, and helped themselves to all the best in Finland, usurped the land and imposed their own government on the Finns. The worst of it was that they had proved unable to defend Finland against the claims of the Russians, who menaced from the east. The Swedes had given up their claims to the country in 1809, but that signified little in Johan's reckoning. It galled him that the Swedes still had the best jobs, still got the best education, still controlled the country's wealth and its land. "And they still look down on Finns," he groused.

Finnish only recently had been declared one of the country's official languages. It was bad enough not to be able to read in any language. But to have court proceedings of your own homeland conducted in a foreign tongue and legal documents written in a language you could not hope to understand—that was intolerable, Johan reminded anyone who would listen.

"My ancestors settled this village in the 1500s. Now look what's become of us—shoveling Swedish manure! What more can befall us?"

Marie tried not to imagine the answer. Exhausted by the baby's demands and those of her masters, she hardly dared sleep for fear of not hearing the cock crow at dawn. Hardening herself to this joyless new life, she tried not to dwell on what otherwise might have been.

Until that day Nikolai sauntered so casually into her life.

THREE

DREAMS OF AMERICA

When Nikolai and Marie finally reached Juho and Siirka's cottage, Henrik glowered at Nikolai with frank suspicion. Henrik hid his broad, earnest face and tender heart under a bushy beard and gruff manner. But as soon as Nikolai began to question him about the allure of the north, Henrik was won over.

"Come to Ruija," he urged, pulling on his pipe as the two men lounged companionably on a bench just outside the cottage door. "You can soon enough have a farm of your own right by the sea, or tucked up in a little valley against such mountains as you've never seen in your life. And all the fish you could ever hope to eat! You would never starve there."

"I don't know," Nikolai mused. "It seems a harsh life. I think I'd prefer America myself."

"America! And how are you going to get to America, I ask you? All you have to do to get to Ruija is put one foot after the other and walk, man!"

"Walk? But it's seven hundred kilometers, and over desolate mountains."

"It's not so bad. Hundreds of people are doing it every year. You should see them swarming over the countryside. The Lapps call it 'The Road of the Four Winds.' It's their ancient migration route to the Arctic Sea. Now it's chock full of Finns, walking or riding on carts and sleds over the mountains and down to the fjord at Skibotn. They just stroll up along the Tornio River valley . . ."

"Stroll! But it's a wilderness!"

"Well, you do have to plan your route carefully so you have shelter at night," Henrik conceded.

Nikolai shook his head doubtfully. "I've seen those poor fools carrying all their worldly goods on their backs, wandering the countryside, begging, starving."

"Look, lad. You don't have to starve or beg. Some people do carry their worldly belongings on their backs. That's their mistake. They're prisoners of their goods. I carry only goods I can sell as I go—trinkets, needles, thread, buttons, wood carvings I've made myself. I sell my labor for food when I'm hungry or for a bed when I'm tired. A man doesn't need all that baggage to get through life. He has to be free to see the world and find himself, right? He shouldn't be chained like an animal to other people's chores and possessions. All he needs is food and drink along the way . . . and maybe the company of a good woman from time to time." Henrik grinned broadly and winked.

Nikolai laughed good-naturedly. "I'm afraid it's my lot to aspire to more than that . . . or my curse, you may say."

Now it was Henrik's turn to shake his head. "There's no future in Finland for the likes of us, Nikolai," he said somberly. "Come to Ruija. Hard it may be, but it's a life better than this, where a man can't even provide for his own children. And who knows how much worse it will get here?"

"I know," Nikolai agreed dejectedly.

"So what will you do?" Henrik persisted.

Nikolai furrowed his brows and stared at the ground. "I wish I knew. I'd like to find a way to earn enough money to have my own bit of land, just enough to put up my own cottage and keep a cow or two, some chickens, a pig perhaps, a garden, and maybe grow enough barley and wheat for the table—and have enough left over for some coffee in a good year."

Marie, listening in the doorway, thought he sounded suddenly embarrassed.

"And if you could find land, how long do you figure it will take you to save enough to have it?" Henrik demanded quietly.

"Well, I've managed to put by a small sum, very small, but . . ."

"Well, then, Nikolai, figure it out for yourself. How many years will it take to save the money to get your own plot of land, providing anyone is charitable enough to part with it, which, in this crowded landscape, I very much doubt."

Nikolai's face hardened, but he said nothing.

"My father slaved fifteen years, and here's what he got for his trouble!" Henrik waved contemptuously across the farmyard. "You can't do it in twenty years, man! And even if you could, do you realize what a broken being you'll be in twenty years, slaving from dawn to dark to enrich another man? It's impossible!"

Nikolai stared at him in mute, naked misery.

"Well, Nikolai, never mind. We all have to have our dreams, don't we?" Henrik laughed mirthlessly and clapped Nikolai on the shoulder.

"I can see why you've grown fond of him," Siirka whispered teasingly to Marie when the men moved out of earshot.

"Don't be ridiculous, Siirka! We're just . . . it's not like that," Marie protested. "You know I'm much too old for him even if I were interested, which I'm not. And he has too many plans to worry about women." She tried to keep her voice normal.

"Plans?" Siirka asked quizzically.

"You heard him. He really means to have a farm of his own."

"Don't they all?" Siirka laughed dismissively.

Marie didn't see much of Nikolai after that day. Whenever she did, she felt unwell. He had never asked a word about the circumstances of Sofie's birth, and she knew no decent way to bring it up. So who could know what he really thought of her? Perhaps he hoped to use her in the same base way. The young men in the village—and many older ones, for that matter—still leered boldly at her and freely teased her with lewd, mocking suggestions. She knew she was a marked woman, forever to be a target of unwanted advances. So she avoided being alone with any man, young or old, married or single. She was considered damaged, thus available, goods. A man faced much less risk of censure for misbehavior with her than with a "respectable" woman. The child at her skirts was an inescapable talisman of shame that proclaimed her status as a fallen woman. She had proven she could not be depended upon to guard a man's virtue.

Still, except for the way he sometimes stared at her, Nikolai had been nothing but proper toward her. Was that because he regarded her as spoiled goods unworthy of affection? Don't be a fool! He's a mere boy, and a hopeless dreamer at that, she reproached herself on those nights when Nikolai's smiling face stood between her and sleep. She successfully wrestled that image out of her mind for weeks, sometimes months, at a time.

But whenever she did see him, an awful rush would paralyze her limbs. And with time her affliction, as she came to regard it, grew worse, not better. She began to dread the thought of seeing him as much as not seeing him. Increasingly desperate, Marie lived on the memory of Nikolai's smile. It nourished her through the long, backbreaking interludes when his physical presence didn't momentarily grace her bleak, hopeless life.

"Rubbish! Make your mark here, boy! Don't listen to all that foolish talk about America."

Erikki and Nikolai were at it again. Marie, against her better judgment, had come to visit Brita Kaisa. It was spring, and she came upon the men repairing the wooden pole fence that lined the lane and kept the cows from wandering. Cut in winter, the poles were set at an angle, one leaning on top of the other. Nikolai was ripping out the remnants of the old ones while his father replaced them. Nikolai had now filled his twenty-first year and become a full-grown man, as anyone could plainly see. Coming here had been a mistake, Marie immediately realized. But Nikolai shot her a quick smile and scooped Sofie up into his arms.

"They say a man can get free land there, as much as he can farm, all just for the taking? What a fairy tale! America, indeed!" Erikki disgustedly jammed the last pole in place.

"No, Father, it's all true. I've seen the letters myself. There is free land."

We all knew about America in those days. Everyone in Rantsila knew someone who had gone there or someone who had gotten a letter from there filled with the wonders of a life without want, one where hard work was not a condition of unrelenting servitude but a passport to a better life. Every month, it seemed, someone from the village left for this golden land, leaving behind envious, admiring neighbors and grieving, proud relatives. New York, Hancock, Astoria, Deep River, Duluth—the names rolled as familiarly off our tongues as if they were the next parish. What began as a trickle grew to a torrent as Rantsila's young men fled to that fabulous, irresistible land where dreams actually came true.

"Father, they call it the 'Land of Opportunity.' Every man can become whatever he's got the gumption to become."

"'Land of Opportunity'!" Erikki scoffed irritably, wiping his brow.

"Especially in the west," Nikolai continued enthusiastically. "There's farming and fishing and in valley after valley, mountain after mountain, farther than any human eye can see, there are trees to fell that are so big that twenty men linking arms can't reach around them. And the trees are taller than three hundred houses stacked on top of one another! Not like these puny poles," he added derisively.

"Trees taller than three hundred houses! Do you take me for a simpleton?"

Nikolai laughed. "I swear it's true. Toivo Aho has gone as far as the Pacific Ocean to a place called Astoria in Oregon Territory. I've read his letters. Lots of Finns have settled there. It's by a huge river, larger by many, many times than our own poor Siikajoki, and brimming with enormous salmon. The Columbia, they call it. Its banks are lined with magnificent trees, and there's endless rich farmland just for the taking."

Marie forgot herself and listened in open wonderment. She had never heard Nikolai so enthusiastic on any subject.

"Fairy tales!" Erikki repeated glumly. "These poor fools that go chasing halfway around the world after riches will come to a bad end, mark my words. Better they should make the best of such opportunities as present themselves right here at home where they belong."

"What opportunities?" Nikolai shot back bitterly.

Marie felt a sudden twinge of dread. She left Brita Kaisa that day with renewed resolve to forget Nikolai once and for all. She plodded determinedly through her cheerless life as anxious summers passed into anxious winters. On the occasions when she encountered Nikolai, she avoided being alone with him. Still, he rarely left her thoughts.

As the summer of 1879 warmed to its full glory, the farm folk swung into frenetic activity, leaving Marie little time to think of anything but the next burdensome task. Cows were turned loose to graze in the pastures. Potato fields wanted tending, pigs wanted fattening. Soon the cotters were swarming over wheat, barley, and hay fields, wielding their long, curved scythes. The womenfolk, hair bound tightly in scarves, followed behind with wooden rakes. All across the countryside the fields bustled with the purposeful tempo that attends the promise of a successful harvest. This year there would be no famine.

The barking of dogs startled Marie one cool, crisp morning as she trudged from the barn to the house, a wooden bucket of milk in each hand. The dogs were dancing about a tall young man with nothing on his head against the weather but a heavy shock of dark brown hair.

"Nikolai!" she sang out in surprise. "Whatever brings you here?"

"Haven't you heard? I'm to help with the harvest."

"You are?" Transfixed, she stood gazing up at him. It had been months since she'd last seen him and years since they'd really spoken. They stood awkwardly for a long, silent moment. Then a blond, rosy-cheeked young woman with icy blue eyes appeared in the doorway, Elsa Suorsa's daughter, Anna. She gave Nikolai a cool appraisal.

"Father's behind the barn. He's expecting you." Anna quickly closed the door, but Marie noticed that she went to the kitchen window to stare at Nikolai as he passed. Anna immediately took a transparent interest in his whereabouts and served him solicitously when the men came in from the fields to eat. Stamping methodically at her butter churn, Marie made silent note of Anna's frequent trips to the window whenever Nikolai was in the yard.

Once again, against her own dearest wishes, the old, conflicting emotions troubled Marie's sleep. She resented his intrusion into the cloistered routine she had created for herself and her child. Still, each day she awoke energized by the hope of seeing him and she flew through the days with a light step. Despite an occasional warm, wry smile or a piercing, unbearable stare, Nikolai's attitude toward her remained unfathomable. She longed to reclaim the unspoken intimacy she remembered—or that she thought she remembered—even though she feared feeding the dampened fire of her misery. So an awkwardness suffocated their brief exchanges. She existed on alternating tethers of giddy hope and nervous despair.

She went home to Juho's cottage for a visit when harvest was over. Siirka wasted no time in quizzing her about Nikolai, but Marie feigned disinterest.

"Poverty and love are impossible to hide, Marie, just as the proverb says," Siirka chided gently as they warmed themselves before the hearth. "Oh, I just don't want to see you hurt after all you've been through. Can't you be satisfied with one of the other lads?"

"You mean one who'll have me even after what I've been through?" Marie snapped. "Who might that be?"

"Marie, don't say such things! That's not what I meant. It wasn't your fault."

"And who's to know that?" Marie spat out. "What decent Christian man is to believe any such thing after the priest has branded me a sinner before all the world?"

"Oh, Marie . . . ," Siirka murmured.

Marie turned to stare into the fire so her tears could fall unseen. She was thirty-one, past prime marriageable age, the mother of a seven-year-old illegitimate child, and foolishly infatuated with a man years younger, someone from whom she had not the remotest realistic hope of ever hearing a proposal of marriage.

W inter came early that year. At first the snow fell in wet sheets, turning the lane and yard to muck. Then, when the roads were all but impassable, the winds roared in from the east and the temperature dropped. Still it snowed, and the drifts piled high against the houses and barns. The fields were draped in a white cloak, and green pines and birches stood trimmed in twinkling layers of white. Life slowed to a muted pace.

In late October, Elsa Suorsa's husband Vilho suddenly died. She barely seemed to notice, except to complain how shorthanded they suddenly had become.

The whirling snowflakes of a dark December afternoon peppered Marie's face as she carried steaming buckets of milk to the house. Sheets of ice covered the yard, but that shiftless Johan Frantsila hadn't troubled himself to do a thing about it. She picked her way gingerly across the ice, frowning irritably as the cold pierced her clothes. She hadn't been warm in weeks.

"Marie!"

She looked up in amazement to see Nikolai striding toward her. Before she could summon a reply, she felt a foot slip out from under her. Tightly clutching the buckets, she wobbled a precarious moment, then fell on her rump in ungraceful slow motion. She sat stupidly on the ice, both buckets upended, as warm rivers of milk puddled around her.

"Oh, no!" she wailed. Now there would be hell to pay. There was hardly any milk left in the cows as it was; every drop was precious.

"Marie, are you hurt?" Nikolai was kneeling beside her, his face suddenly next to hers.

"Oh, no, no." She was too fearful of Elsa's wrath to be embarrassed. "But I'm in for it now." Suddenly, against all reason, she started to chortle. Nikolai bit his lip, then gave in to a wide smile. They looked at one another for only a moment before they burst into giddy laughter. When they regained control of themselves, Nikolai rose and extended his hand. "Let me help you up."

Without thinking, she put her hand in his. The moment his fingers closed around hers, a stab of electricity shot through her limbs. She caught her breath as he pulled her effortlessly to her feet. She dropped his hand as if it were a hot coal. They stood frozen for an intimate eternity in that snowy farmyard, Nikolai suddenly flushed, Marie stunned, their eyes locked.

"Marie Kurola! Whatever have you done?" Elsa shouted from the doorway.

"Oh, Dear God," Marie groaned, picking up the buckets. "I slipped on the ice and spilled all the milk." A hint of a smile tugged at her mouth.

"You clumsy cow! I don't pay you to throw my milk away!"

"It wasn't her fault," Nikolai interjected. "I startled her and she lost her balance."

Marie shot him a quick, amused look.

"What are you doing here, anyway?" Elsa demanded, turning her fire on him.

"I came to see if you could use me in the woods this winter. Your husband told me he might . . ." He trailed off uncomfortably.

"You're a pair of bumbling fools. Why we should have to rely on the likes of you is beyond me," Elsa grumbled as she motioned them inside.

"I wouldn't have slipped if something had been done about the ice," Marie complained, aiming her barb at the feckless Johan, who sat snug by the hearth, whittling. He shot her a hard look, but she didn't care. She was afraid even to glance at Nikolai.

Nikolai came to the house nearly every day after that, though he rarely came inside except for the midday meal. Anna once again fell to spinning an artless web around her prey, but Nikolai seemed oblivious to her machinations. Whenever Marie dared look at him, his eyes were intense with frank longing. Terrified and ecstatic, Marie let herself smile freely at him when no one was looking. His returning smile would see her through her long, restless nights. It fed her hungers.

At Christmas, Marie happily accepted Brita Kaisa's invitation to visit. She put on her best wool dress and brushed her hair into a bun before she and Sofie set off.

Handsome in his homespun, collarless shirt, Nikolai clung to Marie's side the whole afternoon while a hubbub of lighthearted conversation flowed around them. No one seemed to notice how they kept their eyes fastened on one another. After the meal, Erikki turned his attention to Marie and Nikolai, who were sitting on the floor in the straw, playing a game with Sofie.

"So, Marie, what's your opinion of your mistress Anna?" he asked casually, drawing on his pipe.

"What?" Marie asked, nonplussed.

"Your young mistress Anna. Will she make a good wife, do you think?"

"Oh . . . well . . . I . . . yes, I expect so," she answered uncertainly, shooting a quick, puzzled look at Nikolai. She saw him stiffen.

"I think so too. She'd make a fine wife for Nikolai. Her mother will think so too, once she gets used to the idea. Elsa would come around right enough if Nikolai just put his mind to it. But fool that he is, he won't hear of it. Maybe you can try to talk some sense into him, Marie. He'll listen to you."

"Father, please!"

"The girl likes you, Nikolai. Everyone in the village knows it. Don't you see that this is your real chance to better yourself? To have some of that precious land of your own that you want so dearly?" Erikki waved his pipe for emphasis.

Nikolai jumped up, anger flashing in his eyes. He reached for his coat, but Brita Kaisa put her hand on his arm. "We'll have no quarreling on Christmas. Come and sit."

But he stomped out and the room fell silent. Marie saw Brita Kaisa wipe away a tear.

"I'll try to talk to him," Marie offered. Both parents shot her a grateful glance as she pulled on her coat and stepped out into the farmyard. His footprints led into the barn. She found him there leaning tensely against a wall, arms folded across his chest.

"What's happened, Nikolai?"

"You heard it. My father wants me to marry Anna."

She took a cautious breath. "Do you want to marry Anna?"

"No!" He wheeled around, his back to her, slamming his fist into the wall.

Her heart pounded in her ears. "Then what do you want, Nikolai?"

He turned to face her. "Not Anna Suorsa, that's for certain." Then he reached for her and Marie felt herself falling into his arms, tumbling into an abyss, her stomach constricted as if in a free fall. He found her mouth and kissed it, but she knew she must fight against it. Instead, she kissed him back, hungrily, both hands caressing his face.

"Nikolai, Nikolai, we can't," she whispered. "We can't."

"Marie," he groaned, "I've wanted you from the moment I saw you."

She stepped back, gripping both his hands. "We have to talk. We have to think . . ."

"I can't think about you any more than I already do," he protested. "I've tried not to think about you for years."

"I have to tell you something," she insisted. "About Sofie. It wasn't my fault . . ."

"Oh, Marie, I know that. Mother told me years ago how it happened."

"I don't want you to think I'm that kind of woman . . ."

"Oh, no, no, no. That's one reason I've never said anything about how I feel. I know how they've treated you. I didn't want you to think that I thought you were that kind of woman . . ."

"I have to go in, Nikolai. We can't stay here any longer." She pulled away, knees shaking, leaving him staring hungrily after her. "I had better go home."

"I'll hitch up the sled and take you," he said softly.

The night was windless, crisp and clear. Stars threw glistening diamonds of light onto the crusty snow; the frosty trees glittered. Marie settled Sofie safely between them under a heavy woolen robe, and the child slipped into sleep. Nikolai held the reluctant beast to the slowest of trots. They slid silently along, hardly daring to speak.

When they turned into the Suorsas' farmyard, Nikolai finally spoke. "When can I see you alone?"

"I don't think we should, Nikolai . . ."

"I want to see you."

Before Marie could answer, the dogs began to bark and Anna threw open the door. Nikolai helped them out of the sled and hurried away. Anna gave Marie a cold, speculative look, as if seeing her for the first time.

Weeks passed with Marie giddily propelled by nervous energy, Nikolai mutely hovering, Anna single-mindedly circling. Elsa was on constant patrol, sniffing the air like a suspicious spaniel, jumping up from her handiwork to assess the comings and goings in the farmyard, barking occasional sharp commands when Anna trailed Nikolai too closely. Nothing changed but the weather, which became bitterly cold as deep winter settled in.

Finally, on a Friday in mid-February, seven weeks after Nikolai and Marie embraced in the barn, Nikolai stole a private moment with Marie to whisper an urgent plea. "Wait for me in the sauna tomorrow evening after everyone has gone back to the house." He knew it fell to Marie to put things right in the sauna after the others were finished.

Marie bit her lip and nodded. Her heart in her throat, dreading the moment she yearned for, she stumbled nervously through Saturday's chores. That evening, after everyone else had finished in the sauna, she watched to be certain they all disappeared back into the house. Her stomach was a tense knot, but she had made up her mind to give in to her heart.

"Better once too much than always too little," she told herself when she heard Nikolai's soft tap on the door. "They've done all they can to me."

She was wrong about that, of course.

The next morning after Sunday service, Nikolai sought out the pastor to take communion. Parishioners normally did so once a year as a matter of form; those who were more devout might do so more often. Communion entailed confession of sin, and Nikolai chose this day because he was overwhelmed with remorse.

"I'm so sorry, Marie," he told her miserably on Monday morning when he found her alone in the barn. "It should never have happened. It was wrong, a sin." His face was ashen and his voice shook. "I've confessed to the pastor and I think you should too."

Astonished, she stared at him in utter disbelief, blood turning to ice in her veins. "Of course it was a sin!" she finally managed to say. "What did you think it was?"

"I didn't think! That's the trouble! All I could think of was wanting you!"

"Well, now you've had what you wanted," she told him stonily.

"Don't say that! It's not like that!"

"Then what is it like?" she demanded.

"I don't know . . . I wanted . . . I want . . ."

"You're a fool! You don't know what you want, Nikolai!" she hissed angrily.

Before he could reply, Anna appeared in the doorway. "Do you two intend to work today?" she sneered.

Nikolai spun angrily on his heel and left the barn. They studiously avoided speaking to one another for the next few weeks. Marie, furious at him and herself, gave no sign that she cried herself to sleep each night. Then he was gone again.

Early one evening in late May, Nikolai unexpectedly reappeared at the farm. He found Marie finishing up her chores.

"Will you walk toward home with me? I've something to tell you," he said without ceremony. Marie nodded, paralyzed by warring emotions of joy and apprehension. She had been planning to speak to him.

The long light was back now and the sun was still shining when they set out down the lane. It was almost as if it never happened, Marie thought as she strode along beside him. But when she dared look at him, the searing memory of it shot through her and she had to look away. It would always be like this, she realized. She would never be through with him.

They walked in leaden silence. "Let's sit by the river," he suggested when they had gone a good distance. They scrambled down to a spot with mossy rocks to lean against just out of sight of the road. Marie sat facing him, legs folded under her long skirt, hands folded primly in her lap, her scarf tied loosely around her neck.

"It's gotten worse now at home," he began awkwardly, pulling on a blade of grass. "My father wants me to get married, as you know. To Anna. So I can have my farm." He was bareheaded in the sunshine and had laid his jacket in the grass beside him.

"And have you changed your mind?" she asked evenly. She was long past the point of playing the coquette with him—or anyone else, for that matter. But her heart raced wildly.

"No, no, that's not how I want to get land. I want to be my own master, not indebted to some shrew . . ."

Her stomach turned a cartwheel, spinning on hope. "So what will you do?"

"I'm going to America." He pressed his lips together and studied the grass.

"America?" She felt faint; the blood seemed to be draining from her limbs.

"It's all arranged." He cleared his throat nervously.

"But how?" Off in the distance, tiny and far away, she could hear her own voice. It sounded normal.

"I've borrowed money for passage from Grete's husband and my brother Matti. With the wages I'll earn in America, I can pay them back in no time and save for a farm, too."

She wanted to shout at him, to plead with him to stay, but no words came. If he had any genuine feeling for her, why would he leave? It had been impossible from the beginning, she'd always known that. What could he want with a woman her age, used goods to boot, with an illegitimate mouth to feed? A woman he'd already had his way with?

"It's the only hope I have, Marie," he said, eyes downcast. "You must understand why I can't stay here. I can't marry with no prospects."

"Other people marry with no prospects," she heard herself say. "Most of Finland has no prospects. So that's not really why, is it? I'm not good enough for you, am I, Nikolai?"

"Oh, Marie! Don't say such things!" he groaned. "It's not true! What can I possibly offer a woman? A place beside me on a straw pallet at someone else's hearth? A lifetime of slaving and drudgery like my parents for someone else's profit? That's not a life!"

A wave of nausea washed over her. She looked away, her hands working her apron.

He reached out and gently turned her face to his. "Oh, Marie, it's only because there's no hope here. I have just this one chance to better myself, and I have to take it. I can be back in five years a rich man! I'll never forgive myself if I don't go and try."

Just as you'll never forgive me if I keep you here, she thought. How could she tell him now? He would grow to hate her for destroying his life, just as she hated Paavo for destroying hers. That she could never bear. This time she truly had made her own bed; she knew that full well. There was no one to blame but herself.

He reached for her, but she jumped to her feet and ran across the grassy meadow to the road, tears stinging her face. He shouted after her but she ran faster. When, sobbing breathlessly, she finally paused to look over her shoulder, she saw that he was not following her. He was walking down the road in the opposite direction, a tiny figure receding in the distance.

July first should have been hot. But it had been raining, and a white mist lay against the green fields, obscuring the stand of trees that grew along the river by the Suorsa farm.

Nikolai stood stiffly outside the cottage door in the flat morning light. He was dressed in a new dark gray suit and collarless shirt. He asked, in a solemn voice, to speak with Marie. When she saw him, she stepped outside and closed the door. Her face was white, her body rigid, and she kept her hands folded carefully in front of her apron, her anguished eyes searching his. When he removed his cap, his hair fell forward over his eyes and he impatiently brushed it back just as she had seen him do that first day so long ago. A canvas bag lay at his feet in the soggy grass.

"I'm leaving today for Oulu to catch the boat to Stockholm. Wherever I land, I won't get there for weeks, but I'll write to you when I arrive."

"Why?" she managed to whisper, biting her lip.

"I won't forget you, Marie," he promised softly. She didn't answer.

He put on his cap, carefully adjusting the fit, and reached for his bag. Only then did Marie cry out.

"Nikolai!" she sobbed. "Oh, Nikolai, I'll never see you again!"

He dropped his bag and held her in a brief, anguished embrace. Then she broke free and stepped back into the doorway.

Nikolai picked up the bag and strode down the muddy lane. He did not look back. So he did not see Anna at the kitchen window, pale and subdued, staring morosely after him until he was out of sight.

And he did not see Marie, paralyzed in the doorway and blinded by tears, pressing her hands against her imperceptibly swelling belly.

Four

America Widows

I was born that November in the sauna on Uncle Juho's farm. My mother named me Brita Kaisa, after my grandmother, who at first refused to believe I was her grandchild.

In late August my mother had appeared on Brita Kaisa's doorstep with Sofie in tow. The moment she opened the door to them, my grandmother's hands flew to her mouth. She backed away, eyes wide.

"Marie! Who did this to you?"

"Nikolai," Marie answered dully.

"Nikolai! That can't be!"

"He didn't force me, if that's what you mean."

Brita Kaisa flushed. "You're . . . you're an older woman and certainly you, of all people, ought to have enough wits about you to keep such a thing from happening again," she remonstrated, shock warming to anger. "Especially after what you've been through!"

"I came to tell you myself, before you hear it from others. I've just been thrown off the Suorsas' farm. I have to go home and tell Juho now." Her voice trembled. "I've nowhere else to go. If it were just me, I might manage to find another solution, but there's Sofie . . ." My eight-year-old sister mutely gripped our mother's hand as the two women tensely faced one another in the doorway. Mother had come harboring a thin, desperate hope that she might be offered refuge by her unborn child's grandparents. But Brita Kaisa regarded my mother with the cold eye of someone who had been betrayed.

"Does Nikolai know?" Brita Kaisa asked.

"No. I couldn't tell him. He wanted to go so desperately."

Brita Kaisa's faced softened. "You knew and you let him go without telling him?"

"He would have hated me if I had kept him here because of this."

"You love him, don't you?" Brita Kaisa asked, incredulous.

"It wouldn't have happened otherwise."

"Oh, child," Brita Kaisa sighed heavily. "Come in."

She went to the cupboard and got a small wooden box. "His first letter arrived just two days ago. I was going to send you word. You should read it for yourself."

Marie sank onto a stool by the window and, hands trembling, carefully unfolded the precious sheets of paper.

"Dearest family," he began. "All is well. I arrived safely in Quebec, Canada, July 31. The ship journey to Stockholm went well and the train journey to Gothenburg was a wonder. How easy it was to travel such a long distance! But there was an awful hubbub on the docks when I was ready to depart Gothenburg. Agents swarmed over us, hawking passage on various ships. I bought my passage from a Swede who spoke Finnish. He said Quebec was the cheapest fare, owing to the lack of a landing tax as in New York.

"The trip across the North Sea from Gothenburg to Hull, England, was an omen of what was to come. The hold of the deck where I was to sleep was filled to capacity and there was no fresh air, so I kept on deck with my bag. But I was forced to go below when a storm blew up, and I got very seasick. I felt better again by the time we landed and I boarded a train to travel across England to Liverpool to start the final leg of my journey.

"We were ten days en route across the Atlantic from Liverpool with six hundred and fifty passengers aboard a ship that I later learned was authorized to carry only five hundred. I was in the hold with a strange sect of religious people who call themselves Mennonites. They were orderly enough but the rest were a rough lot. We were each required to draw out our own sleeping space on the floor with chalk and write our names on it to keep the peace. But it did little good because we were packed in like sprats in a barrel and I saw more than one set-to of fisticuffs before it was over. People who were seasick rolled into their own—or someone else's—vomit whenever the ship pitched wildly, which was most of the time. You can't believe the stench in that hold after two days at sea! Worse, there were not nearly enough places for such a crowd to relieve themselves. Food was scarce and unfit to eat. We had only stale bread crusts, slimy herring and a few half-rotten potatoes. I ate the last of the bread and meat you sent along, Mother, long before I left Liverpool, where I had to wait many days to get aboard ship and where I had to sleep in such places I hope never to see the likes of again.

"There were all sorts of people aboard the ship, not just Englishmen and Germans, Norwegians and Swedes, but Poles and other such ilk. I kept to the Finns. Two of them told me about the place they are going, a copper mine in a place called Hancock in Michigan, where one of them has a brother. They've invited me to come along and I will, since I don't understand anything the people here say. It will be better to stick together until I learn the language. They say Hancock is many days travel from here by train, boat, horse and wagon, and then boat again across a big lake called Superior.

"As soon as I get to Hancock, I'll write again. Don't worry about me. I am safe in God's care. I pray you are all well. I hold you all dear in my thoughts. I can hardly believe I am here at last. Give my greetings to Marie. Your loving son, Nikolai."

Blinking back tears, Marie handed the letter back to Brita Kaisa and rose to leave. "It's like he's left the earth," she managed to say.

"Shall I tell him?" Brita Kaisa asked.

"Oh, no!" Marine answered, alarmed.

"But he must be told . . ."

"When the time is right. You must not tell him before I can, Brita Kaisa. Promise me that."

Reluctantly, Brita Kaisa nodded her assent.

Nothing Marie had dreaded in her worst moments matched the look on Juho's face when she and Sofie staggered hand in hand into the farmyard. Juho stood stock still in the cottage doorway, the color draining from his face, speechless rage burning in his eyes. Siirka nearly dropped their firstborn child, Elias, when she caught sight of Marie's swollen belly.

Marie stared unflinchingly back at her brother, knowing she could not bend to him. Would not.

"How dare you come here like this again?" he hissed.

"I didn't come here for sympathy. I came for shelter. I have no place else to go."

"You disgrace us! Again! Isn't once before the congregation shame enough for you?"

"Juho, understand this much: nothing you or anyone else can say will ever make me feel shame about this child. But will it not shame you in the eyes of the church to turn away your own sister at a time like this?"

He dropped his eyes, and she knew she had won. But it was Siirka who invited her in. "Of course you'll stay here, Marie," she said, giving Juho a look.

At the end of October, two weeks before I was born, my mother received a letter from Nikolai. It came from Hancock, where he had found work in the mines, but it was not to his liking. "It's unnatural for a man to spend his days under the earth, seeing no daylight for hours on end. Our maker surely didn't have this in mind when he commanded us to go forth and earn our daily bread by the sweat of our brow. But the pay is good and I shall have to stick to it to repay my debts. A year from now I will be free of them and then I can start to save for myself. I think of you often," he concluded without elaboration.

A year, Marie mused. Very well, then, give him the year. She wouldn't tell him yet.

Once again my mother was forced to spend forty days in isolation. And once again she was hauled before the congregation to confess her sin. This time the pastor upbraided her even more harshly and the worshippers glowered at her even more scornfully. She knew that much as the pastor might prattle on about forgiveness of sin, most of them thought she was beyond redemption. She was a hopelessly shameless, incorrigible sinner. But Marie was beyond caring. This time she sat through her public humiliation in a trance, hardly hearing her cue to rise and confess.

Juho had refused to come inside the church to witness his sister's disgrace, so it fell to Siirka to escort her outside to Juho's waiting sled when the ordeal was finished. Some boys lying in wait outside the churchyard threw snowballs filled with rocks after them as they passed. Flaring, Juho turned to shout something. But Siirka put her hand over his arm to restrain him.

"It's over, Juho. Let it be."

But it wasn't over by any means.

Uncle Juho had no choice but to make room for us, so he reluctantly added a room on the other side of the hearth for his own family. Mother and Sofie and I slept in the trundle bed in the kitchen.

Meanwhile times in Finland did not improve. With every month, more of Rantsila's landless men, both married and single, left for America. Often they left behind a wife and children, promising to send money for passage as soon as they could earn it. Many were never heard from again, and anxious wives—"America widows" the villagers began to call them— waited as long as they prudently could before making other, often scandalous, domestic arrangements.

"Have you heard that Pedder Usitalo's wife Josefina is expecting a child? Pedder's not been heard from now these four years," Siirka clucked her tongue over the latest village gossip.

"I'll be the last to cast stones at these poor women whose foolish husbands are infected by America fever," my mother always replied to such tales. With great difficulty she had written Nikolai a Christmas letter. "We think of you often and hope you are well," she had allowed herself to say. She did not say how much she ached to see him nor how often she cried herself to sleep at night. And she made no mention of me.

A reply came from him in late spring of 1881. "You would not believe the winter we have endured here! The snow is well above our heads. But the pay is good and I'll soon be free of debt. When I have saved some money it will be time to think of what to do next." This time his tone was more personal. "I think of you a great deal and the time we spent together, Marie. I wish you were not so far away."

Hope flew into her heart. Perhaps he would offer to send for her one day soon after all, without knowing anything about his child. She went about her chores with a lighter step, daring to lose herself in dreams of America. Her next letter to him was less stilted. "I'm glad you haven't forgotten me," she wrote after much anguished debate.

His reply didn't arrive until Christmas. "I can finally speak a little English and I have begun to put by money of my own. Some of the men here spend their money as fast as they get it. There's much drinking and fighting, but I don't hold with that. There are a few decent, God-fearing fellows here, most of them single like me. Unfortunately, there aren't many Finnish women here considering how many men there are to fight over them. You are much in my thoughts."

Marie decided the time was ripe to tell him she was living back home with Juho. She didn't reveal why, except to say she'd had a "falling out" with Elsa. "Juho is as difficult to live with as ever he was," she wrote, hoping her ploy was not too transparent. "I think of you often, Nikolai, and hope you are well." She debated for two days before giving in to the impulse to close with the dangerous words: "I miss you."

We moved before he answered. The situation with Juho had become intolerable and Mother found a post with an ill, childless elderly couple willing to let her keep two children under their roof.

When his reply reached us that spring of 1882, Nikolai was full of complaints about another hard winter of miserable work and his plans to move west, where good land was still to be had. "They're building a northern rail line to Oregon Territory now and as soon as it's finished, I mean to be aboard that train."

Even though he closed his letter with "I miss you too, Marie," she read this news with deep dismay. He was going even farther away! Yet in his Christmas letter later that year he assured her: "I haven't forgotten you."

It was June of 1883 before she got another letter, this one written in May. "I have been so busy investigating the best route for my trip west that I was delayed in answering your letter," he began. "But now I'm as ready as I can be, though it's not certain the new rail line will be finished by the time I want to leave. So I shall go south to Chicago and then west across the plains as far as the rails will carry me, then on to the Pacific Ocean by stagecoach. I'll leave before the summer is out. I look forward to it with great anticipation. At last I shall see the great trees of Oregon! And finally I will have my own land."

It was the last letter my mother received from him.

The summer blossomed, withered and died. Fall froze into winter. With each passing month, my mother's anxiety grew as she awaited news of my father's safe arrival in Oregon. She knew there were murderous Indians and diseases lying in wait along the way. Everyone knew the stories of the dangers faced by settlers in the American West. Oh, why did he have to go to such a wild, uncivilized place?

"Because he's different from the rest of these louts," she would tell herself. "He wants to make something of himself." Pride, anger, longing and despair warred unceasingly within her as Christmas came and went without word from Nikolai. When January had bled into February and still no word had come, Marie could bear it no longer. She left her children in the mistress's care and set out for Brita Kaisa's. She hadn't been there in more than three years, ever since that awful day she'd told her about Nikolai's child. Marie had not been able to summon the will to call on her again, and for her part, Brita Kaisa had made no effort to visit her grandchild.

"Can it really be you?" Brita Kaisa exclaimed when she opened the door. A shadow passed across her now deeply wrinkled face, but she motioned Marie to a seat by the fire.

"I must know if Nikolai has arrived safely in Oregon," Marie blurted out without preliminaries. "I've heard nothing from him since June."

Brita Kaisa's wrinkles sagged against one another as her face fell. "He's been writing to you all this time? Oh, Marie," she mumbled, turning away.

"What? Is he well? Has something happened to him?"

A long, tense silence fell between them.

"He's married." Brita Kaisa did not look at Marie when she said it.

"Married?" The room seemed to tilt; she was afraid she would faint.

"Yes. Married."

"But . . . but when?"

Brita Kaisa opened the little wooden chest and took out the last letter stacked on top of the neat bundle that lay inside. "Here. Read it for yourself," she sighed.

Marie's hands shook so badly she could hardly unfold the letter. Her eyes wandered unseeing over the page. Then she suddenly sprang up from the bench and rushed out the door. Steadying herself with one hand against the cottage wall, she vomited into the snow while Brita Kaisa stood stricken in the doorway.

Some time passed before she could reach for a handful of snow to wash her face. "I'm all right," she assured Brita Kaisa. "I'll read it now." Weak and shaking, she sank down by the fire again and stared at the familiar, neatly formed words flowing across the page.

"August 14, 1883

"Dear Family, I have much good news. I am safely arrived in Astoria, Oregon, after a long, difficult journey. And yesterday I claimed a bride, a Finnish woman I met in Hancock shortly before I was to leave. I feel God meant our paths to cross as we so nearly missed meeting one another.

She had recently arrived from Finland to live with her brother but could see right away that this would not be the life she hoped for. We met quite by accident through friends and quickly found we have common interests. When I told her about my plan to go west, she was immediately enthusiastic and ready for the adventure. On account of our not knowing one another well, we decided the wisest course would be to put off marrying until we had survived the rigors of the trip west together. We agreed between ourselves that if we managed that, we surely would survive married life. And judging from her uncomplaining comportment on the journey across America, I have made an excellent choice of a woman to stand by me in the tasks ahead. Her name is Maja Liisa, and she's a fine, upstanding Christian woman. We were the first couple married in Astoria's new Finnish church, and quite a fuss was made over us. I only regret that you could not be there to see it.

"For the time being we shall live just across the Columbia River in Washington Territory in a lumber camp called Deep River, where I have obtained work felling trees. And yes, Father, they are every bit as big as I told you! And the salmon are just as astounding. You should see their great size and unbelievable numbers! The nets are so heavy with salmon that they use horses to pull them in, and Astoria teems with fishing boats and sailing ships and canneries. Even Chinese laborers have made their way here to work in them. We travel from Astoria by boat across the great mouth of the river, which is really more like traveling on the open seas, and right up to a dock at the camp, where there is a little store and barracks and cabins for workers and their families, all quite serviceable. We feel fortunate to have secured both work and lodgings and soon will save enough to buy land of our own.

"Once we left the din and dreadful confusion of Chicago, the trip west across the flat, treeless plains was even more astonishing than I had imagined. We traveled out of Des Moines and into Oklahoma and then Nebraska territory, where we began to catch occasional glimpses of Indians. It was very hot and windy, and monstrous storms with thick, black clouds blew up without notice. Such lightning and thunder I hope never to see again! When it wasn't stormy, the sun shone so mercilessly that some of the women passengers fainted. Several times we passed gruesome piles of old, decaying buffalo bones discarded in careless heaps near the tracks. The buffalo are all but gone now, they say. This is a hard land.

"The train follows much of the same route along the Platte River used by the original settlers traveling to Oregon Territory on foot. We were grateful as we looked out on this awesome expanse that we were not required to walk or ride a wagon across this continent to make a better life for ourselves. By comparison, our trip was luxurious and we felt little cause to complain. Still, we were much relieved when at last we could discern a thin blue line of mountains rising in the western distance. These were the Rocky Mountains. You cannot believe their size, even when you see them.

"We got off the train in Ogden, Utah, which lies in a salt-encrusted valley near the headquarters of a settlement of polygamist religious fanatics who call themselves Mormons. They are well known for their efforts to lure the unwary into their licentious traps with promises of Paradise on earth. A number of passengers bound for nearby Salt Lake City broke into hymns of praise when the train first descended into this valley. We were anxious to be on our way lest we have to fend off this sect's zealous agents, so we took the next train onward with just the briefest overnight rest.

"Now we traveled north through the most inauspicious of landscapes— low, sandy hills covered with something they call sagebrush and tumbleweeds. The whole effect was uncommonly ugly, and it continued well past a junction called Pocatello, where many ill-clad, sullen Indians swarmed about, and across another dreary, treeless desert called the Snake River Plain all the way to a settlement named Boise. By now I was worried that Oregon would turn out to be like this forbidding landscape and that we had been duped. For the first time, I had doubts about my decision. The wind howled unceasingly, blinding us with sand; our skin was raw and our throats parched.

"The train tracks ended in Boise, so there we boarded a stagecoach drawn by a team of horses for the next leg of our journey. Mercifully, not long after we left that place and began to climb higher, the landscape began to change. We could see green mountains rising to the west and north. We passed through lush, green valleys and then finally reached the banks of the Columbia River. There we boarded a boat for the trip downstream to Astoria, where, God be praised, we arrived safe and well.

"It is green and mild here, and there are many Finns. We look forward with gratitude to our new life together . . ."

Marie put down the letter. A tight band was squeezing her throat shut and a heavy stone seemed to have settled somewhere in her chest, yet she felt lightheaded. "I won't forget you," he had promised. Indeed. What man would be likely to forget a woman who had thrown herself so shamelessly at him? What a hopeless fool she had been!

My grandmother folded and carefully put the letter away. "How is Brita Kaisa?" she suddenly asked.

"She's a lovely child. She looks like Nikolai, as you would see for yourself if you visited her," Marie replied accusingly.

"I've respected your wishes and told no one, not even Erikki, waiting for you to tell him yourself. Men can't keep secrets," Brita Kaisa answered defensively. "But now, how can we tell Nikolai?" she wailed.

"Do what you want. I don't care. It's of no interest to me," Marie replied tonelessly. She left without another word. Nikolai was as good as dead.

FIVE

SISU

I grew up content with a meager supper of rye bread, thin porridge and sour milk and the doting affection of my mother and sister.

I adored my sister Sofie, who hovered quietly in the shadow of our lives. She was small-boned and frail, and in her large brown eyes there was an impenetrable sadness that haunts me to this day. Even at that age, it was clear she would come to look just like our mother. She was fiercely protective of me, and I wept bitterly the day my twelve-year-old sister was sent to a neighbor's farm to live and work as a dairymaid.

"We can't all live here," Mother explained with unusual curtness. "They don't need her here. Sofie's lucky to have landed in a place where they treat her well." But something in her voice sounded as if Mother didn't think Sofie was lucky at all. We visited her as often as we could.

Inconsolable, I longed for my protector. Once when I was six, I burst into tears when a child I was hoping to play with called me a name. That was nothing new; the other children teased us unmercifully and I often cried. Usually Sofie pretended not to hear their insults. But this time my tormentor persisted in taunting my tears. "Cry all you like! Your mother's still a whore!"

Sofie, who had been working nearby, came running to my side, her eyes flashing. In one swift step she grabbed the child by the arm and slapped her hard across the face, not uttering a word. From then on, they took care to tease me only when Sofie was out of earshot. I don't remember ever seeing Sofie laugh. But then, few of us had much to laugh about in those days.

Uncle Henrik was the exception. One day shortly after Mother's employers died and we had moved back to Uncle Juho's, Henrik came plodding through the spindly trees along the muddy path, a grizzled vagabond in unkempt clothes with a birch knapsack on his back.

"Henrik!" my mother shouted as she rushed to embrace him. "It's been so long!"

He peered down at me, and I stared up at him, bug-eyed with curiosity. "Do you remember your Uncle Henrik, Kaisa?" I nodded even though I didn't really. My mother wiped her eyes and smiled at him. Cautiously, I stepped closer. He was all bushy beard under a frayed hat, and he smelled fiercely.

"You've become a pretty little thing, Kaisa. How old are you now?" he asked playfully. His blue eyes twinkled under shaggy brows.

"Seven," I whispered timidly.

Uncle Henrik settled in with us at Juho's and helped with spring planting. During the long, sunlit summer evenings, he busied himself carving wooden spoons, thimbles, and other saleable goods. Sometimes I came upon Henrik and my mother in earnest, hushed conversation that always stopped whenever I came into earshot. But I could tell that his voice was urging and hers hesitant.

As summer waned he became restless. "You're fine for the planting but never stay to harvest what you sow," Juho complained when Henrik announced his intention to journey north again. I could see that my mother grieved his departure.

"I'll come back to see you one day soon, Kaisa," he promised gently.

Two years later he was back, a little grayer and smellier but otherwise no worse for wear. This time he and my mother spent many evenings talking long into the night. Once I heard them softly arguing.

"Not before she can read and write Finnish," Mother whispered. When I awoke, I thought I had dreamed it.

In early spring of my twelfth year, just as the frozen roads were melting and becoming impassable, Uncle Henrik came home again. This time, something was different. My mother didn't seem as glad to see him, and whenever I came upon them talking together, they fell awkwardly silent, their faces guarded and glum. Mother held me more tightly to her in the evenings, and sometimes her eyes unaccountably brimmed with tears.

One day she cheerily announced that I had grown so big that I would need new clothes for winter. I was nonplussed at this attention. I had grown, true enough; I already was taller than my mother. She set to work fashioning not one but two long woolen skirts and new woolen undergarments and heavy leggings. All this seemingly cheerful industry on my behalf made me uneasy. Then, one day in mid-October, my mother set off on an errand to the pastor. When she returned, she divulged nothing, and I was afraid to ask. She tossed and turned all night in fretful sleep, keeping me awake. Something terrible was about to happen, I was sure of it.

I was right.

The next morning everyone disappeared, leaving us alone in the cottage. My mother carefully arranged two stools before the hearth and asked me to sit down. She took both my hands in hers and looked intently into my face. I could hear my heart pounding in my ears.

"Kaisa, I've prayed for the words to tell you this, but I don't know how." Her voice was steady, but I could see tears rising in her eyes. My heart raced faster.

"You must understand it's for the best, that it's the only hope I have for you. I'll do anything I must to give you a good life, Kaisa. I don't want you to live as I have had to live, with no prospects and no hope of happiness. I don't want you to live as Sofie will have to live."

I could only stare at her, terrified and uncomprehending.

"I want you to go with Henrik to Ruija, Kaisa," she said quietly. "I've been to the pastor and gotten your travel certificate."

I couldn't speak. Surely I had misunderstood.

"Henrik's found you a good home there with a warm-hearted Finnish woman who will treat you kindly . . ."

"No!" I cried, throwing myself into her arms. "Don't send me away! I don't want to leave you!" I clung fiercely to her, sobbing, while she stroked my head gently.

"Shush, now. It's not so bad as all that. You'll like it there, you'll see . . ."

"Don't make me go!" I wailed.

"Oh, Kaisa, dear child," she murmured, "It's for your own good . . ."

I pulled away and looked at her through my tears. "Don't you want me any more?"

She broke into wracking sobs then and buried her face in her hands. I had never seen my mother like this. Finally, she wiped her eyes on her apron.

"You must understand that if you don't go there now, you'll have to take a post as a dairymaid. You're nearly grown and I can't provide for you. You'll be enslaved for the rest of your life if you stay here, even if you do find someone decent to marry. There's no hope for better times here in Finland for poor people like us, child. You and your children will live forever hand to mouth, never knowing when the next famine will strike. You must get away now, while you can!" Her voice was filled with such urgency it frightened me.

"But it's so far! I'll never see you again. I'll never see Sofie again!"

"Of course you will. You can come back with Uncle Henrik when he comes to visit. We'll meet again one day. You'll see." But her voice trembled with naked uncertainty. "Will you go, Kaisa, to give me peace of mind?" she pleaded. "If you don't like it there, you can always come back."

I threw myself into her arms again, but I knew it was no use. I would have to go. I had always wanted nothing more than to please my mother. I could not deny her wish, even in this.

"Henrik wants to leave tomorrow. Now we must go and say goodbye to Sofie. But first I want to tell you something."

She told me the whole story then, from beginning to end, leaving nothing out, her voice hard. But when she had finished telling me about my father, she gave me a loving look, her eyes glistening.

"I don't know if he knows about you or not. If he does, he's given no sign that he cares. But I can't regret what happened, Kaisa, because it gave me you. You were born of love.

"But let my life be a lesson to you, child."

We found Sofie inside the little shed where she cooked hay for the cows, stirring a large, black, steaming cauldron. When we broke the awful news, her eyes widened in alarm. She began to weep and threw her arms around my neck. "But it's so far away!" she protested weakly to our mother.

"I'll write to you," I promised, in my anguish forgetting that I'd earned nothing but cow pie marks for my poor penmanship.

We left her standing outside the shed. I'll always remember the way she stood there, wiping her eyes with one hand, waving farewell with the other.

Tuesday, October 18, 1892, dawned with threatening skies. The night before, Mother had fired up the sauna and Uncle Henrik and I washed ourselves thoroughly. "Scrub well, Kaisa. It will be a long time before you bathe again," he advised cheerily.

Numbly, without speaking, I dressed in my new underclothes that dreadful morning. I pulled on the heavy wool socks, the new leggings and both woolen skirts, one over the other. Henrik had produced a new pair of sturdy boots for me. They had pointed toes and plenty of room for soft grass that would serve as insulation. "Each night you must take care to dry the grass," he cautioned.

He had made a birch basket that I was to carry strapped to my back. In it Mother placed extra socks, mittens and underthings. After we had eaten an unusually large breakfast, she added bread, dried meat, and butter to it. She attached a small wooden canteen to the wooden pack and filled it with milk. Then Henrik swung his basket over his back and picked up his staff.

"Come, Kaisa, it's time."

As if sleepwalking, I pulled on Mother's old gray coat and tied a new woolen scarf tightly around my head and neck. I must have said goodbye to the family before I shouldered my basket and stepped outside, but I have no memory of it.

What I do remember is Mother taking my hand. "I'll walk a little way with you," she said. The three of us stumbled down the ice-encrusted path into the gloomy forest, my heart frozen in my chest. Would I ever see this place again?

The sky darkened ominously and we stepped up our pace, walking three abreast down the lane with me in the middle. I held tight to Mother's hand. No one spoke.

My mother's face was set in stone.

When at last we reached the main road, we turned north and followed the winding Siikajoki past scattered farmhouses. Shortly we came to a place where the road rose on a little hill, and here Mother stopped. We had a view across the snowy fields along the river and of the road as it curved northward. Ahead of us, the sky hung black across a bleak horizon.

"I must say goodbye now," Mother said, folding me quickly into her arms. I held her tight, muffled sobs wracking my chest. I felt abandoned, cast out into a frightening world to fend for myself among strangers in a foreign land.

Gently, she pushed me from her. "Stand up straight in the world, Kaisa. Always remember you're a Finn, and that we Finns have *sisu*. We can endure what others cannot."

"I don't want to leave you," I wept helplessly.

She embraced me again and kissed me. "Oh, Kaisa, I'll miss you so," she whispered, lips trembling. "But you must make a good life for yourself. Be strong now." She pushed me from her again and looked pleadingly at Henrik. He embraced her and patted her comfortingly, then turned to me.

"Come, Kaisa, we must hurry. A storm is coming and we've a long way to go to our first lodging."

Mother's face crumpled then and tears spilled freely down her cheeks. She reached impulsively for me once again and held me close. "I'm so sorry, Kaisa, so sorry," she cried softly.

"We must go now," Henrik repeated, his voice gruff with emotion. "Stay well, Marie." He pulled me away, down the little hill and into the looming snowstorm. I walked with my head craned backwards, my eyes fixed on my mother, who remained on the top of the little hill looking after us.

When we got to the bend of the road where we would disappear from her view, we stopped to wave a final goodbye. She waved back to us, a tiny, forlorn, indelible figure in black against the white hillside. She and I stood there looking at one another across the snowy distance, each dreading to take that final step that would cause us to vanish from one another's sight.

"Kaisa, come now," Henrik prodded impatiently. I waved once more, my arm a leaden weight. She returned my wave. And then I turned my back on my mother and walked away.

It was the first searing heartbreak of my life. Would that it had been the last!

Sobbing inconsolably, I fell into step beside Uncle Henrik. "Sisu, Kaisa, sisu. Remember what your mother told you. You're Finnish, girl! Endure with strength, without complaint." But my tears would not cease.

It soon began to snow and the wind picked up. Heavy, wet flakes swirled around us, but we put our heads down and plodded on, alone on the road. The snow piled about us in drifts so we sometimes lost sight of the road, but I was too engulfed by despair to care. At some point we stopped briefly to take shelter inside an old hay barn by the road and quickly swallowed some of our rations. Later that afternoon, the wind died but the snow fell more heavily. I followed in Henrik's footsteps, stretching my legs to match his stride.

"On a good day we would have been there by now, but this storm has slowed us fearfully," Henrik said when we had been walking in the dark for some time. "We still have a good way to go."

I was exhausted. My feet hurt in my new boots and I was afraid. Here we were, out alone in the dark with wild beasts doubtless stalking us! Slowly, my despair warmed to anger. We all knew better than this. From early childhood we were warned against being out in the dark lest we fall prey to wild animals. Yet Henrik plunged heedlessly on, even past the pinpoints of light that shone from occasional farmhouses.

"Why can't we stop at one of these houses?" I finally demanded crossly. "They can't turn us away." In those days, it was considered un-Christian to lock one's doors at night lest travelers such as ourselves should need shelter. And to deny a stranger food and a warm place at the hearth was unthinkable. Still, then as now, the mantle of Christian charity rested more easily on some shoulders than others.

"No, they can't. That's true. But I know where we're most welcome along this road. You'll have to trust me in that, Kaisa. It's a humble place but full of good cheer. We'll be there soon." He dusted snow from my shoulders and patted me reassuringly.

When at last we arrived at the farmhouse to a warm welcome, I was numb with fatigue and cold. Someone took my coat and mittens and someone else handed me a steaming bowl of porridge. I was given a place by the fire to eat, but I don't remember finishing it. I awoke on a bed squeezed between several children and their grandmother. Henrik was shaking my arm. "Time to rise, Kaisa. We must be on our way."

Blinking sleepily, I sat up and studied the room in alarm. Where was I? Then it all came back, a bad dream continuing after waking. At our hosts' urging, I gulped some sour milk, stuffed a crust of bread in my basket and put a ladleful of milk in my canteen. Then we were on our way. I never even learned their names.

It was not yet fully light but it was clear and much colder. Horses and sleds occasionally passed us on the road, making walking on it much easier. The air was so crisp that ice crystals danced in it, yet I was inconsolably despondent. Never since I left Finland have I seen such lovely, brilliantly clear skies as after a Finnish winter snowstorm. But all I could see that day was my mother waving at me from the top of the hill. I marched along sullenly, lost in my sorrow.

Darkness fell just before we found shelter that night. As we hurried along, the sky suddenly flared alive. Shimmering, unearthly colors stretched across the horizon: violet, silver, pink and gold. I'd seen the Northern Lights before, of course, but never so large and beautiful as this. We paused to admire the shimmering lights, then hurried on again, our way lit by the flickering Aurora Borealis.

"The old Lapps say the Northern Lights are a sign from the spirit world," Henrik remarked. "They think they're omens of things to come."

"Do you think that's true?" I asked, curious.

"Maybe."

"Is it a good omen or a bad omen?"

"I don't know. A good omen, judging from their beauty."

"I hope you're right."

A sliver of hope crept into my breast. Perhaps all this sadness would come to a happy end after all, and these lights might be a sign sent to tell me so. That night I lay down at the hearth of another strange cottage, very near Oulu, with a less heavy heart.

We awoke to leaden skies. A raw, wet wind blew in from the west. "We're close to the sea now. You can feel it in the air," Henrik said.

The sea! I had never seen it and it had not occurred to me that I would see it now. The morning had hardly taken hold before we saw a church spire in the distance, and then the city gradually unfolded before us. Beyond it lay the gray, windswept Gulf of Bothnia, whitecaps roiling its surface. Ice was starting to form at its edges.

"There's fine seal hunting here when the gulf closes for winter. But it's miserable work trying to get close to the creatures while lying on your belly on a sled—especially when there's no wind to fill the sails. Still, I've managed to kill a few in my time," Henrik said modestly.

When we entered the town, I could only stare in amazement. The buildings were so large and so fine! "You might as well see something of the world while you're passing through it," Henrik smiled. He led me down to the docks, a place of much turmoil and shouting where men were rolling barrels of tar about in the snow. Large ships bobbed at anchor a short distance from shore, and smaller boats were ferrying the barrels out to them. In those days, we cut down our forests and burned them to make tar.

"Your father left for America from this dock," Henrik said casually as we stood surveying the hectic scene.

"He should have stayed home and married my mother," I spat back bitterly. "Then I wouldn't be making this journey at all."

Henrik sighed impatiently. "Come then, we can't stand here gawking all day. I have to earn some money." He led me to a spot where the workers would have to pass him, and as I stared in astonishment, he unpacked a few items from his knapsack—a pipe, wooden spoons, a thimble and some carved buttons, needles and thread and a pair of scissors—and with great flourish laid them on a faded piece of cloth on an empty, broken barrel. I stood a little way off, ashamed and shivering. By dusk, a few coins jingled in his pocket.

"Now we'll find a merry place to sleep," he promised. Before long we were knocking on the door of a large house where bright lights shone through the windows. I could hear loud laughter and harmonica music. A buxom redhead threw open the door to us. "Henrik! You again!" she shouted. "Who's your little friend?"

"My sister's child. We're going north. I need a place for her to sleep tonight, Kristina."

"Come in, dear," she commanded. "Let's get you cleaned up." I followed her wide-eyed, staring about me in scandalized wonder. The room was filled with tobacco smoke and the smell of beer, and the men and women were clustered together, not seated separately on their own sides of the room as at home. The men were playing cards. I knew that to be a sin; the pastor had said so.

Warily, I let Kristina feed and attend to me, then I climbed gratefully into a bed in the loft above the hearth while Henrik fell in with the noisy camaraderie below. I awoke the next morning to the smell of stale tobacco and beer. Only Henrik and I remained. Kristina set a bowl of sour milk before me. "Thank you, " I mumbled shyly.

"She's nearly deaf. You have to shout," Henrik told me quietly. "But she's a fine woman for all of that," he added with an impish twinkle.

When we paused briefly later that day to rest and drink at the outskirts of a small village, Henrik cleared his throat. "They say your father's wife is from here."

I considered this information for some time before I asked, "Why did he marry her and not my mother?"

Uncle Henrik took his time in answering. "I don't know. Sometimes a man has to do what he has to do."

"What does that mean?"

"Well, it means . . . it means a man can't always do what he might otherwise prefer to do."

"Didn't my father prefer to go to America?"

"Well, yes, he did, true enough. Still, if he could have stayed . . ."

"He could have stayed!"

"Kaisa, you must understand that sometimes a man is given a poor set of choices . . ."

"And my mother?" I broke in. "What choices was she given?" The look on my mother's face as she waved goodbye swam before me.

Henrik sighed heavily. A cloud dropped over his eyes. But he had no answer.

For the next few days we followed the sea. Raw winds, wet snow and overcast skies dogged our path as we plodded along in melancholy silence. We hurried past the sawmills at the port of Kemi, where many log rafts floated in the river. Each night we bedded down among strangers, some more welcoming and generous with food than others. Finally we saw the church spires of Tornio rising against a lifting sky. We now had reached the place where the sea ends. Shortly we would begin our climb to the mountains.

"This is the finest town you'll see," Henrik enthused, "even if the Swedes did steal half of it and name it Haparanda." We paused on a rise looking eastward to what appeared to be an island floating in white mist in the wide mouth of the Tornio River. An imposing church rose high above a cluster of buildings. The whole city seemed suspended in air.

"For hundreds of years, this was one town. Then, when the Swedes lost Finland to the Russians, they carved Tornio in two and used the river to mark the border between Finland and Sweden—or Russia, if you like." He pointed to another cluster of buildings and yet another church spire on the western side of the river.

"That's Haparanda over there. First we'll go to Tornio and then cross over on the bridge to Haparanda. That way we can keep to the Swedish side of the river as we go north. The post roads are better and there are more settlements along the way."

Henrik studied the arresting scene pensively. "Even thousands of years ago, when they had to make their way in the world with only stones to help them, people were living here," he mused.

I studied the river uneasily. How would we get across? I trembled at the thought. Henrik must have forgotten that I had never been in a boat; he seemed not to notice my anxiety. He wandered off in search of a boatman while I stood rooted to the spot, terrified. When they returned, he and the boatman wasted no time lifting me aboard. They plunked me down in the bow, where I sat rigidly grasping the gunwales as the tiny craft smoothly slid through the thin membrane of ice forming on the water. As we neared the shore of Tornio, a heavy, sweet smell wafted over us. I looked quizzically at Henrik.

"Beer. There's a brewery here." He licked his lips in anticipation.

Henrik paid a coin to the boatman and we disembarked into a town crowded with fine new buildings and many old ones leaning together, and the streets swarmed with people. Some of them were very short and strangely dressed. They wore high, four-cornered hats, and silver spoons dangled from belts girding fur garments that reached nearly to their knees. Soft leather boots with upwardly pointed toes exactly like my own covered their feet.

"Lapps," Henrik whispered when he saw me studying a group of men clustered in lively discussion outside a shop.

So these were Lapps! Wiry and weather-beaten, the men strutted about like proud roosters on short, bowed legs, some with pelts slung about their shoulders, all with pipes clenched between their teeth. Some were dark haired with fierce black eyes; others blond with blue eyes. They spoke a language of unrecognizable sounds.

"Why do they wear such strange hats?" I asked curiously.

"They say the four corners point to the four directions. They come here to trade their pelts for silver trinkets, and they're very fond of spoons," Henrik explained. "Tornio is known for its fine silversmiths," he added, as if that could explain such strange taste.

I regarded them warily. I had heard that during the bad times desperate Finnish parents paid Lapps to take their children to Ruija to find them new homes where they wouldn't starve, but the Lapps instead sold the children into slavery to Norwegian farmers. At least my mother didn't send me away with a Lapp! Suddenly I regarded Uncle Henrik in a new, more grateful light.

"Do you think they have any Finnish children with them to sell in Ruija?" I whispered.

Henrik gave me a sharp look. "Where did you get such ideas? The Lapps have carried many a starving Finnish child away from misery in Finland, to be sure. But they're not slave traders! When they agree to take a child, it's an act of Christian charity to keep it from certain death." He paused, pulling thoughtfully on his beard. "Now it may well be that at the end of their journey some have asked for recompense for their expense in transporting and feeding the child," he conceded. "But that's hardly the same thing as selling it!"

Perhaps not, I thought. But I was glad I didn't have to travel with them. Christians they well might be, but they looked uncivilized to me.

"It's time for a drink of beer," Henrik announced. "We shan't have another opportunity such as this."

I looked at him with worried puzzlement. We still had hours of daylight before us and good traveling weather to boot. Nonetheless, shortly we were seated in a large room with a motley group of noisy travelers. Some were dressed in woolens much as ourselves, others in furs that bespoke an outdoor life on the tundra. Several chatted in strange languages. Henrik immediately fell into animated conversation while I huddled by the fire, grateful for the warmth and a filling bowl of hot porridge. Our rations had gotten very low and I had begun to hoard mine.

When Henrik finished his first mug, he ordered another, and then another. And still another. He spent a merry night in his cups while I dozed miserably by the hearth. The next morning he was up, chipper and tranquil, indifferent to my own foul mood and, apparently, to our dwindling rations. We set out for Haparanda, crossing the Tornio River on a long, rickety wooden bridge that swayed fearfully beneath our feet.

"Why are you so glum this fine morning?" Henrik asked with a sidelong glance at me. It was indeed a fine morning, clear and still, but I pursed my lips and remained silent.

"Do you disapprove of my taking a drink, is that it? You women are all alike!" he fumed, lengthening his stride irritably.

"It's not that!" I protested, scrambling to keep up. "It's just that we have so little food left and . . ."

Abruptly, he stopped on the swaying footbridge within a stone's throw of Sweden and sighed impatiently.

"Kaisa, you must learn to enjoy such moments as present themselves for enjoyment in this life and let the rest take care of itself. We have few enough of them as it is." That said, he stalked off, leaving me to stare unhappily after him.

I turned to look toward Finland. Maybe I could retrace our steps and soon be back in Rantsila with my mother and Sofie. It seemed an eternity since I had left them. This would be my last chance, I knew. Once we entered the wilds of Lapland, there could be no turning back. Sick with longing for home and filled with dread of what lay ahead, I stood in acute anguish on that bridge in the rosy morning light, unable to go forward or back. Then a boatman ferrying a passenger slid out from Tornio into the flat water, breaking my reverie. The boatman! I didn't have as much as a coin to pay him to ferry me back to shore.

I realized it was hopeless. But I could not tear my eyes away from the road south. In that direction lay home, and my heart ached at the thought that I might never pass this way again.

"Kaisa! Are you coming?" Henrik shouted from the shore of Sweden.

I hurried toward him, resigned to my fate. Sisu, I told myself. Sisu. Sisu. Somehow it must all be for the best.

SIX

THE ROAD TO LAPLAND

"This road goes all the way to Pajala," Henrik said as we began our trek out of Haparanda. "The Swedes keep it open to take the mail up there once a week by horse and sled."

The road was busy. Handsome sleds pulled by stout horses often sped past us. None stopped to offer us a ride. It dawned on me that we two must make quite a sorry spectacle, trudging along like destitute beggars with all our earthly possessions on our backs.

"Pajala? How far is that, Uncle Henrik?"

"As far as from here to Rantsila. But we'll turn off the road a bit before we get there, at a place called Lappea near where the Tornio and Muonio rivers meet, and cross back to Finland."

"But what will we do when the road ends?"

"We'll take to the river. It will be frozen solid. It's faster and easier to walk on and there's less chance of getting lost."

"Are we going to walk on the river all the way across the mountains?" I scanned the northern horizon anxiously but could see no sign of the mountains we were to cross.

He laughed. "No, we'll throw ourselves on the mercy of the Lapps."

"The Lapps!"

"They'll be traveling from Karesuando to the Skibotn Market to sell their goods. We'll travel with them the last leg across the summit."

"Skibotn Market?" I knew what a market was. We had a summer market in Rantsila until the pastor put a stop to it on account of rowdiness and drinking. But I never went there and I had never heard of Skibotn.

"It's a very old one," Henrik began, warming instantly to this subject. "For five hundred years—and likely thousands of years before that— people have been coming over these mountains from as far away as Tornio to trade at the Skibotn Market in Lyngen with the people who live along the Arctic Sea. They've always followed this very route; some call it the Road of the Four Winds. They still come every year—Lapps and Finns as well as Norwegians, Swedes, Germans, Dutchmen, Russians—regardless of weather, on the second week of November. It's the biggest event of the year and many hundreds of people come. Sometimes there are even musicians and magicians. The merchants come from the south in large ships with sugar, fabric, flour, tobacco and spirits. They trade with the fishermen for dried codfish. And the mountain Lapps come down to the sea with their reindeer harnessed together one after another in a long line, their pulks and sledges filled with furs, frozen ptarmigan, cloudberries, reindeer meat and butter. It's a sight to behold, Kaisa. But to get there, we must reach Karesuando before the Lapps leave for market. We have no time to waste."

"It's so far!" I cried. Now that we actually were about to begin our ascent into the wilderness, I once again was seized with dread.

"Don't think about how far it is, Kaisa. Take it one step at a time, one day at a time. Enjoy each day for itself because you never know what tomorrow may bring. I've traveled up and down this road for twenty years now, and that's how I do it. There's always something new to see."

At midday we stopped at a row of fishermen's huts lining the riverbank. High, rickety wooden platforms extended out over the partly frozen river. "They stand on these platforms using long poles to net the fish," Henrik explained as we approached one hut where smoke wafted through a hole in the roof. Sure enough, long poles with nets fastened on one end leaned against the outside wall of the hut. Inside, three men squatted around the fire pit roasting fish. The smell made my mouth water. They waved us inside and offered us hot, moist pieces of fish. Famished, I gulped mine down.

The men were brothers from a nearby village. The eldest was regaling his younger brothers with tales of the Lofoten Islands cod fishery off the western coast of Norway when we joined their fire. He had been there the previous year and meant to find a way for all of them to go back the next season. "Soon we could have enough to buy our father's farm from the landlord," the eldest explained.

Henrik shook his head. "That's a hard, dangerous life, Lofoten. If it's land you want, why don't you just pack up and settle in Ruija?"

"We mean to live in Finland, where we belong, not with those stuck-up Norwegians always looking down on you," the eldest retorted. "Besides, have you seen what they call farmland in Ruija? It's hopeless. It's too far north to grow anything even if the soil weren't worthless. The growing season is far too undependable. Finland's seasons are unreliable enough for me."

"Then you must not have cast your eyes on Balsfjord," Henrik replied stiffly. "It's a veritable garden spot, that is. And there are many other places tucked away along the fjords and in those valleys that would make for fine farming with a bit of luck."

"Luck, indeed. I'd rather take my chances in Lofoten," the youngest put in cockily.

"A man can't go broke fishing in Lofoten," the third brother added, his eyes sparkling.

"Many have," Henrik replied drily. "And many others have paid for their fish with their lives. Surely you've heard what happened in the storm of 1870, when one hundred twenty-three men in small rowboats were drowned in less than an hour?"

"We lost some last year as well," the eldest said quietly. All three fell silent.

We thanked them for the fish and pressed on to the next post station, a tidy farmhouse where we spent an uneventful night. We awoke to bitter cold and crystal skies. I wrapped my scarf so tightly around my face that only my eyes were uncovered, but I soon felt my skin tingling. Henrik paused only long enough to rub some snow on my nose and cheeks, then on his own. "It will keep away frostbite," he assured me.

Because the piercing cold hastened our pace, we made good time toward our next stop, Matarengi, which they now call Overtornea. When we crested the hill before descending into the village, we stopped momentarily to admire the wide, pleasant valley that lay before us. Henrik pointed out a structure atop the ridge across the valley on the Finnish side. I could barely make it out in the trees.

"That's the Russian czar's new hunting lodge at Aavasaksa. It's ten years old but he hasn't set foot in it yet." He shook his head disgustedly.

The road into Matarengi wound past a lovely old church that, silhouetted against a brilliant blue sky, looked very like the church at home in Rantsila. It triggered angry thoughts about what had happened to my mother.

No one would ever have call to treat me in such a fashion, I vowed silently to myself.

That night we enjoyed our finest accommodations yet in a big house with two hearths. And our good luck held the next day. About mid-morning we heard harness bells tinkle to a stop behind us. The driver, heavily outfitted in furs, motioned us aboard his sleigh. "Are you going far?" he asked jovially.

"Lyngen," Henrik answered.

"I'm not going nearly that far," he laughed, "but I could use some company to Pello. It helps keep me awake."

Gratefully I climbed in. But it was a mixed blessing, this lift. The cold was far worse now that I wasn't walking. Even though I wriggled them, my toes and fingers tingled, and soon I felt sleepy, lulled by the motion of the sled sliding swiftly along and the men's droning prattle about road conditions and weather. As soon as he saw me sliding into sleep, Henrik roughly shook me awake. Startled, I set to wriggling my toes and fingers again, but there was no feeling in them. A panicked moment later, stabbing pinpricks of feeling returned. After that, I kept my eyes wide open until we reached Pello.

Henrik was enormously pleased. "We've shaved nearly a day's walk off our journey," he told me cheerfully. "You should always travel with me, Kaisa. Then I'm sure I'd have many more such offers of transport," he joked.

But what the Lord giveth, the Lord taketh away.

We awoke to find ourselves encased in fog. It had clamped a lid on the landscape, shutting out light. We set out at the first sign that it might be lifting, but it soon began to snow. We tramped along hesitantly, grateful the searing cold had broken. But by midday a fierce wind had come up and snow was falling so thickly that we could see but a few meters in front of us.

"We'll have to stop somewhere," Henrik said, worry apparent in his voice. "We should come to a farmhouse soon, unless I've completely lost my bearings."

For the first time, a sharp fear shot through me. If Henrik was lost, then we were truly lost! But I knew we had to keep moving regardless. Blindly, I put one foot in front of the other, as Henrik had instructed, and tried not to think of anything but the next step.

We smelled our sanctuary before we saw it. Smoke wafted toward us on gusts of blowing snow, and then we heard dogs bark on our right. "It's up here someplace," Henrik muttered. We nearly stumbled into the cottage door, which flew open at the same moment.

"Gracious! Out in such weather!" A wizened crone stood in the doorway, frowning and sucking on a pipe. "I thought you were my sons. They're cutting wood and should have been back long before this. You didn't see any sign of them, did you?"

Henrik shook his head. "We couldn't see anything out there." We settled by the fire to wait it out while our hostess, whether out of generosity or nervousness, plied us with salted fish and bread and butter. I ate so much and slept so hard that I missed entirely the return of the sons late that evening.

The next morning we set out through new snow and occasional fog. The countryside was not so thickly settled, and fewer travelers were on the road now. I shuffled along as if in a dream, hardly able to believe where I was. I tried to fasten on the memory of my mother knitting before the hearth and Sofie standing by the barn waving, but I felt as if I had never known anything but tramping along this endless road. I didn't know I was crying until I felt tears freeze to my cheeks. Henrik caught me wiping them away with my mitten, but he didn't say anything until we had gone a good bit farther.

"You look like your father, Kaisa, but you're a great deal like your mother. She was always very strong, even as a child."

"What was she like, then?" For the first time, I tried to envision my mother as a child.

"Self-reliant. Quiet. A little shy, but deep. You might not notice her at first, but she was always the most sensible presence in the room whenever there was trouble." He broke into a grin. "She was a stubborn one, that's for sure. Unbendable, even as a child." He sighed and his smile vanished.

"I knew the moment I laid eyes on Nikolai what would happen. She was head over heels in love with him; that was plain to see. And I knew that in the end she would have her way with him, consequences be damned. But I hoped they would marry. And come settle in Ruija."

"Have her way with him?" I repeated, puzzled.

"Your mother knew what she wanted," he answered shortly. "And she knew the risks well enough after what she'd been through."

As we left the post road and crossed back into Finland, Henrik paused to study the sky. "The snow cover is getting shallower, so walking will be easier. Pray it holds off snowing until Karesuando."

We spent an uncomfortable night in a dirty hut in Lappea amongst surly, stinking inhabitants and hastily set out at dawn. I already had noticed that the poorer our hosts, the more generously they treated us; the richer they were, the less they had to share. But this wretched shelter had proven an exception.

The going became slower as we gradually ascended, leaving the Tornio Valley behind. I frequently grabbed a handful of snow to quench my thirst. When we reached Kolari shortly after dark, I was exhausted. But here Henrik had a good friend, an old companion from his seal hunting days on the gulf, and we spent the night in pleasant company with him and his wife and two small children. While the men reminisced on their side of the cottage, the wife entertained me on her side.

"What's a child like you doing on a journey such as this?" she wanted to know.

"My mother had to send me away so I could have a better life," I told her. To my own surprise, a touch of pride crept into my voice.

"Oh, it's like that, is it?" She clucked her tongue. "Well, you're not the first Finnish child we've seen pass by our door on such a journey, and you likely won't be the last. I daresay none have been as fortunate in their traveling companion as you."

I nodded. It was true, I was coming to realize.

When we left, our knapsacks were stuffed with bread, dried meat and fish, and I set out with a lighter heart. Our luck held with the weather. The higher we climbed, the thinner the snow. Soon it barely covered my toes, and we were walking rapidly along on the frozen Muonio River under crisp skies.

"You're getting to be a strong walker, Kaisa," Henrik noted approvingly. I walked faster, prodded by pride. Even then, I was driven by pride.

Later that day we caught our first full sight of the round-topped, snow-capped mountains that lay ahead. I kept one anxious eye on them and the other on the sky. The days had grown noticeably shorter now, so we had less time to walk in daylight. Walking at night in this wilderness was best avoided, of course. The bears might be asleep, but hungry wolves and wolverines were on the prowl.

My thoughts were interrupted by jingling bells rapidly approaching from the bend in the river ahead of us. "Lapps!" Henrik said, pulling me aside. Within moments it was upon us, a single reindeer pulling a sled that looked like a land-going boat. A man dressed in furs rode astride this contraption holding a single rein, and he seemed to be steering it with his feet, which dangled over each side. He whizzed by us with a cheerful wave of his free hand. The reindeer's hooves made a rhythmic knocking sound as it pranced by us, and then we were all alone again in the silence.

"He must be trying to get somewhere before the weather turns," Henrik remarked.

"He's going so fast!" I marveled.

"Reindeer easily outrun a horse. They can fly over the snow for hours on end. They're amazing beasts."

"Ugly ones," I muttered, wrinkling up my nose. They were such gangly, ungainly-looking creatures.

"Don't be so hasty in your judgment, Kaisa. The Lapps manage to get everything they need from just that one animal: shelter, food, clothing, transport, tools, weapons. You may be able to milk a cow, eat her and wear her hide, but you can't make her pull you across the snowy tundra, that's for certain. The Lapps are remarkable, very clever people."

I held my tongue. They looked rough and frightening to me.

When we finally reached the high, open tundra of Lapland, a sharp wind buffeted us unmercifully. The spire of Muonio's church beckoned against a thickening sky, and we hurried to reach that tiny, windswept outpost. It sat on a barren, sloping hillside on a wide bend of the Muonio River. On that wind-scoured tundra, I paused briefly to take one last look behind me. A faint tinge of warm orange and pink colored the sky to the south. I tried to blot out thoughts of my mother and sister and concentrate instead on what lay before me. Here and there, a few short, miserable birches and pitiful pines poked through the snow. The wind howled menacingly, seemingly from all directions at once, sucking the breath from our lungs.

"Now I know why they call it 'The Road of the Four Winds,'" I gasped.

That night we stayed with an old Finn who shared his hut with a Lapp woman. He and Henrik talked quietly about the weather and what lay ahead. I heard something new in Henrik's voice: uncertainty.

The sky was the same color as the ground when we set out the next morning. The wind stabbed through my woolen coat, and for the first time I wished for fur clothing. Icy tentacles wrapped themselves around my bones. Never before or since have I been so cold, yet we were moving at a brisk pace along a flat landscape on a track that was easy to follow. A man passed us on skis and then someone hurried by in a sled; otherwise all was still. At midday we caught up to a ragged man and woman trudging slowly along on foot. They seemed much too old to be out in this wilderness in such weather.

"Are you going far?" Henrik asked.

"Lyngen," came the weary reply from the man, whose face was blue with cold. The woman only looked at us, her eyes wide with worry. We stared at them in disbelief.

"Lyngen?" Henrik protested. "But that's . . ." He broke off, for once at a loss for words.

"We're from Karunki. We've had little to eat this last week or we should have made better time," the man continued half-apologetically. "We have nowhere else to go. We're going north to find our only son. He's in Lyngeseidet, last we heard."

Henrik unslung his bag from his back and reached inside. He handed the woman a packet of dried reindeer meat and two little round loaves of bread. She looked at him with grateful, watering eyes. "Thank you, thank you," she murmured.

"I think a bad storm is coming, so you must find shelter as quickly as you can," Henrik advised. He pointed to a cottage just visible in the middle distance. "That house is just a short way from here and it has welcoming folk inside," he assured them. Then we left them there on the track, plodding slowly along behind us, the woman clutching the man's arm with both hands.

"Do you think they'll get there?"

"They'll make it to shelter tonight. But Lyngen?" Henrik shook his head, frowning. "I've seen too much misery along this trail, Kaisa. This road used to be filled with such vagabonds, destitute people fleeing starvation and often carrying their children on their backs, especially years ago, when my mother—your grandmother—died. And while there are not so many such wanderers on this road now as then, they haven't stopped coming. They never will, so long as the fish lasts in Norway and the hunger lasts in Finland."

We hurried on in the gathering gloom of afternoon. Once, just before we lost the light, I thought I heard a wolf howl. I paused, fear pulsing through my limbs.

"Probably a dog," Henrik said lightly. But I saw that he cast wary, side-long glances into the snow-covered bushes and kept his hand on the handle of the long knife that always hung from his belt. Aside from his staff, it was all we had for protection.

The storm failed to materialize. It hung above us, frozen in place. So the second day of travel across this nearly featureless expanse passed much as the first except that the wind blew harder. It bore down from the east, cutting through our clothes like searing knives. I was hardly aware of my surroundings, knowing only that I had to keep putting one foot in front of the other or die here in this bleak wasteland. We didn't dare stop to rest for fear of freezing.

"Kaisa, look!" Henrik shouted above the wind. He pointed to a rise where a few pines clustered to make a dwarf forest. At first my eyes couldn't make out anything; then I caught an odd movement, something like little brushes waving out of the snowdrifts.

"What is it?" I asked, puzzled.

"Keep watching. There, now look. Do you see it?"

As if on cue, dozens of reindeer heads popped up out of the snowdrifts. Then some set to digging furiously, sending snow flying behind them.

"Those are their tails wiggling. They're digging for lichen. That's what they eat. But you see how nervous they are. They're afraid of wolverines, so they bury their heads in the snow to eat for only a few moments at a time. But each time the reindeer head goes down, the wolverine creeps a little closer. It's a vicious beast, that one, far worse than the wolf. At least you can admire the intelligent way the wolf goes about his business. Wolverines are sneaky, cowardly devils."

Suddenly, at the far edge of the herd, we saw a fur-clad Lapp ski out of the trees with a rifle slung over his shoulder, a black dog bounding at his heels. "He'll keep good watch," Henrik said, waving a greeting as we passed.

Our luck ran out the next day. We had spent a raw night in a drafty hut somewhere on the tundra and were up before dawn, impatient to be off for the final leg of our journey to Karesuando.

"They'll likely be leaving for Skibotn tomorrow, so we must get there by tonight." Henrik seemed worried.

We set out under a stone gray sky. The wind whipped us as before, but it had lost its painful edge. "It's not so cold now," I remarked gratefully.

"We could wish otherwise. Better the cold than snow to blow about and blind us," Henrik grunted. He had barely gotten the words out when I felt the first snowflake on my cheek.

Henrik looked at me grimly. "Can you run awhile, Kaisa? We need to cover as much ground as we can while we can still see."

He took my hand, and with the wind buffeting us, we trotted along side by side, knapsacks bouncing against our backs. We ran until I was sure my lungs would burst. When I gasped helplessly for air, he slowed to a walk. When my sides had quit heaving, he urged me into a trot again. We repeated this over and over, each time running in shorter and shorter bursts. Finally, I could move no farther. My legs were leaden and shaking uncontrollably and my lungs ached. I stopped, exhausted, the snowstorm now swirling in full fury about us. But within moments the paralyzing cold began to creep into my limbs, so we set off again. We couldn't see well enough to run now, and Henrik's eyes were glued to his feet. He used his staff to probe before him. It was impossible to tell what time of day it was or whether mere minutes or hours had passed. Our only salvation lay in pressing blindly into the howling storm. It swooped over our heads, roaring and whistling fearfully. Visibility dropped to less than a meter. Henrik gripped my hand.

"How can we go on?" I shouted into his ear. "We can't see anything!" We were encrusted in snow from head to foot. I was far too terrified to cry. We would die here, I was certain. It was just a question of how. We'd freeze to death if the wolves didn't kill us first.

"You must be brave, Kaisa. This can't last forever." But he sounded as frightened as I felt.

Whenever the river made a bend, we stumbled into its bank. So he carefully probed his way out to the river again by rapping on the ground with his staff until we once more were on solid ice. But each time we turned, I feared we were walking in circles, going blindly round and round in the same spot. I'd heard of people dying this way.

"We should see some lights soon," Henrik shouted as it became noticeably darker. But we didn't, and the storm showed no sign of abating.

"Will we see the lights in this storm, do you think?" What if we went right past Karesuando without seeing it?

"We're still on the river, Kaisa. Hear the ice?" He jabbed his staff reassuringly into the snow, and we plodded on. Was it hours or minutes before darkness completely enclosed us? I can't say. All I wanted was to lie down and sleep.

Then, as if in a dream, we heard it. A dog barked faintly somewhere ahead on our left. We squinted into the blackness, hearts pounding with hope. There! Pinpricks of light!

"We're here, Kaisa!" Henrik shouted jubilantly. "Hurry along now!"

With great effort, accompanied by the frantic barking of dogs, we clambered up the riverbank. We were about to fall against the low door of the nearest hut when someone heard the commotion and threw it open.

"Henrik!" a man shouted. I didn't understand anything else he said. Shaking with relief and exhaustion, I tumbled inside, and someone helped me out of my frozen coat and boots. When I had caught my breath and my heart stilled, I saw that I was in a smoky, round earthen hut ringed inside by wooden poles. A fire blazed in the center of this room and the smoke rose through a hole in the ceiling. An iron pot hung on sticks over the fire pit. Skins were laid out on top of a birch-branch mat. Sitting on them staring at us through almond-shaped eyes were three dark-haired children and four adults, all dressed in skins. Two men babbled excitedly at Henrik in an incomprehensible tongue. Several dogs lay near the doorway, and a baby stuffed in a basket dangled from a pole in one corner. A leather-skinned old woman sucking on a pipe rose and stirred the pot. She handed Henrik, then me, a wooden spoon and motioned for me to eat. Behind her frightening appearance, sympathetic eyes met mine. Trembling with hunger, I dipped into the pot. The stew had a rich, pungent taste, but I gratefully wolfed it down.

When I awoke, dim daylight was streaming through the smokehole and the hut's one glass window. Startled, I sat up, thoroughly disoriented. I had slept so late! Why weren't we on the road already? The men and children were gone but two women smiled at me from the fire, where they were preparing something. They spoke quietly together, glancing at me occasionally. One handed me a steaming mug. A bitter, salty taste seared my tongue and I grimaced. Coffee! The two women hooted gaily and urged me to drink more. To please them I took another swallow, and this time it went down more easily. They watched intently, with kind faces, as I finished my mug. When I handed it back empty, they smiled broadly, but I felt queasy.

Just then Henrik stepped through the entrance, banging his head smartly on the door jamb. Cursing, he carefully closed the slanted, heavy wooden door behind him.

"No matter how long I live, I'll never get used to these damnable door-ways," he said, smiling sheepishly at the giggling women but addressing me. "The Lapps say they build them so low just so the Swedes and Norwegians will have to bow when they enter a Lapp home," he chuck-led. "But you'd think they could make some exception for the Finns."

He sat down beside me, sipping a mug of coffe. "Aslak and the others are loading now. We'll be leaving this evening."

"This evening? We're to travel at night?" I didn't think I had heard him right.

"Yes. All this new snow is too soft for the reindeer to make good time in daylight. But it's getting colder and by evening it will be clear, fine traveling weather. You'll see."

My heart sank. Traveling at night! What now was to befall us?

But when I ventured outside, I felt cheered by what I saw. The smooth-bottomed, boat-like sleds were being loaded with furs, frozen birds, and other goods sealed in wooden tubs. Long poles and rolled-up tents were lashed to some sleds, but others, ones with backrests, were not loaded. I guessed that we were to ride in those. Children, each with a dog trotting alongside, swarmed excitedly about. I remembered Henrik telling me that Lapp children are given a dog for protection as soon as they're able to care for the animal. "The dog answers only to it own master," he had said, and that certainly seemed to be the case here. Cautiously, I studied these strange people as they bustled about their tasks.

"It's a pity we couldn't be here a little earlier in the fall when they round up the herd and castrate the males," Henrik said, his eyes twinkling naughtily. "It's something to see, that is. They pick an old person with a smooth set of teeth so as not to harm the animal, then they throw it on its back and the balls are chewed off, neat as you please."

I stared at him, aghast. I decided he was making it up to tease me and made a disgusted face.

"No, it's true. Ask anyone," he laughed.

When the men brought the reindeer, I eyed the beasts suspiciously. They were balky and their eyes bulged, whether in fear or irritation I could not tell. One by one Aslak harnessed the snorting, skittish creatures to the pulks. They tossed their antlered heads and stamped their wide hooves.

"Are they tame?" I whispered fearfully.

"Not exactly," Henrik chuckled. "But they do follow a leader, once they can be persuaded to the task."

Aslak, a merry gleam in his eye, came over and spoke a few words to Henrik. He pointed to a pulk that was being harnessed to one of the reindeer. Henrik looked at me and cleared his throat.

"Now, Kaisa, you're to ride in that pulk over there. Just for a little practice."

"Alone?" I whispered. I remembered the Lapp who had whizzed by us at frightening speed. Even in my worst moments it had never occurred to me that I would be riding in a pulk across the frozen wastes of Lapland. At night, yet.

"It's easy once you get the hang of it."

I could see plain in his face that he was lying. But there was no help for it; he led me over to the pulk and I clambered awkwardly inside. Aslak held the restless animal's reins while I sat stiff with fright, heart pounding in my throat. A hushed crowd had gathered to watch.

"Aslak will lead you around slowly just so you can get used to it. This is one of the docile ones, so it's all just a matter of holding your balance and moving the rein to the right and left in the direction you want the animal to go. But it will follow Aslak's animal right enough once we get under way."

Just as Aslak was showing me how to hold the rein, the reindeer bounded free in one great leap and galloped headlong away. I had time to shriek only once as we flew across the snowdrifts. Then the animal bolted abruptly to the right, upending the pulk. I rolled out into the snow and the reindeer bounded off. Behind me I heard a chorus of laughter. I sat stunned in the snow while the men scattered in pursuit of the errant reindeer. Henrik came to help me up.

"Are you all right, Kaisa?" he asked solicitously, but I could see he was fighting laughter.

"If that's the worst thing that happens to me on this journey I'll be grateful," I mumbled, embarrassed.

I restrained a wicked urge to box the beast across the nose when the men led it back, spent and panting.

"Don't worry, Kaisa," Henrik chuckled. "You'll be riding in a sledge, and it won't upend you. They were just having a bit of sport."

"Sport indeed," I thought, wiping the remaining snow from my face.

We set out that evening under a black, frosty sky. After a few minutes of wobbly panic as the long line fell into place, I settled back, tightly wrapped in furs. Soon I was mesmerized by jingling bells and rhythmic knocking of hooves as the animals sprinted across the snow. The immense sea of blackness above us grew brighter and brighter as millions of stars, more brilliant than any I'd ever seen, twinkled to life, casting a luminescent glow on the snow. We rushed swiftly along, up and down gentle slopes, past naked dwarf birches and rocky outcrops. My heart raced with sheer joy. Then Aslak broke into song, a wild, full-throated, hauntingly repetitive melody that became one with the rhythm of the clacking reindeer hooves. Suddenly there was a hissing, crackling sound and the heavens lit up with a panorama of pulsating color—purple bleeding into violet and shimmering silver, pink into red, green into blue. The Northern Lights! Would this night's wonders never end?

I don't know how long we traveled before Aslak briefly halted the line so we could refresh ourselves. The reindeer immediately collapsed on their sides, panting horribly, their tongues hanging out of their mouths. Some rolled over on their backs, legs pointing straight to the heavens, sides heaving frightfully. It was a gruesome sight.

"Will they die?" I asked Henrik, alarmed. What if we were stranded out here?

He chuckled. "They'll spring back to life shortly. I told you they're amazing animals. Did you like Aslak's joik?"

I looked at him blankly.

"His song. Did you like it?"

"I did. But what was it about?"

"Oh, probably about the things we passed on our way."

"Things? I didn't see any things."

"You saw the stars in the heavens, the trees and the rocks, the lights and the beauty of the night, didn't you?"

I nodded dumbly.

"Those are some of the things Lapps joik about. It's never the same. They sing to nature, about nature. More properly put, they sing nature. They're not supposed to, mind you. They're good Christians, after all. The church frowns on joiking. Forbids it, in fact." He spat, as I had noticed Uncle Henrik often did when the subject of the church arose. Before I could ask why that was so, we were off again.

The rest of that magical journey is a blur. I was so happy speeding along through the night with the Lapps that I forgot my sorrows and how I had come to be there. It seems an impossible fantasy now, but to this day, I dream of those Northern Lights and racing across the snow to the rhythmic knocking of reindeer hooves and Aslak's haunting joik.

Henrik had told me that when we reached the frozen shores of Lake Kilpisjarvi I would see a high, sharp peak sacred to the Lapps. Then I would know we had reached the summit and were crossing into Ruija. It would be only a short distance then to the famed travelers' hut at Helligskogen, where we would take refuge for what remained of the night. From there it would be a short descent to the sea and the Skibotn Market. And it was all just as he said. But by the time we got to Helligskogen, I was too weary to appreciate how close we were to our journey's end. I found an empty cot and fell into it, dead to the world and its cares.

SEVEN

THE ALPS OF THE NORTH

Our procession fell into line the next morning in wet, heavy snow. "The reindeer will do their best to slow the sledges as we go down," Henrik explained as we prepared to set out. But I had serious misgivings as we began the steep downhill slide. The panicked reindeer ran faster and faster as they tried to outrun the careening pulks and sledges that bore down hard against their heels. As you might expect, our descent from mountain to sea went very fast. Heart in throat, I held on as best I could, shifting my weight from side to side and praying I wouldn't roll over and tangle the line of lurching animals.

I was eager for my first glimpse of this sea, but a thick mist obscured everything below us. Then I smelled it: heavy salt air moving on a gentle breeze. The mist suddenly dissolved and I saw a stunning sight: sunlight glittering on a chain of high, snow-covered mountains that stood guard behind a still, dark blue fjord. Shortly we were on level ground and Aslak drew the line to a halt a little way from a cluster of houses on an icy seashore teeming with more people than I had ever seen in one place. Skibotn!

A wondrous scene lay before us. Noisy mobs of men, women and children scurried about everywhere. Barking dogs frolicked underfoot, and horses and reindeer twitched impatiently in their harnesses. Smoke poured from the chimneys of log houses scattered amid trees and near the shoreline, and men bearing bundles of goods wandered in and out of them. Barrels and boxes were stacked everywhere. Several large ships lay at anchor just offshore, and a fleet of small wooden boats, their brown canvas sails unfurled, rested on the beach.

Down by the seashore, men argued near racks and stacks of dried fish. Large fires blazed on the snowy ground, each with a coffee kettle suspended over it. Around these fires, unkempt men in reindeer skin garments passed bottles from man to man. Some staggered comically about, joiking pitifully before collapsing in their tracks. Here and there in a convenient snowdrift a fur-clad body lay stiff as death, snoring peacefully and reeking of spirits, a worried dog whining affectionately nearby. Well-dressed merchants strutted importantly among the Lapps and their merchandise.

Henrik's eyes shone. "So, Kaisa, what do you think of Lyngen?"

"Even after all you've told me, Uncle Henrik, I never imagined it would be like this." I could hardly tear my eyes from the magnificent mountains and the shimmering fjord. It was a deep, cold blue, not gray like the gulf, and the sharp mountain peaks shot starkly up from the water. These were nothing like the gently rounded hills we had traversed in Lapland. These were real mountains! And this surely was nothing like the flat farmscapes of Rantsila.

"'The Alps of the North,' they call them. And your new home, Balsfjord, is over there, just behind those mountains." He pointed westward.

"To get there, we'll follow this fjord to its head, then cross at a place called Nordkjosbotn, which separates this fjord from Balsfjord. But first we'll pass Horsnes, Kvesmenes, Hatteng and Kitdal, where I hope to conduct some business."

I tried to make sense of the din around me. "What languages are they speaking?"

"Norwegian. Also Lapp, Russian, Swedish, German, even English."

A new worry struck me. "Do you understand Norwegian?"

"Well, I certainly can't read or write it. But I get by," Henrik assured me.

Henrik led me to the home of a Finnish family, and the hostess offered us an alarmingly large portion of boiled codfish and potatoes swimming in salty butter and a thin, flat bread thickly smeared with more butter. Never had I seen so much food on one plate nor accepted it so gratefully. All except the bitter, salty coffee, which I still had trouble swallowing. I ate so much I could hardly breathe or move. But Henrik shouldered his pack.

"Now it's time for some serious trading," he smiled. "I'm short of knives and needles and thread and other trinkets my customers depend on me to carry. This journey has all but depleted my stores," he added lightly.

Henrik saw the dismay on my face. Suddenly I realized that this trip must have cost money. He seemed to read my thoughts. "It wasn't as costly as it could have been," he assured me quickly. "Aslak is a friend and so offered us a good price for the ride. But he's a Lapp, after all. He's a businessman." He paused, as if considering whether to continue. "You should know that your mother gave me all the markkaa she had to see us over the mountains with the Lapps. Even your Uncle Juho gave a few markkaa."

At the mention of my mother, hot tears filled my eyes. I turned away to hide my grief. "Sisu," I told myself sternly. It was too late for tears now. I was here, cast out into a foreign land among strangers whose words I could not understand.

While Henrik went about his business, I wandered off to explore the market. Inside the little warehouses that served as stores, the shelves and floors were lined with an astonishing array of goods: bolts of cloth, bins brimming with salt, sugar, coffee and tobacco, bottles of whiskey. Some stores were entirely filled with large sacks of flour. Others held metal tools, farm implements, knives, glassware, iron pots and pans, household trinkets and supplies of the sort Henrik peddled. Mountain folk streamed in and out bearing pelts, finely carved reindeer bone spoons, soft leather boots or wooden jars of frozen berries. Wouldn't my mother be amazed if she could see all this food and the fine goods!

Once or twice someone spoke to me as I wandered about, but I didn't understand what they were saying. Disconsolate, I wandered down to the shore to gaze at the imposing white peaks of the Lyngen Alps. I felt very small and lost standing there. What would become of me here in this harsh, alien place so far from home and those I loved?

We stayed another day at the market. When it was time to leave, Henrik secured a place for us among stores of flour, coffee and sugar on a small boat going all the way to Kvesmenes. The men hoisted the sails as soon as the breeze came up, and then we were gliding along the deep fjord in a smooth, rolling motion. I gripped the seat, but my fear gradually melted away as my body became accustomed to the rhythm of the gentle waves. I could see that the fjord was narrowing and that massive mountains loomed ever higher over our heads.

All along the coastline on both sides smoke curled up from little wooden huts clinging to rocky outcrops. A few of the houses were low and round and hard to see until we came nearly alongside because they were made of earth and stones.

"Who lives here?" I asked Henrik in wonder.

"Sea Lapps. Some Finns. They're fisher folk who keep a few goats, maybe a cow or two if they are fortunate. Their houses are called *gammes* and they're dug into the earth."

"Sea Lapps?" I had never heard of such a thing. Lapps were reindeer herders, that much I had seen with my own eyes.

"The Sea Lapps say they were the first people to live here along the coast. They claim their ancestors were here long before the Vikings were a gleam in God's eye."

One of the men laughed derisively.

"The Mountain Lapps took to the hills to follow these huge reindeer herds only a few hundred years ago," Henrik added.

The man spat into the water. "You know a lot for a peddler."

That silenced Henrik until we came to a large, flat promontory of land jutting out into the fjord. A few dilapidated huts stood upon it, leaning this way and that. "That's Horsnes, Kaisa. It's said to be one of the old-est settlements around here." This time no one challenged his information.

Shortly we veered toward land at Kvesmenes, a tiny settlement squeezed onto a narrow ledge between a high mountain and the fjord. We helped our sullen companions unload their wares and gratefully scram-bled up the steep embankment to a house, which doubled as a store. Here we would spend the night.

It was warmer but wet when we set out on a narrow path along the shore the next morning. In a light drizzle, we followed it up and down little hills and rocky places. When the rain let up and I could see through the dim light where we were, I felt dwarfed by the huge peaks. Just before we rounded the bend into the tiny settlement of Hatteng at the end of the fjord, the skies cleared a bit. Here I stopped dead in my tracks.

Thrusting impossibly out of the mist was the most beautiful moun-tain of all, its sharp pinpoint piercing the sky. I craned my head back to stare at it, awestruck.

"Otertind. It's very famous," Henrik said, smiling proudly. "They call it 'The Matterhorn of the North.' I always say the walk is worth it when I come back to this place. I'd like to settle hereabouts some day," he confided.

"It's like a fairyland," I said, drinking it in.

We followed a river up a gentle slope into a small, open valley Henrik called Kitdal. It had a pleasant, welcoming feel even though mountains rose high on each side. It felt good to walk again, and we were striding along uphill at a comfortable pace when suddenly something occurred to me.

"What day is this?" I asked.

Henrik thought for a few minutes and then said, "Tuesday."

"No, I mean what date is it?"

He thought again. "The fifteenth of November."

"It's my birthday today," I told him shyly. "I'm thirteen years old now."

"Why, so it is, Kaisa," he beamed. "You'll be a woman before we know it! And a very pretty one at that."

I wondered if it were true or if he was just teasing me. Already I was vain enough to hope it was true.

Henrik did a good business at the houses along the way, so it was dark before we reached the last house at the upper end of the valley.

"Here we are at last!" Henrik sang out as we picked our way past some birch trees and a little creek that emptied into the river. I sensed, rather than saw, high mountains looming all around us. A welcoming light shone through the window of a small log house. The moment a dog barked, the door flew open and a dark-haired woman welcomed us into a room that seemed stuffed with people.

"Henrik!" they shouted gaily, pulling off our outer clothing. Before I could take it all in, someone had thrust a bowl of meat stew under my nose and I fell to eating, ravenous. Not until the bowl was empty did I look around me. There was the man and his wife, plus two girls younger than I as well as two older boys. One of the boys was light haired, the other dark. They all sat laughing with Henrik around the table while I warmed myself on a bench by the fire. When I finished eating, the dark-haired boy came to sit beside me on the bench. He was handsome, stocky like his father, with merry eyes and a captivating smile.

"Your uncle says today is your birthday. So here's a birthday kiss. Welcome to Norway!" he said in Finnish. He bussed my cheek to much laughter while I shrank back, mortified.

"Anton Anders Pedersen!" his mother scolded.

"Utsi! Anton Anders Utsi!" he protested, his brow furrowing momentarily. But she pretended not to hear and continued with her remarks, which I could not understand. Peals of laughter filled the room while I sat uncomprehending, feeling stupid and sure they were making a fool of me. Then the mother, whose name was Nicoline, pushed Anton away and seated herself next to me.

"You mustn't mind Anton," she told me. "He's always full of fun." But something in her tone told me she didn't find him very amusing. "You're very welcome here, Kaisa. What a journey you've had!" She clucked sympathetically, but I sensed there was a sharp edge to her. "My father came that way from Tornio before I was born," she added.

"It was pretty there," I told her softly.

She sighed. "So he always said. I'd like to see it for myself one day. But not if I have to walk! What a stout girl you are to have come all this way!"

"It wasn't hard, really," I answered, flushing with pride. "The hardest part was leaving my mother and sister." My voice broke unexpectedly.

She patted me on the shoulder. "Poor child! Poor Finland!" she sighed again. "Such times they've suffered! They may call our life hard, but I can promise you that you'll never starve here, Kaisa. I only hope Henrik can manage to get a place of his own soon," she added as an afterthought.

The next morning as we were about to depart, I saw Henrik and Jonas, Nicoline's husband, in earnest conversation as they pointed to a farm down valley and across the river. "I'll wager it will be available soon," I heard Jonas predict.

"How old is Anton?" I asked as casually as I could when we had been walking awhile the next morning. It was misty again, and clouds swirled overhead.

Henrik grinned teasingly, as I had known he would.

"He must be twenty-one or so. He's a fisherman. He goes to Lofoten from January to Easter and then to the Finnmark summer fishery, as the men from these parts always have done. It's a beastly existence, fishing. If the sea doesn't take them, disease does."

Henrik fell uncharacteristically quiet as we paused by a tiny farmhouse at the lower end of the valley. He studied it thoughtfully for some time and didn't speak until we reached the main road again. Here, where the fjord ended in a muddy tideflat, we turned left.

We barely had left Kitdal when we came to the opening into another valley. Unlike Kitdal, the mouth of this one was partly blocked by a large hill.

"That's Signaldal, where Otertind is," Henrik said, pointing to the entrance to the valley. It lay hidden from view behind the hill; all I could see of it was the passageway carved out by the river on its way to the fjord and a narrow footpath winding precariously along the shore. "It's a difficult climb into this valley. It's much longer than Kitdal but it seems much narrower because the mountains are so high and close."

As we paused for a moment at the entrance to Signaldal, an odd foreboding, an unaccountable sense of dread, washed over me. But we hurried on toward Balsfjord, though our progress was slowed by the number of Henrik's customers along this road. I didn't lay eyes on Balsfjord until the next day, when we came to a large body of choppy, gray water. A wet, heavy sky hung about our shoulders, but when it finally got light enough to see a good way into the distance, a wide, curving shoreline came into view. The mountains were neither as close nor as imposing here, and gentle flatlands fell toward the water. Well-kept farms dotted the shoreline.

"There's Storsteiness," Henrik said, pointing across the wide fjord. "That's where Jensine lives. We have to walk around to it, but you're almost there now, Kaisa, to your new home." He looked strangely glum.

I peered anxiously into the murk across the broad expanse of water, my heart in the pit of my stomach. How would this Jensine treat me? Would I ever see my own home again? To still my fears, I peppered Henrik with nervous questions. But the closer we got, the quieter he became. I was aching with anxiety by the time he led us to a large, well-lit home.

"This is not Jensine's house," he explained curtly as he rapped on the door. "But there's someone here I want to see."

The woman who opened it hardly glanced at me. Her hand flew wordlessly to her mouth when she saw Henrik.

Then he did something I'd never seen him do: he pulled off his hat and held it awkwardly between his hands. Then he said something to her I didn't understand.

She answered him, then motioned us inside, cheeks flushing. An old woman appeared behind her, scowling. The woman said something to the old woman, who turned her back on us without a word of greeting.

Henrik and I stood uncertainly just inside the door. "Kaisa, this is Matilda," he said.

Matilda said something else, staring intently into his face, but he seemed uncomfortable with her words. She was a plain, serious-looking woman with wrinkles starting to show at the corners of her eyes. She shifted her gaze to me and smiled, patting my arm kindly. She said something to me I didn't understand.

"She says you're very welcome to Balsfjord," Henrik explained.

Then she spoke to Henrik again. It sounded like a question. If it was, he gave a long answer, sometimes looking at her, sometimes looking at his feet. Then she nodded toward a cot in the corner of the room.

Henrik stepped carefully across the room and bent over the cot, where a small child lay sleeping. After a moment, he motioned me over.

"Kaisa, this is my daughter Petra."

"Your daughter?" I stared, dumbfounded, at him, then Matilda, and then at him again.

"Isn't she a sweet child?" he whispered, his eyes glistening.

I could only nod stupidly. "How old is she?" I finally found the voice to ask.

"Three," he said, straightening up. He stepped back across the room to face Matilda. He said something to her in an encouraging tone of voice.

She replied with what seemed another question, her eyes beseeching.

He cleared his throat and answered, then we left her standing in the open doorway as we set out down the road. Even in the impenetrable blackness, I suddenly saw Henrik in a whole new light. Covertly, I studied him through hard eyes as we turned up a little path that took us away from the main road, which continued along the shore. We made our way up a gentle slope to a large farmstead.

"Why didn't you marry Matilda?" I blurted out.

Henrik sighed deeply and stopped. "I knew you would ask me that, Kaisa. It's not so simple. I'm not sure I can give you an answer."

"I expect your answer is no different than my own father's," I shot back acidly.

"Maybe not. But I'm not good enough for these people," he said defensively. "I'm Finnish, and Matilda's mother is Norwegian. She doesn't want me spoiling their good family name, even if it means Matilda must raise a fatherless child. That I'm a landless peddler hardly helps to argue my case." He stalked away up the hill, and I ran to catch up. It was the first time I'd ever heard bitterness in his voice.

"But if you want to marry, why don't you just do it anyway?"

"The truth is, I'm not ready to settle, Kaisa. That would mean working for another man's gain and at his pleasure. One day, I hope to be master of my own land."

The discussion came to an abrupt end before a small cottage some distance from the main house. A large, bony woman filled the doorway in answer to Henrik's knock.

"You're here at last!" she boomed in Finnish, peering past him to where I stood hiding in the shadows, my stomach twisted in a hard knot. She motioned me inside. Hesitantly, I stepped across the threshold.

She was the homeliest woman I ever had seen. Her eyes were set much too far apart, her face was much too long, and her chin was altogether too large. Still, she smiled kindly and her eyes sparkled reassuringly.

"So it's Kaisa, is it? You're very welcome here, child. Very welcome. I want you to make yourself at home." She patted my shoulder.

"Thank you," I murmured. Her cottage was tidy and well kept, not at all like some of the hovels we had slept in en route. There wasn't a speck of dirt in sight. Woven mats lay on the well-scrubbed plank floor and a spinning wheel and loom stood in one corner. Two narrow beds neatly made up with woolen blankets stood on one side of the hearth, where something mouthwatering was simmering in an iron pot. My mother would approve of this place, I thought.

"You must be hungry. Do you like mutton stew?" Jensine asked.

"I've never tasted it," I answered. Suddenly I felt limp and bone weary, more weary than I ever had felt in my life. "I'm tired," I confessed. Jensine led me to one of the cots and I perched on it gratefully while she prepared to serve us.

Henrik sat down beside me. "You can be proud of yourself, girl," he said. "You've walked nearly seven hundred kilometers."

I looked into his face, my eyes filling with tears. The realization of the enormous distance that separated me from home overwhelmed me. How could I ever see it and my mother again?

"You can be happy here, Kaisa, if only you let yourself be," Henrik said gently.

I bit my lip, trying to hold back my sobs, but they forced their way into my throat. I buried my head in my hands and wept. Uncle Henrik put his arm around my shoulder.

"I just want to go home," I sobbed. "I want to be with my mother and sister."

"I know you do. But you must try to be as brave living here as you were getting here."

I sobbed harder. "I'll tell you what, Kaisa," he said cheerfully. "Give yourself some time here. Learn Norwegian. Then, if you still want to go, I'll take you back to Rantsila. You yourself can choose where you want to be."

"Do you promise?" I asked, searching his face through watery eyes.

"I promise, Kaisa. I promise."

"I can't live thinking I'll never see my mother or Sofie again," I told him between sobs. I wanted to be grown-up, to do what was expected of me. And I didn't want to believe, as I sometimes feared in my darkest moments, that secretly my mother had wanted to send me away.

"Hush now, child. Eat. Sleep. We'll talk more about it later."

When I awoke the next morning, Henrik was gone. He left nothing behind except enough money for me to send a letter to my mother. I didn't see him again for several months. But the first time he came back, I reminded him of his promise in nearly flawless Norwegian.

Eight

Learning Norwegian

Not that it came easy.

None of it was easy. Not the backbreaking work in the landlord's barn and fields beside the hulking, good-natured Jensine; not the schoolwork in the classroom where my classmates taunted me because I didn't understand a word they or the teacher said. Even the pastor hectored me as I struggled to learn the scriptures in Norwegian.

But even then I was doggedly stubborn when confronted with difficult tasks, a trait that I fairly may say has served me well through life. And I was proud, which has served me less well.

Lonely and withdrawn, I went through my first arctic winter in a miserable stupor, sullenly aching for home. Not a day passed without tormenting memories of Rantsila—snuggling with my mother and Sofie before the hearth on a winter's evening, running after Mother in the grassy fields at haying time, my mother's face as we said farewell on that dreadful day.

Only with the unfailingly patient Jensine did I speak of my suffering. Her only requirement was that I register my complaints in Norwegian, and she drilled me in them so relentlessly that I became weary of hearing them myself.

In early February, when brief periods of light had begun to pierce the gloom, a letter arrived from my mother. The familiar Finnish words spread across the page triggered a flash of memory of that night long ago when I had heard her say to Henrik: "Not before she can read and write Finnish." My chest tightened with painful comprehension.

"I was so relieved to hear you arrived safely, dearest Kaisa," she had written in a painstaking script. "I hope you are well and happy in your new life. We are all as ever here. I think of you every day and every night, my cherished daughter. I long for the day when I will embrace you again."

Full of hope for a speedy reunion, I had written her of Henrik's promise to bring me home.

As the returning sun awoke the landscape, I too awakened to the beauty around me. From Jensine's cottage, which stood on a hillside a short distance from the seashore, we had a sweeping view across Balsfjord and the peaks that ringed it. All around us were fertile fields sloping to the sea and barns filled with cattle, goats and sheep. We watched fishermen ply the fjord in small boats, hauling in nets choked with fish. I never went to bed hungry, nor did the cows. Among my duties was to gather seaweed from the rock-strewn shore and boil it in a large vat with fish heads and offal. This we mixed with precious hay and fed to the cows. Much content with this fare, they produced rich, salty milk.

Eventually the day came when the sun never set. Night after night, I sat on a grassy hillock near the cottage, spellbound by the sun-burnished landscape. Sometimes sky and water turned shimmering gold, sometimes blood red. On such nights, we hardly slept. Out on the fjord, along the shore and in the grassy fields, meadows, and woodlands, young and old reveled in the life-giving light. Music and merry laughter carried across the water to where I sat moping with my arms wrapped around my knees, alone.

"You're too aloof, Kaisa. Go out and join the young people," Jensine urged. I refused; they would only seize the opportunity to tease me, I was certain. I held back, preferring to spend my free time looking after Henrik's daughter Petra or walking alone by the shore, always thinking of home. From the start, I was determined to learn to answer for myself in perfect Norwegian. No one was going to have the pleasure of shaming me again. That much I knew.

That fall Jensine set me to work baking flatbread and lefse in the farm mistress's kitchen. "You have a talent for it," the mistress declared when she sampled the first thin, crisp rounds of parchment-like flatbread I produced. "Not everyone does, you know." I flushed happily. Once again pride, and, yes, vanity, drove me to greater effort. Soon word of my skill had spread and before long, I was in demand on neighboring farms, where an extra pair of hands was always welcome at baking time. As a result, a few coins clinked comfortably in my apron pocket, and I began to see the possibility of earning money. My self-confidence bolstered by unstinting praise of my baking skills, I began to lose my fear of speaking Norwegian among strangers. I began to mingle with people my age. Even as a child in Rantsila I had been nimble on my feet, and at the first wedding celebration I attended in Balsfjord, I quickly learned to dance. I had a talent for that too, it seemed, and soon I was in demand as a teacher among girls more heavy footed than I. Gradually I came to feel more at ease in my surroundings. Even so, my longing for home hung like a stone wreath around my heart. It blinded me to much of the beauty and kindness around me.

My mother's next letter arrived full of questions. "Are you satisfied there, Kaisa? Is it a hard life, after all? Do you still long for home? Are you keeping well? I miss you so and worry about you every day. I hope to hear from you soon."

"This is a beautiful place but I do long for home," I answered. "It won't be long now until Henrik can bring me back to be with you and Sofie."

One evening in the late summer of 1894 I came in from the barn to find a letter waiting on the table. The instant I saw it, I knew something was wrong. It was too soon for Mother to be answering my last letter. I opened it with trembling fingers.

"My dearest daughter Kaisa," she began. "It is with the heaviest of hearts that I must tell you that your beloved sister Sofie died on the thirtieth of June of a thing they call scarlet fever. It has raged through the countryside here, killing more than twenty-two people in Rantsila alone."

I collapsed into a chair. "Sofie! Sofie!" I murmured, but tears would not come. It was unimaginable. It simply could not be.

"She didn't suffer long and I console myself with the knowledge that now she will be spared the unhappiness of the unforgiving life that awaited her here. But it is a bitter thing to lose both daughters as I have. Much as I long for you, dearest Kaisa, I fear this sickness more. I pray you abandon all thought of returning home for the present."

The following year, after a few weeks of intensive study of scripture, my classmates and I were admitted into the congregation of the Norwegian Lutheran Church at nearby Tennes. The ceremony was held in a little white church on a small hill overlooking the fjord. The whole countryside took confirmation seriously in those days, and on that sunny Sunday they turned out from far and near, rich and poor. Jensine and I joined a parade of people promenading in their finest clothes along the road toward the church. The more fortunate drove past us in wagons, the still more fortunate trotted importantly by in fancy carriages.

Jensine had turned an old blue dress of hers into a new one for me, dressing it up with a white lace collar as a finishing touch. I wore my black hair rolled into a tight bun.

"You should see how lovely you look, Kaisa." Jensine smiled as I drew myself up for inspection before we left the house. "It's a pity that Henrik isn't here to see you. Or your mother," she added somberly. I always took care to hold myself erect, and much to my satisfaction, people already had begun to remark on my handsome carriage. Her praise helped calm my fear.

Matilda and Petra, now nearly six, fell into step with us along the way. When I asked Matilda if she had heard anything from Henrik, she shook her head. A great crowd milled about in the churchyard, anxious to warm itself in the reflected rays of hope that always attend ceremonies of youth. Shyly, I followed Jensine inside, nervous in the company of so many finely-dressed strangers. Happily, the long-dreaded ordeal turned out to be less awful than I had imagined; I was able to answer all of the pastor's questions. I wanted to be like everyone else and I was proud to have learned Norwegian well enough to be confirmed. I was proud too, I'm sorry to say, that people were beginning to mistake me for Norwegian.

As we were leaving the church, Matilda stopped short on the steps and caught at Jensine's arm. "Look," she whispered.

On the edge of the roadway across from the church, an ill-clad, unkempt man stood next to a small crate of red apples. At first, I didn't recognize him. Then I saw that it was Henrik. A flush of embarrassment washed over me at the sorry sight of him.

"Henrik! Whatever are you doing here?" Jensine demanded as we hurried toward him.

"Selling apples," he answered wryly. "Hello, Matilda," he added softly. "And Kaisa! How fine you look!" He smiled at Petra, who hid, wide-eyed, behind her mother's skirts.

"On the Lord's day?" Jensine sputtered as Matilda and I stared at him in speechless amazement.

"This is as good a time and place to sell them as any," he retorted defiantly. "I've just come from Tromsø, where I happened upon a shipment of these fine apples at a good price."

"But the pastor won't like it," Jensine warned.

"The pastor already has made his opinion of me quite clear." He looked meaningfully at Matilda, who dropped her gaze.

"Are you coming to see us?" I interrupted. He well knew why I asked. He had made me a promise.

"As soon as I'm rid of these apples. It won't take long. There are a lot of fine folk here today with far more than the price of an apple or two in their pockets." His voice had a hard edge I didn't remember.

"You promised you would take me home now, Uncle Henrik," I reminded him when the three of us were seated at Jensine's table, sipping the coffee I had learned to enjoy.

"Do you want to go?" He scrutinized me closely.

I paused for just a heartbeat. "Of course. But I don't think Mother wants me to come . . . Well, she wants me with her but she doesn't want me there . . ." To tell the truth, I still had moments when I wasn't at all certain that Mother really cared to have me back.

"What do you want to do, Kaisa?" he persisted.

"Be with my mother again."

"In Finland? With all its misery?"

"I miss it, Henrik. I miss Mother. Do you think things ever will get better there?"

"Never. Not in your lifetime, anyway."

"Do you think . . . Do you think I'll ever see her again?" I could barely get the words out.

He frowned. "Not unless you go there. Or she comes here."

"Do you think she'd come?" It had become my secret wish.

"It's a very long, hard trip, as you yourself well know. And it costs money. It took all her savings—not to mention all the strength she possessed—to get you here. Where she would get either the strength or money for such a trip is beyond me."

I paused to gather my composure before I revealed my plan. "I've been thinking that now that I'm now old enough to take a post, I could save my wages and send for her—if you'll go fetch her."

Impassively, Henrik studied my face, which must have looked so desperately hopeful. "Write and ask her, then, Kaisa," he sighed. "See what she says. Meanwhile take a post. Save your money. See what happens next year."

I found a post as a dairymaid and kitchen help a few farms away. They were a crotchety, childless couple and the pay was next to nothing. I made the best I could of it, dreaming only of the day I would have enough money to send for my mother. For her part, Mother never promised to come, but neither did she say she wouldn't. "We'll see what the future brings," is all she would say. It left me increasingly at a loss to know what she really wanted.

"What if she's too sick to come and isn't telling me?" I fretted to Jensine, who had replaced me with a little orphan boy she was raising. What most worried me was that like Sofie, my mother would die before I could see her again.

Ever more churlish and unpredictable, Uncle Henrik continued to wander in and out of our lives. I missed him. He was my only link to Rantsila and the memory of it was becoming ever more faint. Sometimes I felt as if I had never lived anywhere but Balsfjord, and that worried me.

One hot Friday afternoon in the summer of 1898, Henrik appeared unexpectedly as I was hanging out washing. I was seventeen now, and Henrik raised his eyebrows when he saw me. "What a lovely thing you've become, my little traveling companion," he teased. I blushed. It was true that I had begun to arouse the attentions of more young men than I cared to bother with. But I never forgot what my mother had said: "Let my life be a warning to you." So I kept to myself and avoided their overtures as best I could.

On this day Henrik was nearly beside himself with good cheer. He was on his way to Kitdal to see about obtaining his farm at last. And nothing would do but that I go with him. Little did I know he was doing Anton's bidding; he had asked after me for some time, as it turned out, and Henrik obligingly had promised to bring me for a visit.

"It will be just like old times. Only this time I've arranged to cross the fjord by boat." He brazenly bullied my employers into giving me two days leave on what he billed as "important family business." So the next morning we crossed the fjord under a smiling sky and fell into our familiar pace on the road toward Kitdal. I asked him how he had managed to find a farm.

"Years of careful cultivation," he grinned. "There's a childless widow in the valley. She's far too old to carry on herself or to remarry. She's agreed to let me work for her as payment for her holdings. I'll get it when she dies. There's already a little cottage on it where I can live meanwhile."

"But I didn't think you liked the settled life . . ."

"I'm sixty years old, Kaisa. I'm tired. I can't keep wandering from place to place forever. I mean to have my own place to settle with Matilda."

"Matilda?" I stared at him, openmouthed. "Matilda?"

"I mean to marry her. I haven't told her," he admitted sheepishly. " I want to get the papers and everything in proper order first. That's why I'm going up to see Jonas. He understands these things."

"Does this mean you won't be going back to Rantsila any more?" I asked slowly.

He must have seen the expression on my face because he hurried to assure me. "Don't worry, for heaven's sake. When and if it comes to that, I'll go to Rantsila to fetch her."

When we came into their yard, Nicoline and Jonas were sitting on two wooden chairs in the grass just outside their cottage warming themselves in the sunshine, the picture of contentment. No one else seemed about.

"They've all trooped up to the mountain, and we're grateful for it. It's the only peace we get," Nicoline laughed. Henrik and Jonas went inside to settle at the table, deep in legalities. Nicoline and I stayed outside, chatting idly in Finnish. I shared my worries about my mother and she listened sympathetically. Then the girls came running down to the cottage, followed by Anton and Erik. They all stopped to stare when they saw me sitting there. It was Anton who stepped forward to greet me.

"No, Kaisa, can it really be you?" he said, addressing me in Norwegian.

"Hello, Anton," I smiled hesitantly. He looked just the same, only more handsome and manly than I remembered.

"You're . . . You've become . . . You've grown up!" he sputtered stupidly. Then he broke into that radiant, captivating smile.

"Of course, she's grown up, fool. Did you think she'd always be thirteen?" Erik teased. They all laughed uproariously, but this time I didn't feel as if it were at my expense.

"Get up, Mother, let me have that chair!" Anton pleaded. "Last time she was here you pushed me away from her and took my seat. Now you can just give it back."

They all laughed again and Nicoline obligingly relinquished her place. Anton pulled his chair very close to mine. "Tell me everything that's happened to you since you were here," he commanded in mock seriousness. "Everything!"

"Surely you don't want to know everything," I began, flushing with embarrassed pleasure.

"Your Norwegian's perfect!" he exclaimed. "Mother, did you hear how well she speaks Norwegian? That should please you!"

This time no one laughed, and I sensed he had jabbed some raw wound.

There was just enough breeze to keep the mosquitoes at bay while we all spent a wonderful afternoon in the yard, laughing together under a cloudless sky. I had never seen Henrik so happy, not even in his cups. After supper Anton invited me to take a walk with him. One of his sisters begged to come along.

"For pity's sake, how am I ever to find a wife if my sisters chaperone me everywhere I go?" he joked, playfully pushing her away.

He led me across the little stream that ran by the house and up a steep hillside softened by mossy tussocks and tiny birches. Towering behind us, a massive blue glacier spilled from a fold in a jagged mountain; below us the green valley unfolded under the azure sky, framed by stark peaks. We found a comfortable rock to lean against and studied the breathtaking view. Far below, someone in the farmyard waved up at us and we returned the wave.

"It's beautiful," I said after we had sat in awkward silence for a few minutes.

"I know. I love it here," he answered glumly. "I wish I could stay."

"What do you mean?"

"When I marry, I'll have to find someplace else to live. My older brother Erik will inherit the farm, of course. That's one reason I've not hurried to find a wife. I hate the thought of leaving."

"But it's such a big farm, the biggest around here," I ventured. "It's a pity you can't stay."

He nodded. "My grandfather bought this land in 1846, the moment the law was passed that made it possible to buy land in North Norway. Before that, none of these poor farmers could own the land under their farmhouses. My grandfather was one of the first settlers to break ground here."

"Where did he come from?" I asked idly, wanting to keep the conversation from getting too personal.

"Karesuando."

"Karesuando?" I looked into his face, confused.

"His name was Peder Utsi. He came down to the coast to fish. That's what all the poor young men without means to build a reindeer herd of their own did, even then."

I continued to stare at him, still bewildered.

"He was a Sami. He married a Sea Sami from Horsnes."

"You're a Lapp?" I stammered, wide eyed.

"Sami, Kaisa, Sami. Don't call us Lapps. It's an insult. I'm more than half Sami, though my mother won't hear of it. She's Finnish, you know, though for that matter, she too is half Sami. But as far as she's concerned, we're all Norwegian."

"Oh," I mumbled, stunned.

"She insists our family name should be Pedersen but I think it's only right that it be Utsi. She's very firm on this point, and my brother holds with her. She thinks we harm our prospects by acknowledging our Sami blood and she forbids us to speak of it. And she's probably right," he concluded ruefully.

I had to agree. I had lived in North Norway long enough to understand the order of things: first and foremost came the smug Norwegians, though many of them were as poor as the rest of us. But it was always Norwegians who held the best positions and lived in the finest houses. They were the doctors, teachers, priests, sheriffs, shipowners. They controlled our destinies. They were the upper class and they were at great pains, much of it at our expense, to conduct themselves accordingly.

Then came we sorry Finns. We were much to be pitied for our poverty, much to be admired for our pluck and industry. But we Finnish women were suspect. I had heard on more than one occasion the snickering allusions to our supposedly easy morals. It made me ashamed to admit I was Finnish for fear of what people would think of me now that I had grown into womanhood. I was fully aware of how men already were staring after me.

Moreover, we Finns were not to be trusted in our allegiances. Outside the settlements where Finns banded together for protection there was a constant undercurrent of grumbling by Norwegians about the growing numbers of Finns settling in North Norway. They accused us of plotting to turn it into a Finnish province for Russia's benefit. "Norway for the Norwegians," they said, though in plain fact, of course, Norway was ruled by the Swedish king.

Last in the order of things were the so-called Lapps, the Sami. Not that anyone paid them any serious mind. They long since had been Christianized under threat of death, their shamans' drums destroyed. Still, the secretive Sami came and went in answer to their own ancient rhythms, traipsing after their herds in the mountains in winter, chasing them out to the coast to escape the tundra's tormenting mosquitoes in summer.

People said they were rude and cunning, totally unpredictable, blowing hot one moment and cold the next, not caring what they said or who they said it to. But I always remembered the Sami I had met in the mountains. They had been openhearted, merry and kind. Earlier, when I had first begun to understand the cruel remarks many Norwegians made about the Sami, I had demurred, daring in my ignorance to defend them. But I soon learned it was a profitless undertaking. Most Norwegians regarded the Sami as more to be pitied than scorned. It was generally understood that whatever their individual merits, Sami could never be truly civilized beings. But sometimes when I saw them going blithely about their age-old business, I couldn't help but think that they were the ones playing us for fools.

Still, I had to hold with Nicoline: the less said about these things the better.

Anton sat for some time without speaking. Occasional bursts of laughter rose from the farm below. Finally he turned to me.

"But tell me about you, Kaisa. What was Finland like?"

"It's becoming harder to remember it," I admitted. But I told him my story. He listened intently, staring into my face the whole time. When I finished it must have been very late because the commotion in the yard had ceased. "We'd best go back now," I told him firmly.

"I'd like to come visit you sometime."

"That would be nice." I hoped my face didn't betray too much joy.

He came almost right away. After supper that first evening in Balsfjord, we went down to the shore and spent the entire sunlit night sitting in opposite ends of the little boat he had borrowed to row across the fjord.

"Tell me about Lofoten," I asked shyly. "Henrik says fishing is a terrible life."

"Oh, no, Kaisa. It's a wonderful thing to be out on the rolling sea under sail! There's nothing so thrilling as pulling in a thrashing net full of huge, glistening cod. They're so thick under your boat you can practically walk across their backs to shore. It's not easy work, mind you, getting up long before dawn to row far out into a roiling sea to set and haul in heavy nets and lines, often with not a bite to eat until you return in the afternoon. But you should see all those fish! And you should see all those boats! And, Kaisa, you should see how beautiful Lofoten is. I've never seen such wild, spectacular mountains as those that ring that fishing ground. And when all those brown sails whip in the wind, the boats look like giant, seagoing butterflies floating on the water. The best mornings are when the sea is perfectly still and flat and the snow on the mountains lies right down to the waterline. We're all lined up by five o'clock, hundreds of boats. And when the signal sounds to start rowing to the fishing grounds, the splash of thousands of oars on the water at once is like a clap of thunder. It's a mad race!" When he smiled at the memory, his whole face lit up irresistibly.

Listening to him rhapsodizing about fishing, I decided there was much of the blind optimist in him. But I liked him for that. There was plenty to be gloomy about, but Anton always made me laugh.

"Lofoten seems such a long way from here."

"It is," he nodded. "We must hope for strong winds at our backs to get us down there. Otherwise, we have to row, and then we're exhausted before we arrive. But when storms blow up, we have to row for our lives. Of course, if we have money, we can hook up to one of the motorized ships heading south. I've been on trips where as many as thirty boats were tied to a single ship, in two long rows. That's the way to travel."

His face clouded over. "But it can be dangerous. I was on one trip when a sudden storm caught us and the boats became hopelessly entangled in each other's lines. It was a terrible blow and all we could do was hang on and pray. The boats crashed against one another and some were damaged beyond repair. None of them sank that time, but we had to throw lines to the men in two boats so they could leap to safety in the howling wind. I hope never to relive such a thing.

"Not everyone is so lucky," he added. "The woman Erik is engaged to marry, Hansine, lost her husband just that way. He left her with two children. They'll be living on the farm, so it will get even more crowded soon."

I could see he was about to drift off into musing about his troubles at home, so I prodded him for more information about Lofoten. "Where do you sleep?" I asked.

"In the boat," he answered.

"In winter?"

"I prefer it to the bunk houses. They're not much warmer anyway and there's always someone in them who's sick. We're in a secure harbor in Henningsvaer or Kabelvag, so we ride out storms nicely. We have a little cabin aft and a tiny stove for heat and we line our bunks with sheepskins and blankets. We can't stand up in there, of course, but it's quite cozy once you get used to it. When we go to Finnmark for the summer fishery, it's light all night."

"But you didn't go there this summer."

"Lucky for me. Otherwise I might not have known what a beautiful woman you've become." He looked at me intently, his face an open book.

I knew then that I was lost. But I hoped to keep it from him.

Just before Christmas of my nineteenth year, a long letter arrived from my mother. "I have something to tell you, dearest Kaisa. Your father has been here to see me." I scanned the page in disbelief.

"He came striding into the yard as he always did, but this time finely dressed in a suit of good clothes. 'Hello, Marie,' he said when I opened the door. I gasped in shock when I saw him on the stoop. I recognized him instantly. He was still handsome, but his temples have turned gray and his face looked worn. He asked to come in, and I let him. He stood just inside the door, fidgeting with his hat. He told me he had just come back from America and learned that he has a daughter. 'Why on earth didn't you tell me?' he wanted to know.

"'Why did you marry?' I countered. My heart was pounding wildly.

"His eyes dropped to the floor. In that moment he looked just as irresolute as I had remembered him twenty years ago. 'It was never what we had between us,' he finally said in a low, wavering voice. I stared at him, unable to speak. He stared back at me. 'I've never been able to forget you, Marie,' he said quietly.

"A rage I thought long buried rose to constrict my chest. But still I said nothing.

"'Mother says you've sent her away to Ruija. Why?' he demanded.

"'For the same reason you went to America. So she could have a better life. She's in Storsteinness in Balsfjord, among good people. She has enough to eat and hope of a life without endless sorrow or an early death. And no one to shame her because she has no father.' I looked straight into his eyes as I said it.

"He flinched and flushed. 'I've worked hard, very hard, Marie. I've lived a miserable existence in a desolate lumber camp at the end of the world. I've saved my money and invested it in property and a little store. I want to give you some money now. And I came to tell you I want Kaisa to inherit all I own. I have no other children.'

"'*You've* lived a miserable existence!' I could barely choke the words out.

"As I stood there looking at him, a fury such as I've never known engulfed me. To think what I had knowingly risked for him! For the thousandth time, I saw myself before that hateful congregation, standing despised for all the world to mock. I could barely trust myself to speak.

"'Get out,' I told him, but he just looked at me as if he didn't understand. 'Get out!' I repeated. I took a step closer to look him full in the face. 'We don't want your money! It's too late, Nikolai! It's too late!'

"I didn't cry, and I never gave him so much as the slightest inkling of what I've suffered on his account. He left without another word passing between us. I wanted you to know exactly how it was between him and me, Kaisa.

"We may be poor, but always remember that there is one thing far more valuable than either love or money, and that's self-respect."

NINE

COURTING

The following spring, shortly after Henrik settled on his farm, Matilda suddenly collapsed and died. I volunteered to take him the news, though I admit I was tempted to simply let him find out for himself the next time he troubled himself to visit her. But the memory of what we had been through together immediately made me ashamed of such a cruel thought.

I found him in the yard, sharpening a scythe on a grinding wheel. He put it down when he saw me and pushed his hat back on his head, smiling in surprise.

"I don't know how to tell you this, Uncle Henrik," I began, untying my scarf and wiping my brow with it. "Matilda died yesterday."

He looked at me as if he hadn't heard. Then he sat down directly on the wet grass. His hat fell off, and bareheaded he suddenly looked old and vulnerable. I knelt beside him, tears welling in my eyes despite myself.

"What are you saying?" he asked dumbly.

"Matilda died, Henrik."

"But I was going to speak to her about marrying soon, after everything here was in order," he protested. "I couldn't ask her to come live in the cottage like it is now." He stared at me as a child would, perplexed.

"She just collapsed and died. She's to be buried tomorrow, if you care to come pay your last respects. I'm going up to visit Anton for a little while. You can walk with me to Storsteinnes when I come back. If you care to." With that, I stalked up the valley, seething. It was unkind to leave him there alone, I knew that. But he was such a fool!

Anton was preparing to leave for the Finnmark summer fishery. Nicoline was assembling thick woolen socks, underwear, sweaters and blankets for the wooden chest he would take with him. The girls were preparing stacks of dried fish and meat, flatbread, goat cheese and butter for both boys, though Erik preferred to remain on land. He was about to depart for Kiruna, just across the border in Sweden, to help build the new railroad line to Narvik on the Norwegian coast.

I shared my sad news about Matilda and sat awhile watching their busy preparations. Anton was glowing with excitement at the prospect of being on the sea again. Fishing seemed to be all he lived for, and this did nothing to improve my mood. I didn't stay long.

My disenchantment grew as summer wilted into fall. I had hardly any more money saved now than when I started. Mother wrote to say that my grandmother Brita Kaisa had died. Even though I had no memory of her, I felt a sense of loss. And it increased my worry over my mother's health.

So when I saw an ad in a newspaper for a live-in maid in Tromsø, it set me to thinking. Several girls I knew had answered such ads and come home bearing tales of a glamorous life in the city. I for one was determined not to waste my life in endless waiting for some fool of a man who could not make up his mind about what he wanted. I had seen enough of where that led, thanks to Henrik and my own father. In Tromsø at least the pay would be good. It took me a while to get my courage up, even so. I had never been to so large a city.

Nonetheless, one morning in 1901 not long after Anton left for Finnmark, I put on my confirmation dress, rolled a few belongings into a cloth bag, said my goodbyes, donned a worn coat, and walked to the boat pier at Tennes, and with the ticket sent by my new employer, boarded the boat to Tromsø. "Tell Henrik to come visit me," I told Jensine.

I stood on the deck of the little steamer craning my head in delight as the town came into view. It lay on a long, low island fringed on top by a green swath of trees. Below the forest, a band of grassy fields sloped down to a thick settlement of wooden houses. Rows of warehouses fronted by long piers were crowded along the shore. Large steamships lay at anchor out in the bay; smaller sailing vessels moored closer to shore. The docks bustled with chaotic activity and the streets were filled with people—men in black top hats carrying canes, fine ladies in wide brimmed hats and long, broad-shouldered coats tucked in tightly at the waist. They looked so elegant!

I swallowed my trepidation. I was going to like this place.

And I did. My employers, a sober-sided doctor and his flighty wife, were patient with my ignorance of city ways. When first I knocked on the front door of their grand house, I had to fight down a wave of panic. Surely this could not be the place! It was two stories tall, painted a pale yellow and had fancy white trim work and many windows. At that time, I was too ignorant to know that hired help never came in through the front door. But I quickly learned what was expected of me, and when they discovered how well I could bake flatbread, I could do no wrong. My favorite duty was airing the couple's two young children, since it allowed me to promenade through the streets dressed in my maid's uniform with a child hanging on each hand, drinking in the sights, admiring the goods in the windows of fine shops. I made careful note of the clothing, carriage and mannerisms of the smartly dressed people who strolled out of the city's best hotels. The streets were filled with foreigners and endlessly interesting people going about their affairs. Even Sami, looking outlandish and out of place, wandered the streets. When they passed, people often snickered, wrinkled their noses or made rude remarks.

There were many other servant girls about and I soon made friends among them. On long summer evenings we gathered for band concerts in the park or went down to the Lovers' Pier to dance to accordion music. I always danced until my feet were sore; I was never allowed a moment's rest. I think the other girls were envious of me. I was more quiet and shy than the rest, but I learned to enjoy myself. It was a wonderful, magical time.

I never let on to any of them that I was a Finn.

In late September Anton appeared at the back door in his best suit, a visored cloth cap tucked respectfully under his arm. He was clearly agitated.

"Why didn't you tell me you were leaving?" he asked reproachfully.

"I didn't think you'd mind," I answered forthrightly. "How did it go in Finnmark?"

"It was a poor season. I barely recaptured the expense of the trip. It's good to see you, Kaisa."

"It's good to see you, too, Anton. I've wondered how you were keeping." That was true, of course.

"At first I couldn't believe you were gone. I was on my way to see you when Henrik told me you had left."

"How is he?" I couldn't help smiling at him; he looked so upset.

Anton shrugged. "As always. Older."

Maybe he saw something in my face. He paused for an uncomfortable moment before he said, "Is something the matter, Kaisa? You don't sound like yourself."

I didn't know what to say. I didn't tell him that my father had appeared at my mother's door after all these years and that she'd thrown him out of the house. But I brooded about it, wondering if she'd done the right thing.

"Oh, it's just that Henrik's been such a fool! He should have married Matilda long ago if he wanted to marry her. Every time I think about it, I get cross."

Anton shifted uncomfortably from foot to foot. "Do you like it here?"

"Very much. They treat me well and city life is lively. And I'm able to save money now to bring my mother here."

"I never thought of you as a city girl." His dismay was plain to see. Anton was always an open book; I liked that about him. You never had to guess what he might be feeling. And he never put on self-important airs, like some of the cocky Norwegian boys I met at the dances, the ones who asked to walk me home in hopes of stealing a kiss. I never gave them the slightest satisfaction, but they never ceased to pester me.

"I came to see if . . . if you would still like me to come calling on you. It's a long way," he added in an injured tone.

"It's always good to see you, Anton."

It was true. The instant I saw him at the door, I realized how deeply I missed him. I hadn't wanted to miss him; I was quite determined not to. But there it was. I hadn't been one to sit in front of a mirror staring at myself on Christmas Eve, hoping to see the reflection of the man I would marry, as did some of the girls I knew. Still, I knew well enough when a thing was fated.

He brightened and, right there in broad daylight on the back steps, gave me a long kiss on the lips. He flashed his irresistible smile, and then he was gone.

And that was how matters stood between us. He visited me as often as he could and stopped in on his way to and from the fisheries. He talked openly of a future with me now, but his brow furrowed whenever anyone brought up the subject of marriage. "If the fishing is good this year, I may be able to take a wife," he'd say, only half in jest.

It was the truth. Each time he set out to sea, he went into debt for supplies with Jensen, the local merchant at the bottom of the valley who acted as banker to the community. Often as not, Anton came home owing a debt he could not pay. Then he could only hope that Jensen would extend his credit until the next fishing season, when a bounteous harvest might wipe out his debts and allow him to put something by for the future. They all lived that way, from fishery to fishery, on the raw edge of survival.

In July of 1902 I returned to Kitdal for a visit for the first time since moving to Tromsø. It was a spectacular day, and I expected to find Henrik happily at work outside. But I found him inside, seated on his cot, his old knapsack at his feet. He was loading things into it—thimbles, spoons, carvings. The look in his eyes was awful to see.

"What are you doing?" I demanded.

"I have to leave, Kaisa." He wouldn't look at me.

"Leave? Whatever do you mean?"

"It's true." His chin quivered.

"Why, Henrik? What's happened?"

"They say I can't buy this farm. Or any other farm, either."

"What on earth are you talking about? Who says so?"

"The government. They've passed a law that forbids Finns from buying land in Norway."

I sank down beside him on the cot. "I don't believe it. Someone's lying to you."

"Oh, it's not just the Finns. They don't put it like that. It's anyone who doesn't read, write or speak Norwegian. But it's meant for the Finns."

I recalled the disgruntled murmuring I'd overheard from idle knots of men on the streets of Tromsø. "Norway for the Norwegians," they'd hiss whenever someone they took for a Finn passed, spitting manfully after him. Now their venomous spittle had spawned this.

"Henrik," I began earnestly, taking hold of his arm, "listen to me. I'll teach you to read and write Norwegian."

He turned to face me, eyes brimming with despair. "Kaisa, I'm sixty-four years old. I can't learn to read and write Norwegian. I can't even read or write Finnish!"

"But what will you do?"

"I'll go on the road again. What else can I do?" he asked plaintively.

I had no answer for him.

So Henrik resumed his rounds. Now he went from farm to farm buying up cow, sheep and goat hides that he tanned and sold. He bore his heavy bundles strapped to his back, and it wasn't long before he began to list to one side when he walked. My heart ached for him, but he turned away all suggestions of sympathy.

About the same time, a letter came from my mother. "I hear your father has brought his wife from America and they've bought a farm near Kemi," she wrote without elaboration.

And then, shortly after my twenty-second birthday, a letter came from Jensine. "This letter came for you here," she wrote. "Whoever sent it must not know that you've long since moved." Her note was folded around an envelope addressed in an unfamiliar script. I opened it with great curiosity.

"Dear Kaisa, I have long debated with myself whether you would welcome this letter," it began in Finnish. "Your mother has made it plain where she stands. But I cannot know whether she speaks for you as well, and I will have no rest until I know the answer. You're a grown woman in your own right now, and I fervently hope you will choose to form your own opinion of me. You surely must know that until very recently, I did not know that I had a daughter. I deeply regret that your existence was kept from me. I hope that you are well and thriving in your life in Norway. With the hope that you will use it, I am sending my new address here in Kemi, where I am now settled. I'm enclosing a photograph of myself. I would like nothing more than to receive one of you. With all best wishes, Your father, Nikolai Okkonen."

I stared in amazement at the small portrait. So there it was, the rest of me.

He was handsome, to be sure. He had a mustache and wore his thick, straight hair slicked back over a high forehead. I instantly saw myself in his high cheekbones, finely shaped nose and the serious set of his dark eyes.

"And now what, Kaisa?" I asked myself. Should I ignore his plea for contact with his only child? Was that what he deserved? It seemed so, from what I understood. My mother's anguished face from that day so long ago when we parted still haunted me; even now I could never think of her without a dull ache in my heart and tears welling in my eyes. How could I answer a man who had caused her such unspeakable grief?

I put his letter away unanswered, but I did tell Mother that he had written to me. Her reply surprised me. "It's up to you, Kaisa. Write to him if you wish. He is your father, after all. Just remember your self-respect."

So I wrote my father a short formal letter, glowingly describing my life in Tromsø and making it plain I had no call on his services. And I spent some of my precious savings to have three small portraits made of myself. That Christmas I sent one to my father, one to my mother, and gave one to Anton. He was still suffering the effects of the disastrous winter season of 1900, the worst in fifty years, and his debts were mounting, since the ensuing years had not been much better.

January of 1903 arrived unusually stormy, so some of Lyngen's Lofoten-bound boats were forced to wait out the bad weather in Tromsø. The harbor was full of vessels crowded together at every available pier and the dark, gloom-ridden streets were full of idle, nervous fishermen. Every day in port they were using up precious food and supplies.

Worrisome as it was, for Anton and me the bad weather was a gift. The mistress granted permission for him to take his meals with me in the kitchen to save on his own supplies. His fishing companions whiled away their hours over card games at the taverns, but we spent our evenings walking hand in hand in nearly empty, rain-washed streets, talking wistfully of our future.

On the twenty-first of January the fleet was still in port, but no one seemed to care, for this was the day the sun returned. Near midday we saw just a tiny sliver of heartening light when the sun peeked ever so briefly over the horizon. Even so, it was enough to wake the city from its winter stupor. Rich and poor, young and old took to the streets in celebration. Anton and I stood quietly in the middle of a hilly street, away from the hubbub, eyes fixed on the spot where the sun would make its appearance.

"The Sami say you can have three wishes when the sun returns," he told me, smiling teasingly. "What are yours?"

"To see my mother again," I answered unhesitatingly.

"What else?"

I pressed my lips together. "You tell me one of yours," I hedged.

"I wish you would marry me, Kaisa," he said solemnly. He reached deep into his pocket and opened his palm carefully to reveal a thin gold band. I looked at him openmouthed, not breathing as he slid the engagement ring over my finger.

"But wherever did you get the money?" I stammered.

"Never mind that. You must know that I love you, Kaisa. I want us to be married in the fall as soon as I return from Finnmark."

"But can you afford to marry now?" I was still astounded, unable to believe that what I had so long wished for was coming true.

"I'm thirty years old, Kaisa. I don't want to wait any longer. I can't bear to wait any longer." He swept me into his arms then, kissing me hungrily, right there on the street in broad daylight, such as it was. But it didn't matter. People were laughing and shouting and acting crazy all over town.

My joy at receiving his proposal and the ring was tempered by a sharp foreboding that I might never see him again. Now that he had declared his love and honorable intentions, I feared even more than I had before we became engaged that I would lose my husband-to-be to the sea. So when he asked me to come with him down to his boat that evening, I barely hesitated. The next morning he left for Lofoten.

While he was gone, I tried to banish my worry with work, but I was very apprehensive. When he returned after Easter, I was overjoyed to see that he was safe. But he looked grim. "We did poorly, Kaisa. Very poorly."

My chest tightened.

"I'm going home to see if I can get Jensen to extend me through the summer season in Finnmark. It's the only hope I have of paying my debts."

"How did he come to loan you the money to begin with?" I was baffled by this seemingly hopeless financial arrangement.

"On the strength of my father's reputation. But Father has his own debts as well as mine to worry about, and now Jensen is threatening to take part of Father's farm for payment." The worry in his face was undisguised. Even so, he kissed me and held me close; then, before the day was out, he was gone again. He didn't say a word about our marriage. And I didn't know how to tell him.

It wasn't long until the mistress realized I had a child on the way. After the initial shock, she took it quite well. We were engaged to marry, after all, and such situations were common enough in those days. "Of course you'll stay here. We'll just get someone to help you when it gets to be too much for you," she told me sympathetically. "When will Anton be back from Finnmark?"

"September sometime," I murmured, my mortification tempered by a panic I tried to disguise. What if he didn't come back? What if something happened to him? In my mind's eye, I saw my mother standing humiliated before the congregation in Rantsila and the people spitting on her afterwards, and I felt sick.

I could have written to tell him, of course. And I almost did, numerous times. But each time panic threatened to overwhelm me, something stronger stopped me: pride. Even with my mother's wretched example before me, I wanted to know Anton would come back on his own—now that I'd let him make love to me.

I tossed through the endless, sun-filled nights on my cot under the stairs, fighting nausea and despair. The larger my belly became, the more my anxiety grew. What if he refused to marry me? What if he didn't believe it was his child?

In the midst of my deepest anxiety, a letter came from my father. "I treasure your picture more than you can know," he wrote. He described his difficulties in making his farm productive and asked me to write soon. But I was too overwhelmed by my situation to concentrate on composing an answer.

That July, the entire town went into a celebratory mood over the visit of King Oscar II of Sweden and Norway. Festive banners greeted the king, and I was swept up in the excitement. I ventured outdoors, taking care to hide behind a crowd of strangers lest anyone I knew see me in my condition.

August vanished into September but Anton did not come. Frantic, I wrote a letter addressed to him in Kitdal, certain he would have returned there by now. Then I tore it up. He finally appeared on the doorstep the second week of September, dressed in his best suit. When I opened the door, the smile fell from his lips and the color drained from his face.

"Dear God, Kaisa! Why didn't you let me know?" I smiled weakly, too relieved to speak.

"I would have been here sooner but there was trouble on the fishing grounds this summer. A blockade, arrests. Russian agitators and fools, mostly. But never mind. I'm here now," he continued, wrapping me in his arms.

We were married the next day. Anton never blinked an eye. The possibility never occurred to him that this could be anything but his own child.

I loved him for that. I had grown to love him long before, but never so much as at that moment when I understood how deep his trust in me was.

Our baby, sickly and weak, was born three weeks later in my little room under the stairs with the doctor of the house attending. It was a difficult birth and our son died in that little room twenty-two days later. With the dark cloud of this loss weighing heavily upon us, Anton and I went home to Kitdal to begin our married life in his parents' house. I did my best to summon cheerfulness, to dismiss the gnawing fear that this tragic beginning to our life together was an omen of worse to come.

Another cubicle, this one with a curtain drawn over it for privacy, had been added to the main cottage for Anton and me, but it was terribly crowded in that house. In addition to Nicoline and Jonas and their daughters, Erik and his new wife, the widow Hansine, also were living there with her two children.

I liked Hansine. She too had known loss, and so we fell into an easy companionship. She had lively brown eyes and kinky brown hair that she forever was fighting into a tight bun. She was very thin but for some unaccountable reason wouldn't touch pork. Her widowed father Aaron, who lived down in Hatteng, said pork was unclean and wouldn't permit it in the house, she explained, and that was that. Hansine had been born in Hatteng but her parents met in Tornio, where Aaron had washed up after a shipwreck on the Gulf of Bothnia en route from his native Germany.

"How could someone from as fine a family as I end up in this God-forsaken place?" Aaron was known to complain when he was in his cups. He too had kinky hair but Hansine fortunately did not inherit his prominent nose, which over the years he rubbed bright red in absent-minded agitation over the twists of fate that had led him north.

Despite the crowding, for the first time since I left Rantsila I had a real family to call my own and someone to share my worry about Anton when he was at sea. Nicoline, Hansine and I spent cozy evenings at our handiwork while Anton, Erik, and Jonas sat around the table discussing their debts. Jensen had appropriated part of the farm, and Jonas fretted unceasingly about how to find the money to buy it back. When they wearied of that topic, his sons talked politics.

"It's hopeless," Erik would admonish Anton. "You can't bring back the past. You have to live in the time you live in."

"I just want the respect we deserve. No more, no less. And it's not right what they're doing to the Finns, any more than it's right when they do it to the Sami."

"But don't you see that you'll never have any respect if you insist on parading around as a Sami? Finn, Sami, what does it matter, anyway? We're Norwegians now, man! If you want to get ahead in this world you have to act like one!"

"You may be Norwegian. I haven't forgotten who I am."

"What's so terrible about being Norwegian, for God's sake?"

"We're Sami, that's what!"

It always ended there, with Anton smugly stubborn, Erik offended, and both of them angry. I could never tell what Jonas thought. He just sat there, sucking on his pipe, occasionally glancing uneasily toward Nicoline, who unfailingly championed Erik.

As the second son, Anton had no legal right to any of the farm's land, and these arguments only spurred his determination to find us a home of our own.

The following September, a few days after Anton returned from Finnmark, our second child, a sturdy girl, was born. I lay in the main room of the cottage, surrounded by a roomful of prying eyes and anxious faces. I don't know which was worse, the pain or lack of privacy. They took the wailing child from me and set her in a tub of warm water into which Nicoline had thrown three glowing coals from the stove. I was too weak to ask why. But I had observed that Nicoline, for all her modern pretensions, quietly held fast to the old beliefs. On New Year's Day she set out a pail of water and ladle so the trolls could drink and not be provoked to mischief. And I had seen her spit three times after someone about whom she had misgivings left the house. She never permitted anyone to whistle, since that called evil spirits. I was just grateful that all that was required to protect my daughter was three hot coals in her bathwater.

This baby came into the world fighting, her face contorted in protest, wailing loudly. "Listen to those lungs, will you?" Anton laughed. We named her Berit Sofie Antonsdatter Utsi, the scowling Nicoline notwithstanding. Anton, who had firmly settled on our family name when we married, doted on his daughter, and she on him. There was a special bond between them, some innate understanding.

Nicoline cooled toward me after the christening. It wasn't an obvious thing, but I noticed a distance in her voice when she addressed me. I had been the center of her attentions when she welcomed me into the family's daily routine, but now she turned increasingly to Hansine in small but ever more telling ways. I knew I wasn't imagining it the day she asked Hansine to be in charge of the flatbread baking. She knew good and well no one did that better than I. It was as if she held me responsible for Anton's refusal to be ashamed of who he was. Perhaps she blamed me for indulging him. But if it were up to me, I would have sided with her. There was no shame in being Sami, I had long since concluded. But neither was there any great profit in advertising it to people who believed there was.

Henrik arrived in Kitdal not long after Berit was born. Of course he knew we had lost our first child, so maybe he was only trying to reassure me. Or maybe he knew something. In any case, he bent down to study Berit in her basket where she lay kicking her strong, stubby legs and waving her arms insistently. Then he straightened up to look at me, his face serious.

"You could leave this child stark naked on a bare rock and she'd survive," he proclaimed solemnly. He wasn't far off the mark.

TEN

SIGNALDAL

The fishery, and our fortunes, finally improved and Anton at last cleared his debts. One rainy afternoon in May of 1905 he came home, his eyes dancing with excitement.

"I've found it, Kaisa! A place we can call our own!"

"Where?" It had been an endless topic of frustrated conversation between us, especially since Berit's birth.

"Signaldal." He smiled, well pleased with himself. "I can rent a little plot of land with the understanding that I can buy the entire thing one day."

"Signaldal?" My face must have betrayed my disappointment. I had never imagined we would move from Kitdal, where I had come to feel so at home. And I remembered the strange feeling that had washed over me the first time I stood at the entrance to that valley. But Anton was enthralled.

"Oh, just wait until you see it, Kaisa. It's not too far away. It's only a short distance up the valley. It lies close to the river on a grassy little spot, just at the base of Otertind."

So one bright June morning not long afterward, Jonas hitched up the horse and wagon and we loaded our few possessions into it. Chief among them was the spinning wheel Anton had made me and a belated wedding gift from Anton's parents, a small, black cast-iron stove. I was to have a kitchen of my own at last. That thought brightened my outlook as we said our goodbyes and made our way down valley to the shore of the fjord. Shortly after we began our climb into Signaldal, I saw my new home: a deep, narrow valley nestled between high mountains. We paused on the crest of a little hill near the house where Olsen, our landlord, lived. Anton proudly pointed down to a tiny cottage nestled in a sea of grass a stone's throw from the river. It was old and dilapidated and seemed to lean to one side. A small, broken-down barn stood nearby. Behind the cottage loomed the massive presence of Otertind. Across the river, the stark peaks that separated us from Kitdal rose into the sky. The whole effect was to wall us off in a spectacular slit of earth. I could not imagine anything more unlike the open, flat plains of Finland.

"What do you think?" Anton asked anxiously.

"The valley seems very narrow here," I answered.

His face fell. "I think you'll come to like it," he said uncertainly. "We'll fix the barn and get a cow . . ."

"The first thing we'll have is a sauna," I interrupted firmly.

His face lit up in a broad smile. "Finns! If it's a sauna you must have, a sauna it shall be."

Olsen came sauntering out of the house just then, running his hands speculatively through a very long, bushy beard. He greeted Jonas and Anton, who put his arms around me proudly. "This is my wife Kaisa," he said.

Olsen gave me a long, appraising, almost insolent look. "A fine looking wife you've got yourself," he said slowly, never taking his eyes off me. "Mine ran off with a filthy Lapp."

Jonas tapped the horse's rump with his whip and we rolled away. "Can't say I blame her," he muttered. Anton and I chuckled, and I slipped my hand into his.

"I'm sure I'll grow to like it here," I told him.

And I did, once I had brought the place up to my standards. Before I would allow anything to be brought into the house, I sent the men off to the riverbank for sand and water—there was no well. They unloaded and placed our things about in the grass while I scrubbed the ceiling and walls and the rickety table and the wooden platform that stood in a corner that would serve as our bed. Then, while the men rustled about in the barn, I got down on my hands and knees and scrubbed the worn floor with sand until it gleamed nearly white. Through the long winter nights in Kitdal I had woven old rags into fine floor mats and I was not about to lay any mat of mine on any floor without scrubbing it clean. Finally, while the floor was drying, I swept the dirt away from the front stoop.

"Whatever are you doing now?" Anton asked good-humoredly.

"The outside of the door should be just as clean as the inside," I told him firmly, quoting my mother.

He rolled his eyes to heaven and shook his head. "Finns!" he laughed. But when he and Jonas had installed the stove and our other belongings were safely inside, he looked about the humble but sparkling cottage with gleaming eyes. I could see how happy he was. And that made me happy.

With his father's *ard*—a simple wooden contraption that in those days served as a plough—Anton immediately set about turning up a small potato patch. When it was planted, he set to work on the sauna. He cleverly fashioned a hearth and nailed together an enclosure around it from lumber felled in his father's forest. Some of that wood became our firewood and some was used to repair the barn. One evening he came home from Kitdal leading two woolly sheep and a black and white cow with large, sweet eyes. She was mooing mournfully.

"Here's the rest of my inheritance," he called out gaily as he dragged the wary beasts into the yard. "What shall we call the cow?"

"Palma," I said after a moment's study. "She looks like her name should be Palma. And I think she desperately wants milking," I added, laughing. On my hip, Berit squirmed, straining to touch the cow.

"Palma it is." He led the animals into their new home, then came to stand beside me in the warm sunlight. He slipped his arm around my waist. The valley was at its finest that day, bright green and lush, and the river gurgled softly near our doorstep on its way to the sea. High above our heads Otertind, capped in white, stood guard, reaching into the heavens.

"Isn't it wonderful, Kaisa? We have our own cow for milk and butter, a pair of sheep for wool, a patch for potatoes and vegetables and our own roof over our heads and a stove as well as the wood to warm us. I can catch enough salmon in this river before I leave for Lofoten to see you through the winter. And I have enough money left to buy the salt and flour you need. I've arranged to get some mutton from Father when he slaughters this fall, and our supply of salt cod should be more than enough to last until I get home with more."

His proud recitation should have made me glad—and it did, to be sure. I had seen enough of want to know how fortunate we were. But it also reminded me that he soon would leave again. This time, I would be alone among strangers with a child to care for through the long darkness.

And with one more on the way. I was nearly six months pregnant when he left that January. "I'll be back before the child is born," he promised.

"Be very careful, Anton, please," I whispered as I held him close. Each time he left for the fishery, I had to fight the fear that this time he might be among those who did not come back. But I would not indulge such thoughts. It was impossible to imagine how I could manage without him.

Since the narrow road up the valley passed right by our cottage door, we came to be on familiar terms with almost everyone in the upper valley, especially Edgar and Jenny, who lived just above us at the next farm. When Anton left for Lofoten, they made it their business to keep a close eye on me and often stopped in to check on my welfare. As the wet, gray mist of winter settled over us, I was grateful for company. The first storms laid a coat of ice on the ground, and in my condition, I was afraid to venture farther than the river for fear of slipping and falling. There was no light outside, and the wind howled mercilessly through the drafty cottage. The sleet fell in sheets and Otertind was obscured, but even in the worst impenetrable fog I felt its presence hovering over me.

Berit was my salvation. Her antics made me laugh until my sides ached. She was an excitable little busybody from morning until night; she was never still. She had a vivid imagination and, luckily for me, could amuse herself for endless hours in her fantasy world. As she got older, she followed me everywhere and aped everything I did. Even then, she was stubborn. I have myself to thank for that, I suppose. From the time she was an infant I could see how willful she would become.

This solitary existence was a far cry from the life I had lived in Tromsø, or even Kitdal, for that matter. Since it was out of the question for me to go there to visit the family in my condition, I expected them to come visit me. And Jonas did come two or three times that first winter, but alone, bearing mutton, a sack of wool, news of the family—and once, a letter from my father. I glanced at the envelope, suddenly heartened and immensely grateful.

"Is everything going all right, then?" he asked gruffly on his first visit.

"Very well, thank you," I replied, standing as erect as my condition would allow.

"You'll send word if you have any need of us . . ." he said, his voice trailing off. He seemed ill at ease.

I nodded. "Do you know where Henrik is this winter? I haven't seen him in months."

He shook his head. "But I'll tell him where you are when he turns up," he promised.

Uncle Henrik showed up on my doorstep a few weeks later, leaning heavily on his staff, his gait slowed, his hair stark white. I threw my arms around his neck and cried when I saw him, embarrassing us both.

"Please stay," I begged him. "There's plenty of room and plenty of food but not nearly enough company."

He stayed. He seemed relieved, and I certainly was. When he wasn't fetching wood or water or amusing Berit with some new toy he had carved, we spent pleasant hours by the stove, happily reminiscing about our journey so long ago. It seemed like an unbelievable dream to me now. But with him in the house, my thoughts turned ever more sharply to my mother.

"So are you happy here now, Kaisa?" he finally asked.

"When Anton's here I am. But I won't rest until I see my mother again."

A long silence, prompted by his old promise, fell between us.

"I've been thinking about that," he finally said quietly. "I'm in a mind to take a trip back home, as it happens." He said it casually. Altogether too casually.

"Home? You mean Rantsila?" I asked incredulously.

"Why not? It's been years since I was there."

"Henrik, don't talk nonsense. You're too old for that trip now."

"All the more reason to go now. I'm sixty-seven. I'm not getting any younger."

"Oh, Uncle Henrik, please be sensible."

"She'd come now if I went to get her, Kaisa. I know it. She wants to see her grandchild—her grandchildren," he amended with a grin.

I stared at him, thunderstruck. "She's fifty-seven years old, Henrik! And who knows what her health is like? She'll never say a word about it in her letters."

"I couldn't get there this year, you understand," he continued as if he hadn't heard me. "But by next Easter I can bring her over, just before final thaw. There's more daylight then but the road is still passable. The only question is how to pay for her trip from Karesuando." I had no answer, and I dared not hope after so many years of longing. But if not now, when? I still could not think of her without tears.

"I'll speak to Anton when he comes home," I told him dubiously. "Maybe, if he has a good season, there will be something left that he can spare for her journey."

Karl was born in April, two days after Anton came home. Henrik stayed through the whole thing, fetching the midwife when my time came and water for the sauna, and keeping Berit occupied until it was over. Anton was beside himself with joy over his son. I could have asked him for anything at that moment. So when I asked him from my bed for money to bring my mother to visit me, he smiled.

"The fishing went so well this time that if that's your dearest wish, that's how it will be."

"I have another wish," I told him, slightly feverish with happiness. "But maybe it's too costly." He looked down at me expectantly. "I'd like to go to Tromsø and have photographs made of all of us together. For my mother . . . and father."

"As soon as you're ready, we'll go," he promised.

As matters turned out, he had to leave for the Finnmark fishing season before I was well enough to travel. But he left me the money for Tromsø anyway, and a little extra, feeling expansive with his run of good luck.

"It will do you good to get away for a little visit to the city. I know it's hard being here alone so much of the time," he frowned. "Visit Jensine on the way, why don't you? I'll ask Edgar and Jenny to look after the animals while you're gone."

When the weather was at its warmest, I arranged to ride along on a wagon with a neighbor bound for Nordkjosbotn, and there I hired a boatman to row the children and me across to Storsteinnes. Karl slept peacefully in my arms the entire trip. Berit sang and chattered the whole time. When Jensine saw us struggling up the hillside to her cottage, she ran out to greet us.

"Look at you!" she cried, scooping Berit into her arms and chuckling with delight at the baby cradled in my arm.

"It's been so long, Jensine." I gave her a teary hug. "I've so much to tell you."

Berit settled at the loom, where she industriously set about tugging apart the strips of cloth Jensine was weaving into mats. I dragged her away and shook my head apologetically. "I've taken to tying a goat bell around her neck because she's always running off into the woods and disappearing. She's never still a moment," I sighed.

I t was Jensine who suggested I ask Petra to come along to Tromsø to help with the children, and that's what I did. I was glad for her company. She was sixteen now and, as we sat on the deck of the little steamer admiring the splendid views of fjord and mountains, she was full of anxious questions about her father.

"What's to become of him, Kaisa?" Her serious face was pale with worry. "I try to give him things when he comes by but he'll never take a thing, and he won't ever stay long."

"He's painfully proud, Petra. It runs in the family." I smiled wryly at her, hoping to lighten her mood. But I worried about exactly the same thing myself.

When our turn came at the photographer's, the usually placid Karl turned rigid and commenced to howl, and nothing we could do would still him. Finally Petra took him outside. I, stiff and solemn, held Berit, wide-eyed with curiosity, her short limbs momentarily at rest, alone on my lap for our first family photograph.

I could not know then that the next one would break my heart.

I had forgotten how short she was.
Maybe she'd gotten shorter with age. Or perhaps it was that I'd grown so much taller than she. But she had always loomed so large in my memory that when I first caught sight of them coming over the rise of the hill in the soft sunlight that chilly April evening in 1907, I didn't realize who it was.

The snow had melted from the path and it was turning to mud. I was coming back from the river with a bucket of water in each hand. Anton, just home from Lofoten, was repairing the barn.

They walked slowly, he just ahead, bent over his walking staff, his timeworn knapsack strapped to his back, his battered hat low over his eyes. Behind him was a small figure in black, head tightly wrapped in a scarf. She too carried a knapsack on her back and clung to a walking stick. But she marched steadily along, straight, proud, full of purpose. I understood who it was the instant I recognized her walk.

"They're here!" I shouted.

I flew down the road toward them, heedless of the mud, skirts flapping, Berit in gleeful pursuit, the goat bell around her neck clanging merrily.

When they saw us running toward them, they stopped and stood there waiting, side by side, resting on their staffs. When I reached her, she dropped her staff and held her arms out to me. I only got a glimpse of her dear, deeply wrinkled face before we were buried in one another's arms. Neither of us could speak. We must have stood so a long time, our silent tears washing one another's cheeks. Then Berit tugged impatiently at my skirt.

"Is this my grandmother?" she demanded, looking up at us with her wide-eyed expression.

I wiped my eyes on the back of my hand and smiled at Mother. "She wants to know if you're her grandmother," I explained in Finnish. I barely could get the words out.

Smiling, her face wet with tears, Mother bent down in the muddy roadway and peered closely into Berit's face. My daughter stared back in wonder at my mother.

"I don't see any of us in her," Mother finally said in a choked voice. She formally held out her hand to Berit, who shyly reached up to grasp it, eyes still fixed on her grandmother's face. Then she curtsied prettily, as she had been taught.

"She takes after her father's people," I told Mother, smiling and crying at once.

Henrik, who had stood silent through it all, picked up her staff. Then, one hand tightly clasping mine and the other holding Berit's, Mother walked slowly between us to the house, where Anton stood cradling Karl in the crook of his arm. She shook his hand warmly and he wordlessly handed her the baby. She cradled Karl in both arms, studying his face.

"Nikolai," she said when she looked up. A small, rueful smile tugged at her lips. "He takes after Nikolai."

"God help him, then!" Henrik boomed. We all laughed through our tears, grateful for this moment to gain control over our emotions.

Her dark hair had turned gray, wrinkles creased her face, and her hands were terribly worn and calloused. Otherwise, she seemed unchanged in the fifteen years that had passed since we parted. She carried herself as erectly as I remembered, and her spirit seemed as indomitable.

"It wasn't so hard," she said when I questioned her about their journey. "If I had known how easy it could be, I would have come long ago."

"Easy?"

"We went very slowly. But it's just a question of putting one foot in front of the other, as Henrik says. And that's what I've done all my life."

"I think you're wrong about Berit, Mother," I chuckled. "I think I see much of you in her."

"Maybe." She smiled. "She does seem to have a mind of her own."

We spent a wonderful summer together, Mother, Berit, Karl and I. Anton left for Finnmark in much better sprits than usual knowing I wasn't alone. Henrik came and went, regaling us with gossip and stories from the road. We paid a visit to Kitdal, and Nicoline received us most cordially. Only once, when Berit was tumbling through the grass in front of the stoop where we were all sitting together enjoying the sun, did Nicoline bristle. Berit had stopped rolling end over end for a moment, bent over, poked her head between her knees to look backwards at us through her legs.

"Stop that at once!" Nicoline commanded, alarm flashing in her eyes. She gave me a harsh look. "Don't you know that when a child does that it means someone will die?" she scolded.

On our visit to Balsfjord, mother took a special shine to her niece Petra. "It's a shame the way you treat that poor girl, Henrik," she scolded. "The girl needs a father to look out for her."

"I can barely look out for myself," he retorted crossly. But I thought I saw guilt in his eyes.

When the moment was right, I brought out the letters from my father. Mother read them silently, her lips pulled tight.

"He's still part owner of that little shop in Astoria, I see," she mused. "And it seems he's not satisfied with his farm in Kemi. It won't surprise me if he gives it up, and Finland too. Nothing will ever be good enough for that man."

Her bitter tone, and the naked hurt in her eyes, made my heart ache. I felt helpless and at a loss for words of comfort.

"Has he ever offered you money?" she suddenly asked.

"No. I'm sure he understands I would never accept it," I answered firmly.

I paused, hoping not to hurt her further. "I'll be civil to him because he is my father, after all," I ventured, watching her face to see how she took this. "But I'll never forgive him for what he did to you. And I'm certainly not going to let him buy my forgiveness."

She nodded, apparently satisfied. We never mentioned him again.

All that happy summer I begged Mother to stay, but she refused. "You and Anton are just getting started in life. He'll need all the money he can save if he's to buy this land. He doesn't need another mouth to feed."

"But Mother, we have plenty to eat. It's true the cottage is tiny, but we could add a room . . ."

"I'm not that old yet, Kaisa, for heaven's sake. I'm still able to provide for myself." Eyes flashing, she drew herself up to her full height and I had to smile despite my frustration.

"Later, Kaisa, when you're established and Anton has his feet under him, then I'll consider it."

"Do you promise, Mother? Will you come live with us?"

She nodded. "Why, this year they've even opened that railroad line from the gulf on the Swedish side all the way up to Norway on the coast. I could take the boat from Oulu across the gulf to Sweden and then go on the train north to Kiruna and onward all the way to Narvik on the Norwegian coast. From there I could take the steamer to Tromsø. Henrik has explained all about it. It would be easy."

"But think of the cost!"

"It's just a thought. But you see what might be possible later, in my old age. In any case, I rather enjoyed my walk, to tell you the truth. It was nice to see a bit of the world. I've no qualms about doing it again."

I sensed a false heartiness in her speech but in the end I had to be content with her promise to return. So in the fall, close on the heels of the first good frost, she and Henrik set out across the mountains again. This time we said our goodbyes cheered by the expectation that we soon would be together again.

The seasons flew happily by. The children and land blossomed under our diligent care, and our faithful Palma never failed us. We looked to the future with good reason to hope: our stomachs were full, and each year Anton was able to meet the rent payment as well as put something aside. He even could afford to sleep inside the barracks at Lofoten. I'm the one who insisted on it. It made me less anxious to know he was safe on land each night.

The dark, lonely months in the tiny cottage seemed a little less so with two children to care for. And Henrik continued to drop in for extended visits. I always begged him to stay, but he refused. I don't know if it was wanderlust or pride that kept him on the road.

Our reward for suffering the dreary darkness of winter was a glorious summer. Golden light beamed down on us twenty-four hours a day and turned the narrow valley into a slit of paradise. The sparkling, clear river ran thick with salmon as it tumbled down a verdant valley carpeted in lush meadow grass. Shy red foxes, bronzed by the glittering sunlight, sprang through the meadows in pursuit of mice. At the edge of the forest, moose browsed nervously. Overseeing it all, the awesome spire of Otertind reached into a brilliant blue sky where sea eagles soared.

I had come to love this place.

Nikolai continued to write. "I pray the Lord watch over you," he always said. Over time, I concluded he was sincere in his interest in my welfare, perhaps from religious impulse, perhaps from guilt. In any case, my sympathies toward him gradually warmed. It was a novel, and to some degree a comforting, sensation after all these years to know that I too had a father who took an interest in me. So I wrote back to him with growing pleasure, telling him about his grandchildren and our plans for the future.

In July of 1909, while Anton was in Finnmark and I was in the last stages of pregnancy with our third child, Jonas died. Anton came home in late August, too late for the birth of his second son or his father's funeral. Given his father's death, I expected Anton would want to name the boy after Jonas.

"No," he said firmly, coughing into his hand. "We've agreed on the name. Paulus Nikolai it is."

ELEVEN

ANTON

A raspy cough clung to Anton through the fall. I doctored him as best I could, and he seemed to be on the mend when he left for Lofoten. But when he came home at the beginning of April, he looked gray and worn. His cough was worse, a wracking one that began deep in his lungs. I promptly sent him to bed and he didn't protest. For three weeks I kept him down, feeding him rich, hot porridge made with generous portions of Palma's cream, meat stew full of dried peas, carrots and potatoes, lefse thick with butter and bracing cups of coffee. I was numb with worry. But one morning he sat up in bed and smiled.

"I feel rested this morning," he said cheerfully. Weak though he was, he began on the spring chores. I tried to hold him in check.

"I wish you wouldn't go to Finnmark this year," I told him. "We can manage somehow. It's better for you to stay home and get completely well."

"Oh, don't worry. By then I'll be as good as new." He wouldn't hear of anything but going fishing, since it had been a poor year in Lofoten. "We'll need the money to keep up the payments on the farm," he reminded me. "We don't have that much set aside."

For the first time in our married life, I lost my temper and raised my voice to him. "You're completely unreasonable, Anton! How can you even think of risking your health by going to sea in your condition? You must think of us now!" I glowered at him, more furious than I'd been in my life.

"I am thinking of you, Kaisa! That's why I have to go. Don't you understand that?" He was instantly angry too, weakened and frustrated as he was. "What choice do we have?"

As it happened, a choice presented itself only days after our argument. It came in the form of a letter from Nikolai.

"I have concluded that I was right the first time and that life in Finland is not for me. So I have bought property in Seaside, a little settlement with great promise on a wide, lovely beach not far from Astoria in Oregon, and I have made up my mind to move back to America. I will sell the farm here in Kemi forthwith unless you and Anton wish to take it over. I offer it to you on any terms you desire that might help you get started on a new, perhaps less harsh life. Whatever its drawbacks, the land would be your own to do with as you please. Please write to me at once, since we leave as soon as the harvest is complete."

We regarded one another warily, each trying to read the other's thoughts. "Kemi?" I whispered, half to myself. Anton's eyes were riveted on my face.

"Do you want to do it?"

I studied him thoughtfully. The sea would never cease singing in his blood, I knew. Generation upon generation, he had been untold years in the making. His fate was sealed the moment the first fishhook was dropped into this icy, unforgiving, life-sustaining sea. Yet this was my chance to keep him safe from the sea. But could he be happy away from it? What of our children? What would become of them in Finland with all its miseries? And my mother? What of her? Here was my chance to be with her again. But would she want me back on these terms? I knew the answer to that well enough.

"Do you think you'd come to regret turning down the opportunity to have a farm of your own, even if it meant going to Finland to get it?" I asked, parrying.

He shook his head emphatically. "We'll have our own farm here one day."

"I'm glad, because I think it would dishonor my mother to accept. I can't betray her that way. He's not going to buy forgiveness for what he did."

I wrote Nikolai a long letter thanking him politely for the offer but making it clear we were in Signaldal to stay and that we meant to make our own way in the world. He returned to America that August.

One month later Anton came home from Finnmark coughing blood. Wild with worry, I sent word to Kitdal. Erik came right away. After one look at Anton wheezing and gasping for breath in his bed, he pulled me aside. "I'm going for the doctor."

"We can't afford a doctor . . ." I whispered helplessly.

"I'll take care of it, Kaisa."

The doctor arrived two days later. He didn't stay long. He examined Anton on his sickbed, then he motioned me outside, his face grim.

"It's tuberculosis, I'm afraid."

I could only stare at him. His voice sounded so far away that I could hardly hear what he was saying.

"He's been fishing at Lofoten, hasn't he? Those barracks are disease-ridden hellholes."

"It's my fault. I insisted he sleep there . . ."

"Don't blame yourself. There's not much we can do for him now except let him rest. He may pull through; people do. So it's not as if there's no hope," he added gently. But I could see in his eyes that it was hopeless.

"What about the children?"

He shook his head and shrugged his shoulders. "Keep them away from him, and yourself too, as much as you can."

"But what if they've already been . . ." I couldn't finish.

"Only time can tell us that," he sighed. "For now we can only do what we must."

I went back inside, moving as if in a daylit nightmare. Paulus, a year old, lay cooing in his crib. Karl, three, was playing quietly on the floor near his father's bed. Berit, six, sat still as a frightened hare on a chair on the far side of the room, staring up at me with wide, fear-filled eyes. For once she didn't ask me anything, and neither did Anton.

I went over to his bed and saw that his face was wet. Tears ran down his cheeks and his chest heaved painfully. He didn't make a sound. I took his hand in both of mine and squeezed it, then wiped his face with a wet cloth.

"I heard him," he wheezed. "It's not good, is it?"

"He says you need rest," I heard myself say. "Try to go to sleep now."

When I was sure he was asleep, I pulled Berit and Karl to me, one on each side. "Now you must listen carefully," I told them. "Papa is very sick, and you mustn't get near him or you could get sick too. And you must always remember to be quiet so he can sleep and get well again."

"Will Father die?" Berit asked, her lips trembling.

"Shush, child, no. Of course not."

She fell mute, her lips drawn down at the corners. She didn't cry but neither, I was sure, did she believe me.

The children and I slept at the opposite end of the cottage. After the first heavy snows fell and they could no longer play outside much, I kept them confined to that part of the room. Berit and Karl grew withdrawn and listless. Family and neighbors came and went quickly, bearing food and solace. At night after the children were asleep, I sat alone in the darkness with Anton, cooling his brow with a wet cloth, holding his hand in mine or cradling his head to my bosom, quietly humming a soothing tune. During the day, he kept his eyes fixed on my face, but the merry light that had so enlivened them was extinguished. Sometimes he tried to tell me with that wonderful smile how much he loved us. To this day I don't know how I lived through it.

Two days before Christmas in 1910, I sent word to Kitdal that they had better come if they meant to say goodbye. Erik and Hansine came and pressed his hand, each in their turn, then quickly left. Nicoline stayed at his bedside, eyes red, wiping his brow with a cloth.

"I want to say goodbye to my children," Anton whispered weakly.

Only God could have given me the strength to take Karl's hand. "Come now and say goodbye to Papa," I whispered. Trustingly, he put his hand in mine and looked questioningly into my face. "It's all right. You can give him a hug now."

Anton lifted an arm and pulled Karl to him. "Be a strong boy, Karl. Always mind your mother," he wheezed.

"Goodbye, Papa," Karl whispered, his eyes large and uncomprehending. Anton pulled Karl to him once more and then turned his face to the wall. I had to look away. When I regained my composure, I turned to Berit, huddled in the corner with her arms wrapped tightly around her knees. I held out my hand to her. "Come now, Berit," I whispered.

She shook her head, mute.

"It's all right," I urged quietly. "You too must say goodbye to Papa." I took her hand and pulled her from her perch, but she broke into a wail.

"No, no, I don't want to! I don't want to!" she howled, holding fast to the edge of the table.

"Oh, Berit, please be good now," I begged.

Anton held out his arm to her. "Come give me a kiss goodbye, my dear little Berit," he pleaded hoarsely.

"No, no, I won't! I won't!" she screamed, her face white.

"For shame!" Nicoline exclaimed. "For shame! Come outside with me!" She grabbed the shrieking Berit by the shoulder and hauled her out the door. I quickly scooped Paulus, from his crib and brought him to Anton's bedside. He reached for the baby's foot, but his hand dropped away. He gasped once, then his chest collapsed and his eyes rolled back in his head. I heard a long, anguished animal wail. For a moment, I thought it was Berit.

Then I realized it was me.

We followed his body to the storehouse down by the church where the dead were kept until spring thaw. His eyelids were closed with two coins Nicoline placed on them, and a Bible was tucked under his chin. We left the cottage door open while we were gone, as Nicoline instructed, and later I burned his bedding and his clothes, as was the custom.

"See now? That child knew something," Nicoline hissed at me as we left the churchyard in a wet flurry of snow after the funeral service. "You shouldn't have let her look at us through her legs that way."

I was beyond answering.

Anton had not left enough money to pay the rent for the whole year, but I was determined to find a way to stay where we were. I just needed time to think it through. For his part, Olson wasn't long in coming to the cottage—or to the point.

"With your man gone, you'll be hard put to provide for yourself and all these children," he said, stroking his beard. "But I'm a reasonable man. I'm an understanding man. And for a little understanding from you, I think we can work out an arrangement that will let you and your children stay here as long as you like. What do you say?" There was no mistaking his meaning.

For answer, I went to the box where Anton kept our money and counted it out. "This is all I have," I said, handing it to him.

He made a great show of counting it himself. "Well, it's not enough for the whole year, of course. But it will see you through the summer, anyway. Suit yourself," he shrugged as he opened the door to leave. He paused to give me a nasty look.

"You hold yourself quite high for a Finnish woman," he sneered.

Suddenly penniless, I sank down on a stool by the table and looked about me in despair. I had hoped to bargain with him, to buy some time, but I could see where that would lead. I could owe him no favors. At least I had secured the roof over our heads for the time being, but I had to feed and clothe the children. Mentally, I took stock. We had a cow, two sheep, our winter's supply of potatoes, fish and herring, enough wood and flour to last . . . to last . . . How long? I dared not think of it.

I cast my narrow options about in my head. I could throw myself on the mercy of my in-laws, but I much preferred to manage without them. The kindness of strangers would be easier to accept; the repayment would be less humiliating. Besides, aside from food to keep his children alive, they had offered little but sympathy since Anton died.

Nikolai would gladly help, I believed, but that was unthinkable. Worse to take his money now when I needed it than when I didn't.

I had to find work. I thought briefly of returning to Tromsø, but discarded it as impossible. Where would I get a house post with three children in tow?

So I resolutely set out up the valley, house by house, offering my services as baker, cook, and household help. I had several takers, perhaps more out of sympathy than need. My last stop was at Jenny and Edgar's, who had a child of their own. They too had known serious poverty and Jenny was kindhearted. She assured me she could use my help. I made my last call just down valley, where I was hired on part-time by Terje, an unpleasant churl whose invalid wife could no longer care for him and their two grown sons. In this place, at least, I could see my services were sorely needed, though I'd never much liked the looks of the inhabitants, especially the sons. Both Arne and Emil were known for their loutish, drunken behavior and they ran with a gang of the worst the district had to offer. But I needed the work and they were rarely about. When they were, they made insinuating, lewd remarks about Finnish women. I just ignored them, as I always did whenever some man spoke to me that way.

Through snow, sleet, rain or shine, I trudged up and down the valley, dragging the children behind me, each day at a different place, washing down walls, scrubbing floors, boiling laundry in big tubs, and baking big rounds of crisp flatbread and soft lefse. I put Berit, always eager for something to do, in charge of minding Paulus, and Karl, always calm, in charge of himself.

Our desperate circumstances were a blessing, in their own way. It forced me to concentrate on keeping food on the table for my children when all I wanted was to lie down and weep. It was impossible that Anton wouldn't be back in spring as always, smiling that wonderful smile and holding me close. Even though I was exhausted with work and grief, I lay awake night after night, tormented by the unbearable knowledge that if I hadn't insisted he sleep in the barracks, Anton would still be alive.

Erik came in late January with a load of firewood, a small wooden barrel of salted herring and a side of mutton. "How are you managing?" he wanted to know. He stood awkwardly at the table, turning his cap in his hands.

"Well enough," I answered. "I earn what little I can here and there in the valley. People have been kind."

"Yes," he replied, looking momentarily ashamed. Or so I thought.

"Thank you for all this, Erik," I told him stiffly. "I wouldn't accept it save for the children's sake."

"You know that if there's anything else we can do, you only have to ask . . ."

"Thank you." I was not about to ask for what I most desperately needed. If they couldn't see that and offer it themselves, it could only mean one thing: they didn't want us there. True, Erik was growing a large family of his own. Each year, regular as clockwork, Hansine dropped yet another baby into their crowded household.

"Will Olsen let you stay on here, then?" His voice sounded hopeful. Probably they thought that, once over my initial grief, I would come to my senses and quickly do as his own wife had done: remarry. It was the only real option available for a widow answerable for children. It was her duty, in fact—if any man could be found who wanted her badly enough to accept the burden of another man's offspring.

"Until the end of summer, at least," I told him. The relief on his face was unmistakable.

It was well into February before I could bring myself to tell my mother what had happened. "I feel so helpless, so helpless," she wrote back. "Do you know where Henrik is? I hope he has been of some help to you. Tell him I want to come to you as soon as he can come for me."

But I didn't know where he was. This time, he seemed to have truly vanished. With my mind on all my troubles, it hadn't quite dawned on me how long he'd been gone. Petra came looking for him in late May, her face an anxious mask of worry, an engagement ring on her finger. We exchanged congratulations and condolences.

"I'm afraid he won't come visit me any more," she confided.

"Why ever on earth not?"

"Oh, Kaisa, I was just trying to do the right thing. He's too old to be out wandering from pillar to post in all kinds of weather. I think he's sick, but of course he won't say. So last time he came I told him I thought the time had come for him to live with me so I could look after him. I tried to let him know how glad I would be to have him." She paused, her eyes watering.

"But do you know what he said? 'You haven't received any upbringing from me all these years, and you shall be spared the trouble of having to care for me in my old age.' Then he walked out, just like that, his nose in the air, and I haven't seen him since."

She stared at me with sorrowful eyes. "I'm afraid he thinks I want something from him, his money, perhaps. But as far as I know, he doesn't have any money. That's why I'm so worried about him."

"Oh, Petra, he's so proud," I said, giving her a hug. But suddenly scenes from the high tundra flashed through my mind. What if he'd taken it into his head to walk to Karesuando or some other mountain settlement without telling us? He could have died up there and none of us would know it for months, perhaps never.

"Yes, you told me that once. You said it runs in the family. But I'm not proud. I don't care what he thinks of me. He's seventy-three years old now, and he needs a home and someone to take care of him."

"He cares about you, Petra. You should have seen the look on his face the day we came to see you when I first came from Finland. 'Isn't she a sweet child?' he said."

I meant to cheer her up, but her lips began to tremble. "I get so exasperated with him sometimes," I added. "He is so stubborn. But try not to worry so. I'll send word as soon as I know anything." I tried to sound reassuring. But another heavy burden hung itself around my aching heart.

TWELVE

HOMELESS

At midsummer there always was a celebration down by the fjord. People came down from the valleys and built big bonfires. But I thought midsummer was sad; it meant the days would get shorter and I saw no reason to celebrate that. Worse yet, there were always those looking for any excuse to drink themselves silly, and this day provided one of the best excuses of the whole year for rowdy behavior. So I had never bothered much about it, even in happier times.

This midsummer I was worn out from a day of boiling and scrubbing the laundry—we boiled our clothes and bedding in perpetual warfare against lice—at Marianne Paulsen's place at the far upper end of the valley. They were good people, childless and welcoming of my brood, unlike some of the places where I knew the children's presence was resented as just more hungry mouths to feed. Marianne was a thin, fair-haired woman with a kind smile and cheery word for everyone.

I dragged myself and the children home that day and quickly fed and tucked them into bed. The baby slept with me, and Berit and Karl slept in the other bed. It was still light outside, of course, but I darkened the room with a heavy curtain over the window and soon we were all in deep sleep.

I don't know how long we slept. All I know is that they crashed through the door before I could come fully awake. There were three of them, in their shirtsleeves, laughing and stinking of beer.

"Get out!" I shouted as soon as I understood what was happening. I leapt from my bed in my nightclothes, frantic with fear. "Go away! Go away!" I shouted over and over. But one of them grabbed both of my arms and pinned them behind me; another grabbed the baby and threw him in the other bed. Paulus began to wail, and Berit and Karl sat up to stare in sleepy astonishment.

I recognized the one who held my arms. It was Emil, Terje's son. I craned my neck and bit into his arm as viciously as I could. He yowled in agony.

"Help me with this Finnish bitch if you want your own turn," he shouted furiously at the others, struggling with me. Cursing, he fumbled with his trousers as the other two threw me back on the bed and held me there. I screamed when Emil threw himself on me. I could hear Berit echoing my scream, almost drowning out Paulus's wail. She never let up screaming the whole time he was on top of me.

"Hurry up, man! Let's get out of here, for God's sake," one of them shouted at Emil. He shuddered and rolled off me and they left as abruptly as they had come, leaving the door wide open in their haste.

I managed to raise myself up on one elbow. Across the room my three children sat bolt upright on the bed, two of them howling in terror, the third perfectly still, his eyes huge.

In August, Olsen came about the rent while I was milking Palma. "Your time's up, you know. Unless you've changed your mind." He leered expectantly at me while I finished the milking in silence.

"I don't have anywhere else to go. Winter is coming and I have three children to feed. I had to sell the sheep so I could buy flour." I recited this without emotion, without looking at him, without expectation of sympathy.

"How do you propose to pay the rent, then?" he persisted.

Helpless, I looked him full in his lecherous face.

"Palma," I answered woodenly. "What will you give me for the cow?"

He arched his eyebrows and tugged at his beard. "The cow? You'd rather deprive your children of milk . . . ?"

"What will you give me for her?"

"Six months." He spat it out. "That will see you into February. Then we'll see what your tune is." His confident leer widened into a sickening smile.

Without another word, he untied Palma and led her away. We stood silently looking after them, Berit's face a dark, scowling cloud, Karl's filled with sad confusion.

By the end of September, I knew the worst. I was pregnant. I collapsed on my bed and wept, wanting nothing more than to die.

I lay there curled up and sobbing like a child for what may have been hours. I was dimly conscious that Berit and Karl came to my bedside looking at one another helplessly.

I had told no one of what had befallen me. When it happened, I had been overwhelmed with shame. I knew it was an article of Norwegian faith that Finnish women were not respectable, so I understood they would blame me for it. To talk about it would only heap needless shame upon me if, God willing, nothing came of it. I prayed each day that I had not conceived; then no one would be the wiser. But now despair engulfed me.

When I awoke from a fitful sleep, Berit was sitting on one stool with Paulus on her lap. Karl sat next to her on another. Three pairs of eyes were glued on me. The fire was out and the house was cold.

"Are you going to die too, Mother?" Berit asked.

I sat up. They stayed on their stools, so vulnerable and trusting. I buried my face in my hands, beyond tears, beyond grief, beyond sensation.

"Of course not," I told her wearily. But I could see in her eyes that she didn't believe me.

I kept my secret as long as I could hide it. When I no longer could, I left it to Providence to decide who would keep me on and who would not. As many kept me on as didn't. Those I trusted, like Jenny and Marianne, I told enough that they understood what had happened.

By November, I knew there was no help for it. I would have to go and confront Terje about his son. I hadn't been there since the rape. But we needed money if we were to survive the arrival of another child.

"I didn't know you were in this condition," Terje said when he saw us on his doorstep. He regarded me with wary, narrow eyes.

"Your son Emil did this," I said quietly, my face aflame. "He forced me. I want him to provide for the child. It's only right. He attacked me in my own house."

He looked stunned for a moment. Then he burst into laughter. "My son forced you? He's never had to force a woman yet. Especially not a Finnish one. Be on your way, slut!" He slammed the door in my face.

There was more to come.

Christmas was just two days away and heavy snow lay piled against the houses. I had been busy with Christmas baking at Marianne's and gratefully was carrying home a few cookies for the children. I had nothing else for them for Christmas, but Berit and Karl were beside themselves with anticipation of their treat. I remember thinking how fortunate children are. Neither of them seemed to remember that it was Christmas when their father died.

I saw that something was wrong before we got there: a lamp was shining inside our cottage and the door was flung open. My heart throbbing in my throat, I hurried along as fast as the snow and my condition would allow. Whatever could have happened? Then, as we came near, I saw it. The light from the cottage door fell on our stove, which was sitting askew in a snow bank. Around it lay our other belongings—clothing, bedding, floor mats, the spinning wheel, cooking pots, wooden bowls and plates, two wooden chests. Everything we owned had been thrown out into the snow.

Olsen must have heard my cry because he came to stand in the doorway, hands on his hips.

"What's the meaning of this?" I demanded, fury nearly choking the words. I stood a short distance from him, large with child, clasping Paulus in one arm, my two other children pressed protectively to me with the other. "What have you done?"

"I want you out of this house!" he growled.

"Are you mad? It's winter! My children . . . We have nowhere else to go!"

"You had your chance. But, oh no, you were far too fine for the likes of me, weren't you? Now look at you! Finnish whore! You're all alike!"

"It wasn't my fault! I was forced!"

"Go tell it to your fancy in-laws, then. Surely they'll believe you and take you in." He spat into the snow before my feet. "Get away from here, you and your damn brats! I'm sick of the sight of you!"

I felt the world falling away under my feet. Clutching the baby, I dropped to my knees before him in the snow.

"Please, for God's sake, for the children's sake, show some Christian mercy on us," I begged. "We've nowhere else to go."

"I want you out of this house tonight!" he shouted.

I may have sat there in the snow for some time, or perhaps only a moment. I can't say. I picked up what we could carry—a pair of blankets, the small wooden box in which I kept our money, the letters from my mother and father, and Nikolai's photograph. Then we turned into the darkness and began to walk back the way we had come.

"Where are we going, Mother?" Berit asked. Her tremulous voice sounded tiny and far away. "Mother, where are we going?" she repeated. I realized she was crying.

"We'll have to go to Jenny's. Don't cry, dear Berit." But I was weeping myself and she paid me no heed.

When they saw us on their doorstep clutching our belongings, their mouths dropped open in amazement.

"He threw us out. Everything's lying in the snow. Everything. I have no place else to go," I told them stonily. "We need a place to sleep."

It was the hardest sentence I had ever uttered.

Jenny's husband Edgar and their son Pol wasted no time in hitching up the horse and sled to go fetch our things. I left the children with Jenny and rode with the men the short distance back to the cottage. None of us spoke. When we got there, Olsen was gone. We had brought a lantern and could see that everything else lay as it had been, strewn about in the snowdrifts.

"It's shameful!" Edgar muttered. "Un-Christian! What kind of man would do such a thing?" He spat into the snow.

While they loaded the stove onto the sled, I took the lantern inside and took one last look at the little home where I had known so much joy and anguish. It seemed a dream inside this nightmare. I closed the door, softly, and turned my back on it.

Pol drove ahead with the load and Edgar and I shuffled slowly up the road; I had to steady myself against him in the darkness. "You see what we have, Edgar," I began. "A few provisions, a good stove, a lamp, a spinning wheel, dishes, mats, cookware." I couldn't see his face nor he mine, and I was grateful. "My time will come soon and we must have a place to stay until I'm able to work again. I insist you take our stove and other things as payment."

"Kaisa, Kaisa, of course you can stay," he protested, "There's to be no question of payment."

"No, Edgar, it's not right. I can't ask you to house and feed us. I can't accept that."

"We'll talk to Jenny and see what she says," he answered evasively. But in the end, I prevailed.

My son Inge was born in March of 1912. It was the occasion of great scandal in the valley and it set eager, vicious tongues to wagging. "You could always tell from the way she walked that she held herself better than other folk," people said.

And, I suppose, truly so.

I had three strikes against me, I now realize: I was Finnish, I was pretty, and I was proud. None of it served me well.

It was April before I could form the words to tell my mother what new misfortune had befallen me. "Oh, my dearest Kaisa," she wrote back. "I feel helpless so far from you! I blame myself for sending you from me into what I so hoped would be a better life than mine. I should never have sent you away. I can only pray for you and for God to forgive me."

By then, I had written as well to Nikolai in America at the address he had sent me before Anton died. Pride has its limits, at least when children are involved. I told him what had happened—everything: Anton's death, the rape, Palma, being cast out into the snowdrift at Christmas, Inge's birth. I spared no detail of what had been visited upon me in the short time since he had offered us his farm.

And I asked him for money. It was easier than I thought. He was my father, after all. Were it not for him, I would not be here, far from home suffering like this, I finally told myself. Nor would my children. I told him all that too, desperate and angry as I was.

When I was well enough, I went back to my chores at those farms that would have me. I now had four children, one of them nursing, to drag after me from place to place, and it was clear that often as not, my children were far from welcome. Only pity kept people from turning us away, I knew that. But I had to swallow my pride and accept their pity for my children's sake. Sometimes I arranged to work for room and board. The rest of the time we slept either at Jenny's or Marianne's. In my heart, though, I knew we could not continue indefinitely in this itinerant beggar fashion. My children had to have a home. I had pinned my last hope on Nikolai.

One day in early May I left the other children with Jenny and set out with Inge to Kitdal. I had heard nothing from them, but I was certain they'd heard about me. With time and suffering, my shame had hardened to anger; I wanted them to know the truth. And I had another reason for going there.

Nicoline's eyes widened when she saw me on her stoop with a baby in my arms. She invited me in; she and Hansine had been drinking coffee at the kitchen table. I wasted no time on niceties.

"I want you to understand what happened, Nicoline." She had aged, but not mellowed, I could see that in her eyes. But I told them my story, looking each of them unflinchingly in the face the whole time. When I was finished, Hansine rose and patted my arm.

"Oh, Kaisa, I just knew it couldn't be true what they were saying about you." She poured a cup of coffee and handed it to me.

I swallowed the words that sat screaming on my tongue: "Then why didn't you come to see for yourself?" I could live to be two hundred and still never understand these people.

Nicoline had sat silent, her face a wrinkled, impenetrable mask. "So that's the way it is, is it?" she finally said. "I'm relieved to hear it. What do you propose to do now?"

I understood then that though she might pretend otherwise for the sake of the family's good name, in her heart of hearts Nicoline harbored doubt about my innocence. But I had to let that pass.

"I wouldn't ask except for the children's sake, but I wonder if I might bring Karl to stay for awhile, just until I can get back on my feet. There are so many of them now for me to take with me from place to place when I'm working . . ."

"Of course, Kaisa. Anything you need. You only have to ask," Nicoline answered smoothly. "You know that, of course."

Once again, I bit back the words that lay so heavily on my tongue: "Where I come from, I wouldn't have to ask." But I said nothing.

"What are your plans?" Hansine asked.

"I'm hoping for some money from America soon," I told them. Strangely enough, I felt more pride than shame in this confession. "My father lives there, you know."

"Yes," Nicoline murmured. The disdainful way she said it made me realize that she now saw me in a new light. My illegitimacy had never elicited anything but her sympathy before. Was she thinking, "Like mother, like daughter?"

Oddly enough, when Karl came to stay in Kitdal, Nicoline spoiled him so shamelessly—perhaps to ease her conscience—that Hansine's children resented him. They teased and trounced him regularly, and he cried. When I came to visit him, I found a changed child, morose and withdrawn.

"I don't like it here," he told me sullenly. I couldn't bear to see him hurt, so I took him back with me. It would be just until I heard from Nikolai and could make some other arrangement, I told Petter, the ancient, half-deaf widower who owned the farm where we were staying then. What that arrangement might be I had no idea.

When Nikolai's letter finally arrived, a wet May had dissolved into a glorious June, and even I had been heartened by the renewed life springing up around me. I opened the envelope with trembling fingers.

It was a short, formal note. "Dear Kaisa," he began. "It is with much sadness and disappointment that I read of the life you have fallen into upon the most unfortunate death of your good husband. My financial affairs here have not turned out as well as I had hoped. Nevertheless, I'm sending you a small sum that I trust will be of some help."

I stared unbelieving at the words on the paper. "The life you have fallen into." So he didn't believe me, either. Was he too thinking, "Like mother, like daughter"? He, of all people? A cold rage seized me. The insulting sum he sent might at best buy a sack of flour. Overwhelmed by fury and disappointment, I didn't write to thank him for it. More than a decade would pass before I repented of my anger. But the letters I then so belatedly sent never produced a reply.

I didn't use Nikolai's money for flour, as matters turned out. In the end, I invested it in something more lasting.

I knew that I had now exhausted my options. We lived as beggars, ragged and threadbare, wandering from door to door in hopes of food and shelter, increasingly more objects of scorn than pity. To some, my predicament was satisfying evidence of the inescapable wages of sin. Even those who granted me the benefit of the doubt as to my innocence still found it fitting that someone who had held herself as high as I had was now paying the price for the sin of pride. And, of course, more than one man saw my fallen circumstances as an invitation to satisfy his baser nature. Even that old fool Petter was pestering me.

I knew I had to accept the truth. There was no recourse but the one I had been so dreading, the one I had been trying so desperately to avoid all along. I must find homes for the children until I could get on my feet.

I could throw myself on the mercy of my in-laws, but stooping before Nicoline was unthinkable. I knew I'd never be able to stand up again. Besides, I wanted my children where they were welcome and happy. They had endured grief enough for a lifetime. In any case, Nicoline was not well.

So I began with Marianne.

"Oh, Kaisa, we'd be so pleased to keep him here with us," she beamed. "I've often thought of offering, but I didn't want to upset you by mentioning it. You know how fond Johan is of Karl." It was true; Johan already treated Karl like a son, teaching him how to fish in the river and showing him how to trap mink in the woods up behind the house.

The next day I brought Karl to their house alone. He must have suspected something from the start. He gripped my hand tightly as we walked along and looked up into my face for reassurance with bright, watchful eyes. But he said nothing.

When it was time to leave him there, I sat down with him on the front stoop and explained as best I could, promising to be back soon. I held him in my arms, but he hid his face in his hands and cried piteously. I left him weeping on that stoop with Marianne's comforting arms around him. He was five years old.

Giving away my children did not get easier with practice.

Next, the rest of us walked all day to reach Jensine's at Storsteinnes. The following day, I left Paulus there, wailing in terror. The sound echoed after us as we retraced our steps. It rang in my ears long after we were out of earshot.

I hear it still.

Now we were three, and I caught Berit looking up at me with a new fear in her eyes. I squeezed her hand and tried to reassure her with a hollow cheerfulness. "We'll soon have them both back with us," I told her.

"Will you give me away now too?" she asked, chewing nervously on her lip.

"No, Berit, dear. I need your help with the baby." She didn't say anything more, but I feared she had stopped believing me long ago.

I had worked out a plan, and on our way back to Signaldal I made it my business to stop at all the finest houses along the way to inquire if they needed a well-trained, live-in housemaid. Most people heard me out before they said no, their unfriendly eyes traveling up and down to admire the pathetic spectacle we presented. One woman gave me a coin, and I took it, thanking her through wet eyes. I was far beyond pride or shame.

When we had walked well past Nordkjosbotn we came to a well-kept house I often had admired. It was much smaller, but reminded me a little of the place I had worked in Tromsø; perhaps that's why I nourished secret hopes about it. I knew the man who owned it was a sea captain who had a fishing vessel of his own.

When I knocked on this door, a graying, sour-faced woman answered. "I'm seeking employment as a live-in maid," I explained, holding myself as erect as I could with the baby burdening my back. "I'm a widow. I've had three years experience in a doctor's house in Tromsø."

Mistress Dahl eyed me coldly. "I don't take housemaids with children," she answered haughtily. But she didn't close the door.

"My daughter is a good worker for her age. She's had to take a lot of responsibility."

"And the baby?"

"She looks after him while I work. She doesn't eat much, really."

"What's your name then? Where are you from?"

"Kaisa Utsi. I'm from Signaldal."

"Utsi?" She arched her eyebrows and peered more closely at me, frankly examining my features. Her watery blue eyes moved to Berit, and she sniffed the air disdainfully.

"I'm Finnish," I told her quietly. As I said, I was without shame.

"Finnish. They say you're good workers. Perhaps I should try a Finnish one. The Norwegian ones certainly have been a disgrace. I'll keep you in mind."

I had no way of knowing how rapidly her house help turned over, nor why. But before long, she sent for me.

It wasn't much, just a narrow sleeping chamber next to the kitchen heated from the back of the chimney. There was a small bed and a washstand and space for Inge's crib. Above the bed was a tiny window, at the foot of the bed stood a chest to store our belongings, and pegs for hanging our clothes were fastened to one wall. Whatever misgivings I might have about our employer, it was a room of our own at last, a roof over our heads, food for our bellies and a small wage. I was vastly relieved.

"Isn't this wonderful?" I whispered to Berit as I tucked us into bed the first night. She had been subdued all day as I went about learning my duties under Mistress Dahl's fussy tutelage, and I wanted to cheer her up.

"The mistress doesn't like me," she announced.

"Oh, Berit, of course she does. She's just a little cranky. She's not used to children, that's all. But she'll get used to you soon enough." I tucked her into the crook of my arm and held her close. "You'll like it here, you'll see."

"No, she doesn't like me," she repeated adamantly.

"Shush now, go to sleep. Everything will be all right."

But it wasn't. Every time Inge cried, the mistress complained. When I had to take time away from my duties to quiet him, she became angry.

"I'm going to have to let you go," she said crossly when we had been there a couple of months. "You're a good enough worker, when you can work. But I warned you I didn't want an infant in the house."

I had been half expecting it; I'd learned to anticipate the worst.

"Could we stay on if I didn't have the baby?"

She looked at me curiously, as if seeing me for the first time.

"I suppose so," she answered slowly.

I took Inge to Jenny's the next day. "It will just be until I can get on my feet," I told them matter-of-factly. And maybe I believed it. In any case, Jenny took him, eyes shining, and cradled him to her bosom. Blinded by tears, I stumbled out the door.

Henrik died in the spring of 1912 and Nicoline in the spring of 1913. But it was more than a year after his death, while on a visit to Signaldal to see Karl, before I got word about Henrik.

"Have you heard, Kaisa?" Marianne asked as soon as we came inside. "They say a wandering peddler died a year ago, in March, over in Salangen."

"Was it Henrik?" My heart constricted.

"They don't know his name. But he was the right age," Johan said. He was at the table, showing Karl some trick for preparing a fishhook. I could see how raptly Karl's eyes followed Johan's every move and how they lit up when Johan smiled approvingly at his efforts.

I knew then that I had lost him.

Marianne regarded me with pitying eyes. "There was no one to follow his body from the church to the graveyard, so the pastor asked the confirmation class to attend his funeral. One of Johan's nephews was in that class. That's how we got wind of it," she added.

"Where's Salangen?"

"Several days' walk from here. It's close to the coast. There's some kind of mine works there," Johan answered.

"Could Henrik have walked there at his age, do you think?"

"I suppose so . . ." he mused.

"Then so can I."

Both of them looked baffled.

"I have to know if it was him. He's been missing for so long! I'll never rest until I know what's happened to him, and neither will my mother. It's not right that he just vanish with no one to mourn him properly."

"But, Kaisa! It's so far!" Marianne protested.

"At least one hundred and twenty-five kilometers," Johan added, shaking his head.

"Henrik taught me to walk. My mother taught me to stand up, and Henrik taught me to walk. If he could get there, so can I. The least I can do for him is to make certain he got a decent burial. If it *was* him."

"You can't be serious, Kaisa," Marianne said, her eyes large in alarm. But she could see that I was.

I set out a few days later. It took all my persuasive powers to get Mistress Dahl to let me go, but I brazenly shamed her into it by explaining it was my solemn Christian duty to see to the disposition of my uncle's remains. I left Berit behind, staring after me with mournful eyes. I was tempted to bring her but realized I could move, and get back home, much faster on my own.

It was light all night and I walked much of it, falling into the old, familiar cadence. I almost felt as if Uncle Henrik were striding along beside me, that cheerful smile on his face. I strode along as if my life depended on it, my mind a perfect blank. I quenched my thirst from streams whenever I came to one and stopped at farmhouses to ask directions. Nor was I shy about asking for lodging; Henrik had taught me that too. "Oh, yes, he's been by here," some of them said at farmhouses where I asked after him. "But not for some time."

Salangen sat by the sea, against a mountain. When I at last found my way to the church and explained my errand to the pastor, he nodded sympathetically.

"That's him. I'm so glad you've come. We didn't know his real name.

They just called him Kven." That was what Norwegians called Finns. Often as not, it was meant as an insult.

"How did he die?"

"He was sick, apparently. He had complained of pains in his stomach. They found him one morning outside near the mine works."

"Outside? In March?"

He nodded, lips pressed together, and sighed sympathetically. "He seems to have gone there in hopes of selling his wares to the workers."

He led me to the grave, a simple wooden cross with "Kven" and the death date etched into it. "We'll put his right name on it," he told me gently.

"Was there . . . Did he leave anything behind?"

My reason for coming all this way was just as I said: I had to know if he was dead. But I would have been glad to learn that he had left something behind that I could use to provide for my children. I knew he would have wanted it so if he knew my situation.

"Nothing of value, I'm afraid."

I stood there a moment before Uncle Henrik's grave, considering that. Then I looked right at him, anger and sadness making me bold.

"You're quite wrong about that," I told him.

On the way home I detoured to Storsteinnes to see Paulus and pass on the sad news to Petra, who accepted it with tearful resignation. I spent that night with Jensine venting my sorrow, holding my child close. He was inconsolable when I left the next morning.

"Mama, Mama, take me with you!" he cried, wrapping his tiny arms around my neck. "Take me with you!" He clung so tightly to me that Jensine had to pry him loose.

"Mama! Mama! Don't leave me here! Mama! Mama!" he screamed after me as I fled. I was able to hold myself together until I was away from the house. Then an unstoppable dam of tears broke loose as I sobbed out my desperate grief on the deserted road.

The sky was a sheet of lead. It melted and wept down on bleak, uncaring mountains and into an indifferent, charcoal sea.

You had to be made of stone to survive in this place.

THIRTEEN
THE BIRTAVARRE MINES

My despair turned to a faint glimmer of hope the day I happened upon a newspaper advertisement seeking cooks for the mines in Birtavarre, which lay some distance beyond Skibotn. The life was hard, it was said, but the pay better than any woman otherwise could earn. At least it would be more than I could earn at the Mistress Dahl's. I had come to realize that if I stayed there, I would be there forever—or until such time as she threw us out. At Birtavarre I could make more money quickly and get my children back sooner.

The only problem was Berit. She was nearly nine now and an industrious worker, eager as always to please. She helped me in the kitchen, washing dishes, peeling potatoes and sweeping the floors. Maybe the mistress would let Berit stay until I could come for her?

I wrote to Birtavarre and promptly received a reply offering me a post. With Berit out of earshot, I broached the subject of leaving her with the mistress.

"Are you dissatisfied here?" I could see she was exasperated.

I assured her I was not but explained that I needed employment that would enable me to get my children back as quickly as possible. In truth, I already felt them drifting irreversibly away from me. That was more than I knew how to bear.

"I hope you can find it in your heart to help me," I told her humbly.

To my surprise, she agreed. I hadn't lived long enough to wonder why.

I had noticed another advertisement in that newspaper as well. A photographer was to be at the chapel ground in Hatteng, near the entrance to Kitdal, on an upcoming Saturday afternoon. I mulled it over, unable to make up my mind about spending so much when I had so little. But when I was accepted at Birtavarre, I knew it was the right thing to do.

So I went first to Storsteiness and got Paulus. The next day we all went to Signaldal to gather up Inge and Karl. Then we set out from Jenny's under a flawless sky, my heart a stone in my chest.

The photographer was waiting beside a white sheet hung outside on the chapel wall. I told him what I wanted—one small copy for each of us, plus one for my mother—and I handed him the money Nikolai had sent. The photographer seated me on a chair with the baby in my lap and arranged my other children around me. Afterwards, we waited quietly to see the photograph. When he handed it to me, I stared at it in profound shock and sorrow. I saw a beaten, tight-lipped woman surrounded by wary children. Karl's once serene face had turned grim. Berit's mouth was drawn into an angry scowl, her once merry eyes grown hard. Paulus, vulnerable and frightened, clung close against me. Even Inge looked hollow and misused.

Why hadn't I noticed? I looked closely into their faces, one by one, and saw that the camera had captured them truly. I thought I had steeled myself against bidding them farewell. But now, with this accusatory photograph to sear my memory, my heart broke once more. I dated and signed each one "Your loving mother" lest they forget me. Or one another.

I dreaded leaving Berit the most. On the morning of my departure, her large brown eyes filled with tears and her lips trembled. She looked at me with . . . I can only describe it for what it truly was: hatred.

"I'll be back soon," I said, embracing her. But she stood mute and stiff as a board, her small arms at her sides, tears rolling down her face. Blinded by my own tears, I left her there in that house. But her accusing eyes, filled with betrayal, followed me all the way to Birtavarre. And beyond.

It was far from what I had envisioned. But once at Birtavarre, I had no choice but to remain.

I was assigned to a barracks with twelve men. We all slept in the same room, they two to a bunk, I on a cot in the corner by the kitchen with a curtain drawn for privacy. A pastor once was sent to inspect our quarters in answer to outraged rumors about the scandalous living arrangements in the nation's mines. He concluded that we cooks were safer sleeping in the same room as the men, since everyone could see us—and each other.

The wind howled between the boards of the barracks, and in winter the bedding froze fast to the walls. The men were infested with lice. I hauled water from the stream below the barracks to boil their bedding and their clothes. I scrubbed their floors and cleaned their wounds. Up long before they stirred, I lit the stove and cooked their meals on another stove in a tiny separate kitchen, which they knew better than to enter without my permission. Each day they came back after ten hours in the mine, surly, exhausted, and covered with grime. They washed themselves in the big room by the stove with water I had hauled and boiled for the purpose. In the evenings they played cards, wrote letters to their wives by the light of the oil lamp, or threw punches and chairs in rage. On Saturday afternoons they were permitted to drink, and more than one of them traded all his wages for whiskey.

When I first saw my new home I gasped in dismay. The mine lay in a high, narrow valley. There was hardly a tree or bush to be seen. A handful of buildings were scattered about, and a small stream ran through the camp. A little distance away, out of sight of the barracks, a bridge crossed the stream. There, under the bridge, on a flat ledge hidden by a large boulder, I escaped on summer evenings to think my own grief-stricken thoughts while cooling my feet in a little pool. It was my sanctuary, my only respite from their demands and quarrels.

From the first day, they fought over me.
When they filed through the door the first evening to find me waiting with their meal, they fell silent. Some of them removed their hats. All of them glanced at me with interest. They washed themselves, some more ambitiously than others, and seated themselves at the table. They were a rough lot, young braggarts in their twenties, some not so young ones in their thirties, a few old men in their forties and some broken ones in their fifties.

One of them, a tall man with piercing dark eyes and a full head of wavy black hair that lay in accordion pleats across his skull, said loudly, "Well, let's see what this one can do. Is the food ready or must we wait all night?"

I took this as my signal to begin. I had in mind to serve their meals with the same formality I had learned in Tromsø, and that's what I did. They seemed dumbfounded by it because they ate in near perfect silence, looking at one another with raised eyebrows. Not one of them smiled and not one of them complained about the food.

When I retired to the kitchen at the end of the meal, the commotion began. "Keep your hands off this one, Heikki. She can cook!" someone said.

"Why? So you can have her for yourself, is that it?" There was an explosion of laughter.

"It wasn't me who ran the cook off!"

"This time!" someone else interjected.

"Settle down, for God's sake. Leave her be. We've got to eat if we're to survive this hellhole," a new voice chimed in.

"Who are you to tell me what to do?" the one they called Heikki retorted.

"Keep your hands off me, too. Just leave well enough alone," the same voice repeated.

"There's more to life than food," Heikki growled, but the commotion ceased.

I waited until they were all in bed before I dared come out of the kitchen to lie down on my cot. I hastily drew the curtain and undressed, feeling twelve pairs of eyes on me in the darkness. It was my imagination: most of them were already snoring. But my mind was long since made up. No one was going to trifle with me again. I slid a long, sharp kitchen knife under my pillow.

The next morning when they seated themselves for a hot breakfast, I stood erect at one end of the long table with my ladle poised over the porridge bowl, waiting until every eye was fixed on me.

"My name is Kaisa Utsi," I told them, my voice steely. "I'm here because I'm a widow with four children to support. I aim to do everything I can to fulfill my duties. In return, I'll thank you to treat me with the same respect you'd treat any mother, including your own."

There was a short, astonished silence. Then someone sang out, "My mother was a filthy whore!"

Before I could see who said it, someone reached across the table and lifted the brute out of his seat. I saw a fist fly and connect and a body slump backwards onto the floor.

"Let's eat! We're late!" someone shouted, and I hurriedly fell to serving them, my hands shaking. The one on the floor got up, dazed and glaring. When I got to the one who had come to my defense, I paused. He was light haired with a prominent nose and well-trimmed mustache. "Thank you," I told him quietly.

"You're quite welcome, Mrs. Utsi." He nodded his head formally. "Don't pay any mind to Heikki. He needs his brains knocked into place once a week." I recognized his voice; it was he who had argued with Heikki. "My name is Kalle Pertu," he added, smiling.

Heikki jumped Kalle on the way back from the mine a couple of days later and slashed Kalle's arm with a knife. They more or less settled down after that. Word went out that Mrs. Utsi ran a strict, first-class hostelry where table manners and certain civilities were required. It was my baking that won them over.

Yet when winter came, tensions rose. Trapped together underground all day, trapped in the barracks together all night, they exploded at the slightest provocation. I dreaded Saturdays, when they drank and fought, sometimes with knives. If one of them was only slightly injured, I was expected to patch him up. If it was serious, he was carried off down the mountain and a new man sent up in his place.

Once a month on Sunday, I wrote to the children. I lived for the letters with news of my children from Jensine, Jenny and Marianne. My mother was still a faithful correspondent, full of anxious despair over my worsening lot. No letters came from Berit in reply to mine. She herself couldn't yet write and Mistress Dahl apparently was unwilling to write on her behalf.

The suffocating guilt I felt at leaving my children was my heaviest burden, and I welcomed the hard work as a temporary distraction from my pain. I fought to keep them from my thoughts; otherwise I feared I could not go on. At Christmas, I tried to make things as cozy for the men as I could, given our barren circumstances. I had my own Christmas sorrows to forget and was anxious to keep busy lest my anguish overwhelm me. But after I had served the Christmas Eve porridge and retired to the kitchen, a wave of grief washed over me. Stifling my sobs, I leaned against the pantry, my face buried in my hands.

"Mrs. Utsi? Are you all right?" It was Kalle, poking his head cautiously through the door.

I wiped my face on my apron. "Yes, thank you." I kept my back to him. "You should leave now."

"I just wanted to be sure nothing serious was wrong," he said softly.

I turned to face him despite myself. "It's just that my husband died at

Christmas. I miss him very much." The words just fell out of my mouth. I had hardly spoken two unnecessary words to a soul the whole time I had been there for fear of causing trouble.

"I'm very sorry. It must be hard for you to be in this place."

"I do what I have to do."

"I admire you for it," he answered somberly, then ducked out of the doorway.

I couldn't help but notice him after that. I had kept my eye on him since that awful incident on my second day, figuring he could be counted on as an ally should trouble arise. I had quickly learned who could be depended on to act decently and who couldn't be trusted. But I treated them all with the same polite propriety and took care never to play favorites, with either their portions or my attentions.

I noticed that Kalle kept his eye on me too. But then, they all did. And they watched each other watch me—that was the worst of it. Sometimes I felt as if I were walking on eggshells, afraid to lift my eyes to look any one of them straight in the face for fear of causing a riot by the rest. Heikki was the most unstable of the lot—a drunkard, always spoiling for a fight, forever regaling the men with bawdy jokes that he made certain to tell in my presence. I never gave him the satisfaction of so much as a blush. And in retrospect, I think that goaded him.

Early one February afternoon, two men came from the mine dragging Kalle between them. He was unconscious, bleeding from the head.

"A rock fell on his head," they told me, throwing him in his bunk. "He's probably not badly hurt but he needs looking after."

By then I had become quite adept at the minor surgical arts, but I had never had an unconscious patient before and I dearly wished my first one could had been someone else. I washed his bloody wound and rubbed a smelly salve into it. As I was struggling to wrap a bandage around his head, his eyes opened. He tried to raise his head.

"Lie still," I told him sternly.

He fell back on his pillow, grinning weakly. "It's a small price to pay to wake up like this."

I ignored him.

He touched his head and winced. "I saw it coming but couldn't get out of the way," he groaned. "Is there any whiskey in the house? I think it would do me a world of good."

"Don't get up. The bleeding hasn't stopped."

"I've no intention of it now that I've got you to myself. Do you know what a pretty woman you are, Mrs. Utsi?" he teased.

As it turned out, he had me to himself another day while he recovered, and by the end of it we were well acquainted. He had come from Finland, not far from Oulu, over the same route as myself, in search of work. We spent a pleasant time together comparing our travel experiences, spoke of our lives since we came to Norway, and confided our hopes for the future.

"Mining is the fastest, most dependable way to lay up capital. Fishing is too risky," he said when I told him of Anton's struggles. "If I can hold out a few more years, I'll have saved what I need for a farm." Suddenly, he turned quite serious. "It's a lonely life."

I looked away, embarrassed.

He was looking at me tenderly now and I felt myself flush. Fortunately, someone barged in at just that moment. Unfortunately, it was Heikki. When he saw us, his face froze into a scowl. I would have felt better if he had said something, but he didn't. He just gave me a long look. From then on, every time I caught Heikki's eyes on me, they were openly leering. Every time I caught Kalle's eyes on me, they were openly adoring. I should have seen what was coming, but I was too blinded by my sorrow.

The tension between Kalle and Heikki continued to build throughout the spring. One Saturday in April it came to blows again, but they were both too drunk to do much damage. Mercifully, when the light returned we were able to escape outside. I gratefully returned to my solitary musings down by the bridge, trying to devise a future that would reunite me with my children. I was sick with longing for them and I feared they already had forgotten me. So I had concluded over the long, bitter winter that the answer to my plight must lie in Tromsø. Now that Berit was older, surely I could find some post there that would allow me to have her and my other children with me. I could bring them there, one by one perhaps, as my circumstance improved and my employer came fully to value my services. I knew my own worth as a servant and was confident on that score. I had calculated that I would have enough money saved to start out for Tromsø by summer's end, and I wrote to Berit telling her I would come to fetch her then. This time I got a perfunctory acknowledgement, written by the mistress, assuring me that Berit was well.

Late one evening in early May I slipped away to the stream after my evening chores. It was unusually mild weather but dirty, ice-encrusted snow still lay here and there between the rocky outcroppings. Still, I welcomed the chance to be alone.

He must have been waiting for me.

I barely had tucked myself up against the boulder when he was on me. I opened my mouth but he clamped a large, callused hand over it, stopping my breath, and yanked me down. With his free hand he tore at my clothes, then fumbled briefly with his own. I beat at him with both fists, struggling for air, but it was as if he didn't notice. He pried my legs apart with his knee, pressing down with all his weight on my inner thigh until I feared my leg would break. He choked off my yelp of agony with his hand then forced himself between my legs and entered me. He squeezed both hands over my nose and mouth, pressing my head against the rocky ledge. I thought I would faint. But a split second after he had satisfied himself, he slightly relaxed his grip. I snapped my head sideways and screamed. He rolled off me, cursing.

Within moments we heard footsteps scrambling over the rocks.

"She wanted it," he sneered when they got there. He was on his feet by then. I was still lying there, dazed with shock. They looked darkly from me to him; there must have been half a dozen of them staring at us in awful silence.

Then one of them stepped forward. It was Kalle. Without a word, he threw a punch squarely at Heikki's jaw, knocking him backwards into the little pool. While Heikki struggled to get up, Kalle leaped on top of him and pressed his head under the water. The other men began shouting, and two of them jumped on Kalle to pull him off. He turned on them, fists flying. Then Heikki rose up behind him, sputtering, and clasped his fist together and smashed Kalle in the back of the neck. He fell on his knees in the water. The ones still on the ledge jumped into the fray, cursing and shouting. When at last they had exhausted themselves, they turned to me.

I pulled myself up, steadying myself against the boulder.

"I didn't want it. He raped me." I had learned to my unending sorrow with Inge's birth what would come of failing to speak up immediately, so I said this as firmly as I could, but my voice shook. "Do you understand? He raped me!" I sagged back against the boulder, burying my face in my hands.

Kalle crawled out of the water and hauled himself up to stand beside me, soaked and dripping, his hair plastered flat over his forehead.

"I believe you, Kaisa," he said, for the first time using my given name. He put his arm around my shoulder and led me away.

But in the end, after all was said and all was done, I don't think he ever really did.

Heikki was fired and disappeared, and not long after, Kalle asked me to go south with him.

"The money is better at the Meraaker mine and the climate not nearly so harsh as this. We can have a good life there. I would like to marry you, Kaisa."

Rumors were always flying through the camp about how much better conditions were at some other mine. A mine was a mine as far as I could see. But I confess I was torn by his offer of marriage. I hesitantly showed him the photograph of my children. "I'm afraid they've already forgotten me," I told him tearfully.

He studied it with sympathetic eyes. "As soon as we're on our feet and settled, we'll send for them," he promised.

I had grown to depend on his kindness and could imagine that in time I could come to care for him. Not as I had for Anton, of course. That was another thing entirely. But care for him nevertheless. The truth is, given my circumstances, I felt fortunate to have found him and fearful of letting him go.

But I told him no. "I can't go that far from my children," I explained.

He stalked off and from then on refused to speak to me. His bad humor made me miserable, but I soon enough had far worse things to worry about.

It was unthinkable: I was pregnant again.

Devastated, I lay sleepless in my cot at night, helpless tears sliding down my cheeks. Where could I go? How could I possibly care for another child? I had nowhere left to turn. What was to become of me? And my children? I felt as if I had fallen into a dark well where no one could ever reach me to pull me out. I wanted to die, save for my children. For all practical purposes, I knew I was already dead. Only my body didn't know it.

I never went outside alone even though it was high summer. I sat inside on my cot, the curtain drawn, whenever I had a moment to myself.

Kalle sought me out in my corner one evening when the others were outside. "Kaisa, are you all right?" I didn't open the curtain; he did.

"I'm pregnant," I told him lifelessly.

"Kaisa!" he exclaimed, his eyes large. Someone came in then, and he hurried away. But the next evening he was back, standing stiffly in the kitchen doorway. "I asked you before it happened, so you know I mean it when I ask you again. Come away with me, Kaisa. I want you, regardless."

Astonished, I searched his face. A hand was reaching down into the well. "But my children . . ." I protested.

A shadow furrowed his brow. "We'll send for them," he answered curtly. "Tell me: do you have a better choice?"

His tone should have warned me. But I was too desperate and too relieved to think clearly. "All right," I said, trying to smile.

We left the next day for Tromsø, where he bought me a gold engagement ring. "We'll get married when we're settled in Meraaker," he promised. I pinned what hope I was still capable of summoning on that ring.

We boarded the southbound coastal steamer for Trondheim, where we would catch a little train to Meraaker. The second day, in that Northern light that I had come to love, the Lofoten Wall thrust itself in breathtaking splendor from a glassy sea into a crystalline sky, its sharp spires washed in luminous pinks and brilliant gold. The awesome mass of dark blue rock looked to have exploded from the depths of the sea just to give humans something to cling to. Dwarfed under these massive peaks, tucked into rocky folds and fissures, lay lovely little coves and harbors where tawny fishing boats lay snugly at anchor, their mirrored images reflected in a silky smooth sea. Red grass-roofed cottages clung to pleasing promontories or nestled in soft green meadows that sloped down to a sculpted shoreline. Here and there I saw small boat sheds festooned with garlands of fishing nets and wooden racks adorned with neat rows of drying fish.

I could see why Anton had loved it so. As we steamed southward and the Lofoten Islands disappeared in our wake, I clung to the rail and wept for him, and for us, and for our children. I was beyond weeping for myself.

W hat I most remember about Trondheim is climbing aboard the train, the first I had ever seen. I felt a bit grand despite myself as the little wagons chugged along following a river, the train's whistle tooting importantly. Before long, a broad, green valley opened before us.

"I told you it would be nicer here," Kalle beamed.

He was right. Prosperous, well-tended farms climbed from the lush valley floor up the sloping hillsides, and a green fringe of forest capped the mountains. A plume of dirty smoke rose from the far end of the valley. It was the smelter where Kalle would work. Our lodgings were in a room over a carpentry shop on a farm situated high on a hillside with a fine view of the valley. The landlord's wife treated me sympathetically, and I was as content as I could be so far from my children. I lived for the day we could begin to gather them to us. This would be a fine place to raise them, I thought.

A few months later, in February of 1915, Heikki's child, a curly-haired boy, was born. In February of 1917, Kalle's first daughter was born. We named them Ivar and Gudrid.

But we still weren't married.

Kalle became angry whenever I broached the subject. It was always the wrong time to think of such things. It was always next spring or next fall, when he would have a little more money. "It won't be long now, Kaisa, I promise," he would say, and that usually mollified me.

Likewise, whenever I broached the subject of bringing the other children to live with us, he bristled and gave excuses. "We've got two children to feed already. Where's the money to come from?"

But I noticed that he had plenty of money to drink with his workmates, and he drank more as the months passed. If I voiced disapproval, he flew into a temper. "Hold your peace, woman!" he would shout. He was always sorry later, promising not to do it again and treating me with the sweet charm I remembered—until the next drunken episode.

For a time, I believed his promises. When I no longer did, I avoided facing the question of whether I would have come with him if I had known we would not marry. I was afraid of the answer. And I could not bring myself to tell those I had left behind why I had left them—or that now

I had not just one more illegitimate child, but two. I wrote Berit only to tell her where I was.

A few weeks before Gudrid was born, a letter came addressed in unfamiliar handwriting. "I am risking my post to write you but I can no longer keep my silence in these shocking circumstances," it began.

"I am the maid in the Dahl household where your daughter Berit lives. She is treated abominably by the mistress, worse than a slave. You must send her money at once for passage to get away from this cruel life. I will accompany her as far as Tromsø and see that she gets safely aboard the boat. I will write you in advance so you will know when to expect her in Trondheim so you can meet her there." The letter was signed by someone named Grete Johansen.

I had thought my heart could bear no more. The guilt I wrestled daily rose to nearly overwhelm me, but I could not cry. When Kalle came home that evening, I translated it to him, word for word, since he could not read Norwegian. Then I threw the letter before him on the table.

He looked at me with surly eyes. "Do you know this woman?"

I shook my head.

"So we're to send all this money to a perfect stranger, is that it?" He laughed mirthlessly. "I'm not fool enough to send my money to a stranger on the strength of such a tale, you can be sure of that."

"I have no money of my own to send, as you well know. But you made me a promise, and now I'm asking you to keep it." The calmness in my voice frightened even me.

He jumped from his chair, tipping it over. "Be reasonable!" he snapped. "Where are we going to put another child—and a half-grown one at that! Look at this place!" He gestured around the room, angrily kicking at the upturned chair.

"I've lived in worse," I answered dryly. "So have you, as I understand it."

"We don't have the money!" he shouted, banging his fist on the table. "Can't you understand that?"

"I understand we have enough money to keep you in drink," I answered evenly.

A flush of deep red rose from his neck all the way into his eyes, which flashed dangerously. But I ignored it.

"This is the only one of your promises I will ask you to keep, Kalle. I won't ask you for anything more." The words nearly died on my tongue.

The faces of my children swam before me as I said it: Karl, Paulus, and Inge, their eyes vulnerable and accusing; Berit's merry face hardened into a bitter, tear-stained mask.

Maybe he knew better than to tell me no. Maybe he feared my capacities more than he had call to. In any case, he sullenly relented and sent the money.

Not long after, another letter came. I didn't recognize this handwriting either, and I opened it with trembling fingers. It was from Rantsila, from the parish pastor.

"It is with sadness that I must inform you of your mother's passing. She died just before Christmas in the village poorhouse, where she had been living for some time. She died estranged from her family but not from God. I know He has granted her the forgiveness for her sins that they would not. She was a good, devout woman, deeply repentant of her stiff-necked, strong-willed wickedness and attentive to her religious obligations to the end. May she rest in peace."

I read it over and over, dry-eyed and astounded. He described a woman I didn't know. Perhaps it was one he didn't know either but only hoped existed. She surely had never confided to me that she had repented of my conception. Nor had she let me know that she was living in the poorhouse. Whether from pride or a wish to spare me pain, I would never know. But I hoped it was pride.

I so wanted to believe that my mother, at least, had kept some small measure of *her* self-respect.

BOOK II

UNDER OTERTIND

Berit

FOURTEEN

LOSS

Aghast, she froze in a shaft of sunlight just outside the doorway, eyes wide in disbelief, arms full of washing just down from the line.

I was sitting on the floor next to an empty wooden bucket in a pool of brown, muddy water. It flowed outward from the center of the room where I had dumped it, under the table, up against the black iron legs of our stove and under our beds. Floating in the muck were small clumps of mud, which I had gathered near the barn and rubbed, with great cheerfulness of purpose, into the soft pine floors of our cottage.

"I wanted to wash the floor. But it was too clean, so I had to get it dirty again," I explained with a four-year-old's irrefutable logic.

I looked up at her, first with hope, then with increasing apprehension. After a dreadful moment when I feared the worst, she threw back her head and laughed.

"Oh, Berit!" she gasped. "What have you done?" Then she broke into another wave of rolling, helpless laughter.

I smiled cautiously up at her. I liked to hear my mother laugh; it meant she was glad. But it wasn't clear that this was one of those times.

And little wonder: Mother had just finished scrubbing that floor. Several times a year, she went down on her hands and knees to scrub our floor with sand fetched from the riverbank just beyond our doorstep. This took much time and effort but left the aged boards a gleaming yellow, which is what they had been before I set to my task. I tried to do everything my mother did and had memorized her every motion.

"Just look at this, Berit!" She burst into another gale of laughter. "What am I to do with you? Wait until your father hears about this!"

Certainly she must have laughed after that day. Surely she had occasion to smile at life's little pleasures. But I have no memory of her ever laughing so carelessly again.

A little way up the valley, the river that flowed so gently past our cottage threw itself in a wild rush of spray over a tangled precipice of stone that in some ancient upheaval must have calved off the walls of Otertind. Below these falls were deep, alluring pools.

Salmon swam there.

My father sometimes took me to these falls, a homemade fishing pole in one hand, my hand tightly grasped in the other. He tethered me to a birch tree with a long rope not far from the water's edge. Smiling happily, he cast into the still pool.

"Now pay attention, Berit, and you'll see something!" he promised, his eyes sparkling with delight. I'll never forget his smile; it lit up his whole face.

It was my mother's doing, that rope. "Bell or no bell, she'll run off, mark my words," she admonished my father.

It wasn't true. I could sit still for hours watching my father fish. If I idolized my mother, I worshipped my father. I lived for the moment he came home and I dogged his footsteps from my first waking moment until I dropped into bed, lulled to secure sleep by the low murmur of his warm, melodic voice as he and Mother brought the day to a cozy close.

Fishing was our own special time. The sun warm on my back, I lay on my stomach peering into the pools, searching for the telltale whish of a darting fin, or on my back, watching the clouds drift over Otertind. I could see animals in them, forming and reforming themselves in wisps of white: bears, elk, foxes. Once a real fox came to study us from the other side of the riverbank. He didn't seem the least afraid. He just stood there on the mossy carpet under a cluster of glistening birch trees, the sun glinting off his fur. When I moved, jingling the goat bell, he leaped away into a thicket of leafy branches.

Most of the time I simply sat breathlessly still on the riverbank, waiting for our shared, expectant tension to explode the moment Father's pole bent. Then I would freeze rigid, my fists knotted with unbearable excitement as he battled the fish. Instinctively, I felt every tug and play of the line. When the gleaming fish at last lay flopping at our feet, we laughed gleefully. I was never more proud than when my father and I came home bearing our treasure for the table. We didn't have many such moments together, of course. But they were the most joyous of my life.

My earliest memories of life under Otertind—fishing, running free in the sweet smelling woods, rolling in the grass with my little brother Karl, stirring a bowl of flour and sugar for Mother at the kitchen table—these are the memories I prefer. And if anyone asks about my life then, these are the things I tell them about.

Most people don't ask. They don't want to hear the truth. They can't bear to hear it. I could tell them things they wouldn't believe, if they cared to listen. No one really cares anything about it. Oh, sometimes people pretend to care, to be your friend. They'll treat you so well and make such a fuss over you and get you to confide in them. But you can't depend on them, any of them. They just laugh at you behind your back. Not that I care. I'll not be bending before them. You can depend on that.

Ours were lives such as people nowadays are incapable of imagining— or of bearing. Particularly Hanna. It's true, what they say: blood will tell. She's a useless dreamer, just like her mother.

The cloud that was to blot out our sunny lives under Otertind first settled over us the day my father came home spitting blood. It descended and closed ever thicker around our cottage, darkening our lives in daily increments until nothing could be seen in the suffocating gloom except that my father would die. Even at six I knew it: I saw it in my mother's face. He died on the darkest day of the year. And from the moment I overheard the doctor speaking to my mother, I lived in fear that I too would die.

Afterwards my mother never mentioned my refusal to kiss my father goodbye as he lay pleading on his deathbed, moments from death. She never upbraided me for denying him the comfort that my embrace could have offered him in his final moments of life. Yet my grandmother's verdict rings in my ears: "For shame, for shame!" It haunts me to this day. I cannot forgive myself for refusing my father the only thing he ever asked of me. I loved him so. But I was so afraid.

I've told no one what happened next—Mother's screams in the bed as the men held her down, her lying in the bed the whole day, crying. I recall my own helpless terror as acutely as if it were only moments ago. But sometimes, when Paulus's piercing wails echo in my head, I long for someone to tell.

If I live forever, I will never forget the sight of our stove lying in the snow, our home and our lives tossed out like so much manure on a dung heap. It taught me things, early on, about what to expect from people. I do have that much to thank them for.

I clung ever more tightly to my mother as we tumbled helplessly from one crisis to another, desperately wanting to believe her assurances that our lives would soon be set right. I tried to think of ways to please her, to make her laugh again. But she retreated to a place where I couldn't find her. She looked at me but her eyes weren't there. She had gone someplace else, to a place where I couldn't follow.

And then came the day she herself left.

We were living together, just the two of us, in a tiny cubicle at Mistress Dahl's. We had been going from house to house sleeping in strange beds for so long that I should have been glad for a room to call our own. But I wasn't. I sensed something in the mistress. I have always had a sixth sense about people, but Mother wouldn't listen. And in the beginning, when she was there to keep me out of harm's way, things went well enough.

I was only eight, but I had my responsibilities in the kitchen and barn. I always knew how to work, right from the start. And after Mother gave the others away, I was especially careful to do just as she instructed. I understood that with the baby gone she had less need of me, but I put faith in her promise that she and I would stay together. I tried to forget that she had also promised that Father wouldn't die.

I was old enough to understand that we were destitute. And whatever else I lacked by way of understanding of my mother's fallen standing in the community, the neighboring children soon supplied. Whenever I ventured from the house seeking companionship, they chased me home. "Your mother's a slut!" they shouted as I fled. So I kept to the house with no friends to play with in those rare moments when I did have time to be a child.

The only break in my lonely routine was when the Lapps came through the valley with their reindeer herds on their way to the seacoast. We knew they were on their way down through the pass behind Otertind when we heard their dogs barking. Then came wave after wave of animals, bells tinkling faintly, herders whistling. It was a thrilling sight, one that set my blood to singing. The Lapps looked so free, so proud and fine. I envied them.

Mother had told me the story of how she was sent away by her mother as a child. It made me terrified that I too might be sent away. It never occurred to me that she would be the one to go. If she had dug my defenseless heart from my chest with a kitchen knife it would have hurt less. I wanted to shout: "How can you leave me?" But shock sealed my lips. I stood mute before her, eyes blinded by biting tears. I have not felt such grief since. I can understand why it had to be, these many years later. But I'll never forget that day.

No more had she left me than the mistress, who reigned as she pleased during the long periods when her husband was at sea, blossomed into her true colors. She banished me to the floor near the kitchen stove, where I slept on an old floor mat with one thin blanket over me. She rationed my food, and I lived with perpetual hunger. I had to be satisfied with whatever scraps might be left after everyone else had eaten their fill. As her house help came and left in rapid order, she rode me from morning until night, ordering me to an ever-heavier round of tasks: carrying in wood and water, sweeping floors, emptying ashes. Not a minute of my day was I free of her curt commands and carping criticism. It was as if she were driven to humiliate me.

I was growing and soon had no clothes that weren't too small, patched or ragged. I was hard on clothes, even then. When it came time for me to attend school, I tried to get myself ready as best I could. But when I came hesitantly into the schoolyard that first autumn, I was greeted with mocking hoots. They had always tormented me, but now they seemed to know that I had no one to protect me. Some of them ran toward me, pointing and laughing. "Dirty Lapp rag!" one yelled, hurling a popular insult of the day. When I put my hands up to shield my face from them, they did the same. Then they danced around me, aping my every movement, sticking out their tongues and grimacing. Finally our teacher came to investigate the commotion. They fell away as he strode toward us, leaving me standing there, trembling. He peered haughtily down at me over a long nose from a great height.

"You can't come to school in this condition. Go home and wash your face. Give yourself a good scrubbing with soap and water and come back tomorrow clean. Do you understand?"

I ran away, burning with mortification. I always tried to wash myself as Mother had taught me, but the mistress refused to give me soap. When I came running back to the house, she scowled. "Why aren't you in school?" she demanded.

"The teacher sent me home to wash," I told her breathlessly. "He said I had to scrub with soap."

"Oh, he did, did he? Well, he's not paying your room and board. No one is. So you can just get some ashes from the stove and wash yourself with them. They're good enough for you."

After that, I stopped trying to join the other children in play. I spoke to no one the whole day at school, and when my classmates ran outside to play at our midday meal, I hung back inside the schoolroom, ashamed lest they see the plain crust of bread I had tucked in the pocket of my ragged apron. If the teacher called on me in class, they snickered openly, with the teacher's tacit approval, even before I could form an answer. But the truth is, I rarely knew how to answer correctly and I burned with shame whenever he called on me. I ran home from school at full speed every day to escape them. I never understood why they didn't like me. To this day I don't understand it.

The arrival of the Lapps was a welcome diversion from my misery. They made camp not far from our house, and one day when I found an opportunity to slip away, I ventured close to the collection of skin tents perched in the lee of a little promontory overlooking the fjord. It was a lively scene—dogs and children everywhere, mothers and fathers busy at their tasks, laughter and smoke rising from the tents. I stood a safe distance away, studying them as they went about their business in their fine attire. Something drifting on the light breeze smelled so good that my mouth began to water and my empty stomach growled.

Then I caught sight of a little girl about my own age watching me. She stood quietly in front of a tent, staring directly at me, her face expressionless. I stared back, curious. She wore a tight-fitting cap with a band of embroidery around it and a colorful shawl around her shoulders and pointed-toed boots. I knew I should run away; everyone knew Lapps weren't civilized. But some fascination kept my feet planted. When she started walking toward me, I held my ground. She stopped directly in front of me, still looking hard into my face. Then she smiled shyly and said something I didn't understand. When I didn't answer, she repeated it.

"What?" I finally said, finding my voice.

She shook her head and studied me a moment longer. Then she reached out and took my hand, as naturally as could be, and led me toward the tent, smiling reassuringly all the while. My heart beat rapidly. Was I being kidnapped? I knew the stories about Lapps stealing and selling children. Before this fear could overwhelm me, though, she had pulled me into the tent.

It was so dark in there that at first I couldn't see a thing. But the delicious aroma I had noticed outside filled the tent. As my eyes adjusted, I saw a large black pot over the fire in the center of the floor. A woman and two children were seated around it on a bed of skins. The girl motioned for me to sit down, and she and her mother spoke in words I didn't understand. The mother stirred the pot and handed me a small bowl, a sympathetic look in her brown, almond-shaped eyes.

"Eat," she said in Norwegian.

"Thank you," I mumbled. My hands trembled with nervousness and hunger as I reached for the steaming bowl of stew. I wolfed it down ravenously. To this day I can conjure that taste on my tongue. I've never eaten anything so delicious, before or since. When I was finished, the woman took my bowl and refilled it without a word. When I finished my second helping, she refilled my bowl again, and though I was ashamed of my hunger, I ate that one too.

"Thank you for the food," I remembered to say when finally I was satiated.

The woman lit a pipe and regarded me thoughtfully through little puffs of smoke. I'd never seen such a thing and I gaped at her, fascinated.

"What's your name?" she asked after several long pulls on the pipe.

"Berit Utsi."

"Aahh," she said, nodding with approval. "Utsi." She considered this awhile. "Where do you live?"

"At the Mistress Dahl's." The words were hardly out of my mouth before I sprang up, horror-stricken. I had quite forgotten the mistress.

"I have to go now," I stammered, slipping through the tent flap. I hurried through the encampment on anxious heels but paused at its edge for one last look. The little girl was standing beside the tent again, staring after me. She raised her hand in farewell, and I waved back. Then I broke into a run, terrified and thrilled at once.

The mistress sent me to bed without supper. Defiantly, I confessed where I had been but prudently not what I had eaten. "Keep away from those dirty Lapps!" she fumed.

I didn't protest, but I knew what I knew. The Lapps had treated me kindly when everyone else was cruel. I would never forget it.

Letters came from my mother, which the mistress or one of the maids, each sympathetic or indifferent to their own degree, would read to me. I listened to them in stony silence. They were full of promises that she would come for me soon. I believed none of them. I stopped believing her the day she abandoned me. A bitter anger had taken root in my heart, compounded by inexpressible loneliness. At night, when I was sure no one could hear me, I cried myself to sleep. Yet I was desperate to believe she would come for me after all. At last, in late spring, the letter came that I had been waiting for. "I'll come for you at summer's end, dear Berit," she wrote. "It won't be long now."

So I began to count the days.

And when summer began to fade, I stole away whenever I could to sit by the side of the road, my eyes straining to see her approaching, her arms held out to me, a loving smile on her face. My head was filled with happy fantasies about our new life in Tromsø. Summer was waning, and she had promised to come.

But she didn't.

My hope withered and died as the autumn leaves shriveled and fell from the trees. The first frost had killed the grass—and hardened my heart once more—before a letter finally came. Grete, the latest in the endless parade of maids, read it to me.

"My dearest daughter Berit," she wrote. "I pray all is well with you. I am now living in a place called Meraaker far to the south. There is better work here in the mine for the man I am engaged to marry. His name is Kalle and he has promised that you and the other children shall come to live with us here soon. He is a good man who can provide for us all. I know I promised to come for you but I hope you can understand that this will be for the best. I long for you more than you can know, dear Berit, and count the days until we are reunited. Your loving Mother."

I stared uncomprehendingly into Grete's face. Surely there must be some mistake.

"Marriage indeed!" the mistress snorted. "I suppose I'm never to be rid of you. It's costing me money to keep you here and I'm getting precious little in return. I should never have agreed to it."

Grete sucked in her breath but her eyes flashed. A lively redhead, she had taken pity on me. She lent me her soap, washed my hair and combed it, and helped me keep my clothes clean. At night, after our work was done, she helped me with my lessons.

"The child's a good worker, Mrs. Dahl, far beyond her years, especially for being so small for her age. She's a great help to me."

"And what business is it of yours?"

Grete bit her lip, color rising under her freckled cheeks, and turned to stir something on the stove. "It's shameful how she's treated," she finally said in a low, indignant voice.

The mistress glared at her, eyes snapping dangerously. "I'll thank you to concern yourself with the duties I pay you to concern yourself with, Miss." I thought the mistress would fire her on the spot, but she may have been mindful of how difficult it had become for her to find help. In any case, after that the mistress seemed even more defiant in her cruelty toward me. But I saw that I could depend on Grete. She was my only friend in the world.

Not that I had forgotten my brothers. I had sealed my heart against my mother, but my longing for my brothers never ceased. Whenever I looked at their faces in the photograph at the chapel, I wondered if they were as miserable as I. And I worried that they would forget me. I was eleven years old when I made up my mind to visit them. By then, I had thought out a plan for our future. I would start with Inge and Karl in Signaldal.

"But it's such a long way," Grete exclaimed dubiously when I disclosed my plan to visit them.

"I know the way," I told her confidently. "I went with my mother to see them. If the mistress will let me go on Saturday morning I can be back by Sunday night. Can't you ask her?" I pleaded. But she looked dismayed, so I shared the rest of my plan.

"As soon as I grow up, I'm going to fetch them to live with me," I explained. In the long, empty days since I had come to understand that my mother would never return, I had reached one conclusion: I would take care of my brothers if she would not. I, at least, would not abandon them. We would be a family again. They could depend on me.

Grete looked at me sadly but somehow wheedled permission from the mistress. So the next Saturday, I set out under an overcast sky. It was getting on to fall, the cusp of the season when anything could happen with the weather, and Grete saw me off with concern in her eyes. "Be home before dark!" she called after me.

I had no intention of being out alone after dark. I knew what beasts lurked in the woods at night: wolves, wolverines, bears, trolls. The woods where I felt so at home in daylight were alive with evil creatures at night. More than once I had felt them around me in the darkness, stirring or snarling in the bushes. But that day, I skipped quickly along with a light heart, and before I knew it I came to the place where the path turned to follow the river into Signaldal. As the familiar valley opened before me, so did an unexpected rush of painful memories. When I first saw our cottage, I stopped. It looked just as I remembered it. It was deserted, and I hurried past.

When Jenny opened the door to me, her mouth dropped. "Berit! Can it really be you?" Both of our eyes fell on Inge, hiding behind her skirts, his thumb in his mouth. He peered curiously up at me with dark, sparkling eyes under a thick thatch of black hair.

I stared back in shock. He had grown so big! "Do you think he remembers me?" I asked hesitantly.

Jenny pushed him toward me. "He's almost four now, you know. Can you say hello to your sister?" she prodded. He hung back but it wasn't long before he warmed up to me.

"When I'm grown, Inge's going to live with me," I announced as I bounced him on my lap. Jenny's eyebrows shot up and her face tightened but she made no comment. As I continued up the valley to see Karl, I realized after seeing Inge that Karl would be bigger than I remembered him. Still, I was not prepared for the sight of the athletic nine-year-old boy who came running out of the trees behind the house when he saw me walking up the road. He stopped a few meters away and regarded me with a serious expression. He was tall for his age, lithe and blond, and already I could see how handsome he would become.

"Hello, Karl," I said shyly. I wanted to hug him.

He smiled shyly in return.

"Do you remember me?"

"Yes," he answered. He had a friendly face.

"Have they been good to you here?" I asked formally.

He nodded and looked at his shoes.

"I came to tell you that when I'm grown, you'll live with me. You and Inge and Paulus. We'll be a family again."

He didn't say anything. Then I saw someone watching us from the doorway. It was Marianne and a little girl I'd never seen before. They waited there as we walked together toward the house.

"Oh, Berit, I'm so glad you've come," Marianne said, embracing me. "I've so often wondered how you've been keeping." Her eyes traveled over my face and clothes and I could see that she did not approve.

"I've been so worried about your mother." She began ransacking the cupboard to set out a feast of meats and fish. "I do hope this marriage is for the best," she sighed. "She deserves some happiness after all she's been through."

I ate rapidly, without speaking, until my stomach ached. When I looked up from my plate, it was to see them all staring at me. They had finished eating long ago.

"Have you seen anything of your aunt and uncle?" Marianne asked.

I must have looked blank.

"Erik and Hansine. Have you seen them?"

When I shook my head, she drew her lips in a tight line. "Strange," she muttered. Then, in a voice so low I barely heard it: "Shameful."

"I think you're a little too harsh, Marianne," Johan admonished quietly. "Look at all the children of their own they have to provide for—what is it now, ten or eleven?"

"Ten, I think, with the last one. What was it they called her? Inga?" She sighed. "I suppose you're right. With children it's either feast or famine. I should feel for Hansine, I suppose," she added dubiously. "They do have the means to care for them all, at any rate."

Before I left the next day, Karl proudly showed me his fishing pole and then took me to one of his favorite fishing spots on the river, just across the road from the house. Perdy, the little orphaned girl who also lived with them now, tagged along. I could see she idolized Karl, and I noticed with a sharp stab of jealousy that he was very protective of her.

We sat on a rock and I watched him fish, just as I had Father. "Do you remember our father?" I asked after some time had passed.

"Yes," he answered noncommittally.

"Do you remember fishing with him?"

"Once," he nodded. "He turned to smile at me when he hooked the fish. That's all I remember, his smile. I can't remember what he looked like."

I didn't mention our mother, and neither did he.

They all stood on the stoop waving farewell when I set out. "I'll come back and get you," I whispered to Karl when we said goodbye.

How could I have known how many years would pass before we would meet again?

On the way back home, I slowed, then stopped, at our cottage, drawn to it despite myself. I looked about uncertainly before stepping cautiously across the little yard. I stood on my tiptoes and peered in the window.

The planks that served as the bed on which my father died and on which my mother was brutalized were still fastened to the wall. The floor she had so lovingly scrubbed clean was as blackened with grime as that day I baptized it with muddy water. The barn where we kept Palma stood empty, the door askew. The ground my parents had so carefully cultivated was overgrown with grass. The small sauna still stood near the river, its door ajar. A broken wooden bucket lay near the riverbank where, morning and night, summer or winter, my mother fetched our water. Nothing else of our lives remained.

I finally stumbled away under heavy, menacing clouds that had poured into the valley while I had been lost in reverie, oblivious to the passage of time and the sharp drop in temperature. By the time I reached the valley bottom, darkness had fallen. I could barely see the road under my feet and I was uncertain as to which way to turn. So I finally stood still, my heart racing. Should I go right or left? "It must be this way," I told myself aloud to bolster my courage. I set off to the right, eyes vainly searching for landmarks, ears alert to the slightest sound. I had not walked far before I saw dim lights a way off. They were in the wrong place, I concluded, so it must be back the other way after all. I retraced my steps, hurrying as fast as I could in the blackness. What if I was lost? What if wolves—or worse—attacked me? At every rustle of a bush, every sigh of a tree, I stood stock-still, shivering with cold and fear.

There wasn't the slightest warning. Suddenly a blinding ball of lightning exploded in front of my feet. It broke open the darkness, illuminating the landscape in a bright, cold flash. The ground shook. I was paralyzed, awaiting destruction as thunder cracked overhead. But nothing happened. Thick, black silence wrapped itself around me again.

And then I heard it, almost like a tiny baby crying. "Mew, mew, mew!" It was coming nearer. I remained immobilized, waiting to be snatched up by fearsome fangs. Then I felt something rub against my legs. I jumped, shrieking.

"Mew, mew," it cried again, stubbornly nuzzling my ankle.

I bent down to touch it, to assure myself it wasn't a troll's trick. A cat, black as the night itself, had found me out here.

"Kitty, kitty," I said shakily, stroking its back. "What are you doing out here all alone?"

For answer, it ran a few steps ahead, then stopped to mew at me. When I caught up, it ran on a few more steps, then stopped to make sure I was following.

I understood then. The cat had been sent to help me find my way home. Suffused with relief, I stepped along behind it, confident I was being led the right way. Before long I saw the lights I was looking for. I ran along the familiar road, the cat trotting ahead. Just before I reached the yard, it bounded off into the darkness and disappeared.

I called after it, and at the sound of my voice, the door flew open and the mistress filled the doorway. I had quite forgotten her in my terror. Still, she was less frightening than a bolt of lightning. Besides, I now understood, I had special protection.

"You were supposed to be home before dark!" she remonstrated. I didn't answer but slid past her into the kitchen, where Grete regarded me with concern. "Answer me when I speak to you!" the mistress shouted.

"I got lost," I answered simply.

"Lost!" She glared at me.

I thought she should know who she was trifling with. "A bolt of lightning exploded right in front of me, but a cat came to show me the way home."

My tone must have made it clear that I dared her to doubt me, for she stared at me as if confounded. I had never talked back to her. I had always borne her misuse as if it were my due. Now I knew it wasn't.

She must have sensed the change in me, because she turned the screws more tightly. "Wipe that look off your face!" she commanded whenever she caught me staring at her with undisguised hatred blazing in my eyes. She became ever more merciless in her demands, assigning me tasks I could never hope to finish in the allotted time. Finally Grete pulled me aside.

"We have to write to your mother about what's happening here," she told me. I received occasional letters from her and could write myself now. But I never wrote to her. For one thing, I had no money for postage or paper. For another, I had nothing to say to her.

"Why? She doesn't care."

"Of course she cares." I knew Grete well enough to hear the doubt in her voice. "She simply must send you the money to join them."

I turned my face away. "She won't. She doesn't want me."

"I'm going to write to her myself," she said firmly. "I can't bear to see this go on."

"I don't care what you do. It's nothing to me. She won't send for me." But in a hidden corner of my heart, a tiny spark of hope rekindled.

The day Mother's letter arrived, I opened it with unsteady fingers. When the money fell out of the envelope, my eyes flew to Grete's face, searching for confirmation. Could it be true? Did she want me with her after all? Painstakingly, I made out the words.

"I look forward with great gladness to having you with me again after all these lonesome years," she wrote. I read it over and over, to be sure I understood it right.

Grete wrote Mother well in advance to let her know when I would arrive. I was on pinpricks, barely able to sleep at night. Could it be that I was really about to escape my hellish existence and embrace my mother once more? It was like a dream, and I lived in fear of waking. Not until the morning Grete and I boarded the boat for Tromsø did I believe I was going to see Mother again. I ran up the gangplank, heart thumping with excitement. And when I first caught sight of the city, I had to hold tight to the railing to contain myself. It was so grand! With Grete beside me, I walked through the busy streets, open-mouthed with wonder at the tall buildings and fine people going in and out of them.

"Close your mouth when you're staring," Grete admonished, laughing. She had washed my hair and carefully rewoven the long braids that hung to my waist. But I knew I still made a ragged spectacle in my worn coat and too-short dress.

Grete steered me to a grand building. "Here's the new cinema." She read the billing and flashed a sudden smile. "Would you like to see a film? There's plenty of time before the boat leaves. It will be my farewell treat to you."

Of course I was thrilled, though I had no precise idea what a cinema was. We were no more than seated when I nearly fell out of my chair: music suddenly began to play in the darkened theatre. And at the first flash of a jerkily-moving image on the screen, I jumped to my feet. "Oh!" I shouted. "Look!" The audience erupted into laughter and Grete pulled me back into my seat.

"Shush! Just watch," she cautioned, but I was uncontrollable. A comically dressed man with a mustache and cane was taking pratfalls, and I hooted with delight at his every misadventure. When danger lurked, I leaped from my seat, my fists knotted. "Look out!" I shouted.

"It's not real," Grete whispered, trying to calm me. But it was no use. I was captivated. When we emerged from the theatre, I was so flushed with excitement that I hardly could collect my senses. Grete led me down to the dock, where the coastal steamer lay waiting. She followed me on board to show me to my place, and I felt as if I were in a grand dream, my whole existence turned on its head.

Grete embraced me, sniffling a little. "Safe journey and a happy life, Berit. Write me when you arrive, promise?" Then she was gone. Not until I had put my little cloth bundle of provisions beside me on the wooden bench did I fully grasp that I was on my own. I was twelve years old.

The trip south is a blur. I made myself a bed on the table only to roll off when the ship began to pitch from side to side. The next day the ship picked its way through a sea of mountains. "Lofoten," someone said, and passengers trooped on deck to see. I followed. I remembered Lofoten. This was the place that had killed my father, so they said. I stood on deck in a stiff wind under a dirty sky, staring at the fantastic peaks that shot out of the sea. I tried to imagine him in this strange place, pulling in nets filled with fat fish. I hung on the railing a long time, until I grew too cold and sad to bear it.

When the ship at last docked in Trondheim I was rigid with anticipation. Long rows of bustling warehouses lined a quiet seaway, and in the background the spires of a large stone church rose against gentle green hills. But I hardly noticed.

My eyes were riveted on the expectant throng that stood on the dock looking up at us. I anxiously scanned the crowd, searching for her face. The gangplank was lowered and the passengers started down but I stood where I was, searching, heart thudding heavily. I held my hand over my eyes to shade the spring sunlight. She must be there somewhere.

Finally I scampered down the gangplank with my bundle into the thinning crowd, staring intently into the face of every woman I encountered. What if she didn't recognize me? Or I her?

The crowd quickly melted away, leaving only the crew busily unloading and loading cargo. Why wasn't she here to meet me? What should I do? Where could I go in search of her in this large, strange city? I knew no one. I stood utterly alone on that dock clutching my bundle, helpless and terribly afraid. I paced nervously back and forth, craning my neck to look along a street that led to town. She must be coming this way, I reasoned. Surely she would be here soon.

I sank down on an empty crate, numb with fear and despair. An awful, stomach-cramping eternity passed, perhaps an hour.

Then I saw her.

At first, I didn't understand who it was. She carried a baby in one arm and with the other clasped the hand of a small, dark-haired boy who walked solemnly beside her. A light-haired man stumbled unsteadily along behind them. But her carriage was as erect as it always had been. That's how I recognized her.

I rose to my feet. She stopped a meter from where I stood, heart racing.

"Hello, Berit," she said in a tone I didn't recognize. She offered me a tight little smile. "Welcome." She didn't move to embrace me.

I ached to fling myself into her arms, but she was unrecognizable, distant. Her eyes were not the eyes I remembered, nor was her face. There were hard lines around her mouth and eyes that I had never before seen there.

"Hello, Mother," I murmured shyly, swallowing hard. "I'm so glad you came." I could barely force out the words. "I was so afraid you weren't coming."

Her face tightened and she looked at the man accusingly. But all she said was: "This is Kalle, Berit. He'll look after us now. He sent the money for your fare."

Kalle swayed slightly and pulled the corners of his mouth up under his mustache. His eyes were gray and cold. He nodded but said nothing.

"I'm sorry you had to wait, but Kalle was detained and we couldn't get here any sooner," Mother added, giving him a bitter look I'd never seen on her face.

"You're so grown up," she said, her tone softened with wonder and, I thought, sadness. When she saw me eyeing the children with what must have been obvious amazement, she said, "Their names are Gudrid and Ivar. Your half-brother and half-sister."

I stared at them in disbelief.

"Let's go, then," Kalle cut in impatiently, grabbing Ivar's hand. When we had gone a few meters, Mother turned to me and slipped her hand in mine. "I'm so glad you're here at last," she told me quietly. This time when she smiled her eyes did too, for a brief moment radiating the familiar warmth I had so missed these four long years.

I was glued to my seat as the train began to roll down the tracks. Never had I known anything so fine as this! I smiled from ear to ear, giddy with speed and relief.

Once, when I caught Mother studying me wistfully as we sped along, she smiled and patted my arm. For a moment, I thought I saw tears in her eyes, but I may have imagined it. She was not the mother I remembered, but she seemed glad to see me, I concluded. This time I would take no chances. I would make myself indispensable to her.

Our quarters, above a carpenter's shop, were crowded. But I luxuriated in being with my mother and tending to her every need. My formal education was over but I was well schooled in working from morning until night, and I flew through my chores with the lightest of hearts. Only Kalle's brooding, unpredictable presence tempered my joy.

That summer there was trouble at the mine. The men worked ten hours a day, and after a Finn came to speak to the workers about the injustice of it, there was a work stoppage.

"They always expect Finns to do the dirtiest, most dangerous work for the least pay. It's time we stood up for ourselves," Kalle said when he came home from the demonstration. My mother watched him non-committally but with troubled eyes.

I had only recently learned that she had changed her name. People called her Karin now, not Kaisa, and she and Kalle used the last name Nelson. When I asked her why, she was evasive.

"People don't care much for Finns, Berit," she finally said. "Many people think we should be sent back to Finland. They're afraid we'll join with the Russians to take over North Norway. So Kaisa just causes trouble. People look down on you with a name like that."

One late fall day Kalle startled us by storming angrily through the door at mid-day. Mother was at the stove; I was feeding the children.

"Pack up. We're leaving," he told us curtly.

Mother stared at him in bewilderment. "What's happened?" she asked, searching his face.

"They've given me the boot."

"But why?"

"Me and a few others, all Finns, of course. They take exception to our organizing activities. We're just trying to get decent working conditions. We deserve that much. But they call the tune, so there you are." He spat out the words as if they tasted vile.

Mother looked at him in consternation. "But what can we do, then?"

"We'll go to Sulitjelma. There's plenty of work there."

"Sulitjelma?" Mother said doubtfully. "Where's that?"

"A mine north of here. Near Bodø."

"That far north?" Suddenly she was interested. I knew what she was thinking: the boys.

We set out for the train station the next morning, carrying luggage and knapsacks strapped to our backs. It was snowing lightly, but Mother paused briefly on the lip of the high hill where we had lived for a last look at the pleasant valley that lay at our feet far below. "I liked it here," she said regretfully.

"Me, too, " I told her. "But maybe Sulitjelma will be just as nice," I added, anxious to cheer her.

When I imagine Hell, I think of Sulitjelma. The only difference I can see is that it was harder to get to Sulitjelma.

I do think of Hell from time to time, as all good Christians should, and of the people who are going there. They're rich, mostly. It's the money that turns them into devils. As soon as they get it, they turn their backs on ordinary folk, the poor, hardworking, honest ones. But we'll have our just rewards and they'll have theirs, you can depend on that. The Mistress Dahl, for example. That one got a good taste of what she deserved the day her husband drowned at sea. She went wild with grief, they say. Finally lost her mind, and people thought it was awful. But I laughed when I heard it, years later. I knew all along that one day she'd pay for her cruelty to me.

We got off the steamer in Bodø and boarded a small boat that took us inland up a river, then along a lake. When we had gone so far that the lake was frozen solid, we got off the boat and boarded a small train that ran right on the icebound lake itself. Every spring, the railroad tracks had to be torn up before the rail bed melted and sank. In summer, people and supplies were portaged over hill and dale between the waterways that connected the isolated settlement of Sulitjelma with the coast.

The town clung to a rocky outcrop on the edge of another long, thin lake. The whole business—mine, town and lake—was buried in a narrow cleft of stone surrounded by magnificent mountains. It should have been beautiful and probably once was.

But everything had died.

A thick plume of acrid smoke belched from the smelter and lay gathered in folds, suffocating the valley under an opaque, poisonous blanket. It rose to nestle against the denuded hillsides, smothering every living thing down to the last lichen. The trees that had not been felled to fuel this enterprise had been killed by the fumes that rose from the Devil's own smelting furnace. The lake where fish once swam was now stained with wastes. It too had died, and every wild animal within breathing distance had long since died or fled. Only the wind seemed alive. It howled down from the mountains with the fury of an avenging angel, sandpapering our faces with icy grit, choking us in swirling billows of dust, freezing our lungs to our bones.

They say that when the Lapps got wind of what lay in store for their ancient reindeer foraging ground near the mine, one of them put a curse on it. "The day the church spire is raised in Sulitjelma is the day Sulitjelma will be laid to waste," the old Lapp prophesied. So the usual spire was never built on that church, which stands to this day on a ledge overlooking the town. A cross was erected on top instead.

They tried to fool the old Lapp, but it didn't work. It never does. You can't fool Lapps. They know things. You'd have to be blind not to see that the old Lapp's curse came true.

For all of that, there was reason to be happy that we were living in Sulitjelma: we didn't have to live with Kalle. He got on at the smelter straightaway, but smelter workers were required to live in the squalid barracks with the other men. Of course, the people who ran the mines built themselves fine houses on the hillside overlooking the lake a good distance from the smelter. Mother immediately found work as a live-in maid. Understandably, good house help was hard to come by in that place and they accepted all of us without grumbling. I was to look after the children while Mother worked, but I also made myself useful with the daily chores.

These houses were the finest I'd ever seen. There were many rooms—ours had a large formal dining room, a drawing room with a piano for after-dinner conversation and entertainment, and a separate smoking room for the men and their fat, stinking cigars. There was even indoor plumbing with a separate toilet for us under the stairs. We had a sizable bedroom of our own with a sink and closet. They treated us properly and fed us well, and our room was a cozy, blessed haven.

But there was trouble at this mine as well. The men from the mines were not allowed near the houses. A fence had been put up to keep them out. I was glad for it, and I sensed my mother was too. It was hard for Kalle to get permission to visit us, and when he came, he was on his sweetest behavior. I could see at these times how my mother might have imagined in the beginning that he was a different man from the one I knew.

In summer, we sometimes climbed a steep, narrow footpath behind the house to bathe in a large, icy pool in the bare rocks. It was a refuge from the inhospitable ugliness that surrounded us on all sides. Once, shortly after we arrived, Mother and Kalle took us on an outing up in the hills on the far end of town, high above the death line, where trees still grew and where marshy, rolling tundra stretched toward clean, white mountains. I felt as if I had climbed out of a grave.

On April 1, 1918, a snowy Monday, my mother dressed the children in the best she had for them and marched us all up to the church with quiet, fierce determination. Kalle followed in his best suit and an air of irritated resignation. Mother and Kalle presented three-year-old Ivar and one year-old Gudrid to the pastor for baptism. Afterwards, she took Kalle and Gudrid, but not Ivar and me, to the photographer for a family portrait to mark the event.

That was the day I realized that Kalle was not Ivar's father.

Suddenly I was full of troubling questions I knew my taciturn mother would never answer. She never spoke of the past. Not once had she mentioned Signaldal or my father. And she never made the slightest reference to the life she had lived while we were apart.

Only once, not long after I came to live with her in Meraaker, did she ask me about my life during those years. I described it, hot with anger, while she listened impassively. Until I mentioned the soap and ashes. Then she put her head in her arms on the table and wept.

"I'm so sorry, Berit, so terribly sorry," she sobbed.

We never spoke of it again.

Four days after the children were baptized, all hell broke loose in Sulitjelma. There was always an undercurrent of strife and dissension at the mines, as the workers felt ill used. And so they were, if you ask me. Their working conditions were dreadful, even I could see that. But that's what you can expect from the rich—they just live to take advantage of the poor. And it seemed the Finns were especially put upon, to hear Kalle tell it, anyway. We knew he worked long, hard hours at the smelter, and I think that's one reason Mother put up with his drinking. She knew from her time at Birtavarre just how bad the mine work was, and she sympathized with the miners. She understood the feelings of hopelessness and frustration that led them to behave poorly.

The first we knew of the trouble that day was when hundreds of shouting men came running down the road from the mine works, roaring with anger. The tumult of their fury reverberated against the stony, snow-clad walls above the street and echoed across the still lake. The boiling mass rolled to a stop at the railway station just below the embankment of the house where we lived. We ran out into the yard to peer down over the fence at the commotion below.

"Police have come up after one of them, a troublemaker of some kind," someone shouted. "But they're not going to let the policeman take him."

It was impossible to tell what was happening. We could hear someone shouting orders, then someone else shouting threats, then a surge of noise as the crowd pressed forward. Later, people said the crowd disarmed the policeman and sent him packing.

A few days later four hundred military troops arrived to put the whole town under house arrest. Sulitjelma was aflame with gossip, but I understood none of it. I only knew something wonderfully exciting was happening. Mother, for her part, was openly worried.

"I just hope Kalle isn't mixed up in it," she told me. "We can't afford to have him lose his job."

But he did.

One afternoon in the fall of 1919 Kalle knocked on the kitchen door. I opened it to him, and Mother came to stand in the doorway. He stood on the stoop, cap respectfully in hand.

"They're laying us off. Some of us, anyway. The ones they've got no use for, if you take my meaning." He paused. "They've let me go." He spoke guardedly, his eyes watchful lest someone overhear.

For the briefest moment I thought she would slam the door in his face. Maybe she did too. But the moment passed.

"What will you do?" she asked him, betraying no emotion.

He looked earnestly up into her face. "I've decided to try the fishery. There's always some kind of work with the fish."

"Fishery? Where?"

"Aalesund."

"Aalesund?" She grimaced.

"It's got a big fishing fleet . . ."

"But you've never fished . . ."

"I have to try something else, Kaisa. Mines give out but the fish never do." His eyes were pleading now. "Will you come with me?"

I'll remember her silence forever. We stood there in perfect stillness, he and I, reading her face. "No!" I wanted to shout. But I just held my breath, praying.

Maybe he sensed she was preparing to play for time, preparing a bargain: You go and find work, we'll follow when you have it.

"This mine's finished," he quickly continued. "It's only a matter of time, and not much of that. When it closes, the fine people in this house will go too. Think about that, Kaisa. What will you do then, with three children to support?"

Another long silence. Then a slight nod of assent from her.

"Will we marry, then?" she suddenly asked, stony faced.

In my shock at hearing these words, I almost missed the shadow that crossed his face. But he recovered quickly.

"Just as soon as we get settled in Aalesund, Kaisa."

He looked so sincere that even I, stunned as I was by the news that they were not married, almost believed him.

Fifteen

Aalesund

We first saw Aalesund through wisps of white cloud from the deck of the coastal steamer. It lay on a peninsula below a steep promontory with the open sea on one side and a wide fjord on the other. On an island opposite this promontory, a sharply pointed peak rose from the sea. Along the fjord lay mountains capped that day with a thin frosting of snow.

After Sulitjelma, Aalesund looked like heaven to me. There were especially fine buildings everywhere. "They rebuilt everything in cement and stone after the big fire. Eight hundred wooden houses burned down and ten thousand people were made homeless," Kalle explained. "Even Kaiser Wilhelm helped them," he snorted.

"When was that?" I asked, stumbling along wide-eyed, laden with our luggage. There were fishing boats everywhere, jockeying for position against a long row of warehouses, and the sharp smell of fish and creosote hung in the air.

"In 1904, the year you were born," he replied, eyeing me in a way I did not like. I had just turned fifteen and lately he seemed to take new notice of me.

Mother also seemed cheered by the sight of Aalesund. We had no trouble finding lodgings, but work for Kalle was another matter. Every day he set off to look for a job, but his bad luck held. Day after day, he returned empty handed. Some days he didn't return until late at night, very drunk. The town was full of gloomy men lounging on street corners, hands in pockets, their eyes hard, and Kalle soon found new companions.

"There's no decent work for a man in this town," he fumed despondently.

"But they always need women to salt and pack the herring," Mother answered one day a few weeks after we arrived. "And then the cod." I sensed she had been waiting for this moment. "I know they're needing women to work in the fish packing plants out on the docks at Skarbøvik," she continued matter-of-factly. "Berit can look after the house and children while I'm at work."

He stared at her dully, defeat showing in his eyes, but he had no alternative to offer. So we moved to Skarbøvik, a tiny community clustered around a large fish packing plant just across a narrow expanse of fjord south of town. The little hamlet was nestled under the shadow of the pointed peak, which people called Sugartop. In those days, before the bridge was built, we had to row, or ride a little ferryboat, across the narrow inlet to get to Aalesund.

We took a small apartment in the basement of a house perched on a grassy knoll not far from the bustling packing plant where the boats unloaded their glistening cargo fresh from the sea. The house was surrounded by farms and meadows dotted with grazing sheep and cows. I instantly felt at home. We had a lovely view of the bay and the town, and at night I marveled at the city lights that lit it up and sparkled on the still water of the fjord.

"I like it here, don't you?" I confided to Mother the first day as we were unpacking our belongings. I so desperately wanted her to be happy.

She smiled wearily and patted my arm. "It's certainly much nicer than Sulitjelma. We just have to hope that everything will turn out for the best."

She went to the dock early the next morning. She returned late in the evening, stinking of herring and salt, bleeding fingers raw, cracked and swollen. She carried home part of her day's pay: a string of small, fat herring. She sank into a chair next to the stove, ignoring the sullen Kalle as well as the supper I held ready for her.

"It's difficult work," she sighed quietly. This wasn't like her. She never complained. But I had never seen her look so exhausted.

"Your hands look so sore, Mother. Let me get something to put on them."

"My back is worse," she answered grimly. "But I'll get used to it. "

My mother would spend the next thirty-five years bent over herring and cod, first on the docks in fair weather and foul, then indoors stirring saucepots and tending steaming vats. She was to stand bent all day, year in and year out, as the unending stream of fish swam past, until she was well into her seventies.

Kalle soon disappeared. After a futile attempt to persuade Mother to join him, he left us to look for work at another mine in the north. She had reached some turning point, perhaps because she saw that here she could support us herself. "I'll never live at a mine again," she told him. "It's no place for children. I have work here to support us."

"I'll send money as soon as I can," he promised.

He didn't, of course. But I was delighted to see him go and Mother's spirits seemed to lighten as well. She began to smile and hum again. She made friends among the women on the dock and soon became known as a woman of exacting standards who always expected her children to be on their best behavior. "Don't run in the meadows," she called out sternly whenever one of the younger ones trampled through a neighbor's field. And she was a stickler for cleanliness. "The outside of the door should be just as clean as the inside," she told us as she briskly swept the steps, walkway and grass outside our apartment. She had always done it, ever since I was a child in our cottage in Signaldal.

From earliest dawn to long past dark, she labored uncomplainingly to house and feed us. Even now I can see her, staggering up the hill homewards in fair weather and foul, carrying a string of fish or hauling a sack of coal across her back, doggedly putting one foot in front of the other.

Mother was on good terms with our upstairs neighbor Oddfrid Hansen, a sweet-spirited soul who was mother to a boisterous clan of nine children, seven of them boys. Oddfrid's husband was a carpenter, an unsmiling man who bristled sternly behind a stiff mustache. Their household was in constant commotion. Some of the older boys had already left home and gone to sea, others were apprenticing with their father. Since Oddfrid and I were at home during the day while the others worked, we became friends. I have her to thank for showing me how to use a sewing machine. I envied the young girls I saw in town, strolling along in fine dresses arm in arm with their young men, and was determined to learn to make elegant dresses for myself. No young man was likely to take an interest in me in the rags I was forced to wear. I had seen the sneering looks other girls gave me whenever I was around young people. I was well used to that. As for the young men, they didn't seem to see me at all.

I was seventeen when I first laid eyes on Oddfrid's eldest son Edvard. He was twenty-five, a handsome, dark-haired, debonair seaman who had seen much of the world. I'd heard plenty of talk about him, of course, none of it good.

He had come home while I was out on an errand. When I ran up to his mother's kitchen to borrow something, I found him sitting at the kitchen table with a coffee cup in one hand, nattily dressed in a white shirt with dark trousers and vest, tie loose at the collar, eating my mother's lefse. His mother hovered at his elbow.

"And who do we have here?" he asked, eyeing me from under raised eyebrows. I caught a faint whiff of beer on his breath.

Blushing, I mumbled my name, unaccountably embarrassed.

"Her mother made the lefse you're eating," Oddfrid beamed. "Isn't it delicious?"

"That it is," he agreed. "Can you make lefse this good, then?" he teased, his icy blue eyes twinkling.

I blushed a deeper shade. "No, not yet."

"That's a pity. If you did, I'd have to marry you at once." He smiled wickedly and took a swallow from his cup, watching me over its rim.

"Oh, Edvard, how you talk!" Oddfrid protested. She shook her head in mock exasperation. "Don't pay him any mind, Berit. All the girls are mad for him and he's completely shameless."

I stood my ground, both irritated and fascinated, staring hard at him as he turned back to his food. "You said it yourself," I thought to myself. "You said it yourself."

I admit it: from that moment on, I set my will against his will. He would marry me. As surely as I knew the sun rose each morning and set each night, I knew it would come to be. It was only a matter of time. Meanwhile, Mother would just have to help me learn to make perfect lefse.

At first I kept my plan to myself, simply marveling at how unexpectedly it had been revealed to me and savoring the prospect of my coming triumph. Wait until the other girls saw me march off to the altar with Edvard on my arm! I wouldn't be an object of their fun after that! True, Edvard went back to sea without so much as another word to me. Still, I was bursting to tell Mother.

"There's something I want to tell you," I confided one evening after the others were in bed. I tried to keep my voice normal but she gave me an anxious look. "I'm going to marry Edvard," I announced. I drew myself up as tall as I could. I was still pitifully short though amply developed, more so than most girls my age.

Mother's jaw dropped and the blood drained from her face. "What?"

"He doesn't know it yet. But it's going to happen."

She searched my face. "What are you saying, child?"

"I'm not a child! I'm just saying I know that we'll get married one day, that's all."

Relief flooded her face. "Berit, Berit. Don't you think he'll have something to say about that?" She smiled now, giving me that amused, puzzled look I knew so well. Sometimes she looked at me as if she didn't know who I was or what to make of me.

"When the time comes, he'll do it. He told me in front of his own mother that if I made lefse as well as you, he'd have to marry me."

She chuckled and patted my arm. "Oh, Berit, he was just teasing you. Edvard is an incorrigible ladies' man. Everyone knows it. I hate to think of the hearts he's broken, from what I hear. Besides, he's too old for you."

"I know he thought he was just teasing! But that doesn't mean it won't happen. Anyway, we're the same number of years apart in age as you and Father were," I reminded her.

She sighed then, no longer amused. "You're so like your father," she said quietly after a long silence. "He was just as stubbornly illogical when he set his mind to something. He wouldn't listen to reason either, or couldn't listen. I don't know what it was that drove him. It was hopeless trying to talk sense to him."

A heavy silence smothered us. We rarely spoke of Father or our previous lives. But suddenly I saw him lying on his deathbed beseeching me, just as if he were in the room with us. I had to blink my eyes several times to make the vision vanish.

One day Kalle re-entered our lives. He came sauntering up to the door smart as you please, carrying a suitcase in one hand and a sack of red apples in the other. My heart sank into my shoes when I saw him; I had thought we were rid of him for good. Ivar took one look and ran away; Gudrid stood frozen behind the door, staring at him with big eyes.

"Now there's my girl!" he sang out, smiling. "How about a kiss for Papa?" He thrust an apple at her but she drew away, so he turned his attention to me.

"You're turning into a real woman, Berit." He gave me an oily smile but I just glared at him, hoping to make clear just how unwelcome he was. "Where's your mother?"

"At work, of course," I answered sarcastically. "I'll go tell her you're here." I didn't want to be alone with him, so I grabbed Gudrid's hand and bolted out the door, shouting for Ivar to join us. Sheepishly, he slid out from behind the woodshed. We ran all the way to the dock.

It was a frantic scene. Glistening fish were pouring off the boats onto the pier. Men clad in oilskins hammered lids on barrels while others paced importantly to and fro, spitting and shouting to hurry things along. The women, heads tightly bound in dark scarves, were hunched over brimming, briny barrels, salting down the catch, the wind whipping at their long, dark dresses and white aprons. They looked like a rookery of penguins.

Even here, Mother stood out in the crowd. She moved with a deft, regal dignity. We hurried toward her, ignoring the scowls of disapproval. Children weren't welcome on the docks. When she saw us, she straightened up, ran her forearm across her brow, and waited for me to explain myself.

"Kalle's back," I announced grimly.

Her face fell. At least, I think it did. Maybe I imagined it, wanting it so. All she said was: "Tell him I'll be home as soon as I'm finished here." And with that she turned back to the fish.

He didn't stay long this time either, but it was long enough. One evening several months after his departure, Mother motioned for me to sit with her at the kitchen table. Lately a heaviness had settled over her, slowing her steps. But I was totally unprepared for what she had to tell me.

"I'm going to have a child," she said solemnly.

I couldn't speak. It seemed impossible, poor as we were. True, Kalle had left a little money this time. But how could we possibly cope with another mouth to feed?

"I'm afraid you're going to have to take my place at the packing plant when my time comes, Berit. I don't know what else to do." Her dark eyes flooded and she pressed her lips together. Then she buried her face in her apron.

I jumped up to throw my arms about her. "No, no, Mother, don't cry. Of course I can work at the dock. Of course I can. You mustn't worry about that."

She blew her nose in her handkerchief and wiped her eyes. "You're such a good daughter, Berit," she sighed. "I don't know what I would do without you." She hugged me close.

My heart expanded in my chest, threatening to burst.

"Is Kalle coming back?"

"I don't know," she answered miserably. "I don't know."

So they were no closer to marriage than before. No one here knew they weren't married, of course. Mother had been careful about that. Filled as I was with the shame of it, I nonetheless was glad. I detested him. And never more than on those nights when I awoke to hear my mother's muffled sobs in her pillow.

Sissel was born the following August. Ivar was six, Gudrid four, and Mother was forty-one. I was eighteen, and now Mother depended on me to provide for us all.

At first they didn't want me at the dock because I was so small, but I convinced them I was a good worker. They got their money's worth out of me, I'll say that for myself. I was young and used to backbreaking work, and my fury at our circumstances kept me stuffing fish into barrels with a vengeance long after the others wanted to quit.

When he got the news of Sissel's birth, Kalle sent a little money. It made me angry. I wanted Mother to send it back.

"But it's only right, Berit," she said quietly. "He should pay for the child. Besides, you know how much we need it." I feared that he had grown somehow in her estimation because of the money. He came back the following Christmas to see his children, or so he said. Mother was impossible to read. I glowered silently at the prospect of having him ruin Christmas, but he did as he pleased and tried to steal a kiss from me when he was drunk. Once he even put his hands on me when Mother wasn't there to see. I threw a pail of water on him to sober him up, and he stormed out, cursing.

Mother once again broached the subject of marriage. "We have two children now," I overheard her say one afternoon as I came down the stairs from Oddfrid's.

"We're as good as married, Kaisa, you know that. We don't need any pastor to tell us that," he purred smoothly. I could tell he was slightly drunk.

"But you promised, Kalle."

"It's not a good time, woman, I've told you that." Suddenly he was belligerent. "Look at us! I have to find a steady job first. Something I can count on."

I came into the room in time to see Mother turn away, her face taut and drained. "Then I must ask you to leave us alone," she said, her voice low and steady.

"Leave you alone?" He wheeled to confront her, his face flushed. "Who are you to tell me I can't see my own children?"

"Your children don't know you. They don't have a legal claim on your name. They need a father," she answered. Her voice shook, whether from fear or anger I could not tell.

"I am their father. Aren't I?" he took a step closer to her, thrusting out his jaw. "Or am I?"

"Kalle!" she cried, her eyes wide.

It happened so fast I couldn't stop it. He slapped her across the face with his open hand, sending her head snapping sideways.

"No! Stop!" I rushed at him, butting him hard. He growled at me in surprise, drew back his fist, then thought better of it. Cursing, he grabbed his coat and stomped out.

Neither of us could find our voices. Mother sank down on the bed, her hand gingerly touching her stinging face. Glowering, I sat beside her, my arm around her shoulder. Before we went to bed, I threw his things in his suitcase and put it outside the door. When we awoke the next morning, it was gone.

I had worked out a strategy to capture Edvard's attention. I knew he was due home for Christmas, so I made him a Christmas gift, a fine pair of wool socks. They were thick and soft, white with an intricate black and white design, just the thing to keep a seaman's feet warm while tossing about in the arctic seas. I handed them to him, wrapped in brown paper, without preliminaries on Christmas Eve, just as he was headed out the door. He looked quizzically at me.

"Unwrap it. It's for you. A Christmas gift."

Awkwardly, he unwrapped the bundle and held the socks up and studied them, then me, without a word. I was wearing one of my new dresses that I thought made me look quite grown up.

"Thank you," he finally mumbled. "Thank you very much."

"Do you like them?"

"They're first-class socks, I'll say that for them," he answered slowly.

"I made them myself," I added proudly.

He nodded. "Many thanks," he repeated.

"I think they'll fit you just fine. Your mother said you have small feet for a man. Wear them in good health," I added formally.

He nodded again. "Yes, thank you. You're very good at knitting, I can see that." A hint of his cocky smile played around the corners of his mouth.

My heart soared. That settled it, then. Next time it would be a sweater.

As it turned out, the sweater was a long time in coming. Kalle showed up once more begging for forgiveness and another chance. This time he'd had the wits to secure work in town before he came calling. I felt betrayed when Mother let him stay. I couldn't tell her that he never missed a chance to try to put his hands on me. I stewed blackly for weeks at this unexpected turn of events. Finally, I did what so many other girls I knew had done: I answered an ad for a house post in Kristiania, which is what we then called Oslo. I was nineteen now and ready for something new. I'd heard all the stories about the fine houses and the ballet and music and theatre. It sounded so grand and fine. Surely it would be a better life than this.

I didn't tell Mother what I had done. I hardly spoke to her these days. I just tried to stay out of the house. At first, she tried to humor me and pretended nothing was wrong. But when I wouldn't answer, she got mad. She never confronted me directly but her voice took on a cold edge and she radiated stony anger toward me that only served to fuel my own seething fury.

On the day the letter came offering me the post, I handed it to her without a word. I felt a sweet, satisfying sense of revenge when her face fell.

"But Berit, I need you here," she said tightly. I saw the pain in her eyes but I didn't care.

"You don't need me here. You can stay home and look after the children yourself. You've got Kalle to provide for you now."

"But . . ." She turned away so I couldn't see her face.

"I can't stay any longer with him here," I told her angrily. "I'm going to Kristiania." I hadn't known I actually would go until the words fell out of my mouth. But once said, it was as good as done. "Don't worry, Mother. I'll send money home."

She turned to face me then, as if to check my tone. I couldn't read anything in her pale, strained face, but the sight of it filled me with sudden remorse. If she had asked me to stay then, I would have. But she didn't. "Suit yourself, then," she said shortly.

In the days that followed, she watched my determined preparations without comment. Then she finally broke her silence. "I want us to go to the photographer before you leave," she said simply.

Her words triggered the searing memory of my brothers and me clinging abjectly to her in front of the chapel while the photographer recorded our misery. But the moment passed.

In the portrait we had made that summer day in 1923 with Mother's other children, we all look much more content and well cared for. Once more seated with her children arranged around her, she looks serene, somehow resigned. She's wearing a lovely dress I made for her. When I saw that portrait, I realized how beautiful she was.

"I won't stand in your way, Berit. I just want your happiness," she told me solemnly when we said goodbye at the little ferry that would take me over to Aalesund. I was determined not to cry when she threw her arms around me and held me tight. When she let me go, her lips were pulled into a thin but loving smile. She and the children waved cheerily as the boat pulled away. And I, smiling broadly, waved cheerily in return, determined to ignore the empty, lost feeling that welled up as they shrank from sight.

This time I was the one leaving her behind. She had one child barely out of diapers, a six-year-old girl, an eight-year-old boy and a drunken lout to provide for them all. And three sons she hadn't seen in ten years.

The less said about Oslo the better. Oh, it was a fine enough city and the houses and shops just as grand as I had been led to expect. My employers were tolerable enough, for rich people. I was the youngest of three servants and they also treated me decently enough—at first. I was too industrious a worker, though, and when the mistress sang my praises they held it against me.

I missed Mother and the children terribly and sent money home as often as I could. She wrote often, her letters full of news of the children and sometimes of my brothers in the North. But she never mentioned Kalle. "Edvard is home and asking after you," she wrote in the late fall. That inspired me to use some of my savings to have portraits made of myself for Mother and Edvard for Christmas. I was smartly turned out, my auburn hair shorn into a smart bob, and I couldn't wait for them to see how sophisticated I had become.

One day in my solitary wanderings along the city streets I came across an advertisement for a ballet performance. It showed a lithe, lovely lady held aloft by a darkly handsome man in tights who reminded me a little of Edvard. I decided that I would save my money to see this ballet, and when the long-awaited day of the performance finally arrived, I was immediately transported. I drank in every movement, anticipated every turn. I felt my body soar and leap with the dancers; it was as if we were one. When it was over, I sat riveted in my seat, totally spent.

I was meant to be a ballerina, I knew that now.

I didn't tell anyone, of course. They would only laugh at me. The cook and the nanny never passed up an opportunity to mock me. Still, I knew what I had to do: buy ballet shoes and begin to practice. That turned out to be harder than I had hoped. It was difficult to save the money even for the old used pair I found, and even harder to find a private place to practice. But I stole what moments I could, carefully lifting myself up on tiptoes and leaping into the air as I had seen the dancers do. At night I went to sleep with visions of myself on the stage, arms full of roses, bowing to the adulation of a wildly adoring audience.

One day not long after I embarked on my ballet training, I came upon the cook and nanny drinking coffee in the kitchen. They had their backs to me, deep in conversation, and didn't hear me open the door. I stopped in the doorway to listen.

"I tell you I saw her with my own eyes! In ballet shoes, can you believe it, flinging herself about like a madwoman!" The nanny giggled.

"That ridiculous thing?" the cook snorted. "She's got big ideas, that one. Doesn't know her place. She's nothing but a little Lapp rag, aping her betters, if you ask me."

My blood rose to an instant boil. They must have sensed me in the room because both of them turned to face me. I stood glaring at them with my hands on my hips.

"You'll be sorry one day," I told them evenly. "You'll get what you deserve, mark my words." I slammed the door shut behind me, but I could hear them laughing. I never spoke another civil word to either of them.

In the fall of 1924, Mother, now forty-four, wrote to say she had given birth to another of Kalle's children, a boy. I sent extra money but didn't hear from her for some time. Finally, I got a long letter. "I don't know how to tell you this, dear Berit, but Kalle tried to stab me. He set upon me with a knife when he was drunk and raving. Thank God I managed to get away from him before he could seriously hurt me. I went to the police to get him out of the house, but they just laughed and said I'd want him back in the morning. He's insanely jealous and I'm afraid for the children. But I don't know what to do."

A hot, blind rage blurred the words on the page. It didn't take a moment for me to decide what to do. I marched straight down to the mistress and gave my notice. I left the next morning, dressed in my finest suit. I was still in a cold fury when I arrived home.

I saw Mother in the distance just after I got off the little ferry. She was trudging slowly up the hill toward our house, bent forward under a sack of coal slung across her back. At first I thought it was some old woman I didn't know. When I realized who it was, I felt as if my heart would break.

I called out to her and she dropped her load, staring across the meadow at me in amazement. "Berit, is it really you?"

When we embraced, I felt tears on her cheeks. "Oh, I prayed you would come," she told me. She was thinner and worn. Beaten. Her eyes were dark, sad pools. I saw no will in them.

After I had admired Edmund sleeping in his crib, she sagged into a chair. "How long will you stay?" she asked.

"I'm home for good, Mother. Kalle is leaving. I'll see to that. You're not going to put up with a moment more of this."

Her lips were pursed in a tight line as if to hold her despair in check. "He frightens me, Berit," she confessed. "But how else can we live?"

I couldn't bear the anguish in her eyes nor the hopelessness in her voice. "I didn't want to tell you, but Kalle tried to touch me, more than once. That's why I wouldn't stay."

Her color rose and her eyes widened, then hardened. She covered her face with both hands and slumped forward. Then her body gave way to quiet sobs.

"It's over now," I assured her, patting her back. "You don't have to worry anymore, Mother." I was livid with anger at what this man had done to my mother.

When Gudrid and Ivar came home from school, I took Ivar aside and explained that I might need his help. He was ten and very serious. But his eyes lit up and a wide smile broke across his face when I told him what I had in mind.

"I'll help you. I was planning to do it myself as soon as I got big enough."

"You'll be the man of the house now, remember. Mother will depend on you."

Ivar nodded and puffed out his chest. He already was growing into a handsome boy with black wavy hair. He looked more like Mother than any of us.

Kalle staggered home late, reeking of alcohol. His eyebrows shot up in surprise when he saw me. I had stacked his things near the door but he didn't seem to notice.

"So the fine lady is home from the city, is she?" He leered down at me.

I stepped toward him, hands on my hips, blood racing.

"Get out. We don't want you here."

He stood still, swaying, confused, staring stupidly at me through reddened eyes. "What are you saying?" he demanded.

"Get out." I stepped past him and threw the door open, then pitched his things outside. "Do you understand what I'm telling you? Get out!"

"Are you issuing orders to me?" he growled, raising his arm threateningly.

It was exactly what I had been waiting for. I leaped at him and grabbed his arm, and Ivar, hovering nervously beside me, leapt upon the other. I heard Mother cry out and Sissel break into a howl. Kalle staggered sideways, cursing, trying to break free of us, but we were too quick for him. I jerked him by the coat and spun him around, pulling him off balance. Together, we heaved him through the open doorway. Just clear of the doorstep, he tripped and fell to his knees. I took advantage of this heaven-sent moment to kick him as forcefully as I could in the backside with my new patent-leather shoe, right at the tender tip of the tailbone. He yelped in pain.

"Don't you ever show your face around here or I'll set the police on you. If I ever see you here again, if you ever try to hurt my mother again, you'll have me to contend with. Do you understand?"

His answer was a torrent of vile curses. Ivar and I stood our ground in the doorway while he unsteadily rose to his feet. Now we had an audience; the Hansens opened their door to see what the commotion was about. Slowly, Kalle gathered up his belongings, hurling angry threats. He didn't even give us a last look. He just staggered away into the night.

We never saw him again. A long time would pass before we would learn that he was arrested and deported back to Finland, where it seems he already had a wife.

SIXTEEN

THE CHOSEN PEOPLE

It was a bad time to be a Finn in Norway, however innocent or guilty you might be. Mother rarely let on about being Finnish herself, but that didn't keep their schoolmates from tormenting Ivar, Gudrid and Sissel about it.

"You're as good as anyone else!" I admonished them when they came home upset because someone called them names. It made my blood boil and when I could, I gave their tormentors a good piece of my mind. Ivar was learning to answer for himself with his fists but Gudrid was hopelessly timid. She cried whenever anyone called her a Finn. The only thing worse in those days was to be called a Lapp. People despised them both.

Even with Mother back at the fish packing plant we hardly were making ends meet, so I settled on sewing as a means to get more money into the house. I bought an old sewing machine and before long had almost more work than I could manage, sewing dresses and coats. I had a talent for it.

Life wasn't all work. I took up my ballet shoes again and well remember Gudrid's alarmed expression the first time I hung a sheet on the woodshed wall and danced until I sank exhausted into the grass. On hot summer days, we'd pack a picnic lunch and march the children up the hill and down the other side of Sugartop to the bathing beach. Drugged by the sun, we luxuriated on the smoothly polished rock ledges while the children shrieked gleefully in the water. And there were long, festive summer evenings when Mother's women friends dropped by and, with the coffeepot boiling full steam, she led us in singing and sometimes even showed us a dance step or two. When Mother started to sing again, I realized she was becoming her old self.

One day Edvard came home quite unexpectedly. There had been some kind of row with his father the last time he was home. The talk was that he had been caught sneaking out of a housemaid's attic bedroom through the roof window after her bed broke and crashed to the floor. I refused to listen to such gossip. The moment I saw him coming up to the house, it came rushing back to me with renewed intensity. I had never forgotten about him, of course. But I had been preoccupied with all our troubles and helping provide for the children. He was more handsome than ever, dressed like the finest of gentlemen. But I was older and wiser now. This time I played my cards differently. I ignored him.

It worked better than I expected. Before long he was pestering me. Of course I brushed him off. But he badgered me to go out walking with him. I refused, laughing at the idea.

"Why would I want to go walking with the likes of you?" I scoffed. "I have far better things to do with my time, thank you." As I had calculated, my ridicule only made him more determined to have his way.

"You've grown into quite a woman, Berit," he remarked tentatively one afternoon when he found me hanging out the wash. "Mother brags about you all the time. She told me how you threw Kalle out and how well you look after your mother and all the children. She says you can do anything you put your mind to—sewing, knitting, cooking. Is that true?"

I scowled at him. "Any fool can see Mother needs help."

He flashed a winning smile. "I'm shipping out next week. Won't you go out with me just once before I leave? We could go dancing if you like."

"I'm a good dancer," I told him. It was true. Mother had taught me. "Then you'll go?"

"Maybe," I retorted airily. I left him there in the yard with a half-smile of exasperation on his face. But in the end, I went. I couldn't risk having him lose interest completely.

It was one of those still, warm evenings at the end of summer when little puffballs of cloud take on such a shine of reflected light that the whole world seems rosy. Anything seems possible on such evenings. Aalesund lay glittering before us as we boarded the ferry; I had never seen it look so lovely. I looked quite lovely myself, if I may say so. I wore a pale green, scooped-neck taffeta dress with a lace collar that I had made with just such an occasion in mind.

As for Edvard, he was on his best, most charming behavior, regaling me with tales of the strange things he had seen and daring things he had done in ports from Greenland to the Amazon. He offered me my first cigarette, and I felt altogether a quite sophisticated woman of the world. We waltzed the whole evening away though, truth be told, he wasn't much of a dancer. But I didn't mind. My fondest dream was coming true.

It was, and remains, the best night of my life.

It wasn't until after we said goodnight and I closed the door on him that I fully realized how desperately I wanted him to come back. It fell on me like a smothering weight. "I'll not have you play me for a fool, Edvard Hansen," I vowed. But my heart ached with dread. I certainly wasn't about to let him know that I cared he was leaving, so I treated him coolly the rest of his time at home.

"I'll write," he promised when he came to our door to say goodbye.

"That's up to you," I shrugged, careful to keep my face unreadable. He did write. And I treasured each letter as mounting evidence of an unspoken promise between us.

In the spring of 1928, a letter came that would change our lives. It was from Balsfjord, from my brother Paulus, who was now eighteen.

Mother kept in contact with my brothers all these years, though she rarely spoke of them. I long ago had learned not to mention their names because she fell into a black, withdrawn mood and nothing I said could bring her out of it. We didn't get many letters from my brothers, so each one was a gift. But after she read this one, Mother looked up with an expression in her eyes that I had never seen.

"He wants to come live with us," she said, her voice registering wonder and despair. "He says he can't bear it there any longer now that Jensine is dead."

She handed me the letter. "I so long to be with you, Mother. Please let me come." Suddenly, the words swam on the page. I saw him again at the chapel, face drawn tight, dressed in his little suit with the round lace collar, refusing to look at the camera. A hard lump rose in my throat and for a moment I could neither swallow nor speak.

Mother's voice, raw and bitter, broke my vision. "But how can I feed and clothe another child? We barely have enough to keep body and soul together as is."

"But he's grown, now, Mother. He's capable of working."

She looked crossly at me. "And just where is he to work? Be reasonable for once, Berit! You know very well there are no jobs here for men. Is he to stand in the fish with the women, then? And where is he to sleep? There's barely enough room for all of us here now as it is. Look around you!" She made an angry gesture that encompassed the cramped room and its pitiful furnishings, then sighed heavily. A long, wretched moment passed. "How can I support one more without taking food out of the mouths of the others?" she asked plaintively.

"Don't you want Paulus to come, then, Mother?" I ventured.

Her shoulders slumped in defeat. "Of course I want him to come! You surely must understand that. God himself in heaven knows I have longed for nothing more all these years than that blessed day when my children would be with me again." She paused, her hands working her apron. "You can't know . . . Even now, I hear Paulus's cries as I walked away and left him there. It still wakes me in the night . . ." Her voice broke and she turned away.

"Then we'll find some way, Mother. I promise. We'll surely find a way."

She pulled herself together and looked at me approvingly. "I don't know how I'd manage without you, Berit."

I glowed with pride as her praise warmed me. "So you'll let him come?" A sad, tiny smile tugged at the corners of her mouth. She sighed, and nodded.

"I miss him. I miss them all," she said.

"Just think how much easier our lives would be if only you had your rightful inheritance!" I fumed. She always scoffed, but whenever I saw Nikolai's picture hanging there on the wall it just reminded me how unfair and infuriating it was that we should have to struggle so when my mother should have inherited his fortune. She had told me the story of her mother and father and all that had followed in the wake of their love affair. I often wished that she might have the money that was rightfully hers and never more than at times like this. I knew how deeply she yearned for my brothers to join us. I too had long fantasized about the day we would be reunited.

When the day came to meet Paulus at the dock, we were there well before the coastal steamer was due. We were all in our best clothes—Ivar, Gudrid, Sissel, Edmund, Mother and I. The girls were impatient in the finery I hurriedly had sewn for the occasion and I had to keep after them lest they spoil their clothes. Ivar was leaning on a crate, aloof and sullen in a jacket I had fashioned for him from something Edvard's mother handed down from one of her boys. Mother paced restlessly in a new, long navy skirt and matching sweater I had knit for her, hair swept into a bun, an iron mask of anxiety stamped on her face. Even so, she cut an imposing figure.

The ship slid into its berth and the passengers began to pour down the gangplank. "How on earth are we to recognize him?" I fretted nervously. Mother didn't answer. She stood stone still, barely breathing. I saw her swallow once, that was all.

Then he was standing before us. It was really only a split second, I know. But I can tell you that an awful eternity passed between them the moment their eyes touched. I saw Mother's face break, and then Paulus was upon her, his arms locked around her neck, sobbing. They held one another a long time while I stood silently beside them, blinking away my tears, my throat in a vise, not caring that people were staring and smirking at this grown boy shamelessly crying in public. None of us could speak.

Finally Mother pulled free. "Let me look at you, child," she smiled, her face wet. Shyly he returned her smile, wiping his face on his sleeve.

I got my first good look at him then. He was more handsome than I could ever have envisioned—dark hair and eyes and a smile that could light up the world. There was something elegant about him, even in his shabby, too-small suit. He was his mother's son, that one. Or was it our father I saw in that wonderful smile?

"Do you remember me, Paulus?" I held out my hand to him.

He shook it formally and nodded. "I do. You always took such good care of us." He smiled tentatively. "But you've grown into a pretty lady now."

"You're welcome here, Paulus. This is where you belong."

"Inge and Karl send their greetings," he said when he had been introduced to his half-siblings, who stared at him with great curiosity. "I went to Signaldal to visit them before I left."

I saw a shadow flit across Mother's face. "How are they?" she asked.

"Well. They're both treated well enough, especially Karl. They dote on him in that house. But Inge . . ." He paused and cleared his throat. "Inge wants to come here. He asked me to tell you so."

I shot a quick glance at Mother and saw her face tighten. "We'll just have to see what the future brings," she told him. She slipped through his and patted it warmly. "Let's go home now and eat," him, her eyes smiling.

Of course it was too crowded to stay where we were, so we moved into town. Mother found an apartment right on a dock adjacent to a fish packing plant and just down the street from the fish canneries.

"It's very close to work and the price seems affordable. And there is more room," she told me when she took me to inspect it.

It jolly well should have been affordable.

It was called the Longhouse. It was a dreary, flat-roofed concrete block house where other families in straits similar to ours were housed. We had a two-room apartment on one end of the building, closest to the two dozen stairs we had to navigate down from the street to reach our home on the water's edge. There was a kitchen with a window where the boys slept and a living room with a second window that doubled as a bed-room for the rest of us. In winter when we cooked our meals on the stove that was our only source of heat, the steam ran down the walls in rivulets, pulling loose the paint and nourishing hardy molds. Sissel, who had just started school, was assigned the never-ending task of keeping the walls mopped dry.

Looking back now, I realize it wasn't entirely a bad life, especially in summer. Then the dock was alive with laughing children, and young people congregated there to soak up the sun and swim. Ivar was a dare-devil, happiest when he could spend all day diving off the dock into the sea. The girls already were chasing after him.

Mother and I had steady employment working with the fish, but Paulus and Ivar, certainly old enough to take some responsibility, sat home jobless, mostly keeping an eye on five-year-old Edmund. Gudrid was twelve and had taken over many of my duties at home. Meanwhile, Inge sent pleading letters. One night Mother came staggering home, exhausted after a twelve-hour stint salting herring, to find another let-ter from him.

"How can we make room for one more here? I'm at my wit's end, Berit. I long for him so, and Karl too." Her voice broke, and my heart cramped. This was it, then. I had been preparing for this moment.

"I've been thinking about something lately, Mother," I began carefully. "You know Edvard is coming home soon. He's been a very faithful correspondent and . . . well, I think he might be interested in marriage."

Mother looked sharply at me, whether in alarm or amazement I can't say.

"He ought to be interested in getting married at his age, at any rate," I continued firmly. "He needs a wife and a home of his own. He makes a good salary and I know he's saved up a good bit of money. He's sensible about money. Anyway, I mean to talk to him about it. I've thought it over quite carefully. If we were married, I could have a sewing shop in our apartment. There's good money in that. And with me out of the house, you'd have more room to bring Inge here. And we'd have enough money to send him his fare."

"But he's . . ." She sighed, apparently thinking better of whatever it was. She looked keenly at me for a long moment. "Do you want to marry Edvard?" she finally asked. "Or are you doing this just for us?"

"Yes, I think it would be a good thing."

"So you intend to ask him to marry you?"

"Yes, if it comes to that."

She broke into a smile, shaking her head. "Berit, Berit. Who is it you take after, I wonder?"

I flushed and jumped up. People had made fun of me my whole life. I could put up with that, nothing they said ever troubled me in any way, you can be sure of that. But when my own Mother made me into a figure of fun . . . I marched to the stove, poured myself a cup of coffee and angrily slammed the pot back down on the stove.

"I'm just trying to do the best I can," I told her icily, my back to her.

"I know that, dear Berit. You must know how grateful I am for all you do for us. But you mustn't think that you have to marry just anyone . . ."

I turned to face her. "He's not just anyone, Mother."

She studied me closely. "So that's how it is," she answered slowly. "Well, then, I hope it's all for the best."

Edvard was more agreeable than I had expected. He seemed genuinely pleased with the idea of having his own home. On our wedding day, three days before the stock market crashed in America, he was especially pleased: he got more tipsy than I had ever seen him and played quite the fool. I hid my irritation as best I could. I understood that you had to put up with these things in men.

I found us a cozy daylit basement apartment across from the church and set up a sewing shop, anxious to make as much money as I could while I was able. With Edvard at sea, I started knitting baby things in the evenings with the full expectation that before long my time would be filled with a child of my own. I lived for the day.

Inge soon arrived and was absorbed back into the family with a loving welcome. He was a short, shy, black-haired boy with bright black eyes, a sweet smile and quiet disposition. His arrival caused Mother to change all their last names to Pedersen, the name my grandmother Nicoline always wanted the family to use. "It's easier for the children if they all have the same last name," she said by way of explanation.

The boys did their best to earn money but jobs were scarce. They went fishing, for all the good it did. They would come home from these expeditions with only a few pitiful kroner and clothes stiff with fish slime and blood. If Mother was disappointed, she never said; she just boiled their clothes clean again. But at least she was able to get the family moved into a roomier apartment on the ground floor of a house just up the hill and a block away from the Longhouse. It opened into a sunny little backyard garden where she could dig in the dirt, and it seemed to lift her spirits.

They were living there when, on a Saturday in early May of 1930, a very tall young man came striding up the street and stopped hesitantly before their door. He was dressed in rough country clothes and carried a large pack on his back. It was Paulus who first caught sight of him through the window.

"Dear God!" he exclaimed and bolted for the door. Inge took one look and rushed after him. Mother and I were about to set a meal of mackerel, potatoes, turnips and flatbread on the kitchen table, but we dropped everything and sprang after them, wiping our hands on our aprons.

"Karl! Is it really you?" Paulus asked incredulously.

"Yes, it's me," came the answer. His slow, deep voice resonated with that achingly familiar Lyngen dialect. A big smile spread across his face and his clear blue eyes shone with delight. When he dropped his pack and doffed his cap, a tumble of light hair fell over his forehead. He was incredibly handsome.

The color drained from Mother's face at the sight of him and I feared she would faint. Then she reached for him with both arms and he stepped into her embrace. "Karl, Karl, my dear son," she murmured, pressing him to her. But after a moment he pulled away, his cheeks flushed, eyes wet.

"You must excuse me, Mother. I'm so sorry. But I got infested with lice on the boat," he said with obvious mortification. "Isn't this a shameful thing? To have dreamed of this day so long and now here it is at last and I come to your house full of lice!"

"Never mind, we'll soon have you rid of them. We've learned to take what comes in this family," Mother told him. She patted his arm lovingly as his eyes moved curiously from face to face of those he didn't know: Ivar, Gudrid, Sissel, Edmund. Then his eyes fell on me and he smiled, pleased.

"Berit? Can this be my sister, then?"

I nodded dumbly, searching for signs of that earnest young boy at the riverbank in Signaldal who had groped for some recollection of his father's face. Words were cemented to my tongue. The whole family stood looking up at him, dumbstruck. "Welcome to Aalesund," I finally remembered to say.

He stayed for three weeks. He saw his first apple and cherry trees unfold their blossoms in Aalesund, and we all trooped off together to his first Constitution Day parade to cheer the jovial marchers waving red, white, and blue Norwegian flags along the cobblestone streets. He traded some mink pelts he had brought for a suit of new clothes, and everywhere we went, girls stared immodestly after him. I was immensely proud he was my brother.

From the moment he had shown up on our doorstep, I thought Karl looked somehow familiar. We were all seated in the little living room one day when I happened to look up at the portrait of Nikolai that Mother always hung on the wall wherever we lived. Karl was seated directly under it. My eyes went from his face to the portrait, and suddenly I saw it and smiled to myself. Blood will tell, I always say. When I pointed it out to Mother, a sorrowful expression washed over her face. "I think it could be true, but you know I never saw my father."

We all doted on Karl and hung on his every word. It was plain he lived for hunting and fishing in the mountains. He knew the precise location of every rock and lake and the tiniest pond, the secret lair of every bird and beast. He had tried Lofoten and fishing on the open sea, but he was a mountain man.

To hear him speak of life in Signaldal made me ache inside. It was as if some hurtful, long-trapped thing strove to break through my ribcage. When he told of the red foxes leaping through sweet meadowgrass washed in the amber light of the midnight sun, or of pulling a thrashing salmon as big as a man from the roaring spray of the falls, I felt lightheaded with longing. As for Mother, I had not seen her happier since Father died.

We begged him to stay. "I can't," he answered steadily. He came steeled against us, I think. Or maybe he saw how pitifully we lived and understood how much better off he was where he was. At any rate, he could not have lived in a city. His soul would have withered and died. I understood that.

"I promised Marianne and Johan that I'd come home again. They're so afraid I won't come back," he told us miserably. "They didn't believe me when I said I'd come back." He looked keenly at Mother when he said this, his eyes begging forgiveness.

"I've missed so much of your life," she told him. "Look at you: You're a grown man now, not my little boy. You're their son. I only pray that you can forgive me." She was dry-eyed, stolid, when she said it but the sadness in her voice cut to my heart.

She wouldn't let any of us go to the boat with him when he left. She wanted to say goodbye alone. When she came back, she proudly opened her purse to show me the money he had given her as a farewell gift. "I'm going to save it so I can go visit him one day," she vowed.

Five years would pass before she made good on that vow. Meanwhile, she pestered the city housing authority until she was assigned a place in one of the city's new apartment blocks just above the Longhouse. Here was a proper bedroom and a living room as well as a formal entry, plus a kitchen with a coldwater sink and a fine view of the shipyard and mountains. There was even an attic bedroom for the boys, and, out on the landing of the exterior hall, a flushing toilet shared with the family next door. And a gleaming white enamel bathtub rigged to a boiler and stove was tucked into the basement laundry room.

"It's not a sauna but it will do nicely," she told me, clearly pleased with the turn in her fortunes.

My fortunes too were improving, at least financially. The sewing shop was a great success. But I was not successful at what I most desired to be, a mother. Edvard came home regularly, and, after each visit, Mother offered meaningful hints about the pending arrival of her first grand-child. After five years of marriage and not so much as a miscarriage to show for it, I was in no mood to listen and bristled whenever she broached the subject.

"Don't you mean to have children, then, Berit?" she asked plaintively one day.

"Of course. I just don't want to hear any more talk about it," I snapped.

"Well, it can't be your fault. Look at me. No one can accuse me of not being fruitful," she said ruefully.

I brightened a little at that. My worst fear was that I was somehow to blame. By now I had a forlorn, expectant chestful of booties, blankets, hats and sweaters, but I could no longer look at them. Nor could I bear the sight of other women parading smugly through the streets pushing their prams. I knew they were looking down their noses at me, smirking, pitying me. It didn't matter that I could do everything else better than they: sew, knit, embroider, cook, bake, clean. None of it mattered as long as I was childless.

One blustery morning in the late fall of 1934, Mother and I were drinking coffee at her kitchen table when we head a polite knock on the door. She frowned. "Whoever can be out in awful weather like this?" A sleeting rain peppered the window and the wind howled piti-lessly, churning up whitecaps on the fjord.

Mother opened the door to find two dripping, well turned out young men with bright smiles. Each held a rain-soaked hat in one hand and a book of some kind in the other. They couldn't have been a day over twenty.

"Good morning," one of them said in halting, strangely-accented Nor-wegian. "We're missionaries for the Church of Jesus Christ of Latter-day Saints in America. We'd like to come in and tell you about the true, restored gospel of Jesus Christ."

I came into the entryway to stare at them over her shoulder.

"America?" Mother repeated slowly. "You're from America?" She regarded them with frank curiosity. "My father went to America. Come in," she said before I could intercede. "We've never had visitors from America."

Though I scowled in warning, she took their wet coats and hung them carefully in the entryway, then bade them be seated in the living room.

"Can I offer you some coffee and waffles?" she inquired politely.

The one who had done all the talking smiled stiffly. "No coffee, thank you. We don't drink coffee. Our religion forbids it. We don't smoke or drink, either."

"You don't drink coffee? Whatever kind of religion can that be, then?" I asked.

Mother shot me a hard, warning look, then turned to her guests. "Some tea, then? I think I can find some tea if you prefer it."

"No, thanks all the same. We don't drink tea, either," the same one replied uncomfortably.

"No tea, either?" I hooted. "What do you drink in America, then?" Mother's face tightened but I couldn't stop myself. These two ridiculous creatures put me in a sporting mood.

"It's because of what we call our Word of Wisdom," he explained patiently. "We believe that caffeine is not good for the body . . ."

A burst of incredulous laughter from me stopped him short. "Tell me one thing. Do you dance?" I chortled.

"Yes," he answered calmly.

"You do?" Mother interjected. "You dance?"

"We believe it's one of God's gifts to mankind to make earthly life more . . . joyful," he answered carefully.

Mother seated herself across from him. He had her attention now. "Be so kind as to bring some waffles and milk, Berit. You do drink milk, surely?"

"Yes," he smiled. "Thank you."

I left as soon as I'd served them. I had better things to do with my time than listen to such drivel. "Restored gospel," indeed! Mother could be such a fool at times. I did my best to dissuade her, but she let them come around again.

"They're very nice young men. I don't know why you're so set against them," she retorted when I berated her for encouraging them.

"Haven't you heard about them, Mother? They're Mormons. They're polygamists from a place called Utah. It's in some terrible desert ringed with mountains and no one can escape from it. They go all over the world trying to lure people to come there. Then they take their money and enslave them, especially the young women. They're forced to marry with the polygamists!"

"So what do they want with the likes of me, then?" she demanded quietly.

I was stumped. "I don't trust them," I warned. They were too nice. No one I knew behaved that way. They wanted something from us, I was certain of that, but no one was going to play me for the fool. "Even the pastor has warned people against them," I added. "If you won't listen to me, maybe you'll listen to him."

"The pastor!" she scoffed, eyes flashing. "Aside from the day I married your father, the only pastor I've had any business with threatened not to confirm me because he didn't think my Norwegian was good enough."

To my amazement, she started going to the Mormons' religious meetings in a rented hall down by the bus station. What on earth could she be thinking, I wondered. She had always been so sensible. What if my mother was losing her mind? She was so stubborn, so far beyond the reach of reason once she made up her mind about something that it would be impossible to say whether she was in her right mind or not. When I confided my worries to Edvard, he just laughed. "She's got a mind of her own," he shrugged. "You got that trait from somewhere, after all." I glared at him and changed the subject. There was only one thing to do, I concluded: go see for myself what she had gotten herself into.

So I arrived unannounced one Sunday morning at the meeting hall after the service had started, when I could hear they were singing. I tried to be inconspicuous but the singing stopped just as the door closed behind me, and every member of the congregation turned to stare at me. When Mother saw who it was, I feared her hat would fly right off her head.

They called themselves elders but they were nothing but children. They were fresh-faced and wholesome looking, I'll give them that. They were Americans, after all, and had a certain elegant style about them. The one who had done the talking at Mother's house began to recite a sermon. He was telling about something called "The Book of Mormon," pronouncing "book" not as "*bok*" but "*bukk*." I did try to muffle my laughter but I couldn't help myself. Didn't this fool know a "*bukk*" is a goat?

As I understood it, this Goat of Mormon was the story of Jews who went to America to build a civilization but then disobeyed God, so he cursed them with a dark skin and they became Indians. It was a preposterous tale and I fled as soon as they started to sing again.

I knew Mother would be furious with me so I prudently waited a couple of days before I went to see her. But she didn't say a word about it, probably just to spite me. She had other things on her mind.

"I've decided to go to Signaldal this summer," she announced before I even got my coat off.

"Signaldal?" I repeated, sinking into a chair.

"Gudrid's mad to leave for Kristiania . . . Oslo, so it's best I go now while she's still here to look after the others. But I'm counting on you to help see to it that all goes well here while I'm gone."

Edmund was nine now and Sissel fourteen. The older boys were in and out, doing whatever jobs they could put their hands to. It made sense for her to go now, I assured her. I didn't let on how hurt I was that she was going back there without me.

I waited impatiently for her letters, full of curiosity about what she found there. The first thing that came was a postcard with a picture of a new store at the bottom of the valley. It was addressed to Paulus, not me, and congratulated him on his twenty-sixth birthday. "Here I am back at your father's birthplace," she wrote. "Take good care of the children."

That was followed by a long letter. "Karl has a good life with these people. They treat him like a true son," she wrote. "I'd forgotten about the blessed mosquitoes," she added.

She went to Balsfjord to visit Petra and her children. "We had a good talk about old times," she wrote cryptically. Later, I would learn that she had uncharacteristically unburdened herself about all the awful things that had happened to her over the course of her life, telling them things she had yet to tell me. It was as if she wanted to have some washing away of her unhappy memories on that journey back to the place where so much misfortune had befallen her.

Finally, she went to Kitdal to visit Aunt Hansine and Uncle Erik on my grandparents' farm. "Nothing's changed over there," she wrote. "It's still a madhouse. Half-grown children everywhere—you have many cousins here—and people of all kinds constantly coming and going. There's a painter from Germany living with them, the tents of the Swedish Sami summer school are pitched in the field up behind the house, and carriages filled with American tourists off the ships visiting Lyngenfjord are forever rolling up the valley to gawk at them. All in all, it's quite a spectacle."

That's what did it. "I'm going myself next summer," I announced. Gudrid and Sissel stared disbelievingly at me, then Sissel surprised me. "Can I go with you?" she asked tentatively. "I've heard so much about it, I'd like to see it."

She was so good-natured and responsible that it was hard not to indulge her. She didn't ask for much, I'd have to give her that. She'd be good company on the voyage up the coast, I realized. I gave Gudrid a questioning glance.

"Not me," she said firmly. "I'm going to Oslo."

When Mother came home from Lyngen that fall she sat me down at the kitchen table and made the announcement I'd been dreading. "I'm going to join the Mormon church. I want you to meet with the missionaries so you can understand what it's about for yourself."

I knew that tone. I was powerless to argue.

Though irritated, I agreed to hear them out. I thought it might give me some ammunition to talk her out of it. But on the day the elders came to call on us at my apartment, there was a new one, a little older, and his Norwegian was quite impressive. He had a cheerful sense of humor. His name was Elder Jensen, and when he told us that his great-grandfather had come from Norway, I warmed to him a little.

"I'm from a little town in Idaho called Blackfoot, not far from Salt Lake City, which we call Zion," he explained.

"I've heard that Salt Lake City is ringed with impenetrable mountains and that people can't escape," I told him. "Not that I believe it myself, you understand," I hastened to add. Mother had shot me a look I hoped only I could read.

He threw back his head and laughed delightedly. "Next time I come I'll bring you a picture of the Salt Lake Valley. Then you can see that it's nonsense." He paused, then looked serious. "Do you know why we call it Zion?"

I shook my head.

"We believe God's chosen people are to be gathered there to await the second coming of Christ."

I couldn't think of a thing to say. It was altogether quite astonishing. I'd never heard of such a thing.

"The chosen people?" I managed to ask. "Who are they, then?"

"Those who open their hearts to accept the restored gospel of Jesus Christ. Some people know when they first hear the gospel that they are one of God's chosen," he added. He had a kind voice, and the open, guileless face of a man you can trust. But I still didn't quite trust him.

"Would you like to hear a little bit about what we believe?" he asked.

"Yes, she would," Mother interjected.

I sat back and let him talk, sipping my coffee. He told a fantastic, wonderful story, starting with a young man named Joseph Smith who prayed to God to tell him which church was true. God told him "None of them," and he was ordered to restore the true church on earth. As we sat spellbound, Elder Jensen's gentle voice took us on a journey across America. By the time the prophet Joseph Smith was murdered by a mob in Illinois, I was on the edge of my seat; by the time his successor Brigham Young rose from his sickbed in a wagon above the Salt Lake Valley to declare to his ragged band of pioneers that "This is the place," I was captivated despite myself.

Elder Jensen and his companion came again, a week later. I had mulled the story over and over. Were the chosen people really better than the rest? I wondered.

"God's chosen people aren't the important people, the rich people," he explained. "They're the righteous ones. They often are poor in worldly goods and despised and pitied for it. But such people are richer than the rest because they understand what others are too blind to see: the truth."

His words pierced my soul like a bolt of lightning. In that moment, the ill-fitting pieces of my whole life snapped smoothly into place. I thought of the smug, malevolent people who had abused and ridiculed me all my life. Suddenly I saw a far superior measure to judge who was better among us: the yardstick of the only true gospel.

Mother, Edmund, and I were baptized on January 16, 1936. Edvard and the rest of the family rolled their eyes but held their tongues. But I knew what I knew. I had never been so sure of anything in my whole life.

Seventeen

Hanna

Sissel and I left for Lyngen in June of 1936 and would return home that September. I'd sewn all winter to get us ready, and our suitcases were filled with fine dresses and fabric to make more, as I expected to pay for our keep by sewing for our hostesses. The weather was foul as we set out—the sea and sky formed a sour, solid wall of impenetrable gray. Rain pummeled the deck and the ship pitched and rolled dreadfully. Sissel, now fifteen, was seasick most of the voyage.

The weather lifted a bit by the time we got to Trondheim, so I walked down the gangplank to stretch my legs and look around the dock. It was a mistake. Suddenly I was seized by the vision of myself sitting there on that dock in my pigtails, abandoned, gripping my bundle in wild desperation. I hurried back up the gangplank, my throat constricted. Sissel asked if I was unwell when she saw me, but I told her nothing. I had never told anyone about the heartbroken terror I experienced that day.

When the ferry we boarded in Tromsø steamed into Lyngenfjord, passengers came to stand on deck, awestruck by the Lyngen Alps soaring through the clouds. When we entered the still waters of Storfjord, my blood began to race. And as if on cue, when we neared the dock at Kvesmenes, Otertind burst through the mist in all its majesty to welcome us.

"Oh, Sissel, look!" I exclaimed, inexpressible emotions tugging me in all directions.

I was home.

A tall man stood on the dock, waving his cap in greeting—Karl, of course. He had brought a horse and wagon. There was a new road on the other side of the river now and we slowly made our way along it. Sheep and goats dotted a landscape just as lush with lime-green grass as I remembered. Dainty white buttons of marsh cotton nodded in the gentle breeze. We halted across the river opposite our old cottage, dwarfed under Otertind.

"It's still here," Karl said quietly. "No one's lived there since."

"I see that," I answered tightly. What I really saw was our father, pale on his deathbed, bright eyes pleading, begging me to embrace him.

The first few days I feared it had been a mistake to go back there, though we were welcomed with open arms. Sissel quickly fell in with Perdy, Karl's adopted sister, who had grown into a kind, merry young woman. But I heard ghosts in this narrow, unforgiving valley. I saw visions of things I had long sought to banish from memory.

One day I set out alone down valley on an old bicycle to visit the places I remembered from my childhood—the falls where I had known such joy with my father, the secret places in the woods where I had hidden to act out happy fantasies. I saved the cottage for last. Peering inside through the broken window, it was just as I feared. The whole room came flashing to life, scene after scene vividly unfolding like movie film rolling forward faster and faster. I could hear my mother and father chuckling affectionately over some private joke, their voices echoing softly in the shattered room. I heard Paulus howling in terror as Mother cried out in pain. I saw her writhing on the bed, struggling against her stinking attackers. And once again, my father's face floated from his pillow, his inconsolable eyes following me. And then I was standing outside in the bitter cold while Mother, on her knees in the snowdrift in desperate supplication, begged our landlord for Christian mercy.

"May you rot in hell!" I shouted, blind with tears and fury. That heartless devil had long ago vanished from this place, and a good thing too. He would have had me to reckon with, and I would have made it warm for him, you can depend on that. But he would get paid back in kind, of that I was now perfectly certain.

Something dawned on me as I tore myself away from the dilapidated cottage where my life's destiny had been determined. There had been a meaning in all this, I suddenly understood, for I wouldn't have been properly prepared to come back here until I had received the gospel. Now I knew that those who had wronged us would be punished for their sins, here on Earth perhaps, but surely in the hereafter.

Mother and I had been tested by terrible, unspeakable ordeals, but we had shown them: we had survived. They had done their best against us but they couldn't break us. We *were* the chosen ones, no doubt about it.

Pedaling back up the valley, I felt a new sense of peace. It was as if some crushing weight had been lifted from my chest.

"They're asking after you in Kitdal," Karl announced a few days later. We were fishing at the old spot just across from the house but nothing was biting.

I hadn't laid eyes on my grandparents' farm in twenty-five years. Uncle Erik, who inherited what remained of it after the debts were paid, had died just that spring, leaving Aunt Hansine with a brood of mostly grown children.

I divined from comments Mother had made over the years that there was old, painful history between my father and his family. But I could get no satisfaction from her about what had caused it.

"Karl," I began, trying to find the best words to pose a question that had troubled me for years, "do you know why we didn't go live in Kitdal when our father died?"

He shook his head. "I guess there were too many of them over there."

"But it was a big farm," I persisted. "They had ten cows and a horse and I don't know how many goats and sheep. Think what a difference it would have made in our lives if we could all have stayed together. Why weren't we taken in by our own family instead of given away to strangers?"

I had neither the nerve, nor the heart, to ask this of Mother.

"There's no use thinking about such things. What's done is done." He pulled a tin from his pocket and placed a tiny wad of tobacco carefully inside his cheek.

"I don't understand it, that's all. It doesn't seem right."

"I just think there must have been too many of them there already, Berit," he repeated. "Our grandmother was old by then. I went there for awhile, remember? But I didn't like it."

"Why?"

"Oh, the cousins teased me. They beat me, and then they laughed about it. I was glad to come here after that."

"I don't care what you say, Karl, it's not right. It's shameful. No relation of mine will ever give a child away to strangers if I can help it."

How could I have known how my fine words would come back to mock me?

Mother was right about Kitdal. It was a madhouse, stuffed to the rafters with children, visitors and good cheer. Lapp children and their dogs swarmed in the meadow behind the house, a two-story structure built since I last had been there. The German artist, a dark-browed, brooding man, came and went with his camera and sketches of Lapp life. And whenever their ships dropped anchor at the bottom of the valley, rich, well-dressed American "dollar tourists" arrived to mob the Lapp children in their school tent behind the house.

Somehow in this bedlam Aunt Hansine managed to make room for us. She was a good-hearted person, I quickly decided. Whatever had happened, it surely wasn't any of her doing.

I didn't trust the German artist from the moment I set eyes on him. There was something shifty under those thick brows, but they all fussed over him, especially Inga. She washed and pressed his shirts and waited on him hand and foot. Nothing was too good for him. I said something about it once to Hansine by way of warning, but she chose to ignore it.

"He's been coming every summer for years to draw the Lapps," she assured me. "He's become just like one of the family."

I thought his drawings were terrible and said so. Even Inga, who liked to put on airs, tore up a sketch he made of her. "I look like a goat!" she protested indignantly. She was nothing if not vain. Still, they were proud to have such a distinguished guest in their home.

Four years later, when they saw him marching into the valley at the head of the first column of Nazi troops, they knew I had been right. By then, of course, the damage was done. He knew every rock and stream in Lapland.

The very first day of our stay in Kitdal, I had a real shock. The German had assembled the Lapp children in their school tent for a photograph, and I quickly produced my own camera to record the scene. When I got a good look at the teacher, short but resplendent in her finest Lapp dress, something familiar in her face caught me. I studied her carefully as the German fussed to get everything just so inside the tent, but I drew a blank. Hansine told me her name was Elsa Klemetsen.

"I have the strangest feeling that we've met somewhere before," I told Elsa hesitantly. "But I don't know how that could be. I lived here as a child but I moved away many years ago."

"Have you been to Karesuando? That's where I live," she answered in a melodic Swedish accent.

"Never. And I've not laid eyes on a Lapp in twenty years."

"Sami," she corrected. "We're Sami."

"Of course. Pardon," I mumbled, feeling foolish.

"Where did you live then?" she asked. Her friendly tone had not changed.

"Down by the fjord, near the place where the Sami cross with their reindeer. At the Mistress Dahl's." I spit out the name.

"I came there every year with my parents," she answered slowly. Now she was staring hard at me. As we stood scrutinizing one another, a memory stirred in my brain.

"I visited the Sami there once. I was afraid to get too close, but a little girl came and took me by the hand into a tent and they fed me. It was so good!"

A radiant smile of recognition broke across her face. "You were so hungry," she said simply. "Your name was Berit Utsi."

"You! You were that little girl? Of course you were. I can see it now." Suddenly I felt as shy and at a loss of words as ever I have been in my life. "You remembered my name," I added in wonder.

She nodded. "I looked for you again, every year. I was so worried about you. You were so hungry and looked so sad. But I never saw you again."

A hard lump rose in my throat at this forthright declaration, but I managed to smile all the same.

"You were so kind to me. I've never forgotten that. Or had the chance to thank you properly. Isn't it strange that we've met again?"

She tipped her head to one side and studied me thoughtfully, as if she were dissecting my features. I couldn't imagine what she was thinking. You never know that with the Sami; they're deep, those people. She and I were fast friends from that moment on, and the first thing I sewed in Kitdal was a green silk scarf I gave to Elsa Klemetsen.

It was a wonderful summer. The household was busy and boisterous. The boys were in and out, fishing or felling trees on the steep shoulders of the hillsides surrounding the farm. Sissel and I pitched right in with the chores, gathering eggs, tossing hay to the cows, looking after the goats and sheep. When the hay was cut, suffusing the air with the sweetest perfume on earth, all the women set to work with long, wooden rakes. We vied to see who could last the longest. Only my cousin Jorunn, the eldest of the brood, was still swinging her rake when I collapsed in a heap on the grass.

I hadn't been so happy since Father died.

I fell in with Jorunn right away. She was about my age and had become the very salt of the earth. Her specialties were sheep and goats and knitting. You'd never catch her putting on airs like her younger sister Inga. There was no nonsense whatever about Jorunn. You always knew where you stood with her; she told you exactly what she thought, and I liked that about her. Of all of them, she and I were the most alike. We even resembled one another a little, I thought.

Years later I would hear a story about Jorunn that I instantly knew was the God's truth. It happened after the Nazis had driven the family from Hansine's house and seized it for use as a barracks. One day after fall slaughter on her husband's farm down valley, Jorunn was taking some calf tongues to one of her brothers. A Nazi soldier stopped her on the road and demanded to see what she was carrying. When he discovered it was calf tongues, he wanted them for himself. Even those hopeless barbarians knew a delicacy when they saw it. But Jorunn had other ideas.

"Go cut out Hitler's tongue and cook that and eat it!" she told him angrily and marched off. Anyone else would have been shot on the spot. But no German would dare touch Jorunn.

Inga was another story altogether. She and Jorunn couldn't have been more different. Whereas Jorunn didn't give a fig what she said or what she wore, Inga took great care to make the right impression. The first thing she blurted out when we met was, "You look so fashionable!" I did, of course, and I was pleased someone noticed that I was not the pitiful ragamuffin who had left this place so long ago. She was wide-eyed with admiration for my wardrobe.

Inga had aspirations. She was determined, much against her mother's wishes, to go to hotel school. Hansine thought she should marry one of the local boys who was keen on her, but Inga made it plain he would not do. Blissfully confident that she'd be accepted by the school, she'd already sewn eleven white uniforms.

"Inga's always been such a dreamer," Jorunn snorted one hot afternoon when a group of us sought refuge on a hillside high above the house. We lay about on soft moss, our backs against warm rocks, admiring the breathtaking panorama spread before us. We could see all the way to the fjord, where a couple of fishing boats floated on a mirrored sea. Now and then a cool breeze drifted off the thick tongue of blue ice on the glacier-topped peak across the valley. Below us lay the farmhouse, the size of a button. Inside it, Inga was sweltering over the sewing machine and the twelfth uniform.

"And so stubborn and bossy!" Jorunn grumped. "She has to have things done her way or there's no living with her. You can see how she orders everyone around."

I had to chuckle. There was something likable about Inga for all her silly pretensions. She doted on me and always was asking my advice on this and that, and she took an avid interest in my stories about city life. I thought she was plucky to have dreams. Not enough people have the gumption to dream, if you ask me. Besides, she was lively and full of fun. She had a touch of Jorunn's naughty humor and a winsome smile that would take her far in life, I figured. She was striking to look at—copper red hair, a prominent nose, sparkling brown eyes and freckles. People teased her about her looks sometimes and asked if she came from Egypt or Spain. She didn't look Norwegian, that was certain. She wasn't any taller than I was.

Actually, none of them were. I had always blamed my short stature on malnutrition and hard work as a child, but when I met my cousins, I was both surprised and pleased to see that they too were very short. It ran in the family, clearly.

One day I tried to ask Hansine about my grandparents and how they came to settle in Kitdal, but she didn't seem to know much about it except that my great-grandfather had been the first settler to break ground in the valley who didn't give up and go away. That was in 1846, she said.

"But where did he come from?"

She scratched her chin and frowned. "Sweden, I think," she said after a long pause.

"Sweden? Appalling news."

Hansine chuckled at my little jest.

"Where in Sweden?"

"Someplace in the north. I don't know." I sensed the subject was closed.

"Well, if they've been here so long, it explains why I feel so at home here, I suppose. I was born here, after all."

"So you were. I remember it well." She rubbed her eyes and smiled slightly.

"You do?"

She nodded. "Your mother had a hard time. The house was so small and crowded then. She didn't like so many people hovering over her, seeing her so. But there was no place else for her to be." She paused. "She's very proud, your mother. Always has been." I heard a whiff of condemnation in her voice.

"Your father was proud, too," she added. "He had some ideas your grandparents didn't approve of. So there were raw feelings between them, hurt that didn't have a chance to heal before he died so suddenly. It's a shame it happened that way, Berit, just a shame. It broke their hearts." She dabbed at her eyes and looked out the window.

"What kind of ideas?"

She looked uncomfortable. She bit her lip, brows furrowed. "I'm not sure. Politics, maybe. They used to argue about politics."

"Politics?"

"There was a lot of trouble back in those days, Berit. I really don't remember all the details. All I know is they couldn't see eye to eye and had bad feelings over it." She studied me a moment. "What does your mother say about it?" she asked carefully.

"Nothing. She won't talk about that time. I think it hurts her too much."

Had we really suffered all this because of politics?

I liked spending time with Elsa. I lost all track of time with her because the things she told me about Sami life were so engrossing. One day when four of Elsa's male relatives came down from Sweden with a few reindeer, she asked me to photograph them in their Sami dress, complete with the four-cornered hats that signified they were from Karesuando. Then Sissel and I posed with them, two perfectly turned out ladies grandly seated in our fine summer dresses while they, perfect gentlemen, stood at somber attention behind us, one of them holding his hat respectfully in the crook of his arm.

Then I had a flash of daring inspiration. When I confided it to Elsa she giggled and we hurried off together. In no time, I was back in a Sami dress, a round Karesuando woman's cap with embroidered brim, and a colorful shawl that draped around my shoulders. The cousins greeted me with hoots of teasing laughter. Only Hansine was dead silent.

"Why, Berit," Sissel exclaimed in amazement, "you look exactly like a Lapp!" Her eyes followed me as if she had never seen me before. "I swear, if I didn't know you, I'd take you for a Lapp."

"Sami!" I snapped. "Take my picture."

One of the men dragged a recalcitrant reindeer into the yard and handed me the rein, grinning. I held it as if I'd been doing it all my life, and Sissel recorded the moment. She looked at me again through the viewfinder. "Really, Berit, if only you could see yourself, you wouldn't believe it."

"I will see myself. That's why you took the picture," I laughed. "Wait until Mother sees this."

Hansine's eyebrows shot up. "Indeed," I heard her mutter.

Elsa didn't say a word. But there was unmistakable satisfaction on her face.

A few days before we were to return to Signaldal, Inga got the letter she had been expecting from the hotel school. We all watched her read it, eager to hear the good news. But the lively light in her eyes dimmed as she scanned the page and her face fell into a closed mask. I felt a surge of sympathy and anger even before she uttered a word.

"They won't have me," she announced stolidly. "I guess I'm not good enough."

"And think of all those uniforms!" one of her young sisters wailed.

"Thank heaven, I say," Hansine snapped. "Now you can stay home where you belong."

Inga's eyes were hooded with hurt, anger and humiliation. She pressed her lips together. "I'll just find something else to do, then. I'll find a house post somewhere."

"There are plenty of house posts in Aalesund," I blurted out.

To this day, I can't imagine what possessed me to say it. I felt sorry for her, I guess. I knew only too well what it's like to be belittled and scorned, to have dreams destroyed.

Inga looked at me brightly, fresh hope rekindled in her eyes. "Do you think I could accompany you to Aalesund when you go home?" she asked after the briefest pause.

"Of course. You could stay with me until you find work . . ." I caught a glimpse of Hansine's face out of the corner of my eye. "You'll have to speak to your mother about it, of course, but you're more than welcome."

They had a terrible row after we left to return to Signaldal. But a couple of weeks later Inga came to Signaldal to tell us she was coming with us anyway. She always was willful. Now she was full of plans and questions and seemed to have put her disappointment over the hotel business completely behind her. Inga seemed to have a gift for shutting the door on unpleasantness and walking away. At any rate, she never mentioned it again. God alone knows what she did with all those uniforms.

The two of us had our picture taken together in Signaldal that day. We stood on the road with a mountain peak looming high behind us, nicely framed by trees on either side. She was wearing the flowing, pale yellow flowered dress I had sewn for her. I was in one of my favorites, a beige and navy polka-dotted silk crepe with lace at the neck. We stood there innocently enough in our finery, side by side in the roadway, looking into the distance as if straining to see what lay ahead.

I could not have said goodbye to Karl that crisp September morning if I had known what was coming—if I had known what lay in store for us and for Norway, if I had known that thirty years would pass before we would see one another again. Instead, we left in high spirits, confident we'd soon meet again.

That idyllic summer of 1936 is embedded in my memory as a watershed, the end of a precious era of innocence none of us could know was ending. Not in my wildest dreams could I have imagined that Karl, that profoundly kind, peaceable man, could ever kill anyone.

Hastily trained in munitions after the German invasion, Karl fought in the mountains not far from Signaldal along the border with Sweden and Finland during those first three months when our tiny Norway put up its hopeless fight against Germany. After a bloody skirmish in which many of their close comrades were killed, Karl's unit was inflamed with lust for revenge. They tracked down the Germans who had killed their friends and blasted their position to bits.

"We laughed when we heard their dying screams," he confided remorsefully decades later. "War turns you into a beast."

Still, the medal for valor awarded him by General Eisenhower for service to the Allies and the award bestowed upon him by his mother's homeland for his aid when hostilities broke out between Finland and Russia were his proudest possessions.

When Norway capitulated, Karl and his comrades did not. "We felt betrayed," he said. "We wept." So they vowed to keep fighting underground. They roamed the mountains that Karl knew so intimately, manning the forbidden radio transmitter that beamed to London information they gathered about German troop movements and fortifications. But when the German reinforcements arrived in Signaldal and crowded into his foster parents' house, he knew it was too dangerous to stay. He and Perdy had married by then and had an eighteen-month-old son named Isak.

Karl secreted two pairs of skis in the woods a good distance from the house. At four o'clock one Sunday, on a dark November afternoon, they dressed as if going out for a stroll. Perdy had impressed on Isak that he must not make a peep nor wet his pants. If his diaper got wet, she feared he'd freeze, she told me long afterwards.

With great sorrow and trepidation, they bid farewell to their foster parents and set out toward the Swedish border, pulling Isak on a sled behind them. They passed a German patrol but the little family group out for a Sunday airing aroused no suspicion. When they got to the place where they retrieved the hidden skis, other figures came gliding silently out of the darkness to join them. Karl quietly had passed word to those he trusted that he would lead them to safety in Sweden if they wished to flee. Twenty of his neighbors took him up on it.

The next time they heard a Nazi patrol, they all dived into the woods to hide. Breathless, they crouched behind a sheltering clump of trees as the patrol passed, Isak bright eyed and still as a petrified field mouse. All night the group steadily picked its laborious way up the mountain behind Karl, who led them, sure-footed, over the snow bound trail he knew so well. Perdy, already a stout woman, sweated profusely in the heavy green wool dress she would wear for the next month. By six o'clock the next morning, shaking and exhausted, they reached the first small traveler's hut on the Swedish side of the high, windswept tundra. It was overflowing with other refugees, many of them sick with influenza. Isak hadn't made a sound the entire journey, and when Perdy unwrapped him, his diaper was dry. Fearing the influenza, they moved on to the next hut the following evening. But here Perdy succumbed to it, so they were forced to stop traveling until she recovered. A month would pass before Karl handed his family over to Swedish safekeeping in Dalarna and turned back to the northern mountains to fight.

We knew none of this at the time. All mail was read and censored. Even when their firstborn son Per died not long after the invasion, we could hardly tell from Karl's terse note what had happened to him. Decades later he told me the full story, and even then he barely could choke the words out.

Per was born sickly. When he was just shy of three years old, he was stricken with some minor ailment and the doctor advised he be taken to the hospital for an examination. He would be there just overnight, they assured Karl and Perdy, so Karl made the trip to the hospital alone with his boy. But when Karl returned the next morning to take Per home, the doctor refused to let him see his son.

"There were German soldiers in that hospital," Karl told me, his voice tight with anguish. "Some of them had diphtheria, and one of the nurses who had handled Per fell ill with it. So they told me they had to keep him there for observation, just in case."

Karl swallowed hard. "I was terrified, and so was Per. I could hear him screaming for me. Finally one of the nurses took pity on us and brought him to a window where he could look out and see me." He paused and wet his lips, fighting for composure.

"It was the worst mistake I ever made in my life," he confided, his face ashen with memory. "When he saw me through the glass, he held out his arms to me, howling in fear. 'Papa! Papa! Come and get me, come and get me!' he wailed, over and over."

Karl paused for breath, his chest heaving under his shirt. "I never saw him alive again."

I put my hand on his and patted it, tears stinging my eyes. We sat quietly, weeping together, until he could speak once more. "All I can remember of him now is that helpless, horrible last day," he sighed. "I can't tell you where I found the strength to come home and tell Perdy. But I couldn't stay here at home. I had to go to the mountains to be alone. I don't know how many days I was gone. I sat on the tundra howling like a wild animal. I didn't think I could live through such pain."

He blew his nose on his handkerchief, carefully folded it and put it back in his shirt. Then he turned to look me in the face.

"But you know, Berit, on that awful day when Per was screaming for me in the hospital, I finally fully understood the heartbreak our mother must have suffered when she had to give us away."

It didn't take Inga long to find a house post. And a good one it was too, at the sheriff's home. It was frequented by the fine folks she so admired, and she thrived. She loved to regale us with stories of their grand dinners and fine entertainments. She became quite full of herself.

"We had an ice sculpture for the centerpiece last night," she related merrily one evening. "And for dessert, there was a lady made of ice cream. The bishop was the honored guest, so I had to serve him the ice cream lady first. But do you know what he said to me?" she asked, giggling.

"He said: 'Shall I take the lady from the front or the back?' Some of the men laughed out loud and even some of the ladies tittered behind their handkerchiefs."

"Maybe you should find another post," I said crossly. I was becoming weary of her tiresome prattle about all these elegant people.

"Whatever for?" she asked in amazement. "It's one of the finest houses in the city. I think I'm lucky to be employed there. They only take the best people, after all."

I didn't answer. She was a grown woman for all of her impressionable, silly ways and she could do whatever she pleased for all of me. Still, she continued to rely on me for advice and she was a frequent visitor at Mother's apartment. She always made a great fuss over her Aunt Kaisa, and I think my mother enjoyed it.

I had every reason to think Inga was satisfied with her new life in Aalesund, so I was astonished when she announced that when Gudrid returned to Oslo she was going to accompany her to look for a new post there.

"But I thought you liked the one you have here." I was mystified.

She avoided my eyes. "I have to work too hard there," she answered airily. "I'm tired of it. I want to live in Oslo for awhile."

So we bid them goodbye and Godspeed, as innocent of what was afoot as newly hatched sparrows. Afterwards, Inga swore she herself didn't know it when she left. She insisted she was five months pregnant before she finally went to a doctor in Oslo and learned what was wrong with her.

Some days, I can believe it of her.

The first I knew of the situation was when we got a letter from Gudrid. Wordlessly, Mother handed it to me, her face grim. I understood that something terrible must have happened. When I read that Inga had given birth to a baby girl, I sank into the nearest chair, stupefied.

"She didn't tell anyone," Gudrid wrote. "But it's so terrible I have to tell someone. She needs help, and I don't know what to do. She doesn't want anyone in her family in the north to know. When she wrote to tell the child's father, he told her to get an abortion. I think she tried but it didn't work. Anyway, now she's got an infection and both she and the baby are still in the hospital. She's got hardly any money. Still, she insisted on a private hospital. It's madness. 'This baby shall have nothing but the best care,' she says. You can't reason with her. You know how stubborn and unrealistic she is. But I can't imagine how she'll pay for it. She lost her job, of course, as soon as they saw she was pregnant."

I threw the letter on the table in disgust.

"She's a fool and she's always been a fool. But I can't believe this! How could she be so stupid?"

Mother gave me a hard look. "You don't know how it happened, Berit. You shouldn't judge her. You're too harsh on people." It wasn't the first time she'd warned me about this. She was much too willing to think the best of people. And after all she'd been through!

But I wasn't about to acknowledge my real fear: that the stain of Inga's shame would spread to reflect badly on me. Inga wouldn't have been in Aalesund to get pregnant if it hadn't been for me, there was no escaping that. Even so, who could blame me for it? She was grown, after all, and hardly my responsibility. Still, some of them would blame me, I knew that well enough. They would seize this moment to criticize me behind my back for failing to keep a better eye on her. None of them would say it to my face, of course. They wouldn't dare.

All I said was: "I wonder who the father is?"

"It's obviously someone she knew in Aalesund," Mother answered. We stared at one another blankly. Neither of us knew of any special beau Inga fancied in the crowd of young people she ran with. She clearly was far more secretive than I could ever have suspected. I had trusted her to be who she pretended to be. But all along, when I thought she had been confiding in me because she trusted me and I in return had told her private things I didn't tell just anyone, she had been playing me for a fool.

"Well, it's none of our affair," I told Mother. "If she doesn't want her family to know, there's nothing we can do."

I wrote to Gudrid and said so. And I told her what I thought of her running off to Oslo with Inga in such a condition without telling us. An injured reply was not long in coming.

"I told you I had no idea Inga was pregnant when we left. If I had, I would never have agreed to go with her," she wrote. I could hear her indignant tone just as if she were in the room with us. "But since she has no one else, it's good someone in the family is here with her, I suppose. Last Sunday I went to the christening service. She named the baby Hanna. The adoption seems to be taking a long time, but meanwhile Inga is allowed to see her at the orphanage three times a week. It's a pity she can't keep her. She's such a beautiful baby."

It may be that the idea had been germinating within me from the moment I heard about it. I can't say now, all these many years later, what it was that possessed me. Maybe it was simply the vow I'd made to Karl that long-ago day on the riverbank in Signaldal that came back to haunt me. Or maybe it was Gudrid's pathetic report that prodded me to seriously consider it.

"I think I should go see her," I told Mother after several sleepless nights of turmoil. She didn't seem at all surprised.

I don't know what I expected to accomplish by going to Oslo, really. I told myself it was just an ordinary family visit. But I confess I was stunned when I saw Inga at the train station. My blithe, merry young cousin had turned into a downcast, desperately thin woman. Even in her smart suit, she looked haggard and nervous. She had aged, I could see that, and the light in her eyes was gone. I also could see how grateful she was that I had come. The sorry sight of her softened me towards her, I admit that.

We found a secluded bench and sat down. I didn't see any point in beating around the bush. I demanded to know the whole story. Fidgeting, evasive, she told me just enough so I could understand. Her voice was even and I saw no trace of tears. But beneath her brave words, I smelled something familiar: wild despair.

"It was all quite unexpected, a bolt from the blue," she told me of her pregnancy. "Afterwards, I was sure we'd marry, but it became clear he wasn't interested in that." I noticed a bitter set to her jaw.

"Even when he knew about the child, he wanted nothing more to do with me. Especially then." She paused, then smiled wanly. "Oh, wait until you see her, Berit. She's the most beautiful thing on earth."

The next day we went together to visit Hanna in the orphanage. The spotless room, overseen by a stern nurse, was filled with sleeping babies. Inga motioned me silently to Hanna's crib. The moment I bent over her, she opened her blue eyes, stretched her tiny arms toward me and kicked her feet, smiling from ear to ear. I reached down and gathered her up. What else could I possibly have done at such a moment? The baby squealed happily, wriggling contentedly in my arms. Inga was right; she was the most beautiful baby I'd ever seen.

Inga stood with her deep brown eyes fixed on the two of us. "She likes you, Berit," she said, biting her lip nervously. I don't know how long we stood there, lost in the moment with the infant gurgling happily between us.

Finally I heard myself say: "What would you think, Inga, if Edvard and I adopted her?" I'd not even told him about Inga's baby, but he would be home soon.

Her tense expression softened. "I'd be so grateful to you, Berit, so grateful," she answered in a husky voice. I could see the tears welling in her eyes. "I could never live long enough to thank you properly if only she could stay in the family."

After all these childless years when I had all but given up hope, here at last was the baby I yearned for, truly, as Inga said, "a bolt out of the blue." So there you have it. All I can say is that I only wanted to do everything in the best way I could for both Hanna and Inga. But I should have known that nothing I could do would ever be good enough for those two.

Of course Inga promised to give up her claim on the child. Yet Hanna wasn't but four years old when Inga, at the height of the German occupation, showed up on my doorstep to visit us. She and Gudrid had talked someone out of a fraudulent emergency medical travel pass. If Inga would go to such lengths to see her child during wartime when travel was all but forbidden, what could I expect of her in peacetime? I could guess that answer well enough. If Hanna was ever to be truly mine, I realized, I'd have to take her away from here.

I had toyed with the idea ever since I joined the church, to be truthful. But it wasn't until Inga's visit that I made up my mind. As soon as the war was over, we would emigrate to America.

And once there, I knew I would find Nikolai's fortune for my mother.

BOOK III

SOUP FROM A NAIL

Hanna

EIGHTEEN

HAMSTRING

I took Inga by the hand and tiptoed stealthily to the shiny mahogany dresser crowded against the wall of our tiny living room.

"I want to show you my fine clothes," I whispered.

Mother was busy in the kitchen and I had seized this opportunity to disobey her. Gingerly, I pulled open the dresser drawer I was expressly forbidden to touch. But we had time only for the most fleeting glance at Mother's handiwork before I heard her approaching footsteps. In terrified haste, I slammed the drawer shut.

Inga had arrived mysteriously in our midst without warning. She found us living in the countryside in a red, one-hundred-year-old sod-roofed cottage in Hatlehol, a thirty-minute bus ride from Aalesund. My only other memory of Inga's visit is watching her in the warm glow of candle-light, humming as she worked at Mother's spinning wheel.

Twenty years were to pass before I would see her again.

Mother said we moved to the country to get away from the Germans. She dreaded the sound of their jackboots tramping the streets at night outside her bedroom window in Aalesund. Grandmother, after one visit to our cramped country cottage, threatened not to come back.

"The ceiling is too low," she complained. Mother and I didn't mind. With Father often at sea, we didn't need much room. And besides, we were both short.

But it wasn't just the ceilings. There was hardly any place to sit or stand in the whole house. Adults had to squeeze sideways between the parlor stove and our mahogany dining table and the daybed to get to the small bedchamber in the rear. It was just big enough for my mother's bed and my expandable crib. The postage-stamp kitchen barely contained a black cast-iron stove, a cupboard, a small table and two chairs. A bench next to the back door held a bucket of water and a washbasin. Mother kept firewood in the narrow back hallway, where she also set up the wooden tubs she used to wash our clothes on a washboard. In summer, we bathed in the hallway in one of the tubs; in winter, we bathed in the kitchen, teeth chattering, as close to the stove as possible. She hauled our water, two buckets at a time, on a wooden yoke slung across her shoulders, from a well down the hill below the barn, a good two city blocks away. A fish lived in the well to keep it clean.

In the front entryway, stairs led up to an attic too low for even my diminutive mother to stand upright. But I played there on rainy days, lonesome and undisturbed. From the window that overlooked our little garden, I had a view of our landlady Nelli's barn and hayfields and, in the far distance, the snow-capped mountains beyond Borgundfjord.

We had an inordinate number of relatives, most of whom lived in town. My grandparents on both sides lived in barracks-style apartment buildings overlooking the shipyard. There was—and still is—a distinctive odor in those apartments that seeps into the nostrils and opens the floodgates of memory: an acrid accumulation of boiled cabbage and fish, the faint whiff of coldwater sinks filled with raw potato peelings.

"Besten" and "Besta" Hansen, my father's parents, lived just a block up the hill from Grandmother. The walls around their living room windows had bullet holes in them from a misbegotten effort by our unwelcome German guests to drive home some point or another. Besten was a stern, bespectacled master carpenter who wore a stiff, paintbrush-bristle mustache and matching crew cut. Besta, a gentle, smiling invalid, was confined to her bed in the living room.

Their unmarried daughter, my Aunt Hilda, who earned her keep as a washerwoman, ran the household. Though weary and worn, she rarely failed to entertain us with funny stories when we came to visit. And if she had managed to hoard enough sugar coupons, she sometimes treated me to open-faced sugar sandwiches undercoated with greasy margarine, the treasured delicacy of the day. I was fond of Aunt Hilda.

I was a timid child, frightened of everything. Including my mother's oatmeal.

Mother measured her worth as a human being by her skill at cooking, sewing and knitting. But oatmeal defeated her. Owing no doubt to the lamentable shortage of milk, it turned to steaming gray, gummy lumps.

As she filled my bowl each morning, I sat at the kitchen table, a heavy knot already formed in my stomach. I could not swallow it. But with Mother firmly overseeing the awful ritual, her lips pursed tight in determination, I reluctantly put the first spoonful of coarse, rubbery paste into my mouth and tried to squeeze it down, hoping that today would be the day I would not fail her.

"Be good and eat now," she would admonish. But my throat closed of its own accord, and I gagged and spit it out. "Now you must not be *trollete*," she warned, alluding to the ill-mannered trolls of the fairy tales I cherished. "Eat!"

Obediently I put the spoon into my mouth with the same hopeless results, panic and despair rising with my bile. But it always ended with the same humiliation. "You should be ashamed! Eat your food!" she commanded as I sobbed my helpless protests. I swallowed and gagged, swallowed and gagged, tears salting the tasteless mush, wails of anguish and shame filling the tiny kitchen. Still she forced it upon me, morning after morning.

It was all we had.

Someone later would write of this time: "The housewife became the real heroine of the home front, for hers was the impossible task of concocting palatable dishes out of little—figuratively making soup from a nail with water as a foundation." I didn't know then that my mother was a heroine, but I did know that she was incapable of wrong. The sun in my small, doting world rose and set around her every unpredictable smile and frown, and I ached for assurance that she loved me.

It was said by cynics that Hitler sent his troops to Norway to feed them. Perhaps the Nazis had no real grasp of the depth of the insult they proffered in depriving Norwegians of their food. It was always hard won from the stony soil and stormy seas and thus cherished far beyond mere nutritional value.

They began the plunder of our nation carefully, so as to it make it palatable. First they requisitioned our meat, milk, butter, cheese, sugar, coffee, bread, potatoes, and eggs. Then they ordered increased food production, demanding, among other things, that the hens lay more eggs.

At this point, a popular story has it, a Norwegian farmer sent a letter to a high German official. "Your letter was put up in the henhouse so that the hens themselves could see it. When in spite of this, the hens after ten days still had not resumed laying, I had them all shot for sabotage against the German Werhmacht."

As for the hens, the Germans finally requisitioned them, as well as forty thousand reindeer and two hundred and twenty thousand cows. Finally they requisitioned the farms. In similar predictable progression, they first requisitioned our wool blankets, then our beds, silverware, linens, cash, and finally our houses, including those of my mother's family in North Norway. Nothing was safe: backpacks, rubber boots, motorcycles, and cars were hauled away. They took the businesses, hospitals, orphanages, and insane asylums, all to suit their increasingly demented purposes.

Fantasizing about the glorious day when this nightmare would end, grown-ups sometimes invoked the word "chocolate" with dreamy smiles. My aunts spoke reverently of unimaginable delights: chocolate concoctions with hazelnuts inside, hot chocolate that you drank in cups, even chocolate wrapped around sweet, soft creams, exotic fruits and exquisite liqueurs. Chocolate indisputably was the most wonderful indulgence on Earth. It belonged to the lost world that had gone before, like the stories in the Hans Christian Andersen fairytales Mother read me at bedtime. Chocolate had never crossed my lips, but I knew it was happiness itself. For young and old, chocolate became an unconscious code word, a symbol of what had been taken from us, a talisman of better times.

The Wehrmacht requisitioned two hundred tons of it in December 1940. "There are Germans everywhere, and they eat chocolate spread thick with butter," Oslo diarist Albert Jaeren observed at the time.

I grew up in a society where adults—even my fearless mother—never dared raise their voices, where men stood impotent and silent on street corners helplessly watching the confiscation of the nation, "our knotted fists in our pockets," as chronicler Jacob R. Kuhnle put it.

Even so, there was resistance. We knew from cryptic messages in censored letters that Uncle Karl was still fighting with the underground somewhere in the north. But even the unarmed had their ways of fighting back. Adults refused to sit next to Germans on trains and instead stood in the aisles even when the trains were all but empty. The Germans responded by making standing on trains illegal. Children were dressed in red knitted Santa Claus caps—*Nisselue*—as a symbol of resistance.

The Germans confiscated the caps from their heads. People wore sweet peas in their lapels as a symbol of national unity. The Germans swiftly forbade this adornment.

But as someone in Berlin perhaps should have foreseen, real civilian resistance—and the consequent real reign of terror—was triggered by that other elixir of Norwegian life: milk. There had been unsuccessful but highly unpleasant efforts to force teachers to sign loyalty oaths to the New Order, and the national sports associations had struck, refusing to compete in Nazi tournaments. But when factory workers refused to work because they were denied their extra ration of milk, the Nazis gave up any attempt to woo their Norwegian hosts with friendly persuasion. Trade unionists were shot for their gall. Sixteen months into what was to be a five-year occupation, our radios, the Germans' chief means of domestic propaganda, were confiscated. The gloves were off.

Mother dutifully turned in our radio to the police for safekeeping and, in keeping with the fiction that she could one day reclaim it, was given a receipt. But on certain nights, in a small cubbyhole in the attic of Nelli's farmhouse just across the yard from our cottage, an illegal shortwave radio crackled in the darkness behind black window blinds. Gruff and reclusive, Nelli, who ran the farm with her sweet sister Pernille, wasn't about to give any radio of hers to a German.

I understood that what they were doing was forbidden and dangerous, but I sometimes crept into that room to listen. Huddled together in the darkness, the adults hung on every thundering syllable of a man they called Churchill as his voice rose and faded over the airwaves. On other nights, they sat stock-still as Hitler, whose name and face I knew from the posters plastered all over town, shouted frenzied exhortations. I didn't understand a word either of them said, of course, but I judged the import of it by the adults' tensely whispered commentaries.

"At least when all else disappears, we'll still have the fish," the optimists said. But then even the fish swam off into German pots, confiscated on the docks as the fishermen returned from sea. The ubiquitous, bland, boiled codfish—there was no butter or oil for more palatable preparations— upon which our lives depended became scarce, and everything else had either disappeared or was to be had only on the black market by those brave or cunning enough to obtain it. Even the potato crop eventually failed. We had been issued green and pink ration cards for basic commodities but as the war deepened, these bogus coupons became an ever more cruel joke.

One day Mother and I arrived at our usual bakery in Aalesund to find its quota of bread unavailable. Despite protestations from anxious housewives waving ration coupons under the baker's nose, no bread materialized. So we hurried on to another bakery and queued up at the end of a rapidly growing line. Here there seemed to be bread. When it came our turn at the counter, a grim clerk in a white uniform stared defensively at us, then handed Mother a loaf.

Mother turned up her nose derisively as she inspected the coarse brown lump.

"We don't have anything else," the clerk said crossly. She looked tired and mad, and the other women behind us were muttering rudely among themselves as Mother disdainfully eyed the suspicious loaf.

Contemptuously, Mother threw some kroner on the counter. "They don't know how to bake anymore," she announced loftily as we marched past the restless line of glowering women and hurried out with our parcel. Baking bread herself was out of the question. There was no flour.

That evening, keen with hunger and anticipation, I bit carefully into a slice of this precious bread that had caused us so much anxiety and trouble. Mother had spread it with a thin coat of tasteless margarine, and I chewed diligently. Bread I could swallow.

I bit down on an unyielding particle the size and color of a kernel of grain. But as I removed it from my mouth and examined it with my fingers, the kernel began to unravel and I could see it for what it was: a long, thin piece of brown paper rolled tight to look like a kernel of grain.

Triumphantly, I displayed my clever discovery. But to my dismay, Mother looked as if I had uncovered something shameful.

"It's just some mistake," she sighed. "Never mind. Eat."

Had I done something wrong in showing it to her? When I found more paper kernels stuffed into the loaf, I kept quiet.

It was hard to know how to please her.

From the beginning, the natural world, so sensuous and magical, cast a spell over me: the warm spring days when the first purple crocus popped through the moist earth in our garden; the soft southern summer wind caressing the tender green leaves of the birch trees, shaking them playfully like muted bells; the sweet taste of birch sap painstakingly collected in an old bottle, drop by slow drop, from an incision carved into the bark; luscious black cherries plucked from Nelli's tree while thieving crows squawked indignantly; wild hazelnuts gathered in fall when the woods were weeping red and gold.

The sun-sprung summer days when the long golden light burnished the landscape quickened our spirits. Even we children were allowed to stay up late into the daylit night—struggling to fashion a perfect whistle from a thin green sapling; roaming among wildflowers in fields and meadows; leaping giddily over ancient stone fences to explore the secrets of the friendly, mossy woodlands; tumbling head over heels down gentle hillocks in tall, sweet grass; shrieking with delight as we ran wild in the warm wind, chasing one another with buttercups.

When it came time to bring in the hay, we could hardly contain our joy. It had been dried in the fields, strung along wires attached to tall poles put up for the purpose each season. We followed impatiently as the wagon drawn by Nelli's sturdy yellow horse plodded along the hayracks. When enough hay had been pitched into the wagon, we children were assigned the happy task of hopping aboard to stamp down the load to make room for more. When the wagon finally was well and truly filled, we were permitted to ride, brimming with pride and our own importance, on top of the heap as the wagon lumbered up the ramp into the two-story barn. Dancing with impatience, we waited until the adults had pitched many forkfuls of hay over the edge to the first floor below us. Then came our moment of glory. Dizzy with fear, screaming with glee, we flung ourselves down into the haystack, lurching stomachs tightly knotted, to bounce and tumble in the hay pile. Again and again we leaped into the abyss, growing bolder and more reckless with each jump until finally we dared throw ourselves with mad abandon from the very highest perch.

It was heaven.

At one end of Nelli's barn, over where the cows were stalled, was our outhouse. The human waste dropped directly into a sealed cement chamber on the first floor of the barn. The cow and horse manure was shoveled down into this chamber each day through a trap door. The waste chamber's large double doors on the ground floor were opened only in spring, when it was time to spread the manure on the fields. The initial blast of vile stench when the doors opened could knock a person flat, our parents warned. But we were perversely enchanted at the prospect of subjecting ourselves to this hideous stench, and each spring we eagerly awaited the day the doors of the dreaded, stinking chamber would be unsealed. We made taunting bets as to which of us could endure it the longest. But the moment the first explosive punch of sulfurous stench billowed out, we all ran away, gagging.

In winter, nighttime hide-and-seek was our special thrill. On the cold, crisp, moonlit nights when a hard crust had formed on the snow, we jumped on our *sparks*, the ubiquitous kick-sleds that served as our winter transportation, and sailed off across the glittering snow, we younger children seated in front. Silently, lest we arouse unwanted attention, we chased one another's black shadows, the only sound the hissing and scratching of steel runners as we veered dizzily right and left across the moonlit snowscape.

At these times of revelry in the natural world, the war—the crushing backdrop of our constricted lives—did not exist. For me, a child of the occupation, war was the norm. The adults spoke endlessly of something called peace, but I could not imagine what it meant.

We lived in constant fear of the occupying forces. One winter afternoon Mother and I were in town to visit the family. It wasn't late, but darkness had already swallowed the city and no one was venturing out. In town, people stayed indoors at night to avoid trouble. A thick blanket of snow muffled the city. Heavy flakes swirled around us as Mother and I hurried along the deserted street to Aunt Sissel's apartment, which was in a building identical to, and just behind, Besta and Besten's. She and Uncle Einar had a small tobacconist's shop on the ground floor that in normal times would have been stocked with fruit, vegetables, pop and candy. Uncle Inge and Aunt Anna lived in a small white frame house just a block away.

Suddenly the padded silence was broken by the piercing, high-pitched wail of a siren screaming up the street behind us. I didn't dare turn to look. Were they after us? There was no one else on the street.

"It's the Black Maria," Mother said, her voice steady. The Black Maria was the black police wagon that came to arrest people. No one came back after the Black Maria fetched them away. A numbing fear flashed up my legs and I felt my bladder start to give way. I was torn between running and stopping dead still on the sidewalk. I sensed Mother was frightened too, but she marched steadily along, her hand tightly clasping mine, as if nothing unusual were happening. The ominous vehicle sped past us, then abruptly braked and rolled to a stop near Uncle Inge and Aunt Anna's house, barely two blocks away.

"It surely can't be at their house," Mother said, but I heard anxiety in her voice. The doors of the Black Maria flew open and German soldiers leaped out and ran up the steps to the house next door. They banged on it, shouting. There was loud commotion, and before we could tell what had happened, they sped off again.

"Was someone arrested?" I whispered, my heart still pounding.

"I don't know," Mother answered. "Maybe someone did something wrong, something dangerous."

About this time, Mother unveiled a plan that very well might have brought the Black Maria to our own door. It was called *hamstring*—food gathering on the black market—and it was strictly forbidden. Black market entrepreneurs were a consuming concern of the Third Reich, judging from the posters on walls throughout the town warning against this transgression. One I found especially intimidating showed a huge, sinister rat carrying a large bag over its shoulder. If caught, a black marketeer could count on an unpleasant fate.

Mother explained to Grandmother and Aunt Anna that she had written to Aunt Lina and told her she was coming to sew for any of her neighbors who wanted clothing altered. My fun-loving Aunt Lina was married to Father's jovial brother, Uncle Oscar. Unlike my father, fate had put him on a ship that was out at sea the day of the invasion. He now sailed with the Allies on the dangerous Shetland convoys. Their home was in a remote valley a day's boat ride away.

My plucky Mother, an accomplished seamstress, had developed a lively bartering business altering people's old clothes; she turned the fabric inside out and remade it into new suits and dresses for the next generation. In exchange, she got contraband baskets of eggs, buckets of milk or an extra ration of sugar, and these she shared with our family. Most people's clothes were threadbare, but thanks to her skillful handiwork, I was as well turned out as the most pampered of peacetime children—save for shoes. They had all but disappeared from the stores, except for some made of fish skin and cardboard. My heels bled from the blisters they rubbed on my feet, but there was no help for it, even from my extraordinarily resourceful mother. Aside from procuring shoes, there was nothing she couldn't do, it seemed to me. She could be depended on to take charge of everything. I was very proud she was my mother.

Hamstring was dangerous because Norwegian civil police were posted at all public conveyances and they kept a keen eye on those disembarking from the passenger boats that plied the coast. So Grandmother and Aunt Anna did their best to dissuade her, but Mother countered with her chronic complaint. "There isn't enough food to put on the table to feed the children or keep the old people alive. They've stolen every scrap of food they can find."

Not that Aunt Anna herself lacked spunk. A country woman with a droll sense of humor and a heavy rural dialect well suited to fanciful storytelling, she was one of the few people who seemed to have Mother's unconditional seal of approval.

In the early years of the occupation, Uncle Inge had taken the five-day coastal steamer trip to North Norway to fetch his senile, starving foster parents, Jenny and Edgar, now childless, from Signaldal. When the three of them were about to board the steamer at Tromsø for Aalesund, the half-crazed old man ran away and hid and wasn't found for many hours. I saw him once on a visit to their house, wasted and cadaverous, tied to his bed so he wouldn't eat his own excrement, his mad eyes dancing in fury.

One day when Aunt Anna was coping with all this, a convoy of German troops swept through the rural neighborhood where they were living and stopped in front of their home. Two German soldiers climbed on the roof of their house and commenced to fire.

"They stayed up there for hours, shooting and farting, while I was home alone trying to peel potatoes for dinner and calm the old people," Aunt Anna later complained indignantly. "Germans! A pack of fools!"

In the end, of course, we went hamstring. Nothing ever dissuaded my mother once she had made up her mind.

Aunt Lina's yellow two-story house stood next to a river in a valley so steep and narrow that the farmers staked their cows by the ankles to graze them on the precipitously sloped meadows. In the fall, when they harvested hay from these meadows, the hay bales were sent shooting down the mountainside and across the river on a wire pulley. But even in this idyllic place, the Germans had intruded. Long, deep and narrow, the fjord at the foot of the valley appealed to their strategic interests. They tramped across the countryside on restless patrols, crawling like green lice over the landscape.

We arrived by boat just in time for the winter provisioning. Food was requisitioned here by our self-appointed liberators as well, but these farmers and their wives, far from German bureaucracy, were a wily lot. While Nazi patrols roved the sylvan valley, sausage and salt-cured meats clandestinely were prepared from portions spirited aside after butchering. Butter and cheese were churned from milk withheld on the sly. Flatbread and lefse were baked from mysteriously milled flour. Surreptitious food preparation took place at night in the cellar of a nearby farmhouse where the womenfolk, murmuring and laughing softly, gathered for their illicit task. A lamp hung from a beam, casting a warm glow and shifting shadows. Tantalizing smells of salt-cured meats wafted through the room. Sheep intestines hung drying from overhead beams, awaiting sausage meat. Mother perched on a barrel of brine-cured lamb, smiling broadly as she stuffed sausage into casings and tied off the ends.

She roused me from sleep in the middle of the night that we were to return home with our contraband goods. They were packed into two huge, heavy suitcases that she barely could lift. Aunt Lina rolled me up in a stiff woolen blanket and stuffed me into the horse-drawn sled that was to take us down to the boat. Thick snowflakes were falling all around us, and the horse snorted and stamped its feet threateningly while the suitcases were tucked out of sight. Finally we were under way, Aunt Lina in her fur coat and rakish hat; Mother, as always, in her simple beige, man-tailored cloth coat and high-peaked, navy felt hat. We slid silently down the valley. There were no bells on the harness, no lamp on the sled, not a light to be seen anywhere, but our horse knew the way. Even though the adults spoke in whispers, I could hear the nervousness in Aunt Lina's voice. But the gait of the horse, trotting confidently along in the blackness, lulled me back to sleep and I didn't fully awake again until shortly before we docked in Aalesund.

"Now you must listen carefully," Mother instructed as I wiped sleep from my eyes and we gathered our belongings. "You mustn't say anything to anyone about what we have in the suitcases." Fear shot through my stomach. I could see people standing about on the pier in quiet knots and armed police pacing back and forth. An officer was stationed at the foot of the gangplank, scrutinizing passengers one by one. I looked into Mother's face for a clue to what might happen. I could read nothing in her face.

Suddenly there was a commotion, a woman's cry and a man cursing somewhere behind us. Two of the ship's officers came pushing through the crowd, dragging between them a sobbing woman who struggled to keep her face covered with her hands. Her long, loose brown hair fell unkempt across her face as they thrashed past us. She didn't seem to be wearing enough clothes against the cold.

"Stand back! Clear the gangway!" one of the officers shouted as they shoved the woman down the gangplank.

I stared in horror at this raw, disorderly scene. Whatever had she done?

"Slut!" one of the officers yelled as he threw her into the arms of a waiting policeman. Some of the passengers smiled sourly and shook their heads knowingly. I glanced at Mother, but her face remained impassive.

I wanted to ask what a slut was, but there wasn't time. Mother bent to pick up a suitcase with each hand and prodded me along in front of her. My knees shook as I gingerly made my way down the gangplank behind the other passengers. Once safely at the bottom, I paused to look anxiously back at Mother. She was coming down the gangplank with the air of someone carrying a load of feathers.

The officer eyed us coldly as we came alongside, his eyes narrowing.

"Good day," Mother sang out, nodding smartly as she passed. She never broke her stride.

"Good day," he answered sullenly, turning his steely eyes away from us to scan the next passenger. He didn't give us so much as a second glance.

It was Christmas, and Father had come home. He was full of fantastic stories of wondrous sights from his travels, and I clung to his side, begging for more. They promised me that this year *Julenissen* surely would pay a call at our house. On Christmas Eve, I noticed that Father slipped out of the house. Shortly there was a loud knock on our door, and Mother, exclaiming gaily, went to answer it. Hovering behind her, I saw in the doorway a thin figure in a tan raincoat with a grimacing mask of white whiskers under a red, pointed cap.

"Merry Christmas!" this fearsome apparition shouted as he tried to press upon me a package wrapped in brown paper.

I howled in terror, ran into the living room and slid to safety behind the stove, sobbing. Mother rushed after me, pulled me into her embrace and tried to calm me. "Don't be afraid, dear little Hanna. It's just Papa, see? He brought you a present." He took off the mask and handed me the package. Dubiously, I unwrapped it. It was a green cardboard elephant whose legs moved when you pulled the strings. I was glad for the elephant but distrustful of its provenance. Why had they tried to trick me? And where was the real Julenissen?

Detained by the Germans, Father gamely explained.

He had brought home a bottle of something strong to drink, which he kept in the glass cupboard in the living room. One day when Mother was busy in the kitchen, I saw him pour a glassful from the bottle. He threw back his head and quaffed it down, and then he did it again. I didn't like the look on his face, so I took the elephant and tiptoed up to the attic to play. I don't know how long it was before I heard their voices below in the living room, arguing—hers cold, hard and accusing, his angry and bitter. He swore something I couldn't understand, then shouted that my grandmother was a Finn. I jumped in fright when a chair fell to the floor. Then he keened a string of vile curses, building to a screaming crescendo. Finally I heard the sound of glass shattering against the wall.

I slid down the steps on my bottom, numb with fear. Mother was in the hallway, her face contorted. "Papa is a horrible man. You mustn't believe anything he says. He's a horrible, mean man!" Her face was ashen and her voice shook.

When he left again, our lives resumed as if he had not been there at all.

Pernille was baking blood pudding. I hovered hungrily in the doorway of her large, sunny kitchen, strewn with colorful braided floor mats. The fragrance from the stove was wonderful, unlike any I'd ever smelled. Nelli had just butchered a pig. I wasn't allowed to see the actual killing, but immediately afterward, when the animal was hung by its hind feet behind the barn, I was permitted to watch as the hot, steaming blood from the slit in its throat gushed into a bucket.

"That's for the blood pudding," Nelli told me, grinning mischievously. I was half-afraid of Nelli, even though she patiently suffered my constant presence at her heels as she went about her farm chores. I didn't believe her. Surely people didn't eat blood?

"Blood pudding is unclean. You must promise never to eat it," Mother had told me once when I asked her about it, and I heartily agreed. It was revolting.

But now, assaulted by this mouth-watering aroma, I was unsure. How could anything unclean smell so good? "Mother says blood pudding is unclean," I announced righteously.

"Pish!" Pernille snorted. "I'll give you a taste. You can see for yourself."

"Mother says I can't eat it." My resolve was weakening.

"Well, you can just try a little piece to see if you like it." She smiled conspiratorially. Could Pernille really know something Mother didn't know? When she sliced into the dark brown loaf, the aroma was irresistible. I knew I was lost. After a first tentative taste, I wolfed down the remainder.

Pernille laughed teasingly. "That wasn't so bad, was it? Now you mustn't tell your mother."

Not tell Mother! What had I done? Guiltily, I hurried home to find her knitting by the living room window. Somewhere she had procured black and white wool, and she was industriously at work on intricately patterned knee socks for me. I viewed them with grave misgivings. My legs were allergic to wool, and all winter I scratched at my shins until they bled.

"I ate blood pudding at Pernille's," I blurted out.

The knitting stopped. Startled, she looked into my face.

"But didn't I tell you never to eat it?"

I nodded miserably.

"Then why did you disobey me?"

"It smelled so good," I answered weakly.

She stared hard at me another moment, then threw the knitting aside and jumped to her feet. She dragged me by the hand into the kitchen and seated herself in a chair. Then she pulled me into her lap, backside up, and smacked me with her open hand a half-dozen times.

"You must learn to mind," she said when she put me down. I was whimpering softly, knowing I deserved my punishment.

"Really, I don't know who you take after," she said disgustedly. She always told me that whenever I misbehaved. "One day, when you know the truth, you'll be sorry for how you've behaved," she added ominously.

She often told me that too.

NINETEEN
MAKING PEACE WITH PEACE

I awoke to a flash of light and a sound like bouncing thunderbolts. Mother was sitting up in bed, staring out to the fjord through the little window by her bed. We pulled on our clothes and hurried outside for a better look. Nelli and Pernille were outside too. We strained to make out something in the fjord, but could see nothing. Then came a sudden barrage of explosions, and a huge light arced over the sky, momentarily revealing the outline of a ship. Then blackness again and another explosion of blinding light. Then another and another. Suddenly a huge explosion threw a cascading fireball into the sky as something blew apart in an unearthly display of color and blinding light. Enthralled, I watched the fireball shrink, then burp, bubble and sink into the blackness. Then all was still in the fjord.

The next day, arguments raged among the neighbors about what we had seen. Some said it was a German ship sunk by British bombers. Others said it was a British submarine blown up by the Germans. The spectacular incident, whatever it might have been, was proof to the grown-ups that we had not been forgotten. Each time a bomb exploded over the city, each time an air-raid siren sounded, they were torn between terror and gratitude.

Sometimes these incidents produced more anxiety. One balmy summer evening as our parents gossiped at Mother's back door and we children were perfecting the art of rolling down the grassy hillock by our cottage, someone noticed tiny flames licking the horizon over Aalesund. Then we heard the faint drone of airplanes and soon the skyline was ablaze. Helplessly, we watched the city burn.

Mother paced nervously to and fro outside, scanning the horizon, trying to determine in what part of town the bombs were falling. There was no one to answer and no way to know. She and I caught the first bus to town the next morning and hurried anxiously to Grandmother's. Everyone was safe.

As she had done many times before, Mother implored Grandmother to come live with us in the country.

"Dear Berit, everything went fine," Grandmother assured her. "We all just trooped down to the shelter." She smiled wearily and gave me a little hug.

"But, Mother . . ."

"No," Grandmother said firmly. We both knew that tone. She was not to be pestered further.

Soon, I had the opportunity to see a shelter firsthand. One day Mother dropped me at Aunt Sissel's shop while she and Grandmother went to check on the other church members. Mother was president of the Mormon women's auxiliary, the Relief Society, and she took her leadership duties very seriously. At the outbreak of the war, the missionaries had fled back to America, leaving the small congregation of Latter-day Saints to fend for itself. I liked to see Mother standing in front of the women, teaching them the church lessons and dispensing wise counsel about how to conduct their lives as proper Saints. I could see that they looked up to her.

In the shop, Aunt Sissel, as tall and easygoing as Mother was short and exacting, was presiding cheerfully over her pitiful wares. Despite the poverty of its offerings, the shop was the neighborhood center. Even though tobacco was all but a memory, the smell of nicotine from happier days still emanated from the walls. I liked to watch Aunt Sissel in the shop, dispensing her wares and sharing a good-natured joke with her customers. She had a merry twinkle in her eyes and a wonderful laugh, and she always made a loving fuss over me.

Mother and Grandmother hadn't been gone very long before the painful wail of an air-raid siren split the air. Instantly, Aunt Sissel grabbed my arm and pulled me out the door. We dashed down the cobblestones to the shelter half a block away in a cavernous basement. Sandbags had been stacked against the windows and it was pitch dark inside. I gripped Aunt Sissel's hand tightly as we scurried down the passageway crammed with people and found a place to sit. She pulled me close and comforted me as best she could in a shaking voice. The sirens wailed for what seemed hours, then the all-clear signal sounded. With cries of relief, we jumped to our feet and rushed up the stairs. When we reached the street, we heard people shouting that it had been a false alarm.

A s if bombings were not enough, Mother embarked on another of her high-hazard schemes: She determined to make lutefisk—cod soaked in poisonous lye. This is never a frivolous undertaking, even by the practiced. The fact that she'd never made lutefisk was not to stand in her way. She knew that after the fish was soaked in the lye, it had to be repeatedly rinsed and soaked in buckets of clean water. Properly pre-pared, this dubious delicacy has the consistency of tender, gelatinous lobster, especially when ladled with butter. Of course, we had no butter but counted ourselves lucky to have the fish and some potatoes. Mother set to work, humming happily. I liked to hear her sing; she was vain about her strong, melodious singing voice.

I hovered about the lutefisk buckets, impatient but apprehensive. I'd never tasted lutefisk but I'd heard warning jokes about it. Still, if Mother served it, it must be fine food. When Sunday came and we were to eat it, we seated ourselves solemnly at the table to partake of this rare treat. I chewed the first morsel experimentally. It had an odd taste, a little bitter, but I didn't want to disappoint her. So I picked at it with a show of gusto, but ate more potatoes than fish. Mother heaped her plate and ate raven-ously, then had a second helping. So much food made us both sleepy, and I didn't protest when we lay down in the bedroom for an afternoon nap.

I awoke in terrible pain, my stomach contracting. Then I heard Mother moaning. She was very pale, and sweat poured from her face.

"I have a stomach ache," I whined.

"Oh, poor little Hanna. Do you think you can go to the kitchen and get an empty bucket?" Panicked at the sight of my mother immobilized, I weakly rose on wobbly legs and made my way to the kitchen. I could hear her groaning alarmingly, and I hurried back with the bucket as fast as my shaking legs would permit. I had no more than gotten it positioned under her head when a stream of vomit poured out.

"It must have been the lutefisk," she whispered weakly. "We've been poisoned."

I began to cry softly.

"Don't cry, dear little Hanna. Lie down and rest."

As I crawled back into my bed, a wave of nausea washed over me. I lunged for the bucket and stinking cod pumped from my belly. When it was over, I fell back on my bed, too weak to weep.

When I awoke, my stomach cramps were gone. But something had disturbed my sleep, a strange sound that was coming nearer. Groggily, I sat up. Mother was snoring lightly. But the mysterious sound, like bees buzzing angrily, was getting louder. I tiptoed to the little window by Mother's bed. What could it be? Then Mother opened her eyes. "What's that noise?" she mumbled.

All I could see was a pale blue morning sky and the leafy branches of the large birch tree that grew next to the cottage. Suddenly Mother's eyes widened in comprehension, and she pulled herself up to stare in alarm out the window.

Just then a small open-cockpit plane buzzed over our garden, skimming the treetops. I had never seen an airplane, but this one was so close that we could see the pilot's head wrapped in a leather helmet and goggles. He turned his head for an instant directly toward our upturned, terrified faces at the window, then pulled his plane up in a tight turn for another pass at us.

"Will he bomb us?" My heart was pounding so loud I could hear it over the roar of the airplane. But when he reappeared at our window he merely gunned his engine in an insolent, deafening farewell. We held our breaths a long time, waiting to be sure he wasn't coming back.

Afterwards I related with considerable self-importance the story of the day the German plane flew so close over our house that we could see the pilot's face. It was easier to recount our fright at the hands of the Nazi pilot than to dwell on the fact that we had been poisoned by Mother's cooking. I concluded that something must have gone amiss that wasn't her fault. It was inconceivable that Mother could do something wrong.

I was mad for fishing. I once for a thrilling moment caught hold of a slippery sea trout with my bare hands in a little stream. Another time I brought home a huge crab I managed to catch at low tide with two sticks. I poked at the crab until it angrily seized the sticks in its claws and held fast, then I plopped it into a bucket and proudly raced home to beg Mother to cook my prize. In winter, I liked to watch the armada of tawny wooden fishing boats plying Borgundfjord when the cod arrived.

They came chugging proudly back to port, so loaded with fish that they were almost swamped, for all the good it did us. Germans seemed to have an insatiable appetite for cod.

One day during cod harvest Mother and I were uneasily awaiting Father's arrival home from town. She kept checking and absently winding her gold watch as the dreary winter afternoon wore on, holding it up to her ear and frowning. It was her most treasured possession. Father had given it to her when they were engaged. I was not allowed to touch it.

Finally we heard him coming through the yard, singing. Startled, Mother peered out the kitchen window, gasped in surprise, and ran to throw open the door. Father stood in the doorway chortling, full of himself and beer. Balanced across his shoulders was a monstrous codfish wrapped in paper. He had one arm draped over its head, the other over its slippery tail, both of which hung a good distance beyond his shoulders. Much of the paper had fallen away in the course of his high-spirited journey home, so his overcoat was smeared with slime. He smiled grandly, reeking of fish and alcohol.

She wasted no time attacking it. With one deft stroke, she slit open the belly and freed the large, firm orange mass of roe, then decapitated the fish. The head was a special delicacy. Her dull, worn knife blade sawed raggedly at the carcass. "What I wouldn't give for a sharp knife!" she grumbled happily. It was her common complaint. I wished with all my being that she could have the knife of her heart's dearest desiring. It was the only thing she ever asked for. But knives were not to be had.

While the codfish made a public spectacle of themselves in the fjord, the mackerel made less of a splash. They arrived in early fall and were best taken at night. Mother got wind of a clandestine mackerel fishing expedition that was afoot at a little inlet not far from our cottage. The catch would be discreetly distributed later elsewhere. She wanted a share of it and meant to be there to see it safely brought aboard. So she and I and a half dozen like-minded neighbors set out at dusk, excited children and murmuring adults, through a couple of farmyards and a sparsely treed forest. We came out of the woods on a rocky promontory overlooking a little cove. Here we settled in to wait as darkness fell.

The moon rose, laying a golden, polished sheen on the black water. There wasn't a sound, not a movement on sea or land. Finally we heard the gentle, rhythmic splash of oars coming around the point. A rowboat pulled in below us and shipped oars. We waited in expectant silence and soon heard it: the muffled chug-chug of the motorboat coming around the point. It drew up alongside the rowboat and cut its engine. No one spoke.

The men in the rowboat fell to work, laying out the net. The only sound was the dip of their oars, which left a shining ripple on the dark water. Then the fishermen, backlit by the moon, began to haul in the net, arm over arm, their tensed bodies straining alternately backwards and forwards in an ancient ritual, expertly plumbing the secret depths of the sea, smoothly opening its watery folds to scoop up its glimmering treasure.

When the net broke the surface, we saw an explosion of throbbing, glistening light. The writhing, leaping fish hurled themselves into the moonglow, and the quivering mass hung suspended in the air for a luminous moment, sparkling brilliantly against the blackness. Quickly, the men tipped their shimmering bounty, and a river of quicksilver cascaded into the motorboat. Then, as stealthily as they had come, the boats rounded the point and were gone, leaving just the faintest trace of silver-tipped wake on a velvet, ebony sea.

I had never seen anything so beautiful.

One day toward the end of summer we got word that Father's ship had been sunk by the British near the Russian-Norwegian border and all hands were presumed lost. When Mother explained that he would not be coming back, I tried to read her face, but it held no clue. Father was almost always gone, so we went on with our usual routine. She didn't speak of him to me again, and I asked no questions.

I was awakened one morning some time after that by Mother banging pots and pans furiously about in the kitchen. When I crept from my bed and cautiously opened the kitchen door to see what the commotion was about, she turned on me angrily.

"Look here," she commanded. She held her precious wristwatch under my nose. "It's broken." I could see the crystal was cracked.

"It's your fault. I found it on the floor this morning. You must have brushed it off the table in the night. How many times have I told you not to touch this watch?"

Incredulous, I stared up at her. She knew I didn't get up in the night.

She was the one who got up to visit the commode in the back hallway during the night, not I. The last thing she did each evening before she went to bed was to put the watch on the dining room table.

"But, Mother, I didn't do it," I stammered.

"Yes, you did. How else could it have been broken?" she snapped.

"But I didn't touch it. I didn't come out here in the night." I was desperate with confusion.

"Don't lie to me. You know you broke it. And there's no way to get it repaired."

She went into the hallway to fetch the willow switch while I stood frozen in perfect shock, trying to comprehend why she was accusing me of something she knew I had not done.

I tried again as she dragged me into the kitchen. "But I didn't get out of bed! It couldn't have been my fault! I didn't touch it!"

"It is your fault!" she insisted. She tossed me over her lap and applied the switch to my bottom, but I did not cry. My heart had abruptly turned to stone, caught unawares by deep treachery on a fine fall morning.

"That will teach you to take care of our things!" she said when she had spent her fury.

I could only stare into her angry face in disbelief, the whole order of my world collapsing. I knew she had to have broken the watch herself. I was certain that she knew she herself had broken it. Crushed and bewildered by her willful betrayal, I climbed into the attic in my nightclothes to absorb the heartrending, inexplicable knowledge that Mother had lied, and that she had punished me for something she knew she had done herself.

Bored and lonesome, I was listlessly watching raindrops trickling monotonously down the windowpanes one interminable afternoon in the late fall of that year when suddenly a knock sounded on our door. Mother hurried to open it.

On the stoop stood a skeleton of a man with a duffel bag over his shoulder. He was unshaven and his eyes were sunken into his skull.

Mother's hands flew to her mouth. "Edvard? Is it you?" Her face turned pale.

He smiled thinly. "Yes. It's me."

"Dear God, I can't believe it! I got a telegram that said your ship was sunk and all hands lost. What happened to you?" Trance-like, she helped him out of his thin overcoat.

"Yes, we were sunk, all right."

"Have you eaten?"

He nodded. "I stopped by to let the old people in town know."

"I'll fix something right away. But you must tell me what happened." We went into the kitchen, and he wearily seated himself at the table.

"Yes," he sighed. His voice was somehow different from the one I remembered. "We were in a fjord when the British bombers came over us. We Norwegians forgot ourselves and ran on deck, waving. We were standing there at the railing when they opened fire. It happened so fast that I didn't grasp it until the man next to me dropped to the deck with his forehead blown away. The next instant I felt something sharp hit my leg. I leaped overboard without thinking and swam as hard as I could to shore.

"Two others made it behind me. The ship blew up just as we dragged ourselves up on the rocks. My leg was bleeding, so I tore my shirt and tied it around my leg to stop it. Then we crawled higher and found a little overhang. It kept us dry, anyway, but we had nothing to eat for three days, just drinking water from a little stream. A German patrol boat looking for the ship found us, and they sent me to a hospital to fix my leg."

He grimaced and pulled up his pant leg. A long, ragged scar ran up his shinbone. "It took a long time to heal," he said.

Mother and I regarded him wordlessly, trying to understand what he had been through. Then she turned to me, a smile on her face.

"Isn't it wonderful, Hanna? Papa is home safely. He's all right after all."

Uncle Ivar's wedding was to be the first party I would attend. Shyly, I climbed into his lap in Grandmother's kitchen. I was fascinated by his deep black hair, which lay in tight waves across his head. His straight nose and high cheekbones were a close copy of Grandmother's features. He was full of fun and all the girls chased after him, Mother said. His favorite trick was to show off for them by diving, fully clothed, off ships and docks into the sea. It made Grandmother very cross.

Now he was about to settle down and be married, and they were discussing the wedding plans as I ran my fingers through his hair. Suddenly he coughed, his chest heaving. Mother and Grandmother once again urged him to go to the doctor for medicine, but he once again breezily brushed them off.

"It's nothing," he assured them, bouncing me on his lap.

The wedding feast, such as it was, took place in Grandmother's apartment, the black blinds drawn tight lest the British bombers find our lights. Someone came with an accordion, and he sat on a stool, his cloth cap hanging over one eye, pumping soulful, lusty waltzes from his instrument while the grown-ups squeezed close to dance in the crowded living room. Everyone smiled and laughed as if there were no war beyond those black blinds.

But in the ensuing months, Uncle Ivar's cough worsened. The grown-ups were talking about him now in quiet, worried voices. Then one day Grandmother sat down at her kitchen table and buried her face in her apron. Mother stood behind her, hands on Grandmother's shuddering shoulders as she wept.

I was terrified. Grandmother was a rock.

"Uncle Ivar is very sick," Mother told me carefully. "He has tuberculosis."

He died not long after. She didn't tell me that it was the second time tuberculosis had claimed someone Mother and Grandmother loved.

When the war began to go badly for the Germans, our own lives grew worse. Even our playtime became hunts for food. We children spent days on an unsuccessful scheme to track wild rabbits in the snow and snare them with a thin, precious strand of copper wire carefully looped to seize the animal by the throat as it jumped through a fence.

Mother, as usual, made more successful arrangements. She somehow managed to find a pair of rabbits, and rabbits being rabbits, her enterprise quickly prospered. She kept them in a hutch down by the barn. She killed them sparingly, dispatching and skinning them herself. The white pelts she turned into a muff and hat for me.

As the winter of 1944–45 wore on, rumors intensified. Something was happening, people said. The Germans were on the move, and we had heard that some of them were camped by the road in a field not far from our cottage.

I was playing just outside the door, hopping about in snowdrifts up to my armpits, when suddenly a shot rang out. Mother rushed out to pull me indoors. She slammed the door shut and threw the metal bar across to lock it. She looked frightened, and that frightened me.

Shortly we heard another shot, closer this time.

"Stay away from the windows!" Mother cried.

I dropped to the floor by the living room stove and she took a seat in the corner by the china cabinet, knitting furiously.

Then a bullet ripped into our chimney. We could hear stone and mortar flying loose. It was followed by a brutal volley that whizzed by the corners of our cottage. Then all was still.

Once my fear subsided, I was desperate to go outside to see what had happened, but Mother adamantly forbade it. She kept me inside the rest of that day with my nose pressed against the window in hopes of seeing a German. The next day I begged and whined to go outside until she finally relented.

"Don't go far," she cautioned as I struggled with the straps of my much too long, hand-me-down skis. I was by no means an accomplished skier and they were too long for me to control in any case. The poles were much too tall as well, so I haltingly propelled myself along the snow-bound path toward the rumored German encampment. There was no sign of life anywhere except listless smoke from neighboring chimneys; all was snowy, desolate silence. I poled awkwardly along, dragging my skis under me. It was sweaty work.

Not far from the cottage, a little rise blocked the view of the road. The path bent around this hillock, and, on the other side, was a small open field where we often played in summer. Rounding the bend, I had an unobstructed view into the field, and I gasped when I saw it. It was filled with tents and men in white snowsuits, some standing idly about on skis, some sitting around a campfire. Germans! They must have been the ones who did the shooting! I stood staring as if paralyzed, my fear overwhelmed by curiosity. At first they didn't seem to take notice of me, but then one of them broke away from the group, skiing toward me. I watched just a moment longer to be sure, but there was no mistake: he was coming after me.

I kicked loose from my skis, somehow disentangling my feet from the straps, tucked a ski and pole under each arm, and ran for my life through the deep snow. It was like running in quicksand. I threw a frantic look over my shoulder. Tall and terrifying, the embodiment of all our night-mares, the huge Nazi soldier was poling after me with methodical, mur-derous vengeance. I could almost see his menacing face under his white hood. Shot through with adrenalin, I leaped frantically through the snow, expecting a bullet to pierce my back at any moment. Finally the cottage door was in reach, and I threw down my skis and poles and rushed to the door.

"Mother! Mother! A German's coming!" I shouted as I crashed through the door and slammed it shut behind me.

Mother flew out of the kitchen, eyes wide. A moment later we heard insistent pounding on the door. I dived under the living room table and tucked my knees up under my chin. The tablecloth wasn't long enough to hide me completely.

I heard Mother hesitantly open the door. Uninvited, the German stepped into the hallway. I could see his boots and the legs of a gray-green uniform under his white camouflage suit. They said something I could not understand, and I heard him laugh. Cautiously, I lifted the table-cloth for a better view.

"She's afraid. She's just a little child," Mother said. I realized they were both looking at me under the table. I was deeply ashamed, but not enough to come out.

"You have rabbits," he said in a strained accent.

"Yes," Mother admitted. "Just a few. Just enough for ourselves."

"We require them," he said. "My men have nothing to eat. I can't pay you for them," he added stiffly.

She put on her coat and warned me to stay inside. When the door closed behind them, I crawled out and climbed onto the daybed to press my nose against the window. I could see them down by the barn where the hutches were lined up against the wall. Mother and the Nazi soldier stood there, gesturing toward the cages. After a few minutes, she came back.

"Will they take all our rabbits?" I asked apprehensively.

She nodded. "He says they have nothing to eat."

I remember much milling about near our cottage that historic morning and much speculation about whether our neighbor Marit really ought to take the cows up to mountain pasture just then. I had begged permission to accompany her and her fiancé Jan as they took the milk cows on this annual spring pilgrimage into the forested foothills to forage above Hatlehol. Rumors that the war was about to end had been flying from house to house for days, though as long as I could remember, the adults had been chanting the familiar, hope-filled mantra: "When the war is over . . ." This day, though, they seemed even more distracted by the topic than usual.

But my mind was firmly fixed on the cows. I was six, and it was the first time I had been allowed to help with this grown-up task. I was mad with impatience at the delay.

The sun broke through about noon on May 7, 1945, according to the history books. All I remember is that as the morning wore on, more nervous people came out of their houses to exchange the latest rumors. At some point, Marit must have decided it was now or never. After a messy start at the assembly point by the barn, the animals dutifully fell into plodding line behind the clanging bell of the lead cow. Marit and Jan walked ahead of the mooing entourage, and I scampered proudly alongside keeping order and well clear of hooves. Our presence was a formality, really; the cows knew the way up the narrow, meandering trail among ferns and blueberry bushes.

To this day, I don't know where we were going. Nor do I know what happened to the cows.

When it began, we had been under way for some time, long enough that I could look down from a vantage point high up on the forested bench to see our cottage nestled like a minuscule red toy playhouse in a green meadow far below.

Suddenly, somewhere a long way off, a tiny, musical sound broke the stillness of that sun-dappled day. In the first few moments, the sound must not have registered. But shortly it dawned on us that the tinkling sound we were hearing was not the cowbell. Puzzled, Marit stopped the procession in a sunlit grove and paused to listen.

We could hear it clearly then: "Ding-dong! Ding-dong! Ding-dong!"— a wild, insistent symphony of chimes cascading from steeple to steeple across the countryside, each church bell ringing out nearer and more jubilantly than the last.

It was a sound I had never heard.

We stood transfixed on the path, I anxiously scanning their faces to see what it meant. Marit and Jan stared at one another in what must at first have been disbelief, then ecstatic comprehension.

"Church bells!" she cried. "The war is over!"

He shouted and lifted her off the ground, whirling her round and round in a giddy embrace while I gaped in astonishment. Never had I witnessed such behavior. I can see them still in that fern-rimmed grove, heads thrown back in joyous laughter, a shaft of sunlight falling through the trees to bless their jubilant dance of liberation.

Then they each grabbed one of my hands and we flew back down the path so fast my feet barely touched the ground. They were heedless of everything—bushes, brambles, the cows, my utter bewilderment—save the joyful clamor of bells. Never before had I been dragged pell-mell through the woods by supposedly sane adults.

When we reached Mother's cottage, our usually self-possessed neighbors were gathered at her back door in noisy, animated conversation. Some were hugging one another, others were laughing and joking loudly, their voices bold and careless. A few of the women were crying openly. Even some of the men were weeping.

I was thunderstruck. So this was what they meant by the end of the war: grown-ups acting crazy and undependable.

I sank to the ground, crying quietly.

I don't know how long I sat there sniveling in the grass before Mother noticed and came to bend over me. "Why on earth are you crying?" she asked in bewilderment. I could feel many curious eyes on me.

"I don't want the war to end," I sobbed.

She laughed uneasily and said something in a strained, apologetic voice about my being "just a child who doesn't know any better." Instantly I understood that I had shamed her, and my heart sank in mortification. So I allowed her to persuade me that this was a day to be glad, but I retained my private doubts about the wisdom of throwing the whole world into turmoil for the sake of this thing called "peace."

Not until ten days later would I make my own private peace with peace. On the seventeenth of May, Norway's Constitution Day, we were leaning out the window of Uncle Leif's apartment in Aalesund to watch the celebratory parade. He was Father's youngest brother, and many of the Hansens had gathered for this historic occasion.

I retain fleeting but vivid images of that rain-soaked, cement-gray day:

a band piping a ragged march as I stretched on tiptoe to see over the windowsill; row after row of people dressed in dark raincoats marching solemnly under a forest of dark umbrellas. "Hip, hip, hurrah!" they shouted over and over, and we answered with voices unaccustomed to shouting.

On cue from the band, everyone suddenly burst into an unfamiliar song—people in the windows, people on the sidewalks, people in the procession. I saw adults unashamedly wiping tears from their cheeks as they raised strong, long-stilled voices to sing *"Ja, vi elsker dette landet"*— "Yes, we love this land." I had no idea this was our national anthem, but I was enthralled by the fervent, swelling sound of their voices reverberating along the parade route.

The only color in this gray-on-gray scene was the brilliant red, white and blue of an unfamiliar flag proudly carried by many marchers. With stubborn faith that this day would arrive, they had hidden this forbidden symbol of our nation from Gestapo eyes for five long years. Having known only the swastika, it never occurred to me that there might be a Norwegian flag.

Awed by the spectacle, swept up by song, thrilled by the sight of all those flags, I finally concluded that peace must be a fine thing after all. Anyone could see that this flag was prettier than the swastika.

One day not long afterwards Aunt Gudrid came to visit us, and Mother sent a playmate and me up the hillside some distance from our cottage to fetch a precious can of milk from a farmer she'd persuaded to sell to us. It was the first time she'd entrusted me with such an important, grown-up task, and I skipped proudly along the path, which was pocked with muddy cow prints after a recent rain. The farmer gave us a dubious look but filled our can and tapped on the lid. But when we grabbed the handle, not much more than a metal wire, really, it cut painfully into our palms. We could hardly keep the can lifted off the ground.

Grimly we set out, dragging and bumping the milk can between us. We had to stop often to trade places because of the pain to our palms. We hadn't gotten far when we paused to set the can down at a spot riddled with muddy cow hoof holes. Somehow, the can slipped from our grasp, teetered a breathtaking moment, then fell. The lid popped off and the milk rushed into the black muck. It made creamy rivulets as it flowed into the hoof print holes.

Wailing in terrified anguish, I scrambled after the milk on my knees, cupping my hands in a desperate effort to scoop it up before it sank out of sight. I gathered muddy little handfuls and threw them into the empty bucket. I scraped helplessly at the holes until even the foam disappeared.

Apprehensively, we approached the cottage, where Mother and Gudrid stood waiting for us at the back door, smiling expectantly. But when Mother got a good look at us, a frown fell over her face. "Whatever happened to you? You're all muddy!" she exclaimed.

"We spilled the milk!" I sobbed.

She peered into the can, then turned it upside down. A trickle of muddy swill ran into the grass.

"I tried to put the milk back but I couldn't. I *tried* to put it back," I cried.

"How could you be so careless? That's all the milk we can get! Don't you understand that?" she demanded angrily.

"Berit, you can see the child feels badly enough . . ." Gudrid began hesitantly, but Mother turned on her.

"She has to learn responsibility," she snapped. With that, she grabbed my arm and hauled me into the kitchen. I knew what was coming. She threw me across her lap and slapped my behind with sharp, hard strokes. They hurt, but not nearly so much as my six-year-old's heartbroken shame at having failed her.

On a hot summer day a few weeks after the war ended, Mother put on her best dress and fussed a good deal with her hair for a weekday. She looked me over carefully and tried to run a comb through my hopelessly tangled, tightly matted blond curls. She seemed tense.

"We're going to the bus stop to see if there are any orphans who need a home," she announced as she tugged the comb through my unruly locks. "They're coming on the bus today."

Stunned, I stared into her face, waiting for an explanation. "If we get one, you'll have a brother or sister," she smiled. "Think of those poor children, left without a mother or father, and no home," she continued, clucking her tongue in sympathy.

My chest tightened in anguish. I wasn't a good enough child, and so she wanted another. Heartsick, I trudged mutely along beside her to the bus stop. When we arrived, we learned that everyone waiting there had already ordered an orphan; it was all arranged beforehand. At that news, a fervent hope blossomed in my bruised heart. They were all spoken for, so maybe there would be none for us.

When the lumbering, dark-red bus finally arrived and sagged to a stop, we stared curiously into the windows. Sad-faced children peered back at us through the glass. A woman got out and began to call out names from a list. We stood off to the side until she finished. Then Mother pushed forward, cleared her throat, and addressed the woman in her best voice.

"I can take a child. I didn't know about it beforehand, but I thought you might have some that you don't have homes for."

"No, it's all arranged, thank you," the woman answered dismissively.

One by one, thin, pale, ill-clad, the children stepped from the bus. Their faces were forlorn and fearful. Hanging around each child's neck was a tag, tied with a string, on which was written his or her name and destination. One by one their new families led them away while Mother and I stood wordlessly apart, nurturing our divergent hopes.

When the last child for this stop had been distributed, Mother stepped up to the matron and again began to argue her case. I walked behind the bus and tucked the toes of one foot under the rear wheel as far as I could. Moments later, the driver slammed the door and ground into gear. The bus rolled backwards ever so slightly, just far enough to flatten the tips of my toes, and I yelped in pain. It roared off in a cloud of dust, leaving me hopping on one foot and Mother standing empty-handed in the roadway.

"Let's go home," she snapped curtly.

I limped toward her. When I saw the disappointment in her eyes, a helpless, aching sorrow settled over me. How could I make her happy with me?

"What's wrong with your foot, then?" she asked distractedly when we had gone a few steps.

"The bus ran over it," I confessed quietly.

"Uff da, you're completely impossible!" she sighed crossly. "I don't know who you take after," she added, repeating a familiar refrain. "Thank heavens I've only got one of you to contend with."

With freedom restored our spirits soared, but the shops remained empty. I was given a little bank after the war and dutifully deposited Christmas and birthday money into it with no comprehension of what it might buy. A couple of years passed before the things adults had so longed for began to appear in shops: shoes, soap, tobacco, sugar, fabric, kitchenware.

Knives.

I spotted it in the window of a little shop in town while Mother was next door searching for thread in the fabric shop. The knife shop had always been there, but it had never displayed much in the windows. But Christmas was coming, and there it was: a large, lovely kitchen knife with a wooden handle, just the kind Mother had always said she wanted. And in my pocket I carried the money I had been saving just for this occasion. I already had determined that this year I was big enough to buy Mother her first Christmas present from me.

I made sure she still was preoccupied with the thread transaction, then scooted inside to consult with the shopkeeper. I pointed at the knife and laid my money on the counter. "It's for my mother for Christmas," I explained proudly.

He wrapped the knife in paper and tied string around it. I slipped it into the arm of my coat and ran out the door. I was bursting with happiness.

Mother didn't notice anything until we got on the bus. "What have you got there?" she asked suspiciously. She frowned at the package now visible at the hem of my sleeve.

"I can't tell you," I answered bravely.

"What have you done?" I didn't like her tone.

"It's a surprise," I answered weakly. "It's a Christmas present. For you."

"I hope you haven't bought a knife," she said. "That I don't have any use for."

Her words washed over me like ice water. I turned away from her so she would not see my face, and we rode home in silence. When we got there, she demanded I unwrap it.

My chin quivered. "But it's for Christmas. It's your gift," I protested.

"No, I don't want any Christmas gift." She took the package from my hands and unwrapped it. She held the knife up and turned it over disdainfully.

"How much did you pay for it?" she asked, her voice hard.

When I told her, she scowled. "You must take it back," she told me flatly. "It's too much money. I don't have any use for a knife."

"But you always said you need a sharp knife," I cried.

She was adamant. The next time we went to town, she ordered me to return it while she attended to an errand nearby. Mortified, I entered the shop and handed the package to the shopkeeper. "I have to get my money back," I told him.

"There's nothing wrong with the knife?" He seemed mystified.

"No. My mother doesn't want it."

He studied me a moment, shook his head, then opened the till and with great formality counted the money into my hand. I stuffed it into my pocket and walked wordlessly out the door, face aflame.

"Did you get the money back?" Mother demanded when she saw me.

"Yes," I answered bitterly.

I strode down the sidewalk ahead of her, seared by fury, heartbreak, and humiliation. But I did not cry, and I did not answer when she called after me.

Twenty

America

The fall after the war ended, Mother took me down to the red, one-room schoolhouse just down the hill from our well to see if I would be allowed to start classes a year early. "She's very clever for her age," I heard her boast to the schoolmaster. This was astonishing news to me.

He studied me dubiously. I was only six, and pitifully thin. Children were not supposed to start school until they were seven, but now that the war was over all manner of improbable things must have seemed possible. Perhaps the schoolmaster was just humoring her, but he with great formality took me into the cloakroom and asked me to step on scales that told my weight. Then he lined me up against the wall and measured my height.

"She's too little," he announced solemnly.

I saw the disappointment in Mother's face and was chagrined, once again, not to have measured up to her expectations. But I was relieved. School held terrors. When I did start classes the next year, school was an every-other-day affair and the classroom was dominated by rote learning, the schoolyard by bullies. Once, when my mother believed the schoolmaster knowingly had permitted me to be abused by the other students, she came to the schoolhouse door and delivered a blistering reprimand. Seated at our desks, we children listened, amazed at her audacious bravery, as she vehemently criticized him and—much to my amazement—passionately defended me.

Eventually we moved from the cottage to a second-story apartment in a house in nearby Flisnes, within walking distance to property my parents had bought in Hatlehol. Here they excavated a building site, just in case we were denied permission to emigrate to America. And here Mother raised rabbits, chickens, strawberries, and potatoes. And with a forked willow switch grasped in both hands, she searched for water where our well should be dug. Sure enough, the stick bent firmly down toward the earth right where the water was found, just as she predicted.

Father came home on leave from his ship in time to dispatch the chickens. A little crowd of neighbors gathered that day for the entertainment, knowing, I'm sure, that he was a citified seaman who had never killed a chicken in his life. Before he could get the proceedings under way, one of the hens Mother was holding at the ready suddenly hopped free of her arms and, in an awkward, flapping leap, thrashed skyward, squawking frightfully. The bird came to rest on a tree limb just above the chopping block. No amount of shooing could pry loose her death grip on the branch.

"You'll have to climb up and get her, Edvard," someone shouted tauntingly. Father grinned at this challenge and manfully heaved himself up the tree trunk until he reached the limb where the hen perched, nervously flapping her wings. The little knot of spectators shouted approval as Father slid out onto the limb, the bird nearly within grasp.

The hen hopped farther out on the branch.

Father cursed, grinned, and scooted closer. The hen again hopped farther out. They were at a standstill; the branch was bending, but the bird held on. We could see that Father was in danger of being bested by a hen, and so could he. Briskly ordering up a saw, he stubbornly set to work on the limb that held them both.

"Saw on the other side, Edvard, the other side!" his audience hooted. But Father, sawing away between the trunk and himself rather than between himself and the hen, serenely ignored this prudent counsel, clowning good-naturedly all the while. I had never seen my father so happily at the center of so much attention.

Shortly, of course, the limb broke open and Father and the hen tumbled together to the ground, feathers and curses flying. Before the terrified hen could flee, Mother was on it, and Father jumped to his feet and grabbed the axe. A few quick pointers from Mother and the luckless hen was transformed into a headless, gushing fountain of blood. Mother threw a bucket over the decapitated bird to contain it, but the bucket broke away in a rapid trot, fleeing to the woods. We all laughed until our sides ached, even Father.

This time out his ship had put into port in New York, and there he had bought me my first doll, a lovely large blonde whose eyes opened and closed. It was an unthinkably grand gift, and I relished suddenly being elevated to an object of envy by my playmates. He also brought me a rare, unknown delicacy, an orange. I regarded my well-traveled father, as well as his gifts, with awe. He was so elegant in his new three-piece suit, also from America. I timidly followed him from room to room, raptly hanging on his teasing, fanciful stories. Like all of the adults since the war ended, he seemed in extraordinarily good spirits. A wizard at math, he turned his attention to drilling me, with scant success, in the multiplication tables I was required to memorize in school.

It was about this time that Mother got into serious animal husbandry. She got her hands on a piglet, which she kept in an old pen near the apartment we rented. The pig was a great success; it grew rapidly to astonishing proportions. It pawed and snorted menacingly whenever we got near its pen, and Mother eyed it with both pride and alarm. It was bigger than most men and far heavier. Then, one fine summer day, it happened. Through our open kitchen window we heard a sudden commotion and the loud cracking and splintering of wood.

"Oh, no! The pig has broken loose!" Mother cried. She grabbed her broom and we bounded down the stairs and into the field. The pig saw us coming. It took one look at Mother, approaching at full throttle waving the broom, and leaped into the meadow grass, its legs pumping stiffly in frenzied flight. Mother ran after in mad pursuit, shouting furiously at the fleeing beast. They tore down the meadow, into the woods and out again as if they were both possessed. The pig circled and doubled widely on its tracks, bleating in panic. Each time Mother closed in, the ungainly porker lunged forward in a renewed burst of terror, sprinting in erratic spurts across the meadow. Wild with excitement, I cheered Mother on until the pig abruptly stopped in its tracks, its sides heaving rapidly. She swatted it smartly across the butt with her broom, and the pig stepped dispiritedly along in front of her, its head down, grousing noisily as she prodded it back to its shattered pen. When I saw her face, I knew the pig's fate was sealed. It wasn't long before we were feasting on its rich meat.

Aunt Lina came to visit while we lived in that apartment. I relished her company because she was full of naughty fun and she spoiled me. One day while Mother was outside, Lina opened the kitchen window and hurriedly took a few puffs on a cigarette. "Now don't tell your mother!" she cautioned, frantically waving the smoke out the window. Mother forever was lecturing on the evils of smoking; she detested it as a grave sin. When she came back into the room, though, Mother needed just one whiff to confirm what had been happening. She angrily rebuked defenseless Aunt Lina, who abruptly terminated her visit. I could see that smoking had dire consequences.

When I was nine years old, on one of those perfect summer play days of childhood, my world abruptly shattered.

"We have wonderful news, Hanna!" Mother told me when I came in from the woods. Her face was radiant as she held up a piece of paper. "We're going to America! We got a place on the boat in January." All my life I'd heard Mother's stories about the wonders of America, and I knew we had been on the waiting list for years. But it never occurred to me that an actual day of departure would arrive. So I was dumbstruck.

"But I don't want to go to America," I finally stammered.

She smiled reassuringly. "You'll like it there. You'll see."

"Can we take Grandmother with us?" I pleaded.

"We'll send for her later, after we get settled," she assured me.

"I don't want to leave Grandmother," I wailed.

Nonetheless, the awful day of departure all too soon was upon us. Mother and I were spending our last few hours with Grandmother in her living room, dressed in our traveling clothes, when Mother shooed me into the kitchen.

"Now I'm going to speak to Grandmother alone," she told me solemnly and closed the door. Heartsick, I pressed against the door, straining to hear what they were saying.

"It's so far away. I'll never see you again," I heard Grandmother protest quietly.

"No, no, you mustn't think like that. I'm going to send for you as soon as we get on our feet. We'll be together again in Zion as soon as we can. That's God's plan for us. And I'm going to find your father's fortune and see that you get what's rightfully yours."

"I'm too old to go to America, Berit, I've told you that. And Edvard doesn't want me there. You'll see. We'll never embrace one another again."

"You mustn't talk like that. God will watch over us and soon reunite us." Mother's voice trembled.

"You know I never got back to Finland to be with my mother when she needed me. She died before I could get back. And when you leave, it will be the same with us!" I could hear Grandmother crying softly now.

"Oh, Mother, you know we were parted once before, but we found one another again. You must remember that God will watch over us when we are far apart. And if we don't meet again in this world, you know we'll meet again one day in Heaven."

Here Mother's voice broke and stopped. There was no sound from the room now but quiet crying. The longer they wept, the more terrified I became. But when at last they opened the door, both were composed.

"In those days, seeing someone off to America was like going to a funeral," one of my cousins who saw us off that day told me years later. "You never expected to see them again." It had exactly the somber air of a funeral, only worse: We were *volunteering* to vanish from their lives.

A large crowd of Pedersens and Hansens and church members came to the dock to bid us farewell. My parents milled in the crowd, exchanging formal handshakes and last-minute advice while I clung tightly to Grandmother. Handsomely dressed in a fashionable hat and her best coat, her favorite brooch pinned to a scarf around her neck, she smiled bravely and murmured quiet encouragement as I gripped her hand.

Then, the dreaded moment came, the last boarding call and the unbearable final embraces. We made our way up the gangplank to hang over the railing and wave farewell while the ship's horn blasted noisily.

"Goodbye! Goodbye! Safe journey!" they called as we slid slowly away from the dock.

Grandmother stood solemn and alone at the edge of the crowd, wiping her eyes with a handkerchief. Then she lifted an arm in a dignified wave. To this day I can see her standing there on that dock, waving forlornly after us.

Father was inebriated from the time we left Bergen until the day before we docked in New York. Someone took a picture of us on the Atlantic crossing with the box camera that Mother had used over the decades to record so many of our family's historic occasions. Father is standing on deck hatless in his three-piece suit, his hands stuffed into his pockets. I'm squinting into the camera, my hair an unruly tangle of flying curls gathered to one side with a large ribbon. Mother, as always, is coyly posed. Not one of us is smiling.

As the ship neared New York harbor on January 18, 1949, it suddenly struck something and listed to one side. We were in the dining room eating our last meal aboard when the floor tilted sideways and the dishware slid off our table and crashed to the floor.

"Probably just a sandbar," Father remarked casually as the ship reversed engines and got under way again. We hurried on deck, where people were pointing to something in the distance. He had told me that when we could see the Statue of Liberty, it meant we were in America. Now, I could just make out a tiny statue. It ever so slowly grew larger until at last we were dwarfed under an immense, faded green lady with what seemed to be a crown on her head. With one arm, she was thrusting a torch into the sky. Transfixed, I stared up at the awesome sight.

America!

The ship's horn sounded a long, deafening blast, and the passengers broke into wild cheering. "Hip, hip hurrah! Hip, hip hurrah!" they shouted as we slid past the statue, and the men doffed their hats and waved them in the air. There was clapping and laughter and general pandemonium.

Ships from all over Europe were disgorging passengers around the clock into the cavernous customs sheds of the New York Port Authority. A swirling sea of bewildered immigrants milled under glaring lights. We fell in behind interminable lines of people dragging boxes, bags and squalling children. The din of incomprehensible tongues drowned out the shouted instructions of the uniformed men trying to maintain order and keep the confused hordes moving along. When, hours after we landed, it finally came our turn to be examined, the inspector carefully checked our passports and documents.

When he pulled the large x-rays of our chests from their envelopes and held them up to the light, he frowned and said something to Father in a questioning voice, pointing to a spot on the picture and then at me. Haltingly, his face tight, Father said a few words. Now two men studied my x-ray, then one of them gestured down a hallway and said something more to Father. I understood only the word "doctor."

Father turned to Mother. "He wants you to take Hanna to be examined by the doctor. He says there's something on her lung."

"Tell him we know she's been exposed to tuberculosis but that was a long time ago and she's never been sick," Mother urged.

"They might not give her permission to enter the country," Father said, his voice strained.

Heart heaving in panic, I clutched Mother's hand as we followed the inspector carrying my x-rays down a long hallway. He led us into a little room and left us there. I had been afraid to utter a sound until now. "Why might I not get permission to be in America?" I whispered.

"Shush, everything will be all right," Mother answered, but I could see she was in shock.

When the doctor came, he had Mother undress me while he studied my x-ray on a machine with a light behind it. He put his stethoscope to my racing heart and gestured for me to breathe deeply. When he was done examining me, he wrote something on a paper.

"Okay," he said, nodding. "Okay." He smiled reassuringly at us.

Someone took us back to where Father was waiting with our things. We were waved through the line and discharged with our baggage into the raucous, glistening streets of New York City. It was long past midnight.

The noise was overwhelming. Cars and trucks whizzed by, honking their horns. A mob of taxi drivers, some with black skins, crowded the sidewalk, shouting incomprehensibly. Father gave a taxi driver a card with the name of a hotel on it, and we and our baggage sped into the night. I was glued to the window, captivated by throbbing lights that flashed messages I could not understand. So this was America!

The next day we went to the Norwegian Seamen's Home in Brooklyn, familiar to Father from previous visits to New York and where he now sought advice for our journey to Idaho. Then we boarded a Greyhound bus and rode endlessly westward, pausing each night to sleep at a hotel. I entertained myself trying to pronounce the names of the cities we passed through: Cleveland, Chicago, Kansas City, Omaha. They came and went in a blur. "We have arrived safely. All is well. We are in Chicago and headed west," Mother scribbled on hotel stationery in a short note to my father's parents.

Gradually the crowded cities became fewer and farther between as we headed out into the open, snowy plains. They were immense. In all directions, the flat, white landscape stretched toward the horizon under a boundless sky. Here and there lonely, ill-kept farmhouses and huge, untidy barns bravely held their ground against the snow, and enormous herds of cattle stood about in drifts up to their knees.

"To think they leave their cows outside in winter!" Mother exclaimed. "The poor animals!"

"Can you believe how flat it is here?" she repeated over and over as we rolled over the endless prairie. "There's not a tree to be seen!" Father didn't say much by way of reply. He stared silently out the window, thinking his own thoughts.

When we reached Denver, an impressive scene lay before us. Snow had immobilized the city. Cars parked on the streets had all but vanished under the snow, and buildings were draped with a thick mantle of white. Early the next morning we pressed on, setting out for Salt Lake City under a crystal sky. I was on pins and needles for seemingly endless hours until the bus finally rolled into the Salt Lake Valley. Almost immediately, I caught sight of something I recognized.

"Look, Mother! It's the Temple!" Just then the bus wheeled into the terminal.

"Salt Lake City," the driver announced grandly.

Zion at last!

We disembarked, dazed and disoriented. While Father fussed with our luggage, I dragged Mother out on the sidewalk to look at the Temple just across the street. We stood together on the snowy sidewalk in silence, staring up at its familiar, imposing spires jutting into the sky. Neither of us spoke. I couldn't tell what she was thinking.

We spent the night at the home of a missionary friend we had known in Aalesund and the next morning reboarded the bus for the final leg of our journey to Idaho. Mother and Father were tensely quiet; my nose was pressed to the bus window. We headed north through a treeless, snow-laden expanse that rose into gentle foothills. A few small towns lay listless and uninviting along the route, and we stopped briefly at all of them. They too had peculiar names that I twisted experimentally around on my tongue: Ogden, Brigham City, Malad. When we reached Pocatello, a broad, flat plain lay before us.

Brown-skinned men and women lounged impassively in this waiting room. The women wore long, colorful dresses and shawls, and the men were dressed in high-heeled, pointed boots and short jackets. Both men and women wore silver jewelry on their fingers and wrists. "Indians!"

Mother whispered when she caught me staring raptly. Silent as stones, some of them climbed aboard the bus with us. Then we were off again, humming along an open plain nestled against low foothills to the east. In the west, strange, forlorn formations jutted up against the sky. They looked like mountains whose tops had been sawed off. Within minutes we stopped again, this time at a dilapidated storefront called Fort Hall where the Indians got off. A few minutes later, we rolled into yet another featureless little town choked in snow. Here the bus pulled to a stop in front of a small hotel.

"Blackfoot!" the driver sang out. Our two-week ordeal was over. We stumbled out of the coach and looked about us in amazement. There wasn't a building higher than two stories anywhere in the squat, lifeless town, which seemed to be buried in snowdrifts.

"Berit! Edvard! Welcome to America!" A bald, hatless stranger in a long overcoat was striding toward us, his arms outstretched in greeting, a wide smile warming his face. I knew this must be Elder Jensen.

My parents fell on him in relief. "Robert! Here we are at last," Mother cried as they clasped hands. "Can you believe it? It's like a dream, simply a dream!" she exclaimed happily while Father nodded and smiled.

"I almost couldn't get here because of the snow," Robert said in flawless Norwegian as they struggled to fit our baggage into the car. "We've never had so much snow."

"I'm glad to hear that," Father responded dryly. "We've never seen anything like this at home."

The only immigrants in town, we were treated as celebrities, and Mother gloried in the attention. A furnished apartment had been arranged for us, as had a job for Father. A photographer even came to interview us and take our picture for the local newspaper, and Mother wasted no time sending the ensuing newspaper article home to Norway. Here was proof for all to see of the wisdom of her decision to come to America.

Eight months after we arrived in Idaho, Mother turned forty-five. When a letter came from Grandmother one day, Mother read it silently and handed it to me. Then she did something remarkable. She wept.

It was Norwegian custom to hire amateur poets to put feelings into commemorative verse for special occasions, and that's what my Grandmother had done:

I sit alone and think and my thoughts fly away
To Zion out there in the West
Oh, if only I could follow
Then I would embrace you, Dear, and whisper the most tender words
Express longing thoughts and wishes for you from your mother.
I want to thank you, Berit, you always were so kind and good
You toiled and helped your siblings and were a comfort and help to me
I was left alone with the children
Because your father died so young
I often recall that time because it was so hard for me
Then you were forced out into the world to stand on your own two feet
And you longed so for home and your brothers
When we were together again, our joy was great
But now only God alone knows if in this life you'll see your mother again
So I wish you luck and happiness
Yes, all the best in the world, Berit, I wish for you
And today when you celebrate your forty-fifth birthday
Remember that Mother holds you in her thoughts
And if we don't meet again in this life, then we'll meet at last there
Where never again will we be parted from those we hold so dear
Then we shall sing forever in the joyous heavenly choir
Then we'll forget life's sorrows and all Earthly want and loss
God bless you, Dear Berit.

That poem from my grandmother became my mother's dearest possession. And I'm sure it spurred her determination to find Nikolai's money for Grandmother. By the time I was eleven, I wrote English well enough that Mother set me to work writing letters in search of him and his promised fortune. The replies were disheartening and unfailingly brief: "We have no record of any such person"; "We need more information." But we had no more information to give. Mother remained undeterred, though fruitless months grew into years. Whenever she got a new lead, she would direct me to write more letters. The man had vanished, yet my mother persisted in her stubborn hope.

As I grew older and more American, it fell to me—as it usually does to children of immigrants—to translate the subtleties of American cultural norms to my parents and to try to persuade them to adopt them. My parents, and especially my mother, took this instruction dubiously, if not with vehement protest. In Norway, she had been someone people looked to for guidance on how to behave. In America, she seemed to become willfully incapable of mastering even the most basic of social niceties and seemed to insist on upsetting people with deliberately insulting or inappropriate behavior. The longer she lived in America, the worse her behavior became. It was as if she were striking back in defiance at a society that didn't accept her.

"People need to hear the truth," she adamantly declared whenever I remonstrated against her outbursts. Eventually she alienated herself from her co-workers and every new friend. "Americans smile and pretend to be your friend, but you can't depend on them," she complained. "They'll never tell you what they really think. They're two-faced."

"Don't trust anybody," she repeatedly warned. On that much, at least, my parents agreed.

Meanwhile, the more American I became, the more my parents spoke of America with criticism. The cultural and emotional tensions that separated us became wider and more painful with each year—as did the tensions between my parents, marooned as they were in this high desert, far from home.

I came to see that my mother relished a good fight, especially with my father. She seemed deliberately to bait him just for the satisfaction of seeing him erupt. It was as if she got proof that she mattered to him by provoking him to anger. Afterwards, she would recount each detail of their wretched exchanges proudly, gloating at having gotten his goat. "I got him mad," she would smirk triumphantly, "and then he called me a devil." I was too bewildered by the pride she took in besting him in these bitter exchanges to ask her why such a perverse victory was something to gloat about.

Mother's difficulty in meeting and trusting our American neighbors compounded her isolation. Quick to harsh judgment, she was equally quick to invest each new acquaintance with the attributes of perfection. It would happen suddenly: someone at work or church took an admiring interest in her knitting, sewing, baking, cooking or embroidery. A compliment was paid, and a fast friendship immediately blossomed. "She's such a genuine person," Mother would enthuse in the early blush of these encounters. Then she would step lightly through the house, humming and glowing with good spirits. She could never show enough generosity or kindness to a new friend, or toward someone she took to be among life's less fortunate. She harbored a fierce sympathy for the downtrodden.

When she felt appreciated and admired, my mother was transformed into a person of lively, solicitous charm and exuberant good humor. She was never happier than when she had an audience, with all eyes on her as she told comical stories, often acting out the parts of characters in some lighthearted, droll tale. She relished being on center stage. And when the right mood struck her, she would share riveting stories from her childhood.

Preoccupied as I was with my own teenage angst and excesses, it never occurred to me that I could improve our relationship by the simple act of complimenting my mother on her talents. I now understand it would have given her some confirmation of personal worth that she so yearned for. But lacking the wit and skills to please them or to cope with the turmoil they created, I emotionally withdrew from my parents for the sake of self-preservation. Nonetheless, I was burdened with a nagging sense of my mother's loneliness. So I was always relieved each time she found a new friend. Invariably, though, the day would come when someone who only recently had been Mother's closest friend would suddenly no longer meet her exacting standards.

"Oh, her," she would snort dismissively. "She's nothing. You can't trust her." Mother was a woman of expectations that no one seemed able to meet.

The first house my parents bought in America was a tiny, two-bedroom house on two acres just outside town. Here we grew potatoes and other vegetables as well as chickens, one of which we killed each Saturday for Sunday dinner—Father had mastered the art of dispatching them. Once a week, he opened the gate of the irrigation ditch and flooded the potato field. And I, clad in jeans and a straw cowboy hat, proudly worked beside him, wielding a shovel between the rows and up to my ankles in muddy water.

Both of my parents now worked at the local hospital, where Father was the custodian responsible for the physical plant and Mother for the laundry room. She was asked to cook for the patients but had to give it up because she couldn't read English, never mind such exacting recipes. He polished the floors, cut the lawns, and monitored the oxygen tanks as well as the heating and cooling systems.

With a home of our own, Mother began to press to bring Grandmother to America to live with us. Father was resolutely opposed. "What's an old lady like her going to do here all alone all day? She can't speak a word of English. Be sensible for once!"

They argued about it for years. These arguments, unlike the others, ended with Mother in helpless tears. Finally, she stopped talking about it and began to speak of Lyngen. "You should see how beautiful Signaldal is, how magnificent the mountains and fjords are. The water is as still and smooth as a mirror, and the sun shines on it all night. And the fish! Oh, you should see the fish!"

I occasionally wrote to Grandmother in painstaking Norwegian. Though I had Americanized quickly, I still clung to the images of my childhood by the sea in that green, lovely land that was so unlike this sterile wasteland we now called home. When I sent her a small copy of my first high school yearbook portrait, Grandmother wrote back to thank me. "You've become a pretty, grown-up lady since last I saw you. I have become old but I can't do anything else," she wrote. "Are you thinking that you might sometime take a trip to Norway? It would be wonderful to see you once more in my life while I live."

I lived for the day.

Father continued to drink intermittently. I think he felt—as perhaps did my mother, though she would never have admitted it— disappointed, or tricked somehow, by life in America. Quick to anger, the teasing, witty man I had known as a child all but disappeared, except when he had had a drink. Then he was cheerful—at first. He went about his menial work—tasks much beneath his sharp intelligence—with a hard set to his mouth and eyes that bespoke deep unhappiness. Mother had the church for social support but my father, whose mastery of English never progressed as far as hers, remained isolated and friendless. I never saw, or heard, my mother betray any outward sign of affection for him, but she did set the missionaries upon him in an effort to save his soul.

He delighted in baiting them, and they soon gave up. When he drank, he railed against Mormon hypocrisy—and Mother's search for Nikolai.

So Mother and I lived on sharp pins and needles, never knowing if he'd be drunk or sober, charming or abusive. When she lashed out by heedlessly dumping a load of incendiary criticism on his smoldering fire, he flamed back in white-faced fury. Often she seized the weapon of stony silence, refusing to utter a single word to either of us for days, sometimes weeks. Her face compressed in a fierce scowl, she mutely went about her chores, preparing our meals and slamming the plates down in front of us with contempt.

Finally, in response to a particularly bad bout of drinking, she kicked him out. He went to Salt Lake, leaving us to manage for ourselves. It was a blissful interlude of peace, and Mother and I grew closer than we'd been since my early childhood. She ceased criticizing me, so I hesitantly began to confide in her—something I long had avoided. She seemed pleased by our newfound intimacy and soon proposed that she make me a new winter coat, even though I sensed we were very short of funds for the fabric. I understood that she offered this dearly-bought gift as a token to show that she cared for me, and I tried to reciprocate by letting her know how much I appreciated it. As the months passed, though, she became increasingly quiet and preoccupied. Still, I didn't see it coming until the day she sat me down at the kitchen table to tell me Father was coming back to live with us.

"It's very difficult, Hanna. There isn't enough money. He's promised to stop drinking now." I didn't for a moment believe it, but I held my peace.

Not long after he came back, we bought a bigger, nicer home in town. Gradually, our lives took on a patina of what I held to be American normalcy. I held two jobs after school, and Father surprised me by buying me an old car so that I could get to work. At Mother's urging, he also bought an old boat, which we used to go on fishing and camping expeditions. Mother invariably caught more fish than either of us on these outings. She seemed to have some magical talent for it. "My father taught me to fish," she would tell us, a faraway look in her eyes. Then she would reminisce about her childhood in Signaldal.

It didn't last, of course. The first time Father was drunk enough in public to be jailed for disorderly conduct, she went to fetch him, a much chastened man. The second time, she left him there. It was a New Year's Eve, and while he sat in jail, we went to a movie together at a theatre where I was working as an usher. As we made our way home that night through empty streets along snowy sidewalks, Mother suddenly paused under a streetlamp near our house.

"I want to tell you something, Hanna," she announced solemnly. I understood from her tone that this was an important moment, a time when she would impart some wisdom that should pass from all mothers to their daughters. I dimly had been expecting just such an occasion. I had long felt a growing undercurrent of something unspoken in our house, a sense that there was something of consequence that she needed to tell me.

I was fourteen, self-centered, and focused on my own troubles, not those of my bewildering mother. It did not occur to me that it was the disgrace of having her husband in jail that prompted her to choose this moment to impart to me the sum of what life had taught her.

She spoke solemnly and deliberately. "Life is full of disappointments, Hanna, so you must learn to depend only on yourself in this world. Never allow yourself to imagine that you can depend on anyone else. Always remember that there's no one you can trust, no one to depend on to help you but you yourself alone."

"Don't trust anybody"—my parents had long drilled this sentiment into me, but this was the first time it sounded as though my mother were including herself in that admonition. The implications of what she was saying were clear enough, I thought: it was formal notice that she was washing her hands of me. She was telling me I was old enough that I should no longer expect anything more from her; I was on my own.

Crushed by what I took as a brutally forthright declaration of abandonment, I stood speechless under the glare of the streetlight on that snowy sidewalk. It was the final feather on a crushing load of pain years in the making. My chest seized up in a cold rage. It never occurred to me that I simply might have misunderstood her—or that she was suffering a lifetime of her own deep, inexpressible hurts, that she too longed for love and acceptance.

So that night I vowed to withdraw the last lingering shred of expectation that despite her constant criticism of my shortcomings and frequent anger at my thoughtless behavior, she nevertheless did care for me. I was through trying to please and appease her, through caring whether I made her mad or proud. There would be no more walking on eggshells striving to keep her in good humor, no more fear of blundering into some innocent offense that would set off a tongue lashing or weeks of silent fury.

My parents' difficulties grew more pronounced. One day while I was gone from the house, Father blackened Mother's eye. She filed for divorce, and once again he disappeared from our lives, this time to sleep on park benches in Seattle. Yet, once again, she took him back. This time she broke the news by calling me at school. "The bishop has been to the house," she announced. "He's just married your father and me."

In no time, they fell back into their familiar, spiteful habits. The air crackled with constant criticism—Father blackly cursing Mother, she bitterly berating him, and both of them turning on me when they wearied of abusing one another.

One day not long after my eighteenth birthday, some wayward expenditure of mine triggered a particularly violent argument. Father shouted and pounded his fist on the kitchen table, excoriating my profligate ways. "When are you ever going to learn the value of money?" he roared. I tried to defend myself but he was beyond the reach of reason, his face white with anger. Mother hovered mutely on the sidelines.

A hopeless rage exploded in me, obliterating my fear. "I won't cost you another dime!" I spat out. I threw some clothes in a suitcase and left. I spent the week at a friend's house, never once calling home.

That Saturday, Mother called me. "Come home," she said matter-of-factly. "I have something to tell you. Your father's at work today," she added.

Apprehension weighed my steps as I came up on the porch and let myself in. The house was quiet. Mother was at the kitchen sink, looking grim and resolute as she rinsed a few dishes and laid them on a towel to dry. She didn't say anything by way of greeting but motioned me to sit down at the table. Warily, I drew up a chair.

"There's something you should know, Hanna," she began quietly, wiping her hands on a towel. She pulled up a chair and seated herself across the table from me.

"We're not your real parents. We adopted you when you were just a baby."

I stared at her, my world spinning. Shock—and profound relief—washed simultaneously over me.

"Your real mother is my cousin Inga," she continued, her voice and face devoid of emotion. "Your real father wouldn't marry her. When she realized she was pregnant, she tried to starve herself to abort you. But it was a fiasco. Inga always wanted to be so thin and fine," she added disdainfully. "We adopted you because we wanted to keep you in the family. We've done the best we could. We've always meant to do only the best for you."

I stared stupidly at her, tears welling in my eyes, my throat constricting painfully, relief warring with pity and guilt.

"You were in the orphanage for ten months while they tried to decide who should get you. There was a rich family that wanted you, but I told them we had something better than money to give you—we had the gospel of the only true church. Finally they decided we could have you, but the head nurse didn't like it. The day I came to get you, she threw you at me like you were some dirty dishrag," she concluded, her eyes snapping at the memory.

I got up and awkwardly put my arms around her and tried to embrace her. "But you are my mother," I managed to say. She turned my conflicted protestations aside. Her hands, folded together, stayed on the table in front of her.

"I'm sorry it didn't turn out the way you wanted it to be," she continued evenly, impervious to my labored show of affection. "I've tried to do everything in the best way I could for you," she repeated.

"I know that," I answered, the years of our lives together flashing before me in a new, wrenching light. "I'm thankful for it."

Still, she ignored my attempt to reach out, to make amends. So I sat down again, defeated, not knowing what to do or say.

"There is one thing, Hanna, that you must never do," she admonished. "You must never tell Inga that I told you she is your mother. You're not supposed to know. And no one else must know you're her daughter, either."

Still too shocked to ask why, I nodded assent.

"Who was my father?" I asked hesitantly.

She told me his name. "He never knew anything about you."

It crossed my mind to ask why she had fought so hard to adopt me when she seemed to be at such pains to let me know that she had no use for me. But I assumed the answer was obvious. I had simply turned out badly. She couldn't have known she was getting inferior goods.

That night I moved back in, and we gingerly resumed our lives. I felt free, exuberant, as if a prison door had been flung open. Knowing I did not really belong to them liberated me from the awful burden of guilt I had carried for so long and tempered my bitter, unforgiving anger. Yet in some ways knowing I was adopted made our estrangement worse than if they had been my biological parents. They had chosen to raise me; they had not been obliged to take responsibility for me as they would have been with a child of their own making. They were under no obligation to love me; I wasn't theirs. They had fulfilled their part of the bargain, and much more besides. They had generously housed, fed and clothed me and provided for my every need. No one could fault them there. No more was to be expected.

The morning after high school graduation Mother took time off work to come to the bus station in her white hospital uniform to see me off. I was moving to Salt Lake, where I hoped to earn enough to start college in the fall. We said perfunctory goodbyes and I climbed aboard, giddy with carefully concealed joy. I was escaping this unrelenting hell on earth at last! As I settled into my seat, I glanced at Mother one final time through the window.

In a blistering moment of comprehension, I for the first time truly saw the woman I would always call Mother: a small, forlorn figure, waving stoically in the dusty sunshine, her face fixed in a cramped smile. Behind that mask of determined, hard-edged indifference, I suddenly realized, she was vulnerable and lonely. For the first time, the depth of my failure with her sank in. The image of her face, so fiercely set against hurt and abandonment, haunted me as the bus rolled south across the sunny, arid sagelands.

When I wrote home later that summer to say I would have to postpone college a year to earn more money, Mother surprised me by urging me not to delay. "We'll find a way to help you with money," she wrote.

Loath as I was to sink deeper into their debt, I uneasily agreed. Hope blossomed anew that we could make a lasting peace. But all we could ever manage was a wary truce. Sometimes I suspected she only gave me things so she could accuse me of being ungrateful for them. And I *was* ungrateful, given how dimly I appreciated how hard they worked and how little they had for themselves.

They came from a culture where material things, not loving words or physical touches, were proffered as the best proof of affection, though I was unaware of this at the time. By that standard, they had done more than anyone could ask. Of course, it wasn't really *things* I wanted from them. But I had no way to tell them that.

I was in college when Mother finally went home to Norway for the first time. Nothing could dim her joy at being with her mother and family again, not even the news that Father had been hospitalized after drinking himself into a stupor, perforating an ulcer and collapsing on our kitchen floor. Still, he wrote to her faithfully every week, enclosing a five dollar bill for her upkeep and providing detailed accounts of how the potato harvest was going on the land they were renting on the Indian reservation.

She and Grandmother traveled to Lyngen, and I think that's when she finally made up her mind to move home to Norway. Her letters were full of amazement at the rebuilding and wonderful changes that had taken place since we left. Recovered from the war and determined to eliminate the suffering that poverty had wrought on families such as ours, Norway had established a social welfare system that in time would become envied by the world. "And everyone treats me so royally you wouldn't believe it!" she enthused.

She returned to Idaho via Greyhound late that fall, accompanied by a small barrel of stinking Icelandic herring she somehow had talked past customs. Once again far from all she longed for, she sustained herself, in that cheerless wasteland where her faith and dreams of America had led her, with verdant memories of home. She now lived for the day she could move back to Norway.

Our relationship did not improve. Desperately lonely, Mother glowered with unconstrained jealousy if I brought friends to the house and often as not refused to speak to them or me. When she did speak, it usually was to assert what struck my young, Americanized ears as some harebrained, superstition-laden theory of life. There wasn't a folk remedy that wasn't superior to modern medicine, nor a detail of human life too inconsequential to escape divine intervention. Inexplicably, she had all but given up attending church, but she remained keen on the central tenet of her private faith: divine retribution against the rich for the wrongs done to the poor—especially to her. Hers was a vengeful God.

Increasingly confounded by her fiercely-held, unlettered beliefs and unpredictable, willfully uncivil behavior, I half-jokingly began to account for my mother's inappropriate excesses by saying she was born into the wrong century. It was an admission of defeat.

Yet I indulged in periodic fits of optimism that things could improve. Once I even ventured to bring home two friends from college in a guilt-induced effort to include her in my life. It was a mistake. She lit into me at the breakfast table, serving up surly denigrations with the ham and eggs. "You have no idea how hard we work to keep you in school," she said, slamming pans into the sink.

Anxious to prevent a scene, I reverted to Norwegian. "Do we have to talk about this now?"

"When shall we talk about it?" she snapped.

I hastily cleared the table and began to wash the dishes. But she elbowed me sharply out of the way. "Get away," she snarled.

Melissa, Jane, and I retreated awkwardly into the living room, but she followed us.

"Do you always take friends home when you visit your parents? Is that how all you fine, modern people behave?" she asked them angrily. "You and your fine friends think you're too good for us. Why do you bother to come home at all?"

We hastily piled our belongings into the car while Mother stood in the doorway, hurling accusations after us. Speechless with anger and embarrassment, I roared out of the driveway, tires squealing. When I could get the words out, I apologized for her behavior.

Jane cut me short with a dry laugh. "She's simple," she sneered.

This dismissive insult stunned and shamed me. And despite my fury at my mother, it made me angry. There was nothing simple about her. It was true that she had no more control of her emotions than a vengeful child, spitefully lashing out to avenge herself for her life's hurts and disappointments. But she was my mother and I still felt impelled to defend her.

I didn't bring friends home after that. And because I could not summon the skills or wisdom to navigate this treacherous terrain, I avoided going there myself as much as duty allowed. Poisoned waters lapped at the unstable, crumbling edges of the wide gulf that separated us. The isolated shores on which we lived our lives drifted ever more distant from one another.

I was cheerfully loading my car to return to school one fall weekend in my senior year of college when Mother, who had been watching wordlessly, without warning sank into the faded blue upholstered chair where she sat in the evenings after work, knitting the ski sweaters she sold for extra income. My mother was incapable of sitting still or relaxing for a moment; her hands were never idle. But now she covered her eyes with her hands and broke into tears. She crumpled forward, her shoulders shaking uncontrollably.

"I have no one to talk to," she sobbed, "no one to be friends with, no one to enjoy anything with. Other people have friends. But day after day, I just go back and forth by myself, inside four walls, completely alone. No one cares anything about me. They just laugh at me behind my back."

I was astonished at her honest confession; it was totally unlike her. Not once had it occurred to me that she cared for a moment whether or not anyone laughed at her, or that she cared what anyone thought of her. She always proudly resisted any criticism of her behavior. So the sight of her helplessly crying out for human companionship shocked me deeply. Overcome with guilt and pity, I put my arms around her shoulders and tried to say something comforting, but words failed me. She stiffly rebuffed my embrace. She would accept no consolation, at least not from me.

"Just go," she told me harshly. "You don't care anything about me."

I drove away feeling cruel and useless. The incident weighed heavily on me and influenced my decision to accept a teaching job that would allow me to live at home after graduation. I owed her that much, and maybe our relationship could work now that I was an adult, I told myself. She seemed pleased when she told other people about my decision, but she never said so to me.

There were no major contretemps until just before Christmas Eve, when Father left to go drinking in town. Mother fell into a black, mute mood and retreated to their bedroom to sit stonily on the edge of the bed, arms crossed. Hoping to cheer her, I followed with the Christmas gift I had bought her. But she sullenly threw it aside unopened.

"I don't want any presents," she said angrily. She wouldn't look at me.

I didn't have the common sense to wonder whether she was taking out her anger at my father on me. Instead, the memory of the knife suddenly rose to stab me.

"Fine," I told her tightly. "I'll take it back, just like I did the knife."

She glanced at me for an instant. "What knife?" She said it hesitantly, but I was sure she remembered.

"You must remember the knife? I was eight years old and I wanted more than anything to give you a present, something I thought you really wanted. But you made me take it back. Nothing I do is good enough for you, is it?"

She refused to answer. She just turned a stony face to the wall.

TWENTY-ONE
HOMECOMING

I first laid eyes on the city of my birth from the air. My eyes feasted on red and yellow cottages nestled cozily in rocky coves, sailboats bobbing in Oslofjord, and the deep green forested hills that surrounded the city. My heart raced.

Norway at long, long last!

Inga was to meet me at the airport. Mother hadn't bothered to ask me if I wanted Inga to meet me. I had nurtured an unspoken, growing curiosity about her for the six years since I had learned she was my mother, but I dreaded the meeting all the same. I had no concept of the woman who had given me life. She was a blank slate, a total mystery. Did she even want to meet me? What if she pressed some claim on me? How would Mother react to that?

My head was spinning as I stepped onto Norwegian soil and slowly made my way through the customs line. Nervously, I scanned the crowd waiting behind a glass enclosure. There didn't seem to be anyone there who fit the bill. Maybe she hadn't come after all. Who could blame her? Who would want old sores reopened a quarter of a century after the fact? It must be very painful to be confronted with a grown child whose life you had missed. And hadn't Mother warned me never to let on to Inga that I knew she was my real mother? That must mean she didn't want to acknowledge me. But what was I supposed to do if Inga told me herself? Lie about knowing it already? And what allegiance would I owe Inga then? Would I have to keep it a secret from Mother that Inga had told me she was my real mother? I had been twisting these agonizing, labyrinthine possibilities over and over in my mind for months.

I began, with some relief, to believe that she might not have come, but then my eyes fell on a small woman in a gold dress peppered with dime-sized black polka dots. She was standing in the back of the room, clutching an armful of yellow roses, staring intently at me. But this woman had red hair. I was looking for someone with my own blond hair, blue-gray eyes and fair complexion. As she moved closer, I could see that she had freckles sprinkled on high cheekbones and warm, merry brown eyes.

Surely this couldn't be my mother.

But she was smiling tentatively at me, and as I cleared the line, she stepped forward.

"Are you Hanna?" she asked hesitantly.

"Yes," I answered in Norwegian, careful to keep the incredulity out of my voice. "Are you Inga?"

"Yes," she smiled. "Welcome to Norway!" She broke into a warm smile, thrust the roses at me, and formally proffered her hand in greeting. Her sparkling eyes searched my face, hungrily taking in every detail. Flustered, I shook her hand and stammered my thanks.

"You're so welcome to Norway, Hanna," she repeated, smiling up at me.

"Thank you. It's wonderful to be here." I tried not to stare, but she was so utterly unlike what I'd imagined.

As she drove us to my hotel, I studied her. Her cheekbones and the shape of her face, I realized, were mine. Her delicate bones and small hands on the steering wheel were an eerie, identical copy of my own. Here, then, was something astonishing and incomprehensible: a total stranger who was my own closest flesh and blood.

Dazed, I listened as she chattered gaily, nervously perhaps. I answered as best I could, my brain racing to recapture long-lost Norwegian words as I concentrated on deciphering the tone of her voice. It was a warm, generous, loving one, I concluded, filled with lighthearted humor. "Is it hard for you to speak Norwegian?" she asked solicitously.

"A little. But I understand everything," I assured her.

When we presented ourselves at the hotel registration counter where she had made reservations, Inga stood protectively by me as I handed over my passport. The desk clerk looked momentarily at the two of us standing there side by side. Then he remarked pleasantly, "You two look so much alike you must be related."

Inga blanched visibly but recovered nicely, I thought. "Well, we are in the same family, after all," she retorted haughtily as if in answer to an accusation.

I kept my head bent over the registration form, smiling inwardly. So this is how it was to be.

And that's how it was between us for the next thirty years.

Fifteen years had passed since I last stood in Grandmother's kitchen. Shorter, heavier, more wrinkled, her black hair peppered with gray, she stood smiling wordlessly in the center of the room, tears rolling down her cheeks, arms held out to wrap me in a loving embrace.

They all embraced me as if I'd never left—beloved aunts, uncles, cousins on both sides of the family. And I saw what Mother must have yearned for, so alone in America. We shared our common memories and marveled at all that had transpired since we said farewell on the dock that winter day so long ago. Every visit to a relative's home entailed mandatory, prodigious bouts of eating; there was no want of food here now. My family was living modestly but comfortably in the new Norway, which was so unlike the impoverished, war-torn country I remembered. I went to Hatlehol in hopes of seeing our cottage, but it had vanished, as had Nelli's barn. Both had been erased from the earth and new buildings put up in their place. My childhood seemed to have happened on another planet.

I clung to Grandmother—now aware, of course, that she was not really my grandmother at all but my great aunt by marriage. It was a meaningless distinction: she always had been and would be my grandmother, and I treasured my time with her. She fed and fussed over me, told stories about my mother and held my hand in hers while we reminisced about our life together so many years ago. I wanted to hold her fast; my heart ached at the prospect of telling her goodbye once again. When that day came, we knew this time it was a final goodbye. We both cried. I walked woodenly across the airport tarmac and turned to wave at her a final time. I saw a small, stooped figure in a gray coat and hat, already so far beyond reach. I desperately wanted to run back and embrace her. She raised her hand to bid me farewell, just as she had that day she had stood on the dock so straight and dignified and heartbroken as we sailed away to America.

I never saw her again.

While Inga didn't acknowledge me as her daughter, she did begin to remember me on my birthday and at Christmas with expensive gifts or generous amounts of money, which distressed me. I knew

Mother would take it badly, so I kept it from her as much as possible. I considered returning Inga's gifts, but I worried that then she would feel I was rejecting her. I could see no solution. The dilemma gnawed at me for years, unresolved. Whatever I did, I knew one of them would be hurt.

My parents meanwhile settled on a date to move back to Norway. Mother was in high spirits knowing she was soon to be reunited with her mother and busily set about packing their belongings. Driven to exasperation by her insistence on shipping even the most useless of items, Father borrowed a truck and, while she stood weeping in protest in the doorway, loaded it up and hauled a garageful of her treasures to the town dump.

"Goddamned junk!" he snorted when she recounted this injustice for my benefit. But she persisted in gathering up the objects that represented her life in America, even packing box after box of cleaning rags. Finally he threw up his hands,

"Well," he conceded in uncharacteristic, philosophical resignation, "she's worked as hard as I have while we've been here, and if she's determined to spend her money hauling rags back across the Atlantic, then she'll just have to do it."

Four months before they were to leave for Norway, Mother called me in Salt Lake, where I was living. Instantly, I sensed from her tone that something terrible had happened.

"I had a telegram from Aalesund," she said in a tight voice. "Grandmother has died."

I struggled for words, but nothing came.

"It was Mother's Day there," she went on tonelessly, her voice subdued. "She had been to Edmund's for dinner and he was bringing her home on the bus. When they stood up to get off, she said 'I feel faint.' She collapsed on the sidewalk and never regained consciousness."

"I'm glad she didn't suffer," I said lamely. "I'm glad we got to see her again," I added, my throat constricted with grief.

"I have her last letter here," Mother said. "The last thing she wrote was, 'You're most heartily welcome here, but don't travel in the worst of winter. Wait until spring, when the sun has turned to smile on us all.'"

The years of our lives apart—the cozy chats, the untold stories and unshared memories, the loving laughter and lonesome heartaches—all of it streamed past as Mother talked flowers and funeral. We had lost years of Grandmother's life living here. Now she was gone. I had recaptured a short, precious interlude with her. But, I realized with anguish, I never really knew her.

My parents moved back to Norway anyway. They never once broached the subject of my coming with them, which simultaneously relieved and perplexed me. On the day of their departure, we said our stilted good-byes at the Salt Lake train station, sweltering in the midsummer heat. Mother may have been going home without Nikolai's fortune, but she left well supplied with rags. The train chugged slowly out of the station en route to Ogden, running backwards like film being rewound as my parents returned to their homeland. They stood on a platform smiling and waving happily in the searing sunlight, then receded into the distance and disappeared.

I hoped that Mother and Inga would take up the friendship they had shared decades before. At last Mother would have someone to confide in, I thought. But the first time I went home to visit my parents, I felt the full force of that miscalculation.

"That woman has to boss everybody around. Everyone has to dance to her tune. She's always been like that. Everything has to be done just her way."

Foremost in my mind, as I tried to juggle this emotional minefield, was not to be the agent of pain for either of them. But here it was, exactly what I had been striving to avoid: warfare between my mothers.

I hid my dismay behind a sardonic smile. "But you never boss anyone around yourself, of course."

Different as they were, there were striking similarities in these two women. They could both be hard, unforgiving cases. When her sister Jorunn died and Inga discovered that she was not named in the will, she took deep offense, refused to attend the funeral and went back to Oslo in a huff.

Though never married, Inga had lived with a man who was her business partner in a delicatessen. She was the perfect, well turned out lady, as enslaved by appearances as Mother now was scornful of them. While Inga had embraced the polished, gentle manners and rigid social dictates of the high-class society she served and admired, Mother brusquely condemned anything that smacked of wealth or polite society. It was inevitable, on that basis alone—never mind with me so awkwardly looming between them—that they would come to grief.

"I suppose she had nothing but the best for you," Mother said sullenly after I'd visited Inga. I sensed the seething jealousy that she never could openly acknowledge, her fear that I would like Inga better than her. It grieved me, but I felt helpless to do anything about it. Certainly Inga and I seemed more compatible in taste and temperament. Genes must count for something, after all. Still, Berit was my mother and I longed to make peace with her. It was Berit, not Inga, to whom I owed the duties of daughtership.

Mother eventually found her way back to Salt Lake City for a visit. Norway was not all she had envisioned, as matters turned out, and she longed for America. We stood together on the front lawn of my apartment and looked at the moon, knowing the first humans were walking on it as we studied it. I sensed she disapproved of the notion of men traipsing about on the moon and I ascribed it to her religious impulses. This sort of thing was not in the gospel playbook, after all. I myself was done with the gospel by then, but I was certain Mother's faith was as unshakable as ever. So I was thunderstruck when I discovered that she was secretly smoking, which was strictly forbidden by church teaching. She had railed against Father's smoking ever since I was a child; I could more easily believe Jesus Christ would smoke than my mother. When I offered her an ashtray lest she burn down the house, she blew up and announced she was leaving for Blackfoot.

So I took her to the bus station, where we seated ourselves by a large window and had a cup of coffee, also forbidden by her faith. Behind Mother, a block away, the spires of the Temple loomed. To my amazement, she opened her purse and produced cigarettes and matches.

"I'll tell you something, Hanna. It's your father who's driven me to smoking. He's ruined my nerves." She took short, nervous puffs from her cigarette, then held it aside a moment to take a sip of coffee. For a blindingly mocking, ironic moment she sat there, framed against the Temple, a coffee cup in one hand, the smoke from her cigarette wafting up toward the Temple spires. It was a wildly dissonant and indelible image. Never could I have envisioned it would come to this when we left everything dear to us to come to Zion so long ago.

My parents had a final go at severing their relationship not long before my father died. His abusive binge drinking once again became intolerable, and she kicked him out. He wrote beseeching letters trying to dissuade her from divorce. And once again, they found reason to agree on another reconciliation. Not long after, he died.

"On his last day in the hospital, when the doctors told me it was the end, I tried to put my arms around him, to embrace him," Mother told me later. "But he just lay there in the bed, his arms stiff at his side, cold and furious. He wouldn't put his arms around me," she said, "even then."

Maybe something she saw in my face compelled her to say it.

"I didn't hate him," she added, a strange, worried look on her face. "I never hated him," she assured me.

But I feared she had come to hate Inga. Mother had become obsessed with Inga's faults, and her letters and phone calls were a ceaseless litany of the slights and insults she had suffered at Inga's hands. "She's never given me a single present in all these years," she complained. "And after all the things I've given her!"

"Inga told me she never expected we would spend money on a college education for you," she reported piously.

"When I told Inga how poorly you manage money, she said I should disinherit you," she confided on another occasion, innocently straight-faced. Could that be true, I wondered? What did I know of Inga, anyway? Maybe she too was untrustworthy, just like Mother.

Yet I got no hint from Inga herself that anything was amiss with my character. She was unfailingly affectionate toward me whenever I saw her, although keeping up the pretense that I didn't know she was my biological mother grew more maddening with each passing year. And I felt helplessly under siege from the barrage of Mother's attacks on Inga, who for her part seemed cheerfully oblivious to them.

So I was astounded one Christmas when Mother, brimming with good cheer, called to inform me she was going to spend the holidays in Oslo with Inga. And, she also informed me, they had decided to buy me a Christmas gift together. Incomprehensible as it was, this news filled me with hope. Nothing could please me more than to have my mothers at peace.

Their gift, a large wooden traditional bowl decorated with rosemaling design, arrived just before Christmas. But there was something else:

an envelope from Inga with two hundred dollars inside. I called on Christmas Eve to thank them and found a jolly dinner party under way. When Mother came on the line, I was thrilled to hear how ebullient she sounded. When I thanked her for my gift, I prudently didn't mention the money Inga had enclosed.

"We're having a splendid Christmas," Mother assured me, her voice exuberant. "Inga has thought of everything. You should see the fine table she's set."

It was my best Christmas ever and I wasn't even there.

Mother's letter came shortly afterward. I was expecting a glowing report of her holiday stay in Oslo. I should have known better. "Dear Hanna," she began without preliminaries. "One day when Inga was at work, I was looking through some things she had left on the shelf and I found the receipt for the money she sent you. I have never been made such a fool in my life. She deceived me about your present just to make me look cheap and so that she could look like the fine lady. I thought we were each going to pay half. But she always has to be the best, she always has to impress everyone with how fine she is. She's completely treacherous and untrustworthy. I'm through with her for good."

Mother was as good as her word. Unaware that she'd been found out, Inga faithfully tried to keep up the relationship, but Mother cut her off. My feelings of helplessness about how to navigate through this emotional minefield became even more acute. So I decided to try to nudge Inga to tell me the truth about us by giving her an opening to broach the subject.

"You have to stop giving me all this money," I told her the next time I was in Oslo. We were having dinner at a high-toned restaurant Mother would never have set foot in. "It's not right. Why don't you spend it on an airline ticket to America for yourself instead?"

"Oh," she answered brightly with barely a hint of a pause. "I don't do anything for you that I don't do for the rest of the nieces and nephews."

There then, was my answer. I gave it up.

Out of the blue, Mother astonished me by getting married again. Birger was gentle, sweet, and smilingly good-hearted, a bachelor who rented the basement apartment in the house she and my father bought shortly before he died. Mother seemed truly pleased with Birger's thoughtfulness toward her. Laden with gifts, I flew home for the wedding. I was invested in this marriage and dared hope that with a man such as this, surely my mother at last would find happiness.

On the day of the wedding, I cleaned the house in preparation for the dinner with the family and was about to change clothes for the church ceremony when she stopped me in my tracks.

"You can stay here and clean the kitchen floor," she told me.

It's a testament to how little I had learned about her after all these tumultuous years that for a moment I actually thought she was kidding. She knew perfectly well that the floor had just been cleaned.

I watched from the window as they walked hand in hand to the bus stop in front of the house. When she saw me in the window, she waved gaily up at me, as if it were the most natural thing in the world to order a daughter who had come six thousand miles across the Atlantic for your wedding to stay home and scrub the floor.

I feared not a little for Birger's fate in my mother's hands. He was an innocent, no match for her, I realized as I bemusedly watched them board the bus. But I clung to the hope that he could bring her enough happiness to change her behavior.

While I wasn't allowed to attend the wedding, I was allowed to come on the honeymoon. We traveled on the coastal steamer to Lyngen, where for the first time I was welcomed by my relatives in Signaldal and Kitdal. I immediately felt ancient bonds binding me to this place where my mothers' lives had begun.

Mother showed me the little grassy expanse where her parents' cottage had stood under Otertind. It had vanished. Nothing remained except a slight outline of the foundation—and echoes of laughter and grief that sighed on the breeze in that little meadow.

We visited the family farm in Kitdal, where portraits of my biological grandparents on their wedding day hung on the wall. I could see that my face was a carbon copy of Inga's mother, Hansine, who had died a few years earlier. But no one let on that they knew who I was.

One day I saw Sami for the first time, down by the sea. Their tent was pitched by the roadside. There were two of them, a man and a wife, dressed in their traditional bright blue garb trimmed in colorful red and yellow ribbon. Mother brightened when she saw them, so we stopped the car and got out for a better look. The woman was selling tourist trinkets, and the man, well past half drunk, was quaffing beer from a bottle.

Mother bought something while I regarded them from a distance in contemplative silence. They were strange and foreign-looking, unfathomable beings. No one would mistake them for Norwegian, that was certain.

"The poor Sami," Mother clucked sympathetically as we drove off.

Birger had faults, as it turned out. Mother's complaints began slowly, little drips of acid pitting a polished marble surface. By the next time I came to visit, she was baiting Birger mercilessly, lashing at him with a biting stream of criticism. She seemed perversely to relish it. Blow by blow, insult by insult, she related her mistreatment of him. "Then he called me a beast," she confided with that odd, triumphant pride at provoking a husband's anger. Birger's jovial spirit was crushed. He walked around the house with a heavy air of resignation, a beaten look in his eyes.

When Mother turned seventy-five, I flew to Norway to arrange a birthday celebration for her and her remaining siblings at one of Oslo's hotel restaurants. Aunt Gudrid came with her husband Erick from Sweden; I hadn't seen her in thirty years. Inga also was invited but the party began without her. "She's not coming," Mother predicted. "I can't believe she'd be so rude."

As we milled about waiting to be seated for dinner, a small, anxious-looking woman dressed in black shyly made her way toward us. I didn't recognize her at first glance; she seemed somehow smaller and older.

"Inga! Is it really you?" Mother asked sharply.

"Hello, Berit," she smiled, anxiety vanishing as her face lit up. "Happy birthday."

When Aunt Gudrid saw her, her wrinkled face broke into a smile and she grasped Inga's hands, towering over her. "No, is it really you, then, Inga?" she said softly. "How are you after all these years?" I thought I saw her blink away tears.

"I'm well, very well," Inga answered in her husky, soft voice.

"Just think how long it's been since we first came here to Oslo together," Aunt Gudrid said quietly. My ears instantly perked up, but the others pressed in upon them and the moment was lost.

Radiant, Mother presided grandly from the head of the long table. I seated myself on the other end with Inga next to me. I sensed her discomfort at being in the midst of all these relatives she had once known so well. Did any of them know she was my mother, I wondered as I looked around the noisy, chattering table. Just how secret was this burdensome knowledge Inga and I had been hiding from one another all these years?

The answer was not long in coming. I bent down to better hear something Inga was saying, my head close to hers. After a few moments, I realized the noisy table had fallen strangely quiet. I looked up, my face still close to Inga's, to see a dozen pairs of fascinated eyes riveted on the two of us. It was plain in their faces. They all knew, for heaven's sake!

At that moment, Inga jumped out of her chair and made a great formal show of presenting Mother with a gift, a large silver plate. Glowing with delight, Mother passed it around for all to admire.

"I have a little something for you too, Hanna," Inga announced. She handed me a tiny package. Again, all eyes were fastened on us in pregnant silence as I struggled with the wrapping. When I saw that it was an elegant gold ring set with a ruby gemstone, my heart sank.

Why was she doing this? And why now, here, in this public setting? Why on my mother's birthday, of all godawful times?

I held it up to be admired, wishing I could vanish. Someone asked to see it, and the ring made its slow way around the table. Each of them in turn—aunts, uncles, cousins—took the ring in hand, turned it over, held it up and solemnly studied it, mumbled a polite remark, then passed it on. When the ring reached Mother, she gave it a dismissive glance and handed it on.

"That's a lovely ring. Are you two getting engaged, then?" she asked.

The nervous, awkward laughter that followed did not erase my mortification. I dared not look at Inga. Someone rescued us by changing the subject, and the wretched moment passed.

This would be the last time these siblings would be together— Mother, Sissel, Gudrid and Paulus. Edmund, Ivar and Inge were dead. Of the living siblings, only Karl, far north in Signaldal, was missing.

After dinner and the celebratory toasts, Mother rose to give a little speech. I had forgotten how naturally poised, how eloquent and articulate she could be, how effortlessly she expressed herself in front of an audience, and how leavened with wisdom and sensitivity her public remarks could be. When she stepped into this role, she was transformed into another person, the one I remembered from my childhood. Radiating maturity, wisdom, and kindness, she was the antithesis of her willfully harsh, hurtful persona. As she spoke, I saw her once more through the admiring eyes of the child who had observed her dispensing counsel to the Relief Society women so many years ago. She had an innate gift for leadership, I realized, but it had gone unfulfilled.

Reclaiming her role as the eldest child in the family, she spoke with calm authority in formal, measured tones. "We have drifted apart over the years," she told her brother and sisters, her vibrant voice strong. "We have lived through great hardship in our lives, cruelly separated as children by death and poverty, and suffering as adults through war. We've lived these later years of our lives too much apart. We've become separated from one another, partly by distance, partly by neglect. We've not remained as close as a family should. That wasn't how we really wished it to be. It surely wasn't what our mother would have wanted. My wish now is that we can have closer contact with one another as a true family in the years that remain in our lives."

It was not to be.

The last time I saw her alive, Mother, now once again widowed, had descended into the wild eccentricity to which she had been impelled for a lifetime. Long, unkempt hair falling out from under an odd hat, a much too large coat dragging cape-like across the floor, she shuffled haltingly with the help of a cane across the lobby of the Oslo hotel where we were to meet. I had seen her come in, marveling at the spectacle. But the realization that this apparition was my mother didn't dawn on me until she began to make a rude, loud scene at the front desk. I was shocked at her physical and mental deterioration.

The moment we were alone in our room, she sat down in a chair opposite me, gripped the arms tightly, and began to cry. Shocked and fearful, I could only listen as a terrifying wellspring of long-buried emotions poured forth.

"My father wanted me to embrace him before he died, but I was afraid," she sobbed without preliminaries. "I'm so sorry. I was just a little child.

I didn't know any better. He pleaded with me, but I wouldn't come near him. It must have hurt him so. How could he ever forgive me?"

I tried to put my arms around her to comfort her, but, as always, she stiffly refused to respond. Her guilt-ridden words poured out, some awful dam broken. I had never seen her sob so wretchedly.

"Father and Mother come to me in dreams at night. They knock on the door very loud, wanting me to come. They're smiling and happy, and so anxious for me to come. But when I get up to open the door, they're never there." Her voice trembled.

She stared directly into my face, her eyes wide and beseeching, brimming with tears of regret and fear. And what else did I see there? Longing for the love and comfort that she refused to accept from me? Love I now was past knowing how to give?

I could only stare back at her in helpless despair. She had raised a child but cheerfully left it an ocean away. She had buried two husbands. But, as though she had never progressed past the day she was abandoned by her own mother, it was her parents she longed for.

I did what I could to get her life in order and assure she was looked after for the next few months, though she resisted my every effort on her behalf. I promised to come back in the spring, when I proposed she be ready to come back to America with me.

"No one will plant roses on my grave," she told me bitterly one day. But on the last day I saw her alive, she was full of the fierce self-reliance that had been a hallmark of her life. "You mustn't worry about me," she assured me as we parted. "I'll manage just fine."

She died unexpectedly four months later of heart failure. "Hanna will be here soon. Then everything will be fine," she told church members who visited her in the hospital. She died one day before I could reach her to say goodbye.

She died as she lived: willful, heedless and impossible, driven by warring impulses of kindness and anger, carelessly cruel, cheerfully malevolent, morbidly vulnerable to both sympathy and betrayal, a tragic figure longing bitterly for the love she spent a lifetime ruthlessly driving away.

Inga died nine years later of alcohol-induced liver failure caused by decades of secret drinking. I spent four days with her in her Olso condominium a year before she died. The first evening, we sat down to an elegant meal under the portraits of her parents on their wedding day. She caught me studying them.

"I think you resemble the people in this family," she said carefully.

I stopped breathing. I had been searching for a suitable opening to this conversation ever since Mother died. I had hoped that Inga herself by now might have told me she was my mother, but eight years had passed without a word.

I in the meantime had gotten curious about Mother's unfinished family genealogical records and eventually uncovered the astonishing, clearly documented news that she and Inga had Sami fathers. I sent copies of the records to Inga, hoping she would see this as an opportunity to acknowledge our relationship. Instead, she called me to express profound alarm.

"There have never been any Lapps in our family!" she protested shrilly. "It's just some mistake. It's not true. People always think everyone from the north is a Lapp."

Her reaction dissuaded me from confronting her with the truth about our relationship. If she didn't want to acknowledge her own identity, she wasn't likely to want to acknowledge who I was either, I reasoned. I certainly wasn't keen on forcing myself on her. Besides, who could know what she suffered or how she felt about giving away an illegitimate child?

But now, given this opening, I plunged in. After fifty-five years, it seemed prudent to seize the moment. "That shouldn't be surprising," I said quietly. "I've known since I was eighteen that you're my mother."

She smiled a sweet little smile, seemingly not at all flustered by this news. "I didn't know if you knew," she answered calmly.

"Mother told me I was never to say anything to you about it," I explained.

"When I gave you away, I put it all behind me," she said, as if in answer to an unasked question.

"Does anyone in the family know about me?"

"I've never told anyone." She paused briefly. "But I think my mother knew about you."

"Why?"

"Someone must have told her. All I know is that when I finally went home to Kitdal for the first time in 1946—we couldn't travel during the war, you know—Mother and I were sitting alone on the sofa in the living room one day when she suddenly said something about 'Hanna.' I just pretended I didn't know what she was talking about, and she never brought it up again."

Norwegians! I wanted to scream. What could be more typical?

I tried to read the look in her eyes, wondering how far I could go.

"Why didn't you and my father marry?" I asked as casually as I could.

"He wasn't interested in marriage. It wasn't as though we'd had a long engagement or anything. It was quite a bolt out of the clear blue heavens, quite unexpected." She chuckled and smiled that winsome smile again.

"What was his name?" I asked, testing her. I knew his name.

"Why should I tell you that?" she retorted, prickly for a moment. But she instantly relented and told me. I kept my eyes on her face, trying to read what lay behind her words. Her eyes hardened and her face tightened.

"He wanted me to have an abortion. He never paid a penny for your care. But I was determined you were going to have the best care there could be." Her eyes softened again. "When I first saw you, I thought you were the most beautiful thing on earth."

I couldn't speak.

"If it had been now, I would have kept you and you would have been my daughter," she added simply.

I could only look at her and try to smile.

"I was in the hospital with you for three weeks after you were born. I had an infection. When you were in the orphanage waiting to be adopted, they let me come to see you three times a week. But I was afraid something might happen to you, so I had you baptized."

"You named me?"

"I was supposed to be named Hanna, but the night before I was born, my father dreamed of his Aunt Inga who went to America as a young woman and was never heard from again. So he named me after her. And I gave you the name I was supposed to have."

I could see her alone in a strange city, helplessly hovering over my cradle in the orphanage, cooing at a child she could not keep, stubbornly presenting me to the priest for baptism despite her shame so as to ensure my soul would not go to Hell should I die.

"I'm so grateful to Berit for taking you. I was so relieved you could stay in the family. I'll always be so grateful to her for that. I could never repay her for that."

Maybe she did have the genetic wherewithal to read my mind. Or maybe she saw something in my face. "I never want to hear a bad word about Berit," she warned firmly.

She never did.

When I got the call that Inga was dying, I once again hurriedly flew across the Atlantic to say goodbye to a mother. This time I got there in time. I found Inga surrounded by family and nurses. She was almost unrecognizable: a redheaded skeleton with a huge, distended belly. When I got close enough that she could see who I was, she broke into a radiant smile.

"It's my dear daughter," she announced happily to the nurses. "She's come from America." It was the first, and last, time she acknowledged me publicly.

Her mind was going, poisoned by her failed liver. I stayed by her bedside as she slid in and out of rational thought, stroking her brow and holding her wandering hands still in mine. I kept my composure by fastening my eyes on the tranquil autumn scene outside the window of her stuffy room. The gentle, green hills of the city where she had brought me into the world were dusted with early snow. But a rosy bronze glow warmed the hillsides, as if the sun were reluctant to give in to winter's killing grip.

Inga floated in and out of reality. "She told me she didn't have any choice," one of my cousins reported after a hospital visit. "She said she had to give you away and send you to America because there was a war on and she didn't have any food to feed you." She shook her head sadly. Of course she knew Inga had given me up before the war started. "You can see how it's preyed on her mind all these years."

When I thought she was rational, I tried to thank Inga for all she had done for me when I was born and all she had given me since. "I'm glad you're my mother," I told her. But she gave no sign that she understood.

The day I left her to go home to America, Inga sat up in bed to see me off. "I'll come back and visit you next summer," I lied as I gently embraced her for what I knew was the last time. When I turned to take one last look at her from the doorway, she smiled that wistful, sweet smile I had grown to love and weakly raised her hand in farewell.

I hurried from the room, unable to breathe.

Like Mother, Inga died in February. She too died as she lived: generous, warmhearted, bossy, harshly unforgiving, stubbornly secretive, a dreamer determined to shape her own identity—and life itself—into something far different from what either would have been in the humble valley where she was born and into which she was interred. Her will said that she had no descendants, and her death announcement made no mention of me. That, I suppose, is what she would have preferred.

But whether either of my mothers died knowing who they really were, or whether they lived out their lives ignorant of the ancient imperatives of their Sami blood, I do not know. That too is a secret, and they took it to their graves.

As for Nikolai, at age sixty he began to clear forty acres for a farm of his own in a little hamlet near Astoria. At seventy-five, widowed and alone, lost to his real fortune—his large family of descendants across the sea—he sold his farm for one dollar to a Finnish couple who in exchange promised to care for him and let him live on it until he died. That bargain held for fifteen years. In December of 1948, at the age of ninety-four, Nikolai—like his lover Marie—died in a poorhouse, two days' drive from what would soon become our home in Idaho. He was buried in a pauper's grave on a lovely hillside overlooking a quiet bay of the Pacific Ocean, far from his home in Rantsila.

We missed him by one year and one month.

NOTES ON METHODOLOGY

My mother's stories of her own early life and of the heartbreaking hardships borne by her mother Kaisa provided the inescapable impetus for writing this book. To construct Books I and II, I placed my mother's accounts in factual context with the help of amazingly detailed Scandinavian church and census records, both of which include names and personal information. These records led me to the unexpected discovery of Marie Kurola's dramatic story—and to the discovery of my own Sami heritage.

Academic experts, museum exhibits, and historical accounts of social conditions in northern Norway and Finland in the 1800s provided historical backdrop, as did numerous interviews conducted as I traveled in Finland and Norway tracing Kaisa's life. (These sources are detailed in the Acknowledgments section of this book.)

In reconstructing this story, I was strongly guided by the recorded dates of significant events in the characters' lives. They provided the story's framework as well as clues to suggest a character's feelings and motivations at crucial moments in the narrative.

Though the nature and details of Nikolai and Marie's relationship are of necessity imagined, I relied heavily on Finnish accounts of everyday life among the cotter class to tell their story. He did arrive in Rantsila in 1874 to join his parents. Marie was at that time the unmarried mother of Sofie, whose father and circumstances of conception are unknown. Marie's rape, while imagined, was not atypical of the lot of indentured dairymaids. According to Rantsila church records, Marie twice was publicly shamed for bearing an illegitimate child. These records also attest that Marie was adept at learning; she got only the highest marks in school.

She remained an unmarried dairymaid, came to Norway to visit Kaisa, and died in the Rantsila poorhouse.

Sofie died at the time of the scarlet fever epidemic, and I speculate that her death initially served as an added reason to keep Kaisa safe in Norway. That Marie gave her second daughter Nikolai's mother's name led me to conclude that Marie Kurola and Brita Kaisa Okkonen had enjoyed a close bond.

Following the dates for clues to motivation also led me to believe that Nikolai was religiously enough inclined to repent of his sexual union with Marie. Church records show he sought communion very near the presumed date of Kaisa's conception. He left Rantsila for Quebec on the stated date, and passenger records show that he was aboard an overloaded ship, the S.S. *Sarmatian*, with a group of Mennonites. I do not know if he knew Marie was pregnant when he left.

The description of his travails on the sea portion of his journey borrows from actual accounts of travelers noted in the Acknowledgments. His letters home are imagined. His was the first marriage celebrated in Astoria's Finnish Lutheran Church. He did live in a Deep River, Washington, lumber camp and cleared land for his farm at age sixty. He returned to Finland after some twenty years and had a farm there, which he later offered to Kaisa and Anton before returning to Oregon. He and Kaisa corresponded, but never met. He died a pauper in the Clatsop County, Oregon, poorhouse.

The story of the central dramatic incident upon which this novel rests—Nikolai's return from America and offer of money and inheritance to Marie and Kaisa, and Marie's proud, angry rejection of his offer— came from my grandmother to my mother and finally to me.

I know none of the details of Kaisa's journey from Rantsila to Balsfjord except the date she left. As was the custom, the all-powerful parish pastor granted, and recorded, her travel certificate. I relied on travelers' historical accounts and interviews with museum officials for much of the description of what she might have encountered. I followed the dates of century-old Swedish and Finnish government records to reconstruct weather they likely experienced. Finally, I myself twice traveled along Kaisa and Henrik's route, conducting research along the way. The second time, I set out one hundred and one years to the day after Kaisa's depature to follow her trek from Rantsila to North Norway. It is plausible yet pure supposition on my part that she traveled from Karesuando to Skibotn with the Sami. For this section I'm particularly indebted to early travel accounts.

Henrik was a peddler who was denied the right to buy land in Kitdal.

The major details of Kaisa's life in Norway are factual. She was happily married to a Sami fisherman, then widowed and twice raped. The description of the first rape is from my mother's eyewitness account; the second is construed from a second hand account. Palma the cow was given away to the landlord in lieu of sexual favors, and the family was thrown out of their cottage into the snow. Kaisa kept her children until it became impossible to provide for them, then worked as a cook in Birtavarre, where she met the man she became dependent upon for survival and who falsely promised to marry her. All Kaisa's children but Karl rejoined her years later in Aalesund, where she worked as a "herring wife." Berit and the children threw Kalle out of the house. Karl's visit to Aalesund is real, as are his World War II exploits and the loss of his son.

Berit's guilt-inducing refusal to kiss her father as he lay on his deathbed is factual, as is her experience as a child slave—she was ordered by her employer to use ashes for soap. Her reunion with her mother on the dock in Trondheim is real, as is the poem Kaisa sent Berit on her forty-fifth birthday. Berit's meeting with the Sami girl is imagined, though she did befriend the Sami schoolteacher on her grandparents' farm in Kitdal. The family was in Sulitjelma during the riot. Berit's return to Kitdal and first meeting with Inga in 1936 are factual—as is Inga's fateful decision to accompany Berit to Aalesund.

ACKNOWLEDGMENTS

M any people helped retrieve this story from the mists of fading human memory, and I owe them all a debt of deep gratitude.

Indefatigable genealogical researcher Liisa Penner of Astoria, Oregon, exhumed Nikolai from the basement records storage room of the Clatsop County Courthouse, and staff at Peace Lutheran Church in Astoria subsequently opened church records to fill in important details of Nikolai's life.

Sanna Kurola of Rantsila, Finland, patiently provided assistance with translation and historical research. Maaja-Liisa Kurola, undaunted by our lack of a mutually comprehensible language, offered warm hospitality and assistance during my stays in Rantsila. Pentti Koppekoinen, pastor of the Rantsila church, explained church records and what had been done to Marie.

I'm enormously indebted to my late uncle Alfred Nymo of Signaldal, who shared his earliest and most painful memories and urged me to write this book. Solveig Nymo of Signaldal gave generous hospitality and assistance for this project. Magnus Grønnaas and Ruth Grønnaas of Balsfjord, Norway, rendered especially valuable information. Torleif Lyngstad of Birtavarre, Norway, and Elina Pesonen of Karesuando, Sweden, also offered helpful information.

Mauno Jokipii of Jyvaskyla University in Finland was particularly generous in explaining Finnish migration to Norway. Reino Kero, author of *Migration from Finland to North America in the Years Between the U.S. Civil War and World War II* (Turku: Institute for Migration Studies, 1974), is the source of the information I used to depict the "sprats in a barrel" shipboard conditions under which Finns traveled to the United States and Canada. Emil Larssen's history of Kitdal and Signaldal in *Lyngen Bygdebok* (Tromsø: A.S. Peder Norbye, 1988) proved invaluable.

Scholars at the University of Tromsø, Norway, offered information on matters of Sami history and culture, as did the staff of Tromsø Museum. Johan Albert Kalstad of the university's Sami Ethnographic Department, Einar Neimi of the Department of History, Nils M. Knutsen of the Institute for Language and Literature, and Regnor Jernsletten, professor of Sami Culture and History, all generously shared their time and expertise. Harald Gaski, professor of Sami literature at the university, has supplied faithful encouragement and assistance from the outset. Any errors in the Sami portion of this book are strictly of my own making.

Tom Dubois, then of the University of Washington's Scandinavian Department in Seattle and now at the University of Wisconsin, graciously provided Finnish translation and research assistance, and University of Washington Scandinavian Department chairman Terje I. Leiren offered advice and encouragement in getting the project under way. Carleton E. Appelo, an authority on Deep River, Washington, graciously shared his historical knowledge.

Sulitjelma Mining Museum director Harry Evjen, who unearthed church records revealing the heretofore unknown identity of the father of one of Kaisa's children, was most generous with his time and knowledge. Minna Heljala of Tornionlaakson Maakuntamuseo, Tornio's regional museum, patiently instructed me—with the aid of a children's picture book—in the details of everyday Finnish domestic life in the 1800s. Marita Mattson Barsk of the Tornedal Library in Overtornea, Sweden; Marja-Liisa Pimia of Helsinki's National Board of Antiquities; Kari Ansnes of the Nordiska Museet in Stockholm; Terttu Pellika of Oulun Kaupunki Pohjois-Pohjanmaan Mueso in Oulu, Finland; Eva Gradin of Norbottens Museum in Lulea, Sweden; Laura Johansen of Nord-Troms Museum in Otern, Norway; and Diane Thomson of the National Library of Canada all went beyond the call of duty to assist me in furnishing factual historical context for this fictional re-creation of a vanished moment in history. Again, any errors are mine.

The Finnish Meteorological Institute and the Swedish Meteorological and Hydrological Institute supplied weather records covering the time of Kaisa and Henrik's journey over the mountains. These provided a foundation from which to depict typical weather the travelers may have encountered. The Hoover Institution of War, Peace and Revolution at Stanford University gave me access to World War II documents from Norway, and the Family History Center of the Church of Jesus Christ of Latter-day Saints in Salt Lake City, Utah, offered genealogical records.

I took inspiration from Sami poet Yrjo Kokko's poem "The Road of the Four Winds" in choosing the title for Book I.

A short selection from Book III describing the day World War II ended was published in the *Seattle Post-Intelligencer* on the fiftieth anniversary of the end of the war.

Computer wizards Deb Dahrling and Connie Carman gave freely of their time and expertise to keep the manuscript from vanishing into cyberspace.

Patron saint Joann Byrd, assuming the role of pro bono literary agent, cast her keen editor's eye upon the manuscript and set in motion the events that led to the publication of this book by the University of Washington Press.

I'm deeply appreciative of the unfailing professionalism of the Press—Michael Duckworth, Pat Soden, Marilyn Trueblood, Alice Herbig, Beth Fuget, Gigi Lamm, and manuscript editor Molly Wallace. It was a joy to work with them.

Finally, my most profound and heartfelt gratitude goes to Karen West. Were it not for her encouragement and support, infinite patience and insightful editing of the manuscript over the fifteen years it took to bring this book to fruition, this story would remain untold.

Aarseth, Bjorn, ed. *Grenser i Sameland.* Oslo: Norsk Folkemuseum, 1989.

Alanen, Arnold R. "The Norwegian Connection." *Finnish Americana* 6 (1983): 23–33.

Du Chaillu, Paul B. *The Land of the Midnight Sun.* New York: Harper and Bros., 1881.

Eilertsen, Roar, ed. *Billeder fra gamle Tromsø.* Tromsø: Tromsø Bymuseum, 1978.

Engman, Max, and David Kirby, eds. *Finland: Land, People, Nation.* Bloomington: Indiana University Press, 1989.

Figenschau, Tore. *Signaldalen g jennom 150 aar.* Finnes, Norway: Tekst & Cetera, 1999.

Flatmark, Jan Olav, and Harald Grytten. *Aalesund in hverdag og krig.* Aalesund: Nordvest Forlag A/S, 1988.

Grym, Emil. *Fran Tordendalen til Nordnorge.* Lulea, Sweden: Lulea Bokforlag, 1959.

Hauge, Tore, Finn Solheim, Berit Sivertsen, and Anders Ole Hauglid. *Her bor mit folk.* Tromsø: Lyngens Bygdeboknemnd/Nord Troms Museum, 1986.

Jokipii, Mauno. *Finsk bosetning i Nord-Norge.* Turku: Turku Migrations Institute, 1982.

Kalhama, Maija-Liisa, ed. *Finnene ved Nordishavets Strender.* Turku: Turku Migrations Institute, 1982.

Knutsen, Nils Magne, ed. *Nessekongene.* Oslo: Gyldendal Norsk Forlag, 1988.

Manker, Ernst. *People of the Eight Seasons.* Gothenburg: Svenska Forlags AB Nordbok, 1975.

Niemi, Einar, Ottar Brox, Odd Mathis Haetta, Kjell Jacobsen, and Hans Kr. Eriksen. *Trekk fra Nord Norges historie.* Oslo: Gyldendal Norsk Forlag, 1978.

Punkeri, Elsa. *Rantsila kotiseutumme.* Oulu: Oy. Lliton kirjapaino, 1958.

Qvigstad, J. *Lappisk Eventyr og Sang fra Lyngen.* Tromsø: A .S. Tromsø Stiftstidenes Boktrykkeri, 1921.

Qvigstad, J. *Den Kvenske Invandring til Nord Norge.* Tromsø: A.S. Tromsø Stiftstidenes Boktrykkeri, 1921.

Taylor, Bayard. *Northern Travel: Summer and Winter Pictures of Sweden, Denmark and Lapland.* New York: Putnam, 1858.

Tromholt, Sophus. *Under the Rays of the Aurora Borealis.* Boston: Houghton, Mifflin & Co., 1885.

Vilmusenaho, Risto. *Siikajokilaakson Historia II 1860–1960.* Oulu: Siikajokilaakson paikallishoriatioimikunta, 1984.

Vollan, Odd. *Den tause motstand.* Aalesund: Nordvest Forlag A.S., 1989.

Wold, Helge A., Edgeir Benum, Karl Skadberg, Dag Skogheim, Axel Johnsen, and Rune Hagen. "Industrialisering og arbeiderbevegelse i Nord-Norge fram til ca. 1920." *Ottar: Populaere smaskrifter fra Tromsø Museum* 119–120 (1980): 3–65.